"Step back in time to nation. Amber Lynn Perry transports you to America's Colonial era, where the struggle for freedom is wrought with sacrifice, danger, and suspense. Perry's characters are endearing, her leading men swoon worthy, while her storytelling soothes the reader's soul. It feels like a TV miniseries with characters you come to love and never want to leave."

~ **Paula Scott, author of** *Far Side of the Sea*

"Rarely do I find a book that hooks me from the start and won't let go until the end, but *So Pure a Heart* did just that. The romance was masterfully written, the historical era was vividly portrayed, and the plotline kept me on the edge of my seat. The redemptive thread, so carefully interwoven with the story, took me by surprise in the best way. As with the best stories, these characters will stick with me, and I can't wait to read the next book in this series to get to know them better!"

~ **Heather Day Gilbert, Grace award-winning and best-selling author of** *The Vikings of the New World Saga*

"Oh, this lady's pen—or should I say *quill?* It gets sharper, its words more lyrical, with each tale, whose ink writes itself across a reader's heart. Hannah and Joseph's romance is no exception—so beautiful and poignant, it lingers long after the last sigh. Huzzah, Amber Lynn Perry!"

~ **Tamara Leigh, USA Today best-selling author of** *The Vexing*

SO *pure* A HEART

Book 4 of the Daughters *of* His Kingdom Series

AMBER LYNN PERRY

So Pure a Heart
By Amber Lynn Perry

Copyright 2017 Amber Lynn Perry
ISBN-10:1-945965-00-2
ISBN-13:978-1-945965-00-5

P.O. Box 4723
4801 W Van Giessen St
West Richland, WA 99352
amber@amberlynnperry.com

Cover Design, Seedlings Design
Cover Photo, Danyell Diaz Photography

Published by Liberty Publishing

This novel is a work of fiction. Names, characters, places, incidents, and dialogues are a product of the author's imagination or used fictitiously.

Author/publisher contact information:
www.amberlynnperry.com

To those who sacrifice—may the love of Providence sustain you.

Offer the sacrifices of righteousness, and put your trust in the Lord.
Psalm 4:5

Spying during the Revolutionary War was as real and dangerous as it is today. Only unlike today, it was often undertaken by regular civilians who wished to make themselves useful to George Washington and the Glorious Cause. Men and women alike volunteered to engage in covert operations despite the risk that if caught, their lives would be ended. (So though this story is fictional, much of its roots are based in historical fact.)

The information provided by these valiant men and women made an indelible impact on the war, and without them, undoubtedly the outcome would have been different.

We owe our freedom not only to those whose names we recognize but to the unknown Patriots who risked everything for liberty.

Chapter One

Alone, Hannah Young stared at the dirt-covered mound as the chilled air breached the warmth of her heavy cloak.

Graves are sorry things.

The words her uncle had spoken not an hour past replayed in her mind and held solid the reality she wished not to accept, but must. Her dearest aunt Bea, her friend and confidant—the woman she'd loved as a mother—was never coming back.

Hannah looked up, gazing across the lonely hill, straining to gather any rational thought through the thick fog of sorrow. At the sight of the house a hundred paces away, and Uncle Ensign nearing the plot where she stood, Hannah's eyes burned. There was nothing they could have done to save her. 'Twas Bea's time, and God had called her home. Such knowledge should strengthen, should it not? Lowering her head, she smoothed her cold fingers around the soft emblem in her hand. It should, but it would never quell the pain. That she knew. For still she grieved the loss of ten years past, as if 'twas only yesterday.

"Hannah, you should not still be here."

She glanced up at the sound of Ensign's voice, then turned again to Bea's cold resting place. "Perhaps." She could say no more without weeping.

"The others have long since returned home. As should you." He put his arm around her shoulder and pulled her close as the gray clouds mourned over them. At long last his heavy tone returned to mingle with the air. "She loved you, my dear. More than you can ever know."

Nodding, Hannah's throat grew thick, impeding the reply that wished for release. *And I her.*

Ensign cleared his throat, but still his words came out thick and broken. "We shall always have the memories of our dear Beatrice. And though she is gone from us in this life, I know we shall see her in the next."

Hot streams of tears rolled over Hannah's cold cheeks. "You have such faith, Uncle."

He released a quivering breath before his solemn reply. "I could not bear the grief if I did not."

Hannah allowed his words to rest in the wintery air, consumed by both love and heartache, before the thoughts she'd been forming found shape in her voice. "She was so good to me. She loved me anyway." Hannah glanced down at the tiny knitted booties in her hand, speaking through the tears she could no longer restrain. "Both of you loved me despite everything, and I could never repay such kindness, no matter how I tried."

He tightened his loving grip and whispered in her ear. "There is nothing to repay, sweet child. She loved you as her own, as do I." He coughed to clear his throat and straightened his stance. "Your father gave up a great treasure when he left you to us. He is a lost man. We must pray for him."

The tears halted at the mention of Philo Young, and she glanced up, unrepentant for the truth that spilled out. "I fear I have given up praying for him. He will never..." She couldn't finish the rest.

"Forgive me." Ensign looked down at her, the deep lines around his eyes flaring before he kissed her temple. "I should not have mentioned it. I know how it pains you."

She glanced down at the booties once again and tried to speak through the strain in her throat. "That is not all that pains me."

An audible sigh left him, and he pulled her closer. "I know."

Hannah inhaled a choppy breath, attempting to cleanse away the dark clouds that closed upon her mind. "At times...at times it seems as though 'twas only yesterday. Then in the next breath, I feel 'twas a different lifetime."

The memories she wrestled gathered hard and fast, like storm clouds darkening an already bitter night. She shifted her feet and tucked the booties in her skirt pocket, attempting in vain to tuck away the thoughts with equal ease. "Without Bea—without you both beside me—I..." *I would not have lived.* Hannah looked away, unable to finish the thought aloud. "And now I shall never again be able to tell her how much I loved her, how grateful I am, how I shall never forget her."

Ensign released his hold and brushed his knuckles against her cheek. "I heard you speak such to her every day."

"But it wasn't enough."

"Dear child." He kissed her hair once more, then moved back, one hand still on her shoulder. "You must return inside—I beg you. You have been too long in this chill."

He turned and started down the hill, but she called after him, the cold slowing her lips as she spoke. "Only a moment more, Uncle. I cannot leave her just yet."

Ensign stopped and glanced back at the grave, eyes red. Not moving his gaze, he answered her request with a pained smile to hide the quivering of his chin. Wiping a stray tear from his cheek, he took in a long breath, blinking as if he still struggled to accept the truth, the same as she. His mouth tightened, and he offered a quick nod before striding down the slight slope toward the house.

The cold cinched harder, stinging Hannah's cheeks as she stared at the earthen catacomb of her only and dearest friend. She looked up, blinking against the moisture in her eyes. She had Ensign, true. And Caroline. But her cousin was in Sandwich, and though their treasured letters brightened every week, Hannah could not fathom how she would endure every day without Bea's smiles and humor, her light and wisdom.

Again, she dropped her gaze, recalling Caroline's most recent pleading. *Nay.* She hugged her arms around her chest under her cloak and rubbed them to fight against the cold. Never would she return there, no matter how her dearest cousin begged, no matter how lonely the years ahead might prove. Sandwich was the place of her youth, the place of her formative years, aye. But 'twas the place where her past still lived and breathed.

She reached into her pocket, eyes trained on the clouded horizon. Circling her fingers against the memory, she pushed back the bitterness that pressed against the doors she'd hidden it behind. Here in Plymouth she had discovered the meaning of true caring, true love of family.

Hannah tightened her fist around the soft wool as the face of the one man she longed to forget filled her vision as real as if he stood before her. She looked to the house to escape the illusion of him, but it lingered, forcing the imprisoned emotions to cry for freedom.

'Twas as much your doing as his, was it not?

The wind whipped harder now, signaling the need to find refuge indoors. Loathing to part, Hannah blew a kiss toward the lonely mound, grateful, almost, for the distraction that allowed her to leave her post without weeping.

Walking across the snow, she gripped her cloak, shivering as the memories thumped harder in her chest. Ten years had passed, and still she thought of him. Foolish. For surely he thought not of her.

At the back step she clutched the handle, breathing away her past before she could enter. The light from the house peeked through the small cracks in the wood, like her hope that refused to die.

After all they had done—after all they had lost—and still her heart betrayed her.

She grasped the handle tighter and pushed the door open.

She had forgiven him, aye. But she could never, ever forget.

Waiting at the back door of the Smiths' home, Joseph Wythe peered at his young nephew who stood beside him, leaning against his crutches.

Looking down, Jacob shielded his expression from both the snow and Joseph's questioning gaze.

The cold flakes that had fallen without ceasing since last eve dusted silently atop Joseph's hat. He tightened his grip around the laden sack in his hand and exhaled a heavy breath that billowed white in the midwinter air. "Cold today."

Not looking up, Jacob adjusted his weight on the crutches and shrugged as Joseph knocked again.

"Leg bothering you?"

The boy didn't answer. Joseph's ever-ascending prayer filled his heart for the hundredth time that morning. *Lord, be with him. And please, I pray thee, help him to know why I must do this.*

The sound of hurried footsteps echoed through the house only seconds before Kitty Smith flung the door open, bathing them in warm cinnamon-scented air. "Good heavens! Forgive me. Have you been waiting long?" She swung sideways and ushered them in before resting her hand on the swell of her belly. "Come in, please. Let me take your coats."

"I cannot thank you enough." Joseph watched Jacob maneuver his way inside, carefully placing his crutches on the first step before using his good leg to lead him into the house. Joseph followed close behind. Removing his hat, he closed the door. "You are sure your husband would approve? We are not inconveniencing you?"

Kitty smiled, hanging their coats by the door before taking the sack from Joseph's hand. "You two are old friends. Nathaniel would be aghast if you had Jacob stay anywhere else."

"But you..." He swallowed, unsure how to speak of the growing child in her belly without causing her to blush. "Are you quite sure? Do you feel well enough?"

"Do not worry." She smiled in gracious gratitude and placed the parcel on Nathaniel's desk. "I have never been so vital in all my life." With a polite touch to his hand, she turned to face her new house guest. "Good morning, Jacob. May I take your hat?"

A tentative smile washed over his drooped expression. He removed his worn tricorne and handed it to her. "Good morning, Mrs. Smith. Thank you."

She hovered her hand at the boy's shoulder and led them through Nathaniel's study toward the parlor. "You cannot know how pleased I am to have you."

Jacob answered her kindness with a fleeting nod.

"Do make yourself comfortable." She hurried a few steps ahead and shifted the rocking chair to the side, allowing him an easier path to the couch.

Joseph trained his vision on Jacob's expression as he reached for the arm of the furniture and slowly sat, resting his crutches beside him. Not the slightest grimace of pain. But that didn't mean he hadn't become adept at hiding what ailed him.

Kitty's smile deepened. "Your company during these months will be a godsend, Jacob. Having a man in the house will ease my spirit greatly, I can assure you."

Mouth tight, fingers knotted, Jacob attempted another smile, but it died the second it touched his lips.

Kitty glanced at Joseph, sympathy in the slope of her eyes. She bent to the table, her clear voice singing through the room as she prepared a steaming cup of coffee. "I should like to talk to your uncle for a moment." Offering it to Jacob, she smoothed her hand over his shoulder. "I shan't keep him long."

Jacob looked up, cheeks rosy and eyes hesitant. "Of course. Thank you."

Kitty grinned and turned toward Joseph, motioning back to Nathaniel's study. Once there, she turned to face the parlor, her voice riding a whisper. "How is he doing?"

Joseph's insides churned, and he stared at the nephew he had come to care for as his own son. Matching his volume to hers, he sighed. "The pain in his leg seems to be fading, though I fear somehow the pain in his heart grows." He shifted his feet, swallowing away the rising concern he'd battled to suppress for days. This boy had no parents or siblings, and now he, the only family Jacob had in the world, would leave as well? "I wonder if I am doing the right thing?"

"Do you *really* wonder?"

He met Kitty's gaze, struck with a courage that seemed to reach from the depth of her blue-green eyes to the center of his wearied spirit.

"He is not a child, Joseph. He knows the significance of what you are willing to sacrifice." She extended her arm and touched his wrist, the gentleness in her smile surpassing the vines of worry. "You must join the militia—join my husband and the others. You have waited long enough. Eliza and Anna and I shall keep Jacob well occupied until you return."

Would he return? Would any of them?

A dense fog crept through him, and he lowered his tone even more to avoid the waver that rose in his throat. "Should anything happen to me—"

"I've prepared a room for him."

Kitty's abrupt words cut past the unpleasant thought, as if she knew speaking of such would bring too much gloom upon them both.

"'Tisn't much, but I did worry...considering what happened..." She pursed her lips and glanced to Jacob before she turned to the open doorway behind her. "'Twas the only space I had. Going up stairs would be too much for him of course, but do you think he...do you think I should offer it to him or not?"

Joseph stared at the room only a few paces ahead from where he stood, shocked at how the memory of what had happened there made his insides harden. Stepping forward, he looked over what had been Nathaniel's surgery room. The smell of blood and the gruesome sound of the saw cutting through bone filled his senses, but he shoved them aside. "I should think he would be grateful for a place to call his own. But I cannot know for certain how it...how it would be for him."

Kitty hurried in from behind. "I've removed the surgery table, as you can see." Her expression was sweet but edged with apprehension as she sat on the bed and smoothed her hands along the quilt, as if to prove its worthiness. "You remember Anna Donaldson, Henry's wife? Her father made the bed especially for Jacob. Anna and Eliza made the quilt."

She stood and motioned to the cabinet in the corner. "I've replaced all the medical supplies with books, paper, quill and ink—you said he enjoys reading and art?"

"Aye." He nodded, grinning, and continued to take in the room that resembled nothing of his last visit there. Though 'twas pleasant, to be sure, how would Jacob feel?

"I suppose 'twould be best to have you ask him."

Kitty's sudden words interrupted Joseph's thoughts.

"If he cannot...that is, if he wishes another place to sleep, I will do whatever I can to make him comfortable."

Joseph glanced toward Jacob. "I shall speak with him." He stopped just through the doorway and turned. "I cannot properly express my thanks—"

"Not at all." Kitty grinned sweetly and started toward the kitchen. "I believe the turnovers are just about done. I shall check on them."

She hurried through the study and past the parlor, disappearing into the kitchen.

Joseph neared the couch, pulling the rocking chair in front of Jacob, who still held his drink and sat motionless as the snow fell harder outside the window. Joseph rested his elbows on his knees. "Jacob, I—"

"I want you to stay."

Jacob looked up, the ache in his eyes reaching across the small distance to strangle Joseph's already pained longing.

"I know I shouldn't think such a thing. I know your efforts are needed for the cause, but I cannot help it."

His chin quivered, and he looked down, the small thread of sound hammering Joseph's heart to his ribs.

"I...I cannot lose you as well."

Joseph's throat swelled, and he coughed to let his answer free, but still he couldn't speak. Only eleven years old and already the boy had been made to suffer far too much. Losing both parents in the same day only months ago... Joseph allowed his vision to linger no longer than a second on the neatly pinned pant leg that covered the place Jacob's knee and lower leg should have been. Joseph took the cup from Jacob's grasp and held the boy's hands in one of his. His other he placed behind Jacob's neck with a gentle grip. Binding his gaze with his nephew's, he strained his voice to keep it from wavering. "I shall think of you every day until I return. I *shall* return. I promise."

"If I had my leg, I could go with you." The boy's eyes reddened with tears. "We wouldn't have to be parted. I could fight alongside you and—"

"Jacob..." Joseph checked his words before speaking them, every immediate response lacking the true depth of feeling that pressed in his chest. He smoothed his hand down to Jacob's shoulder and lowered his tone. "I would be honored to fight alongside you. You are fearless, Jacob. I have never known anyone so brave." He released his hold on the boy and straightened, allowing a half smile on his lips. "You would send those Redcoats running, I have no doubt of that."

Grinning wide, the red in Jacob's eyes dimmed to pink. "I'm a good shot too."

"You're an excellent shot."

His face beamed. "Aye? Excellent?"

"Near as good as I, and I'm almost twenty years older."

"Aye, but no one fights like you." Jacob's smile broadened. "You could lick a whole lot of Lobsterbacks all on your own."

Joseph laughed at the well-intended compliment. Growing up, he had been forced to learn how to defend himself against this boy's very father and earned a reputation for strength he'd rather not have gained. Suddenly he debated his previous wisdom in having shared even abridged versions of the scrapes of his youth.

Winking, Joseph sat back. "Perhaps I need not fight at all. Perhaps those Redcoats will take one look at the militia and sail right back to England, hmm?"

"These turnovers are just right."

Kitty entered between their conversation, swirling steam rising from the fresh-baked goods on the tray she carried. She rested the vittles beside the coffee, the scent of such delicious food making Joseph's stomach emit a loud grumble that could not be ignored.

Jacob suppressed a laugh, his boyish face lifting into a wide grin that made his countenance shine.

Kitty made a surprised face and pretended to stifle a giggle, making the boy laugh harder.

"Forgive me." Joseph exaggerated an apologetic frown and reached for a turnover. "I suppose I should take one. It seems my stomach speaks the truth I wished to hide." He winked at Jacob, then looked to Kitty. "Turnovers are my favorite."

"Well then, I'm pleased I made them."

Jacob continued to chuckle lightly and took one of his own, peeling off a corner and blowing on it before stuffing it into his mouth.

Kitty sat beside Jacob on the couch, the expression on her face bright and kind. "Eat as much as you like. I'm so pleased to have someone around that I may cook for." She flung a glance to Joseph before looking once again to Jacob. "What do you think of your sleeping arrangements?"

Hang it.

He should have spoken of that right away. Joseph put down the turnover. "I hadn't spoken to him yet—"

"Oh, I'm sorry." Face ashen, Kitty rose from the couch.

"No, no. Not to worry." Joseph shook his head and motioned for her to stay seated before turning to Jacob. "Mrs. Smith has prepared a wonderful room for you."

Jacob slowed his chewing, looking between them with peaked brow and questioning eyes.

"'Tis..." Joseph looked to Kitty before spilling out the words in a tone he hoped would seem natural, matter of fact. "'Tis a very welcoming space in the room the surgery used to be."

Jacob's eyebrows folded hard as he swallowed the bite in his mouth. He sat back and after a long, slow blink shifted his eyes toward the room he knew so well.

Kitty shot a frantic look to Joseph and spoke to fill the vacuum. "There's a new bed, and I've stocked the cabinet with books and the articles you need for drawing, if you like."

At this he looked up, and she continued, smile coaxing. "'Tis quite cozy. There's a soft quilt and a lamp and—"

"You mean I won't have to go up the stairs?" A hopeful lift in his brow mirrored the ribbon of relief in his voice.

Joseph shook his head, a welcoming relief brushing away a layer of worry. "Nay, you shall not."

Resting her hand atop Jacob's, Kitty answered with a slight tilt of her head. "I hoped you would be happy, but I was...I was concerned that perhaps—"

"Nay, I am pleased. Thank you." He met her gaze before looking again to Joseph. Eyes instantly flooding, Jacob glanced at the ground. He blinked, not speaking again for several seconds. "I suppose you must leave now."

Neck tight, Joseph inhaled a long, pained breath before sliding off the chair to kneel in front of Jacob. He cupped his hands on the boy's shoulders, praying God would mask the agony in his voice with a courage he couldn't feel but needed. "No matter what happens, you must hold to hope, and I shall do the same. Hope will keep our courage alive, will allow us to make this sacrifice of separation. Can you do that?"

The boy swallowed, nodding quick and shallow. "Aye." Tears pooled in his eyes. "I shall write to you."

Joseph smiled his response, then reached around Jacob, pulling the boy into an embrace he prayed would convey the love he hadn't the strength to speak. Moving back, he held Jacob's face. "I shall take you fishing when I return."

Jacob nodded, forcing a strained grin. "Promise?"

"Promise." He planted a kiss to the boy's head and rose to his feet, the urge to flee the suppressing sorrow consuming his muscles as he started toward the back door.

"Joseph." Kitty hurried behind him. "Take these with you."

He turned to see a large knapsack in her hands. She offered it to him, and he peered inside. Journey cakes and rolls, as well as dried fruit and meat, filled the bag to the brim.

"You needn't have—"

"I know you haven't anyone at home to...to make you anything. I hope you don't mind."

"Of course not. I am grateful indeed." He'd thought of the fact he would need food, but not how he would come by it. God surely worked in wonderful ways.

Kitty tilted her head. "There should be enough to sustain you until you reach camp, and when you see Nathaniel...you can give some to him as well." Her voice cracked, but she lifted her chin and forced a smile. "I've a letter for him in the bag. If you would be so kind—"

"I will be sure he gets it."

Kitty reached for his arm, her large eyes brimming and voice faltering. "Thank you."

Joseph grinned, wrestling back the emotion that threatened to choke away his response. "Of course."

He reached for his greatcoat and put it on before he opened the back door. Placing his hat on his head, he prepared to leave, when she stopped him again.

"Come back to us. You must *all* come back."

Joseph glanced over his shoulder and past Kitty to where Jacob sat on the couch, his eyes fixed on

Joseph, his young face gripped with heartache, as if he was ready to spring from the couch and run to him.

Snow flicked Joseph's face and neck, rendering him motionless with grief. *Lord, please give him strength. Give us both strength.*

"Joseph."

Kitty's quiet voice pulled his gaze away from Jacob and back to her.

She lowered her chin, encouragement in the lift of her mouth. "We shall be fine here. Do not worry over us."

He swallowed and shifted his jaw before responding. "The conflict will be over soon." He spoke the words, but hoped more than believed them to be true. "Tell Jacob I will write when I can."

Turning, he left, raising the bag in his hand with a nod and smile of thanks.

Kitty waved and closed the door, cutting the tie that bound him to that awful moment.

Joseph patted his hand on his horse's neck before securing the bag at the side of the saddle. Straining to focus his mind away from the boy that ached for him inside the house, he untied Anvil from the post and slipped his cold hands into his leather gloves. He mounted, and with a quick tap of his heels, the animal started across the snow-covered road. *Keep moving. Don't look back.* The cause. He must keep his mind upon the cause.

As he moved slowly forward, his mind trailed backward, far into the past—to another time he had been forced to walk away from someone he loved.

He clicked his tongue and tapped his heels again to move his mount faster, as if doing so would help him evade the memories that stalked him. But no matter how he tried, the torturous thoughts nipped at his heels. How had she fared these past ten years? Did her mind toy with the pleasant memories of their love the way his did? Did she grieve as deep as he?

He ground the thoughts into submission. Such things were best left untouched, no matter how they festered, like a weeping wound that begged for healing. Of course Hannah Young would not think of him, not after so much time had passed.

Growling low, he rubbed his hand against his forehead. Why? Why could his thoughts not remain buried under the layers of hurt and resolution that piled so thick? He lowered his hand and stared through the snowflakes as they folded on the road ahead. Unbidden, the deep green of her eyes, the merry song of her laugh, the honey-sweet scent of her hair circled and consumed him until he could hardly breathe.

Looking forward, he exhaled his memories into the cold January air. He must steady his mind upon the future—upon Jacob and the liberty for which he would fight.

The snow fell harder, and a brush of wind pulled at his coat. He might have hope for the fight of the future, but he would never be able escape the prison of his past.

Chapter Two

Looking to the clock for the hundredth time, Philo Young rubbed his palms against his black jacket and straightened. Noon. Any moment a knock on the door would signal his brother's arrival. How many months had passed since he'd paid a call? A drop of hope rippled through Philo's chest. This must be a sign of goodwill. He spun from the healthy fire, nodding with satisfaction that everything was in place, the floor swept, the mantel dusted. Hurrying to reposition the first seat, he scooted it an inch closer to the fire. There. He nodded with satisfaction. His elder sibling would have the chair closest the warmth. Philo would sit opposite.

The yet to-be-spoken conversation toyed with his imagination, and a few more splashes of eager anticipation began to rain. *It shall be mine at last.* Again he wiped the moisture from his hands, pacing back and forth in front of the hearth. There was only one reason Ensign would come twenty miles.

The awaited knock jolted Philo like a crack of splintering wood. He shook his head, huffing away his frayed nerves. Hurrying to the door, he swung it open and stepped back with a slight bow. "Welcome, brother."

Ensign dipped his chin slightly. "Philo." Entering, he removed his cocked hat and set it on the table by the door. "Thank you for seeing me on such short notice."

Philo closed the door against the cold. "Shall we sit?"

Hardly so much as a nod of acknowledgment, Ensign moved to the offered chair and sat, but his shoulders and back refused to relax.

Such gray lines under his eyes. Was he ill? At the chair beside him, Philo rested with his hands in his lap. "Your journey was not too unpleasant, I trust?"

Expression drawn, eyes unmoving, Ensign answered with only a fleeting glance. A thread of silence knit back and forth between them. Looking to the fire, Philo rubbed his thumb into the palm of his other hand. He might not have seen much of his brother over the past years—their closeness might have even been strained betimes with anger—but he knew him and could sense some unvoiced woe from the slant of Ensign's shoulders.

"I..." Ensign's voice cracked. He quickly cleared his throat and tried again. "She is gone from me, Philo. I have lost my dearest friend."

Bea.

Philo's stomach lurched. So the illness had taken her, after all her years of fighting. "Ensign, I am so sorry—"

"Hannah feels her loss almost more keenly than I."

At the sound of his daughter's name, a flowering joy bloomed and instantly wilted. Any response he might have spoken fled like birds before a pursuing dog. How many years since he had seen her? Too many. But the rift between them gaped wider with every phase of the moon. What she had done could never be forgiven. Not by him.

"Bea shall be missed." Philo wrestled the phantom that clutched him from behind, struggling to answer as if Hannah's name had not been spoken. "She was a good companion to you."

"She was my heart, my very life's breath." Ensign's throat shifted. "If not for Hannah, I am not sure I could bear the loss."

Must he speak of her? Philo squirmed as the chair became a cluster of upward-pointed nails. The pricking forced him to stand. "I am grieved at your news indeed. And honored, truly, that you would come all this way to tell me." He placed a hand at his back. "But I am sure you did not traverse the ice-covered roads for that alone."

Eyes unmoved from the fire, Ensign sat back, and his chair creaked. "Aye." His voice tapped across the weak thread that bound them. "I have...I have come to a decision."

The silence roared as Philo turned to stare at the orange waves in the hearth, waiting in agony for the words he'd longed to hear. When still the quiet clawed him several moments later, he spun back. The dipped brow and working jaw of his brother made Philo's stomach pitch. Would he not speak?

Skin spiked with anxiety, Philo glanced to the kitchen, then the window, then again his brother. He couldn't long remain here in such torturous quiet. Perhaps Ensign was parched from the journey. Philo should have offered him a drink. "Shall I get you a—"

"I've sold it, Philo."

Philo went still, his mind grinding over the revelation like a millstone over grain. "You what?"

Ensign licked his lips before lifting his eyes to Philo's. "I've sold Eaton Hill."

His former hopes dried in an instant, leaving behind a sandy plain of hate. The grains blew wild in the winds of Philo's rage, stinging his skin, as he prayed his words would do to Ensign. "How dare you. Eaton Hill should be mine!" His volume rose slow and thick, pulse thudding hard through his ears. "You came here thinking to soften me with your sorrows before revealing you have taken from me that which I have longed for all these years?"

Ensign flicked his head up at the outburst. "Believe what you like. But I tell you only the truth."

Philo's neck corded. "Eaton Hill should go to none but me, and well you know it."

Standing, Ensign pulled his shoulders back, his tone staying sickeningly calm, as if the man hadn't the enmity Philo knew was there.

"As the land is mine to do with it what I will, I choose to give it into the hands of one who will work the foundry and care for the land, not simply own it only to place it in the care of an overseer who will use it for profit."

Philo narrowed his vision until he could see only the man who betrayed him. "Faithless sot. I should never have trusted you."

Chest rounding, Ensign's eyebrows evened while the foundation of his words turned to stone. "I did what I felt was best, and I stand by it."

"You lied to me!"

His expression was unchanged, but his voice deepened. "At no time did I tell you Eaton Hill would be yours. Where there is such want, Philo, there is weakness, and you have fallen prey to it."

Philo's fist pounded the air. "You made me think you were coming here with tidings of goodwill, but instead you tear asunder the only thing that could have mended what has long torn us apart."

Ensign shook his head, his brow peaked in the center. "How could I have done it, brother? You know full well I could not let you near her."

There it was. The truth of it all.

The rope that held him snapped, and the pit he'd dangled over consumed him in quenching flame. "This is not about Hannah."

"It has always been about Hannah." Ensign pulled his shoulders back, his height bringing him a full two inches above Philo. "It has been since the moment you turned her out."

"I had no choice. I could not bear the sight of her—it pained me so. Did not she know that?" Head spinning, he looked to the fire. "And yet I am forced to endure the sight of her lover near every day, so it would seem. Though I try, I cannot escape the shame of what they have done." He looked back over his shoulder. "I turned her out, aye, but what else could I have done?"

"You could have loved her as a father should."

The answer spat a muddy truth over Philo's white conscience. "She defied me. She defied God—she sullied the name of Young, and that mattered not to you? How could I allow her—"

"She has suffered enough, Philo. Can you not forgive her after all this time? Surely God has. Surely 'tis compassion she needs, not your disdain." Disgust in his eyes, Ensign stepped away. "I refuse to give you access to her or the land."

The claws of rage stabbed up through Philo's feet. Allowing a curse to strike the air, he stepped to his brother, only a fist of space separating them. "It has always been your wish to rip from my life anything that might bring me joy."

Head shaking lightly, Ensign breathed out, his tone a freshly whetted knife. "Nay, brother." He started toward the door and paused before gripping the handle. "That power belongs to you alone."

"You know what is best for her, is that it? Yet I, her own father, does not?"

Glancing behind him, Ensign held Philo with pointed eyes. "So it would seem."

In two large strides Philo grabbed him at the shoulder and spun him around. "Eaton Hill has belonged to Young blood for near a hundred and fifty years, and now you would see it thrown into the hands of someone else?"

"I have never said it would leave our care." His eyes flitted over Philo, as if he inspected some piece of work and found it unworthy. "Do you not feel Hannah has Young blood? Does she not have any right to the property?"

A sigh breathed out, cooling his frame from scalding to a low, steady burn. "You have bequeathed it to her." Perhaps he still had a chance...

"I have not said that."

Would the man speak in riddles? "Do not play games with me. Is Hannah to own the land or not?"

The sun's mournful winter light dimmed, darkening along with it what glimmer of belief still flickered in the dark corners of his heart. "Ensign, tell me. Who owns Eaton Hill?"

Ensign reached for his hat, holding it in his fingers a moment before preparing to place it back on his head. "One who will care for it. That is all you need to know."

He turned the handle, but Philo gripped his arm. "Tell me!"

Tilting his head, Ensign sighed, as if Philo were a mere curiosity. "Had you any remorse, any showing of caring for her, I would in an instant seek ways to help mend what should be between father and daughter. But until then, I will strive only for her well-being. And you are no part of that."

Ensign pulled open the door, the winter air blasting through the room. With a nod, he strode to his waiting horse, not once looking back.

How dare he!

Philo hurried a few steps after him, stomping through the snow before the weight of his anger made his legs too heavy to move. "Tell me!" The yell scraped up from the ground, hurling through him to shake the very clouds above.

Ensign continued on, the words seeming to die amongst the newly falling snow before they reached his ears. He untethered his horse, mounted, and rode away with only a cursory glance before he kicked his horse to a steady run, leaving Philo to stumble about in the darkness of unknowing.

Streams of hate trickled down his neck to his chest. The land was his. If Ensign wished to relinquish it to anyone, it must be him, not some unknowing, unfeeling stranger who cared nothing for it, as he did.

Nay. His lungs heaved as a hard, heated rage flowed through his veins. The atrocities Ensign had heaped upon him before were mere specs of dust compared to this mountain of dirt. Never would he forgive him. Ever would he make him regret it.

Chapter Three

Hannah leaned back in the soft chair that faced the fireplace, pulling the shawl tighter around her shoulders, the evening's chill as deep as the night was dark. The warmth of the radiating flames reached out to her, comforting away the coal-black sorrows. Sparks popped. The clock ticked. Otherwise, only silence.

A week had passed. Seven days that dragged on and on, the grief draining her tears and parching her heart. Closing her eyes, she rehearsed the Bible verse that quenched her dry spirit like a cool mountain spring. *In the world ye shall have tribulation: but be of good cheer; I have overcome the world.*

Opening her eyes, she stared into the parlor's dark corner where the light of the oil lamp refused to reach. So much darkness in the world, so much pain. She prayed the Lord would impart His grace. They needed it now more than ever.

"You left your supper untouched."

Hannah sat straight as Ensign entered the parlor. Shrugging, she tried to grin away the truth. "Did I?"

Taking the seat beside her, he scowled through his remark. "You are not feeling unwell, I trust?"

"Nay, I am well, Uncle." Sighing, she pressed mirth into her words. The scent of stewed beef curled on the air, and though she tried to find pleasure in it, she could not. "I shall have a few bites before bed—worry not."

He gave an approving nod, then slowly turned his head and stared at the orange flames. "I find I am somehow more fatigued than I have been. Forgive me."

The grief weighed him down, as it did her.

"You take too much upon yourself." Hannah reached out to touch his arm. "It has only been a week. It will take time. I do not wish for you to work harder than you have strength."

"You are too good to me." He leaned back in his chair and stared forward, deep creases lining his brow. It seemed he wished to speak more, but the hard line of his mouth refused him.

After a few more pops of the fire, she forced herself to speak. "How was your work today?"

Looking sideways, his eyes found her, but his mind was still wherever he had left it, the blankness in his pale expression crimping worry between her eyebrows.

He blinked and shook his head. "Oh, 'twas fine." He sighed and leaned forward, resting his elbows on his knees. "Micha Ross's last day. He's leaving for Washington's camp in the morning."

Hannah nodded, the unspoken message of his words ringing loud in her ears. Now they had all gone, every worker to join the Glorious Cause. Panic wound its wiry fingers around her throat. Her uncle would not go too? He'd spoken of his wish to join the brave men-at-arms many a time—how he wished he could lend his hand in the grand fight for freedom. She too championed the cause and wished herself to take part somehow in the valiant efforts for liberty, but how could either of them—

"Hannah?"

Startled, she blinked. "Aye?" The way he swallowed and looked at the ground made her clutch the fabric of her shawl. *Do not say it.* "What is it?"

He licked his lips and cleared his throat, his words spilling out in a choppy mix of fast and slow. "I have...I have been meaning...meaning to tell you something particular for some time now."

"Oh?" *Please do not say it...*

"I..." Still leaning forward on his knees, he rubbed one thumb against the other, the answer dripping with resigned remorse. "I have sold Eaton Hill."

She exhaled, the relief at his answer overwhelming the surprise at his words. "Sold it? Why?"

He stood and moved to the fire, a slight release of air bobbing his shoulders. "'Twas time." He faced her, love reaching out from his smile. "I have many good years left in me, but 'twas time to place the foundry into the hands of someone younger. With no apprentice to leave it to, I could make no other choice."

Hannah shook her head, trying to put her scattered thoughts into place. She stood and rounded the chair, giving her unease a resting place as she gripped the soft fabric of her seat. "Who is the purchaser? Are you sure they will care for it as you have? Have they the same skill? No one can match your work—" She released her hold, the next words so thick with disbelief she could barely form their sound. "Tell me you did not sell to him."

His thin lips flattened, and his gaze gripped to hers as he answered clear and full. "You know I would not." He breathed in deep, his chest rounding, and continued only after a long, heavy sigh. "Though your father has beseeched me these many years, I would not reward him ownership or nearness to you."

Moving to the fire beside Ensign, worry clipped her tone. "He will not relent. You know how he is."

"Aye, I do." His expression sighed away, as if his mind took him to some place he would rather not journey. "If I had any indication he wished to mend what has been broken between you, I would have acted differently—"

"But he does not." After ten years the pain still throbbed like a fresh wound. "I know he will never change. That he thinks only of himself. He cares nothing for me."

Ensign reached out to touch her shoulder. "He allowed you here, Hannah. That says something, does it not?"

Allowed? A generous way to describe it. Releasing a tight breath, she leaned against him, and he put his arm around her. Her head on his shoulder, she stared at the charred wood in the fire, crumpling away the fragile memories and sacrificing them to the flames. "I suppose whoever has bought the foundry must be a man of great talent."

"Aye, and character."

The comfort of his embrace soothed the rising anxieties. "Well then, I shall trust your judgment."

Quiet eased around them, Ensign stroking her arm. "I have only one concern."

She craned her neck to look up at him. "What is that?"

"The only thing that eats at my heart is the thought of what will become of you when I am gone." Tender, but nipped with worry, the answer spilled from him like water from a wintery stream.

"Gone?" Pulling from his grasp, she stood before him, willing his spirit to believe what next she spoke. "Heavens, Uncle, you will not leave me—"

His light chuckle stopped her. "I have many years ahead of me, 'tis true, but selfishly..." He reached out to stroke her cheek. "Selfishly I wish to see you with a family of your own. I wish you to be as happy as I have been."

The tenderness of his statement baited the question. "What do you mean? I have never been more happy."

His kind, worn smile lifted gently at the corners. "I should like to see you marry."

A stiff wind blew across her heart. "You know I cannot." Grinning up at him, she laughed lightly, a barrier against the tender memories that pined for recollection. "I need no one but you. Besides, my heart has grown so accustomed to this place I cannot bear the thought of leaving it."

He pulled her against him. "Then I suppose it is a good thing the buyer has generously offered to allow us both to stay while he lends his hand to Washington...and upon his return, as well."

She tugged away from his embrace. "In truth?"

"Indeed. He has also asked that I stay on and do the books for him."

The goodness of God opened before her like a vast, star-filled sky. Whoever could be so generous? "We must give thanks for such a man."

Ensign looked down, his eyes reflecting the glow of the fire. "That we must."

"Who is it?" The question popped from her lips, her childlike curiosity warming her chest like a summer dawn. "You must tell me, Uncle."

Ensign's chest lifted and lowered, and she moved away, the question of his sudden silence being answered by the sheen of reserve in his stare.

She straightened, that dawn clouding with gray. "You will not tell me."

The answers waited just beyond the kindness that lined his tired gray eyes, but still he would not speak them. "All will be revealed in time."

"What? Why?" She stepped back, letting her arms drop at her sides. "Why can you not tell me?"

"Do not press me, child, I pray you." He shook his head and rested his hands on her shoulders. "There are things that are better left unsaid."

She blinked, trying to flush away the questions that crowded her vision. "Is secrecy your wish? I would not betray a confidence, if that is what you fear."

"Of course not, dear one." He glanced up, his neck working with emotion before meeting her gaze once again. "'Tis hard to keep anything from you, you know that. But this...this I feel is best learned in the future."

"When?" Hannah glanced down, then back up, questions falling thick like the snow that blanketed the ground. "A week, a month, a year?"

He gripped her fingers and shifted his jaw before answering. "When the war is over."

"When the war is over?" The shock of his statement forced her to repeat his words. "That could be endless. No one knows when—"

A loud knock pounded against the door. "Open in the name of the king!"

Hannah jumped back with a gasp, body suddenly numb. *Soldiers.*

Ensign pulled his hand from hers, his voice thin. "Dear God…"

A shiver of disbelief trickled down her skin when the forceful knock once again shook the door. She spun to Ensign. "Uncle—"

A voice called from the other side of the door. "Open now, or we shall force ourselves in."

Ensign hurried to the door. "Coming." Turning, he pointed to the kitchen.

The firm line of his mouth and rigid angle of his arm drilled a pit in Hannah's middle.

Spinning, Hannah dashed for the darkened kitchen and jerked through the entryway just as the front door squeaked open. She pressed her back against the wall, trying to quiet the frantic pace of her breath.

Footsteps stomped loud through the parlor as the intruders entered. Hannah stared down at the floor, the prayers she threw to heaven ripping her soul in two. *Lord, protect him.*

"Are you Ensign Young?"

"Aye."

Her uncle's response rang calm, steady, unlike the madness that raced through her as she listened.

"How may I help you gentlemen?"

"My name is Major Stockton." A deep, gravelly sound scraped its way through the shadows. "I am here to relieve you of your foundry, Mr. Young."

Dear Lord, no! Hannah leaned her head back and rested it silently against the wall. Clutching a thick mass of shawl at her chest, she forced herself to breathe through her nose, straining to calm the swells of emotion that crashed on her like a boat on an angry sea. Shock, anger, disbelief. The number of footfalls told her there were several inside, but exactly how many was impossible to tell.

The man with the deep timbre spoke again. "The king is in need of a foundry, sir. And with such a robust reputation, yours has been honorably chosen."

"Well..." Ensign cleared his throat, his slow steps tapping across the floor. "I fear I must report ill news, gentlemen. I have just sold the foundry these three days past. It is no longer mine to give."

"Nay, it is not. For now it belongs to King George." A chair scratched across the floor and wheezed as someone sat. "Captain Higley, return outside and see that Reece and the others return to camp. They are not needed here."

"Aye, sir."

The door opened and shut before the loathed man continued. "We shall stay here this night, and you will give me a tour of the foundry in the morning."

"I—"

"Lieutenant Greene, go to the kitchen and discover what food this man has to share. I am famished, and that scent is tantalizing."

Hannah stiffened. *Dear Lord! Not the kitchen!*

"No!" Ensign's voice echoed loud through the room. "What I mean to say is, I fear I have nothing to offer you, good sirs."

Not moving—hardly breathing—still clutching the shawl that did little good against the gaining chill, Hannah looked to the door that led through the yard to the barn. Should she attempt it? If she did, they would surely see her as she crossed the stream of soft light that shafted through the doorway. If she did make it unseen, that Higley fellow and the others would surely see her. She gripped her arms and looked upward. *Lord, what am I to do?*

Again, the chair scraped and footsteps started. "You wish not to share your wealth with the king's men, is it?"

"I haven't any wealth. I am a poor man whose family is not here, as you see."

"I do see."

Whoever owned such an ominous tone was likely as imposing as his voice was deep, for his footfall was powerful against the wood.

"Then perhaps there is something else you hide."

Swift stomps toward the kitchen turned Hannah's blood instantly cold.

"Nay!" Ensign rushed to the doorway and turned to face the parlor, his shoulders just visible from where Hannah pressed against the wall. "'Tis only that I am ashamed I have naught to offer."

A shadowed figure neared, darkening the light at Ensign's frame. This time a different voice, equally rich but more melodic, whispered past the doorway. "Do not test me, old man. For I promise you shall lose."

Ensign remained motionless. "The king, as you say, may now own the foundry, but this is still my home, and I will not have you demanding that which I do not possess."

The unseen man sniffed, his shadow lengthening. "Then pray, how is it I smell bread and a hearty stew? Wilson, help me persuade him." With a grunt the man shoved Ensign, but he gripped the doorframe and looked to Hannah, the silent command blaring in his eyes.

Run.

She picked up her skirt and raced for the door.

"A girl!" The soldier barked from behind. "Major, a girl!"

Her heart stopped, but her feet propelled her to the freedom of the door.

"Run!" Ensign yelled.

"After her!"

She yanked it open as Ensign roared. "Leave her be!"

"Out of my way."

"Never—"

A shot cracked the air, and Hannah stopped just outside the door. Shock slowed her senses. White smoke rising, Ensign fell limp to the ground in a heap. Her eyes rose to the man who lowered the pistol and stared directly at her.

Limbs thick and numb, she stared back, unable to find the strength to make her way to safety. Somehow she heard a voice from behind that pulsed blood through her legs. *Run, child. Run.*

Sprinting, she yanked her skirts to her knees and darted to the barn as yells and frantic footsteps raced from behind.

The winter air drove spikes into her heaving lungs and brushed past her cheeks and up her skirts as she hurled herself to the barn, slowing only enough to slip sideways through the gap in the sliding door. Hannah rushed to the nearest horse and flicked the latch of the back door.

Faster.

She gripped the horse's mane, launching herself onto his unsaddled back only seconds before two soldiers rushed in.

"There!" The taller soldier ran forward. "You'll not get away so easily, you trollop." He lunged, when a flash and crack jerked his progress. He bellowed and crumpled forward as the first soldier spun around, spitting curses that sparked in the damp air.

Ensign stood half-bent, weapon in hand, blood gushing over his fingers as he pressed a fist to his wound. He looked to Hannah, a rainstorm of emotions clouding his eyes.

The remaining soldier looked back and forth between them. His dark glare went wicked, and he grabbed for his dagger, lunging and thrusting the blade into Ensign's gut.

Hannah's scream scraped up her throat. "Nooo!"

The soldier yanked the blade back, and Ensign slumped to his knees before falling to the ground.

Grief and shock choked her, as thick and course as a rough-hewn rope.

Slowly the soldier circled back, when once again that gentle voice whispered from the heavens.

Go.

Hannah blinked, helpless against the crippling shackles of confusion and fear.

Go, now!

Compelled by a power not her own, Hannah gripped the horse's mane and kicked her heels. Clutching her mount, she trained her focus on the black road. She must get to safety. But where? To whom could she turn? Who would know what to—

Clear as a summer sky, the answer scrolled across her mind as if written with a heavenly quill.

Militia camp. Nathaniel Smith.

Aye, Nathaniel. She leaned closer to the horse as his head bobbed, heedless of the biting, speed-induced wind that cut against her ears. It had been years since she'd seen him, but he would surely know what to do. His work with the Patriots' cause was renowned.

Tears burned, spilling hot streaks against her freezing skin. She could not think of Ensign now. She must make the forty miles. And then...then she could weep for him. Then she could seek to avenge his bitter loss. For he, she vowed, would not have given his life for her in vain.

Chapter Four

"Aw, good fellows. Look who has finally cared to join us."

Joseph pulled on the reins of his horse and dismounted, chuckling in reply to Nathaniel Smith's jocular greeting. "I figured I ought to lend my services. Heaven knows you poor souls won't be able to succeed without me." He ignored Nathaniel's outstretched hand, instead pulling him into a brotherly embrace. "Good to see you, old friend."

Nathaniel patted him hard on the back before pulling away, his beaming grin and bright eyes preaching both strength and weariness. The collar of his jacket was pulled up, a thick scarf around his neck. "Our little band was not complete without you." He motioned to a young boy who stood several paces back. "Jackson, walk my friend's horse for him, will you?"

The boy rushed forward, taking the reins with a gleeful expression on his whiskerless face. "Aye, sir."

Nathaniel turned to Joseph but motioned to camp. "You can see to your horse later. First, we must talk."

From behind Nathaniel, Henry Donaldson broke from a group of somber troops and welcomed Joseph with a warm smile and firm clasp of hands.

"Welcome, Joseph."

"Good to see you, Donaldson." Joseph glanced past Henry's broad shoulders to the sorry scattering of shelters, where the other volunteers huddled around pitiful fires or inside makeshift huts. "So this is our fearless army, eh?"

"Come," Henry said, gesturing with a flick of his hand. "Allow us to give you a tour of our grand encampment."

Joseph hurried after his horse to unlatch his small satchel from its spot on the saddle, then followed after them. He nodded briefly at a handful of men who eyed him, bobbing their heads as he passed, not a whisper of a smile on their worn faces. Joseph looked up, quickly scanning the other small groups scattered around the clearing. Were they all so gaunt? Washington's petition for more volunteers had swept up and down the coast, and now Joseph could clearly see the need had not been exaggerated. Joseph eyed a weary pair whose matching red hair named them as father and son. Taking note of their threadbare coats and shoes that gaped at the sides, Joseph's gut twisted. The boy could be no older than Jacob. *Dear Lord.* He stared overlong at the innocent expression on the lad's face, praying once again that Jacob would feel God's strength and peace. For once, the tragedy of Jacob's accident seemed almost a mercy.

"Are all these men from Sandwich?" Joseph lengthened his stride to walk beside Nathaniel. "I thought I knew everyone from town, but it seems I give myself more credit than I deserve."

"Nay, these groups are varied and scattered." Henry answered first, nodding at a lone soldier as he passed. "But we tend to stay with your local militia as best we can."

"Connecticut, Rhode Island, even Pennsylvania men, they're all here, scattered along this line, awaiting the British to make their move. Or Washington—whoever acts first." Nathaniel touched his hat as the three of them passed a shack constructed of canvas and old pieces of roof. The men inside lowered their chins, never moving their outstretched hands from the weak fire that waved only inches above the small circular pit.

A realization dawned, and Joseph scowled. "Where is Thomas?"

Nathaniel led Joseph to the largest tent at the edge of camp. Flapping back the door with a loud whack, he motioned for Joseph to enter. "He's been appointed as Knox's right hand. He'll be here this evening."

Joseph nodded, not in the least surprised that the humble, steadfast man had been chosen to help in such a capacity. Ducking to avoid the shallow opening, Joseph grinned in mock surprise. "These are your humble quarters then?"

Henry followed and stopped just inside when a man rushed up to them.

"Captain Donaldson."

"Aye?" Henry looked from the man to Nathaniel, then back again. "What is it, Private?"

"A dispatch rider, sir. Says he must speak with the leader of these groups—that is you, isn't it, sir?"

Henry nodded the affirmative and looked to Nathaniel. "I shall return."

Nathaniel offered a quick bob of the head in reply.

Henry turned. "Let us see what news awaits us."

Both men hurried back into the milky daylight, the tent door flapping closed behind them.

Joseph looked up and removed his hat. His height brought his head only inches from the drooping canvas roof. Nathaniel motioned to one of the two simple wood chairs that waited with arms outstretched, ready to ease any weary traveler. Joseph was all too willing to comply.

He sat with a humph and rubbed his finger and thumb against his eyes. "How long have you been in camp?"

"Three days."

"Three?" Joseph's eyebrows pinched down hard. "And already Donaldson has risen to such a rank?"

"His military experience is more than all the rest of us combined. The men are in desperate need of leadership and discipline."

Looking to the tiny slit of light that wedged through the tent door, Joseph hummed in agreement. "I could not think of anyone better suited for such a position."

Wiping a hand down his face, as if attempting to scrape away the thick exhaustion that dulled his eyes, Nathaniel fought a yawn. "We'd hoped to make the journey from Ticonderoga in only a few short weeks, but the devil had his fingers in the weather—impeding our progress at every turn." Nathaniel took the other chair and sat. He leaned forward, resting his elbows on his knees while he rubbed the back of his neck. An airy sigh, full of memories and sprinkled with amazement, laughed from his throat. "By God's good grace alone we survived the trip, and with the artillery intact. But I shall bore you with the victories and woes of our journey another time. Needless to say, Washington has the cannon and may use them as soon as he wishes. Until then, we wait."

Joseph leaned back, reveling in the blissful stretch he could allow his long, ride-weary legs. He sat, studying the sudden pensive stare that pulled lines across Nathaniel's brow. "You are tired."

Nathaniel released an audible grumble of agreement. "We all are."

The unusual quiet of the man Joseph had known since childhood—a man who always had a ready wit and jubilant nature—made Joseph sit rigid in his chair. "What is it?"

Nathaniel's neck corded, and he pulled his bottom lip through his teeth. "Our situation is grave. More grave than any of us care to admit. Therefore we do not." He spit out the answer like spoiled food.

Joseph stared, his expression growing heavy the longer he awaited the continuation of Nathaniel's unspoken thoughts.

"There are so few men," Nathaniel said. "And those who do remain are plagued by one horrid aliment or another." He stopped and shook his head, his mouth thinning as he stared at the far corner of the tent. "I fear the pox will end this war before it has begun."

The pox. Motionless, Joseph allowed the ugly word to burn in the heated silence before glancing to Nathaniel once again. "How many are afflicted?"

"More than I can number."

Dear God.

Nathaniel rose and went to his desk. Pulling a canteen from the drawer, he took a drink before offering it to Joseph. He took it gratefully and refreshed his thirst while Nathaniel finished speaking.

"I have inoculated a few, those who will allow it, but it races through the men like fire in a wheat field. If we cannot contain it..." Nathaniel returned to his seat with a huff of tangible worry.

Joseph exhaled, resting the canteen on the ground beside him. He'd rarely seen his friend with such deep lines on his face, such a firm set to his jaw. Glancing down, Joseph picked up the bag and opened it, reaching to the very bottom to pull from hiding the lifeblood of Nathaniel's spirit.

"Your wife's generosity kept my belly full on my journey. You've married a good woman."

Nathaniel's head flicked up, eyes round, tone reverent. "You saw her?"

Joseph nodded and extended the note. Nathaniel straightened, joyful disbelief spinning in his expression. Taking it, he caressed the seal with his fingers, as if across the miles her skin could feel his touch against the paper. He looked up again, this time speaking the simple words as if they were a prayer. "How is she?"

"Very well." Joseph looked to the tent door, a twinge of grief tugging at his memory. "I asked her if she would be willing to look after Jacob."

"She agreed, of course."

Nathaniel spoke with such confidence, as if he knew without question how his wife would act. What would it be like to be joined with someone who carried the same mind, loved with the same heart?

He rested the almost empty bag on the floor. "I had prepared to leave earlier, as you know, but Jacob's fever returned, and I could not bring myself to leave him."

"He's improved then? How is his leg?" Nathaniel tucked the precious note inside his jacket, no doubt eager to read it when he could treasure his wife's loving words in sacred solitude.

"His leg is nearly fully healed. The wooden leg and crutch allow him to walk without too much difficulty." He stopped, gratitude burning at the back of his eyes. He chuckled to release himself from the strain of emotion that thickened his throat. "Now, because of your heroism, he's considering studying medicine instead of remaining on as my apprentice."

At this, Nathaniel's white smile beamed through the room. "Well"—he chuckled—"it would be difficult for anyone, indeed, to not be supremely impressed by my skill. Don't take it as an affront to your trade, Joseph. Blacksmithing is...honorable."

"Honorable?" Joseph leaned back, a chuckle on his breath as he rested his hands behind his head. "I should like to see you swing a hammer for days on end. I doubt you could."

He tilted his head, a grin at his lips. "Then again, 'twould seem I *am* the hero."

"Aye, but without my *honorable* trade, you would not have the tools for heroics."

Nathaniel laughed full out. "Touché, my good man. Touché."

Grinning, Joseph rose and went to the table, examining the large map of Boston, neatly organized correspondence, compass, and unlit oil lamp. "Truth is, I, uh...I have recently purchased an addition to my trade."

"Oh?" Nathaniel followed suit and moved around the desk, standing opposite him. "What would entice you to expand in such a way? You needn't the money."

'Twas true. He'd inherited his father's wealth four years ago at his passing, leaving Joseph with the deepest pockets in both Sandwich and Plymouth. Aye, he dressed well when required and donated generously to those in need, but the frivolities of the upper classes never held any allure.

"I know blacksmithing so well—I want more of a challenge." He picked up the compass and circled it in his fingers. "I bought Ensign Young's foundry."

Nathaniel dipped his head, his brows jumping. "As in Philo Young's brother. As in...Hannah's uncle."

The sound of her name stroked Joseph's ears, and he shook his head to ease the seducing sensation. Unable to voice the answer, he nodded with a weighted sigh. "I stopped by on my way here to finalize the agreement." Joseph set the compass back down and turned, resting against the edge of the table. "I regard the man with great esteem. You would be hard pressed to find anyone more skilled or more sincere."

"I do not know Ensign, though I know *of* him, of course. His good reputation is unmatched indeed. I do, however, know his brother." There was disdain in Nathaniel's tone, as if the taste of his statement was as unpleasant as the man himself.

Philo's sneer and hollow eyes heaved from Joseph's carefully arranged memories. He shuttered the image away. "They are nothing alike."

Shadows, haunting and black, snapped at his heels. He too had had a brother—one whose spirit matched more the dank underbelly of earth than the bright sun-gifted light of day. But his brother was dead. And now his brother's son was Joseph's to love and raise as his own.

"There were rumors he was planning to sell..." Nathaniel's words pulled Joseph from the slippery bank he nearly fell from. His friend rounded the desk and stood beside him, staring questions Joseph could read as easily as a handwritten missive.

If he dared speak it...

Joseph gripped the edge of the table, recalling the battle that had waged within him—the battle that still waged. Should he have done it? Would she flee at the mere thought of his taking over for her beloved uncle? Sighing his answer, Joseph shrugged. "'Twas time for me to expand my trade, that is all."

"Does she know?"

There it was. Blinking slow, Joseph faced forward and gripped the edge of the table. "Nay."

"You do know she will find this out."

"Not until the war is over. Ensign has given me his word."

Nathaniel pulled his head back, one eyebrow sloped. "You trust him then."

Standing, Joseph brushed past the overgrowth of frustration. "When I spoke with Ensign only a few days ago, he gave me his word he would not apprise her of my purchase until the conflict is finished and that he would keep watch over the property until I return."

"Then?"

Joseph slanted his head and glanced at his friend, who seemed dangerously curious. "Then they will stay on, and Ensign will do the books."

"What is Hannah to do?"

"I don't know what Hannah is to do." The answer sputtered too loud and too quick. "She is free to do whatever she pleases."

Nathaniel looked down, then back up, the teasing nature fleeing from his expression. "That *is* why we are here. To secure her freedom to do just that."

Freedom. A single acknowledging hum bumped through Joseph's chest. That was why they were there. To ensure the freedom of them all.

He glanced to Nathaniel, who studied the matted grass at his feet. Joseph's gut twisted. He'd never revealed everything that had happened between him and Hannah. Should he tell him? Perhaps 'twould be good to finally relieve his heart of the swelling pressures of the past.

He took a deep breath, piling the courage it would take to form the words, let alone hear them on the air. Opening his mouth to speak, he snapped it shut when a soldier burst through the tent door.

"Doctor."

His tight mouth and rigid stance brought both men to their full height.

"You are needed immediately."

Nary a moment's pause, Nathaniel hurried to the door, speaking over his shoulder as he left. "I shall be back shortly."

Joseph stared after him, his feet at the edge of the cliff he nearly attempted to clear. Speaking aloud the things he kept inside would have been fatal. Hannah was a beautiful, dangerous memory he oughtn't to indulge. If he did, the pain might bring him to that place he loathed to linger. Love—the love he had given and felt in return, the love whose shattered pieces still littered his soul—*that* love was no friend to anyone.

Shouts and pillars of color surrounded her body, which cried out in pain, as her mouth could not. Every movement, every breath stabbed with the spears of cold.

Unable to open her eyes, Hannah slumped against the horse's neck, gripping hard to his mane. Frozen, after hours upon hours of riding in temperatures far too low, she wanted only to sleep. But the blissful black evaded her. Willing her mouth to speak the words her lips were too cold to form, she groaned as best she could. Did she actually voice Nathaniel Smith's name or merely dream it?

Someone neared and strained her fingers from their grasp on the horse's mane, but they were frozen in their solid grip. "You there," he yelled, "bring me your knife!"

An unfamiliar moaning grated from her throat as she attempted once again to call for Nathaniel. Sounds around her grew. More talking. More shouting. More hands grabbing at her waist. Was she even in Cambridge, as she hoped? Were these friends or foe?

One slash, then another, and suddenly her hands were free.

"You are safe, miss. Someone has run to fetch Dr. Smith." The kind stranger gripped her sides and slid her from her mount, lifting her in his arms.

"Thank...you..." The words she produced sounded naught more than a woeful whisper.

As if her body understood what her mind yet did not, the tension, the building terror she'd borne since the moment Ensign's life was taken, began to drip from her muscles, and she closed her eyes, resting her head against the stranger's strong shoulder.

The man quickened his pace, his tone a calming stream of warm vibrations. "My name is Henry Donaldson, miss. Dr. Smith shall be here straight away. Jack, clear off that cot. You—bring me some hot water." The warm stranger rested her on something firm and soft, when his volume suddenly rose. "Someone get me a—"

"Henry, what's happ—oh dear Lord."

Praying for strength to raise her eyelids, Hannah groaned with the pain of it. *Lord be praised.* "Nathaniel."

"Hannah."

He knelt in front of her, and she lost the strength to keep her eyes open.

He placed a hand on her shoulder as a shiver consumed her. "What's happened, dear friend? Why are you here? Henry, I need three heavy blankets and strong coffee."

A grunt of assent and shuffling sounds filtered through the room as Nathaniel's hands covered hers. "We shall warm you up quickly. Not to worry."

If moments or hours passed before a welcome heaviness weighted against her body, she could not tell. The slow, even warmth that started to bring an angry buzz into her fingers and toes was a welcome acknowledgment of a fact she had almost been unwilling to believe. She had made it.

Chapter Five

"There, boy. You did well. As always." Joseph moved his hands along Anvil's foreleg and lifted his hoof for inspection. Happy sounds of boyhood laughter brought to mind the boy he'd left behind. Glancing over his shoulder, he noticed several lads jostling for position in muster practice. Some were men, aye, but several were not much older than Jacob. With a quick shake of the head, he turned back to his mount and examined the next leg.

"You miss him too, don't you." He stood and patted Anvil's neck. 'Twas Jacob who had given the horse his name. *He's strong and black like the anvil in your shop, Uncle. So that must be his name, mustn't it?* No other name could have suited him better.

"Joseph! There you are."

Nathaniel's tone pulled Joseph up and around like a firm grip on his shoulder. But it was the hard set of his mouth and firm slant of his eyes that made Joseph's stomach harden with his next intake of breath. "What is it?"

He heaved through his words. "You'll want to come with me."

Without pausing to question him, Joseph followed Nathaniel's frantic pace down the long, staggered row of temporary shelters. "What's happened?"

Running, Nathaniel stayed quiet until he reached a large tent surrounded by a mumbling crowd of men. He halted and clutched Joseph's shoulder, that same hard look once again gripping the lines of his face.

Joseph swallowed, his mind coughing against the billowing dust of the unknown. Had Jacob followed him—injured himself on the way? "Out with it!"

Nathaniel peered to the tent before stabbing Joseph with a look that went clear through him. "Something has happened at the foundry."

"What do you mean?"

At that moment, Henry exited the tent and maneuvered his way through the thick mass of men to where Joseph and Nathaniel stood. He said nothing, only nodded and passed by as if he'd been ordered to keep silent.

"I don't know the details, only that..." Nathaniel dropped his hand and sighed without once moving his gaze from Joseph.

His blood chilled more than even the air that bit his cheeks. "Tell me."

Nathaniel pointed to the tent, then dropped his hand to his side. "Ensign is—"

"Is what? Is here?" He strangled the urge to yell. "Speak, man."

Nathaniel gripped Joseph's bicep with grinding force. "'Tis not Ensign that is here, Joseph." He paused, his jaw working. "'Tis Hannah."

The force of Nathaniel's words hurled against him, and he stepped back. "Do not jest of such things."

"I do not jest."

The strike of his answer hit Joseph firm in the gut.

Nathaniel released his grip, but not his stare. "She arrived moments ago."

Too many thoughts scrambled through Joseph's mind for him to find a single word to speak, let alone think. His heart began a rapid thumping, bringing heat back into his lifeless limbs. He looked from Nathaniel to the tent.

"Hannah is in there?"

"She is weak and very chilled from the ride but—"

Joseph didn't wait for more. He split through the crowd and launched through the canvas door, his pulse thumping hard in his throat.

He stared, blinking, waiting for the truth of what his eyes beheld to match the understanding he tried to unfold in his mind. Shivering on the cot, under a thick mass of blankets, lay the woman he'd known so well. Red cheeks, hair a tangle of honey-gold knots, full lips chapped. Why was she—

"All I could make of her broken words was that something has happened to Ensign."

Nathaniel's voice snapped the weak limb Joseph had perched upon, forcing him back to the cold ground where he stood.

"I fear he is dead."

Joseph jerked his head around. "Dead?"

"I do not know the details. We must warm her. She must drink and gain her strength. Hold her up while I try and get her to take some of this coffee."

Frozen, Joseph struggled to decipher what his friend had spoken. He didn't honestly expect him to get any closer than this.

Nathaniel spun, wild questions folding hard across his brow. "Come on, man. She must drink."

His lungs slowed their pace. He stammered, trying to find a way to get his tongue and lips to work in unison, but their sudden numbness made speaking difficult. "She...she wouldn't want me to. Why not Henry or someone else?"

Nathaniel shook his head and mumbled under his breath. Stepping to the cot, he pointed with an impatient flick of a finger. "Help me."

Hannah moved her head against the pillow, a petite moan escaping the small part in her lips.

Never had his legs felt so heavy, the short distance from where he stood to where she lay as dangerous to traverse as a lake of fire.

"Hannah..." Nathaniel lowered to his haunches beside her head, the steaming cup of coffee in his hands. "I should like you to have something warm to drink. We'll have broth for you to take later as well. Can you sit up?"

Still shivering, a small hum of reply was the only response she could give, and Joseph's insides turned to liquid. She strained to rise, eyes still closed, but her shaking refused to abate. In a heated rush, all the strength returned to Joseph's limbs, and he lunged for her. Heedless of the danger to his heart—to his past, which had only just begun to heal—he scooped her legs to the ground and sat beside her, cupping her petite shoulders as he helped her to sit upright. Eyes only half open, she leaned against him, her quivering frame unsettling the dry foundation of his spirit.

A stream of murky questions filled his mind. What had happened? Why was she here? Most, had a harm come to her they did not yet know?

He breathed in slow, deliberate breaths and looked to the canvas ceiling. This closeness was deadly ground. Ten years, and she still felt the same in his arms, still smelled of honey and sweet cream. How could he not close his eyes and rest his lips on her hair? How could he not brush his fingers against her cheek?

But he must not. He would not.

Her father's parting words those many rocky memories ago still rang loud in his ears. *You've damaged her beyond repair. She hates you for what you've done.*

She shook harder, dislodging him from the grasp of the wicked past, though in truth, reality was not much kinder.

Nathaniel, still kneeling, offered the cup. "Here, Hannah. I shall help you hold it while you take a sip."

She reached out, her slender fingers so unsteady she couldn't hold on. Nathaniel wrapped his hands around hers, helping her to bring the cup to her lips as Joseph silently blessed and cursed the tender sight.

I should not be here. Though in truth, he wanted nothing more, a dichotomy that ripped him down the middle.

The tent door flung open, and Henry entered, another steaming mug in his hands. "Strong broth."

"Excellent." Nathaniel stood and went to the small table at the opposite side of the tent. He set the coffee down when Henry placed a hand on his arm.

"You are needed elsewhere, Doctor." He looked to Hannah, then back. "She seems in good enough hands here. You must come."

Unfathomed panic sprang to life in Joseph's chest like a sword-wielding beast. He glared across the room, but his unspoken warning of the mortal danger his friend should face if he were left alone with her went unheeded.

"Sit with her until she is able to remain upright. Then assist her with the broth." He followed Henry to the door. "At the first available chance, see that she gives you a full report of what happened."

Then, they were alone.

Her shivering increased, and she rested her full weight against him. "Thank you."

Those two whispered words, so soft and light, floated in the air like a gossamer thread. They all but killed him. If she had known to whom she spoke, he knew she would not have spoken at all.

Aw the bliss of such warmth. Though her ears and cheeks still pricked, only a slight stammering plagued her muscles, and her eyes could remain open, but she chose to keep them only partly peeled, for the light, however faint, still pained her head.

Unspeaking, the kind soul beside her stood, but not until he was sure she could remain upright. He paced to the other side of the tent and busied himself at the table.

Bracing herself with one hand, she rubbed her eyes with the other when the phantoms of two days past moaned to life from their shallow graves. She grit her teeth to keep the sudden burst of emotion from welling. *Dearest Uncle.* A clink of tin brought her head up, a blessed distraction from that which pained too deep.

With a shuddered inhale, Hannah blinked—and blinked again, slowing every movement, every thought as she stared at the tall, broad frame across the tent. *Nay.* Her eyes lied. Gripping the cot with both hands, she squinted, then blinked several times more, shaking her head to clear her fog-laden mind. *Lord!* She clenched the smooth wood harder, her heart already accepting that which the rest of her refused. It could not be.

The shivering halted, and her heart raced at a speed she could hardly endure. 'Twas him. Ten years could not mar the imprint of him that still lingered so deep within. The impossible breadth of his shoulders, the sunny-blond hue of his hair. 'Twas then he turned and stopped hard, his mouth fixed and blue eyes as question filled as her own.

A sparked silence popped in the frigid air between them. Even as he stared, the reality of what she saw could hardly breach the bulwark of disbelief that rose ever higher. His face had not changed. Matured, aye—grown more handsome even—but naught else. The sharp cut of his jaw ticked, as if he struggled as hard as she to find any fragment of thought in a mind crazed with questions.

She swallowed, and unbidden, his name formed not only on her lips but in her voice. "Joseph?"

Motionless, his gaze pricked deeper. Panic stabbed, and the walls of the tent seemed to press closer. Perhaps 'twas not him. Perhaps her mind played tricks upon her.

Slow and calm, he stepped closer, and her heart pulsed impossibly faster. His gait, his strong hands, the small scar on his cheekbone... *Lord in heaven!*

He paused several feet in front of where she rested, a steaming mug of something in his grasp. Still gripping the cot like one clinging to the edge of a fathomless pit, Hannah craned her neck to peer up at him, then followed as he stooped down to rest on his haunches, his head now almost level with hers.

Extending the tin mug toward her, a fleeting grin graced his mouth before it disappeared. "Hannah."

The sound of her name from his lips took her heart and tipped it, streaming out a host of imprisoned memories that both wept and cheered their sudden freedom. Careful to not meet his gaze and to keep her fingers far from his, she took the warm mug.

Her shivering began once more, but she ignored it, sure the sensation would pass and promising herself it had nothing to do with the fact that this man knelt before her.

"Are you all right? Can you drink unassisted?"

The silky depth of his timbre played along her skin and deep into her chest.

She could not speak her answer, only nod. A frown bit hard into her brow as she stared at the tawny liquid, when a burst of realization cut down her spine like a knife through butter. 'Twas he she had leaned against moments ago, his arm that had rested around her shoulder, his warmth she'd relished and kindness she'd praised. Somehow deep within, her soul had known him, had remembered his touch and welcomed it. Traitorous heart.

She popped her chin up, an ounce of her strength returning, and with it the clarity of mind she'd nearly lost. Was this not also the man who'd left her? Was this not the man who'd toyed with her heart only to discard it like an unwanted scrap?

Swallowing, she rubbed her thumb against the warm tin. But that was the past. There was a much greater need now than to linger over a hurt that should have healed long since.

"Have you..." *Be strong.* She straightened on the cot as best she could. "Where is Nathaniel? I thought—"

"Why are you here, Hannah?"

His firm, somber tone forced her eyes to his. Flashes of memory stole her thoughts, and she lowered her gaze once again to the drink that warmed her freezing hands. Ensign's cry of pain as he fell, the vow in the soldier's stare that he would not let her escape... Yet, by the all-powerful hand of God, she had.

Throat a knot of emotion, she spoke without meeting his gaze. "Where is Nathaniel?"

That was the man she'd sought from the moment she fled the barn. Why Joseph was here, she knew not and wished by heaven he would find his way back to wherever it was he came from.

Without looking up, she could sense him turn away before he faced her again. "I know you wish Nathaniel here, and he will return, but he instructed me to discover why you would travel forty miles to a place not befitting a lady."

The weight of his heavy question rested on her gaze and pressed it farther down until she stared at the muddy grass beneath where he crouched.

"Hannah?"

She glanced up, sorrow and fear churning so hard the truth surged from her mouth to splatter in the frigid air. "Ensign is dead."

Joseph's eyebrows plunged. "Dead?"

"Aye." She took a sip of drink, praying the steaming warmth would clear away the clog of grief in her throat. But it did not. "A handful of soldiers came to the house..." She gripped the mug so hard she could have left her handprints on the tin. "They insisted that the king needed the foundry and that it now belonged to them."

Clutching the little vessel offered a strand of courage, and she clung to it. "He tried to dissuade them—"

"They took it by force." Joseph's stare went hard, the lines at the corners of his eyes lengthening as his scowl deepened.

"'Twas their plan." Hannah swallowed, praying God would grant her grace enough to speak the rest. "Ensign told me to hide in the kitchen. When they insisted on taking our food, Ensign refused them entrance to try and protect me but..." Her pitch threatened to rise, but she held it even. "He was shot as I ran to the barn. Then when they came for me—"

"Did they hurt you?" Joseph reached for her wrist, the sudden surge of rage in his eyes tampered only by the concern that softened them at the corners. "Did they touch you?"

His words floated past her ears, but she couldn't quite hear them. She could only see the stain of Ensign's blood and hear the thrust of the blade into his flesh. She pinched her lips against the cry that stormed behind her teeth. Unable to hold his gaze, her eyes burned. *Dear Ensign...*

"Did they touch you?"

Joseph's quiet rumble rustled the stray hairs at her ears, and she looked up.

She blinked, failing to snip the line of his stare. He could not be so genuine, could he? When for ten years he had not so much as—

"Hannah?" Joseph's stare reached out with firm, familiar tenderness, belying the rage that warred behind their blue depths. "Are you untouched?"

"Aye." She swallowed away the storm of emotions, praising the Lord once again for His goodness. "I am unharmed."

His shoulders dropped as a heavy sigh left his lips.

Licking her own, she continued. "Somehow Ensign followed me, despite his wound, and shot one of them, but the other turned and stabbed Ensign where he stood." Her voice severed, and a searing tear streaked down her cheek. "He gave his life for me."

Closing his eyes slowly, Joseph bowed his head, then brought it back up in the next breath. He squeezed her wrist gently before releasing his grip and pushing up to his full height. "You were not followed?"

"Nay."

He nodded and pivoted toward the tent door, his fists working, rippling the muscles in his forearms. He lunged for the door when Nathaniel strode in, another man entering behind him.

The doctor looked from Joseph to Hannah and nodded, a somber tilt across his mouth. "I am pleased to see you are looking so much better." He turned to

Joseph, his tone dropping an octave. "Do you have the full of it?"

"Nay, but enough."

Nathaniel's eyebrows shot up. "And?"

"The king's men have taken control of the foundry." Joseph paused, his throat working. "They killed Ensign. Hannah managed to escape unharmed."

Eyes sharp as a blade's edge, Nathaniel looked swiftly to the man Hannah still didn't know, before facing her. "Why did they take it? Did they say?"

Hannah's shivering increased, and she gripped the little mug harder, wishing its warmth could seep into her soul as well as it seeped into her fingers. "To use it—'tis what I understand from what I heard him say."

"Who?" The stranger neared, his striking face strict with purpose. "A soldier? Did you get a name?"

"Aye." She scowled, scrambling through the ransacked memories, searching for the name she knew must be hidden in the disarray, when she stumbled upon it, like an overturned table. "Stockton. Major Stockton."

The men in the room eyed each other, their jaws ticking.

"Not surprising there, is it?" The man whose name she still did not know clenched his fists.

"Do you know him?" Hannah's bravery saddled her wild curiosity, flinging the question from her lips.

"I do," he said, his tone answering far more than she'd asked. The stranger bowed politely in her direction. "Forgive me. I fear we have not been introduced."

Nathaniel stepped forward. "Miss Young, allow me to introduce Captain Henry Donaldson."

She nodded politely in return as the man pinned his unmoving gaze upon her.

"What exactly did he say? Was there anyone with him?"

Flinging a look to Joseph, Hannah shifted on the cot, ignoring the way her stomach flipped at the sight of him so near. She met her questioner's stare. "There were others. I do not recall their names...Greene, perhaps? There were more, but I don't remember the others."

She glanced between Nathaniel and Joseph, whose brows shot skyward as they fixed their eyes on their friend.

The captain shook his head, then turned back to her. "Pray, continue."

Tension, that ever-thickening weight on her chest, pressed so hard her lungs struggled to rise. She steadied her voice as one might a frightened horse, but still it fought against the tether. "That is all I know."

The three men stared, each with tight lips and hard eyes.

The new fellow spoke low, his head dipping. "We should tell Thomas of this."

"Aye," the others answered in unison.

"Tell me what?"

The door flung open, and another man entered. Near as tall as Joseph, this next stranger nodded instantly, his kind face softening as he glanced toward Hannah before he aimed a thoughtful scowl on the others. "Well?"

"'Twould seem the British have gotten themselves a foundry." Nathaniel's chin dropped before he motioned to Hannah. "An old friend of mine, Miss Hannah Young. Miss Young, Mr. Watson."

Mr. Watson nodded politely before facing back to Nathaniel. "How came you by this knowledge?"

"Miss Young's uncle owned a foundry. And 'twould seem the British have taken it—and his life."

The man's face flattened. "That is terrible indeed." He flung a look to Hannah but quickly turned his attention to the men. "Why would you wish to inform me of such a thing?"

Nathaniel canted his head. "I should think 'twas obvious."

"If you mean to say we take it back, then I am in full agreement." Joseph folded his arms around his broad chest.

"'Tis quite a risk." Mr. Watson shifted his stance. "Though I am in agreement as well, we have no way of knowing their numbers, what munitions they have—"

"If we take them by surprise, I predict a fairly easy victory." The captain's arms were folded, and he spoke to the ground until the last. "Though 'tis difficult to know their strength, the risk is worth the effort. We need the production of guns more than they."

To this, Nathaniel shifted his feet and nudged his chin at Joseph. "What say you? Had you thought of such?"

"I had." A muscle in Joseph's face flexed as his jaw moved back and forth.

Nathaniel continued his pointed gaze toward Joseph, his volume deepening. "Did he say anything to you? Did he suspect?"

Did who suspect?

Joseph's gaze darted to Hannah, and she gripped her arms tighter at the glint of darkness in his glance. The emotion he harbored refused to be named, but that hint of foreboding floated on the blue of his gaze like a boat on a storming sea.

"Who are you speaking of?" Mr. Watson stood straighter, his muscled arms thickening as he crossed them. "It appears there is something I do not know."

Joseph flung a strained look to Hannah, and her already tight shoulders pinched a mite more. She nearly whispered to him to speak the obvious ill, but he turned away when Nathaniel spoke.

"You might as well know. The foundry the British have just taken now belongs to—"

"How many men will we need?" Joseph's voice boomed, his eyes so strained upon his friend that Hannah believed he might actually have strangled the man with his stare alone.

With a nod, Nathaniel crossed his arms, the look on his face suggesting he understood Joseph's sudden interruption. "That is difficult to estimate."

"I shall apprise Knox of this." Mr. Watson rubbed a hand over his jaw. "He will need to know what we plan."

Captain Donaldson shook his head. "Without sufficient intelligence you cannot know what awaits you."

"There cannot be many of them." Nathaniel shifted his weight over his feet. "Our need outweighs all. The men are desperate for occupation, and this will fill the void."

Hannah glanced to Joseph, his arms folded and eyes stern, then to the others, who conversed with clipped words and solemn brows. They spoke of the foundry as if it were nothing more than a place—a winnable, impersonal thing. That was her home, her life for ten years. Her future. And here they planned to make battle on the very soil her uncle gave his life upon?

"But you cannot move forward without more knowledge, Nathaniel. You could be walking into a trap." Captain Donaldson's volume rose, his hand slicing the air. "We can take it, and we will, but not without first sending a scout."

"'Tis a risk, but can be done." Mr. Watson looked to Joseph, then to Nathaniel. "There are many willing to be covert."

"But there are none who know the foundry." Hannah's voice startled even herself as the words seemed to fly from her mouth before her mind fully thought them. "There are few who know the woods and roads around it as well as Ensign and the men who worked there."

"Are they here...the workers?" the captain asked.

"Aye." Hannah's cheeks burned from the gaze Joseph pinned on her, but she feigned the lack of feeling. "But such would be suspect, would it not? A known Patriot returned home—to their very work?"

Nathaniel put his hand to his mouth, his eyebrows lifting as he looked between the men. "'Tis a valid point."

A flash in her mind illuminated the silhouette of a feeble thought. She blinked as she spoke to the ground. "I could do it." She looked up, the men frozen in place.

For longer than a few breaths, they stood without moving. She cleared her throat and tried again, for the once tiny epiphany gained stature as her rising courage nourished it. "I could do it. They would not suspect a woman."

Captain Donaldson cleared his throat, a gentle grin on his face. "Your bravery at even suggesting such a thing is admirable indeed, Miss Young. But I fear you would be engaging in something far too dangerous—"

"Forgive me, Captain, but I am not ignorant of the danger." She straightened as a rod of determination slid down her spine. "I do thank you for your kind regard for my well-being, but my uncle died at their hand. He gave his life for mine. I feel I am as engaged in this war as much as any of you."

Silence gripped the air. The men seemed unable to respond, so she continued. "I have long supported the cause of liberty, though I have not had the means or ability to be of use to it. But now I can—I must."

Turning only his head toward her, Joseph's bass tone teetered quietly across the space between them. "Do not, Hannah. I know your tenacious nature. I know you would wish to do this and your cause is just, but how could we—"

"Pardon me, Mr. Wythe, but you do not *know* me." The gall of him. She shot a pointed gaze to each man, keeping her voice more calm than it had been seconds ago. "Tell me what must be done, and I shall do it."

"Nay." Joseph pivoted to face her, his voice a soft boom. "You have just escaped them. I fear your journey here has stolen your reason."

Nathaniel stepped forward, reaching a kind hand to her arm. "We are not ignorant of the pains you have suffered, but allowing you to take such a risk is unthinkable."

Hannah pulled her shoulders back, straining to keep a ladylike composure on the outside, despite how it evaporated within. "I thank you for your concern." She breathed in, leveling her chin and finishing her statement with unmistakable grit. "My mind is made up. And 'tis you now who must accept my offer. For I *will* do it."

Chapter Six

Anger cooked Joseph from the inside as he stared at the determined slant of Hannah's mouth. Of course she would not listen to him. He ground his teeth. He *did* know her, despite what she professed. 'Twas that determined, fearless spirit that first pulled his heart toward her those many years ago. He knew everything about her—he knew that shadow of a small dimple in her cheek, that rogue curl that framed her ear, and the way her face reddened when she expressed her will to do something others professed she could not. A will he knew would not easily be swayed.

"Hannah, I would speak with you alone." He motioned to the door of the tent.

Her dainty eyebrows lifted, and she tilted her head with her open mouth ready to gainsay him, when he grabbed her elbow. "Come."

She pulled her arm from his hold, full lips pinched and eyebrows raised in shock. "Where are we going?"

He stopped at the door and opened it, speaking across his shoulder to the men who stared with questioning eyes. "We shall not be a moment."

Out the door and away from his friends who certainly wished to be an audience to what would likely be a fantastic display, he marched from camp toward a line of trees where several horses were kept.

The hum of the camp now several dozen yards away, Joseph took Hannah's arm again and pulled her around the largest horse, partly shielding them from any straying curiosity.

"You cannot do it, Hannah."

She crossed her arms under the blanket that still covered her. "You heard them. Intelligence must be had. And who better to do it than I?"

Was she mad? "This is not for you to decide. This is a matter of war, and the risks are—"

"You think I do not understand the gravity of what has happened, what *will* happen?" She hugged the blanket tighter and leaned forward. "I know what is at stake. I witnessed Ensign's death. I know they will not hesitate to kill."

"Then you must understand why we cannot allow you to do it. 'Tis dangerous enough for one with experience in such things."

"Joseph, I—"

"Hannah, no." Her name felt strange and wonderful on his lips. He shifted his weight over his feet, struggling for anything that might help him at last come to fully accept where he was and with whom he spoke.

She pursed her lips, that small dimple creasing in her cheek as she looked away. Finally she returned her eyes to his, and he felt his heart tip within him. "Ensign loved this cause. If he was willing to give his life so that I could have freedom, how can I not do that for others?"

He clenched his fists to keep from taking her by the shoulders. "Your desire is virtuous indeed, but, Hannah, think. It would not be safe for you to return to a den of vipers, especially with no one to help you should something go amiss, for certainly something will."

She looked away, her head slanting.

He paused, pressing out a heavy breath that plumed white in the frigid air. "I know you wish to help. But you have not thought it through. There are too many avenues of discovery that would make such a venture near suicide."

Her dainty throat bobbed, and she glanced up, red rimming her eyes. "I want to do something. I must. Somehow."

Was it the sorrow in her voice or her determination that stalled him? Both, likely. Unable to move, Joseph allowed his eyes to trail over her. Here they stood, speaking as if they were no more than acquaintances, no more than two souls striving for a common cause. *Hannah.* The wilderness of unspoken hurts stretched for miles between them, yet he could reach out and touch her cheek, tuck that curl behind her ear. Here she stood, as real and alive as he had ever seen her. Though so much time had passed, it almost seemed a dream, beautiful and wrenching. All he wished to speak wrestled with what he should. Of course she could not be allowed to do what she willed. Such a thing could very likely take her life. She must be made to understand that.

Willing himself to tear open the sack of protests that weighed heavy in his arms, he stepped forward, mouth open and ready to speak, but 'twas Nathaniel's voice that cut the air between them.

"Joseph."

Both of them looked up to see their friend a polite distance away on the other side of the horses.

Joseph answered. "Aye?"

Nathaniel nodded to Hannah. "Forgive me for interrupting, but I should like to speak with Joseph alone if I may."

She offered a smile in reply before flashing a tight-mouthed expression to Joseph. "Of course."

Stepping sideways, Nathaniel motioned back the way he'd come. "If you are willing, I would be grateful if you would return to the tent and take some broth. Your strength cannot yet be recovered in full, I am sure."

"Thank you, Doctor. I believe you are right." After another quick look to Joseph, she rounded the animal and plodded back toward camp just as Nathaniel neared Joseph.

"You know..." Nathaniel glanced in Hannah's direction but spoke to Joseph. "She may have a point in what she proposes."

"What?" The searing audacity of such a statement nearly melted the snow beneath his shoes. "What can you possibly mean?"

"I mean she could be right—that she could make a good spy."

"Not two moments ago you were as much against it as I." A hard laugh burst from Joseph's chest and echoed through the grove behind him. "You have gone daft."

The usual brevity in Nathaniel's nature never surfaced. He only stared, a slight lift to one brow and twist to his head.

'Twas Joseph now who balked. "You cannot be serious."

"We are in desperate need of intelligence, Joseph. And though the thought of placing her at risk is beyond comprehension, it is a brilliant stratagem."

A slug to the gut would have taken him by less surprise. Nathaniel would actually approve of this? "Thomas and Henry agree with you then." He prayed the statement wouldn't be verified.

"They were the ones who persuaded me."

A rough grunt raked up Joseph's throat, and he stepped toward the trees, hoping the motion would ease the sudden rage that burned his limbs. "You will enable her foolishness." He spun back around. "Surely they cannot be ignorant of the fact that she could be killed."

"Of course they are not, which is why..." He stopped. Amusement flashed in his eyes before earnest resolve curtained the mirth. "Which is why we have devised a plan."

"Oh!" Joseph feigned pleasure at the thought, his voice bright. "You have devised a plan?" He cocked his hip, the theatrics gone. "I have learned to be wary of that glint in your eye."

"She wishes to go, and truthfully, we cannot stop her. But we can insist she have *someone* accompany her."

At this, Nathaniel's smile grew slightly, and Joseph's stomach clenched.

Ha! Truly, his friend had lost his senses. A barrage of protests hurled across the battlefield of his mind, but the fight was too violent to allow any thought to make way to his voice.

He marched for the trees once more, hearing Nathaniel speak behind him. "'Tis the only thing that makes sense."

Joseph jerked to a halt and pivoted back around. "It does not make sense." He choked the words free, still unable to speak as fully as he wished. "I will not go along with it."

"I've never seen anyone fight and shoot as well as you." Nathaniel paused, expression cinching. "I've never seen anyone bluff the way you can. 'Twas as if you were trained for this, Joseph."

The unvoiced message in Nathaniel's words ground like a bootheel in flesh. "Do not try to flatter me. Cyprian's treatment hardened me in my youth, made me fight for myself both mentally and physically, aye." Frustration steamed. "I may have learned to hide my emotions well, but that doesn't mean I am ready for this kind of covert action—and neither is Hannah."

Nathaniel went on, undeterred as if he'd heard nothing of Joseph's protest. "You could pass as relatives—as brother and sister even." He tilted his head, one eyebrow slanted. "And if you two were to 'return home' to Eaton Hill after visiting a Loyalist family up north and simply happen to find the soldiers there...I do believe such a tale would be believed."

"Let us say your plan is accepted and we move forward—how are we to act at the 'news' of our *father's* death, hmm?" He removed his hat and raked a hand over his head. Growling to the sky, he finished the continuous thought. "There are so many flaws in this proposal I cannot begin to name them. Not to mention anything of the fact that you are completely ignorant of the past that lies like a vast ocean between Hannah and me. We cannot be made to spend time together like that, Nathaniel. 'Twould not be proper, no matter how we devised it." Improper, aye. More, 'twould be cutting open a festering wound and salting it through.

"Well…" Nathaniel conceded with a slight tilt of the head. "You are right. I did forget about that. So who would you have accompany her in your place? There are plenty of men in camp who would be more than happy to be her guardian and companion in such an undertaking."

The mention of it forced Joseph's muscles to flex. No man in camp could be trusted beyond his intimate group of friends—and with all of them married, 'twould be impossible for them to accompany her. He looked toward camp, his insides afire at the thought of any other man at her side. A stranger could well take advantage of her in ways unthinkable.

Nay. It had to be him.

Like meat on a spit, he was skewered, the truth spinning him over the heat of a fiery, unforgiving fate.

"'Twould be only for two weeks."

Joseph scowled. "Two weeks?"

"Thomas says Washington is in great need of intelligence regarding their movement, troop numbers, artillery, and this knowledge must be had by mid-February, if not sooner, so the decision of how and when to attack can finally be made."

Rubbing his temple, Joseph grumbled silently. Two weeks was not so terrible, and such a mission would give his mind plenty of action to distract from the nearness of her.

He sighed aloud and dropped a hand to his side. "I shall do it. But we shall go as cousins and name Ensign our uncle."

Nathaniel nodded, trying to hide a victorious lift of his mouth. "Excellent."

Joseph scowled. What had he done? He looked to the camp. There was no going back on it, no matter how his stomach churned. He turned back to Nathaniel, whose wide grin was now fully exposed and close to being smacked. "When do we leave?"

Nathaniel's smile grew wider still. "At dawn."

The morning road was nearly empty, but for a few shoppers and tavern patrons who raced over the snowy roads to find warmth indoors, for there was none to be had in the frigid January air. A thick coat of fog hovered over the road like a sea of floating white. Scents of wood smoke tickled Philo's nose as the muted sound of a ship's bell barely reached his ears from the sea a mile away.

Philo hurried his pace, glancing aimlessly at his mud-covered shoes before putting his attention forward. 'Twas early, perhaps too early for Maxim to be in his office, but even if he wasn't, Philo could wait. The inquiry he'd sent to Plymouth, innocently asking about the sale of Eaton Hill, had yet to receive a response. Perhaps none would come. It mattered little. Philo dodged a pile of manure and continued on. Maxim knew everyone and everything, and with a little persuasion, he could be prevailed upon to do just about anything. Getting this information would be a simple task for such a man as Maxim.

"Uncle!"

Philo looked over his shoulder, the quiet road suddenly less pleasant than it had been as his niece hurried toward him. He faced forward, hoping she would hear his feigned pleasure, not see the irritation in his eyes. "Caroline. How are you?"

She rushed up beside him, a laden basket in her arms. "I am well. And you?"

Her exuberance made her seem younger than the five and twenty years she boasted. Then again, she had always been the most animated of the two— Hannah, in truth, only slightly more reserved.

"Where are you off to?"

Not slowing his step, he glanced at her with his eyes only, dismissing her inquiry with a comment of his own. "I might ask the same of you. Where do you go on such a morning with so large a basket?"

"Oh..." She looked down, shifting the cloth more securely over the contents before flinging him a smile. "'Tis nothing."

Her obvious dismissal of his question was no surprise. They had never been close, despite her congenial nature. And no matter how he wished to ignore the sensation, Caroline Whitney had a strange way of being able to make him more at ease than even his own sister. He glanced at her, struck by how much she resembled Helena. "How is your mother?"

Smile blooming, Caroline shifted the basket in her arms. "She is well, thank you. 'Tis fortunate I came upon you. She requested I seek you in order to issue an invitation to dinner this evening."

His dear sister, Helena, had always been kind to him. 'Twas more than he could say for any other member of the family. That familiar burning, the same he'd suffered since Ensign's ill news, began again. "Give her my thanks, but I fear I cannot accept."

"No?"

"I shall be engaged elsewhere." Philo rubbed the aching spot in his palm.

She nodded with a humming response. "Church related, no doubt?"

Chuckling bitterly, he faced the road. "Isn't it always?"

She grinned and appeared ready to speak again, but Philo beat her to it. "Your load makes me curious...I venture to guess you bring Leo Cooper a basket lunch and plan to sit on a blanket in the parlor as you might by the pond, if it were not covered with ice and snow."

Her cheeks bloomed red like a summer rose, and she looked away. "Nay."

A slight chuckle eased a bit of the chronic blistering in his middle. "He is courting you, is he not?"

Raising a single shoulder, Caroline shifted the basket and made clear she wished not to speak of what he'd mentioned, by changing the subject as they continued around Shawme Pond. "How is my cousin? I have not heard from her of late."

He kept his eyes forward. Then she did not know? Did Helena and Jack? "You know she doesn't write to me."

"Have you written to her?"

The innocence of her question stung like a hand to his face. "My affairs are none of your concern, Caroline."

His cutting response seemed only to fuel her need for discussion. She stopped and pulled him at the elbow, forcing him to halt his progress as well.

"I heard about Eaton Hill."

So they did know.

He tried to pull back, but she'd snared him with the youthful wisdom in her eyes. "We know you are saddened. But 'twould seem for the best."

A bitter laugh popped out. "The best? My brother wishes to cut me off from everything that should be mine. Even my own child."

She dropped her hand back to the basket. "'Tis a two-way road, Uncle. You cannot expect something when you give nothing in return."

Blast. He should not have opened his mouth. She only spewed her mother's own words at him.

The tension between them nipped at his heels, and he widened his stance. He would not be cornered by his sister's child, especially when she only invited him to dinner in order to tell him what was done was "for the best" and "everything will be fine in the end."

"The truth is..." Caroline glanced at some faraway spot on the horizon, her expression solemn but accepting. "Leo is not courting me. Not any longer." She flung him a fleeting look before darting her eyes away. "He wished my affection but wasn't willing to offer any of his own in return."

He stopped, a frown pulling hard on his brow. Poor child. She would think herself an old maid. "Well, the man is a fool, and your future is better without him."

"You are kind to me, Uncle." A slanted half smile pushed up one cheek. "I see now we were not a good match. And he has so many constraints on his time..."

"Constraints?"

She jostled the basket again, and he reached for it, taking it from her arms. Shocked at the heavy weight, he balked with a surprised look, and she laughed, answering his previous question as they continued on. "Leo said he has too much to think about. Now that Joseph Wythe has given him his shop, he must focus on his work."

Philo put his hands in his pockets, his mind leaning back to a word she'd spoken. "Given? Did you say Joseph Wythe *gave* his shop to Leo?"

Caroline bobbed a shoulder but offered nothing more.

He bit the inside of his cheek, gnawing away his rising irritations. Was she too so blinded by the man's pretended goodness? "Joseph simply walked away, hmm? What a generous man he is."

"Indeed." She smiled. "But 'twas no secret he planned to leave for the army."

That had been rumored about. "What of Jacob?"

The travails of years past were known to most everyone in Sandwich. Cyprian Wythe had been a friend to few, and his death—as well as the death of his wife—had left their son an orphan, whom Joseph had taken in.

But the benevolence did naught to soften the man's image in Philo's mind. Still wanton, still selfish and sinful, Joseph Wythe was nothing more than the mud on his shoes.

Caroline's response to his previous question tugged him back to the moment. "Jacob is with Kitty

Smith and will stay there until Joseph returns to fetch him."

"Returns? Ha."

Caroline's delicate eyebrows jumped at his bitter response, but he tilted his head her direction and finished anyway. "Anyone who goes to battle should consider themselves as well as dead."

"Uncle, really." Caroline started forward, and Philo matched her step. She gave him a sideways glance. "You are not a Tory, are you?"

"I am no friend of the British, but I am no fool either. Let the Patriots fight if they will, and all the better for me should they win. I for one would like to keep my head in place."

A sprite laugh breathed from Caroline's mouth. Stopping, she looked at him, a sudden wisdom in her narrowed eyes peeling away his exterior, leaving him exposed, as if she could see what lay open in his soul.

Her eyebrows neared as she stared, and his stomach squirmed. Why should a woman—a young one at that—make him feel the pricks of some unknown conscience? Had he anything to hide?

With a smile that said she reserved whatever it was she'd wished to speak, Caroline took the basket from him and turned to where the road curved right. "I shall give your regards to my mother." Long strides led her swiftly away from him, but she spoke over her shoulder. "You are still welcome, should you change your mind."

He touched his hat, and she turned away, disappearing around the bend in the road. His gut writhed, and he cursed the discomfort. He shouldn't let his niece rile him in such a way. 'Twas not as if she was anything but a parrot of her mother, speaking and doing what Helena would do. The very reason declining the invitation was without question.

"Philo! Philo!"

Frantic steps and the blurted sound of his name spun Philo at the heel. "Maxim. I was on my way to see you. I—" Philo stopped, the round eyes and flushed cheeks of his companion seizing his lungs. "My friend, what's happened?"

Maxim gasped for breath, a hand at his chest. "I've just heard about the foundry."

Was that all? Why such a fuss? Philo fought the urge to growl. "That's what I wanted to speak with you about this morning."

"You do not seem as upset as I would have expected at such news."

"Surely I'm upset, but there's naught I can do until I know who's bought it."

"Bought it?" At that, Maxim's face lost a mite of color. "Then you haven't heard. You cannot have, for I just overheard it from a Redcoat in Newcomb Tavern."

A pin of frustration jabbed, and Philo splayed his palms. "What?"

"The British have taken the foundry. They have taken Eaton Hill."

The words wound around him like the lingering fog, seeping through his mind before a thrill raced up his spine, followed after by a sharp reprimand. Should he not be aghast, enraged? Somehow only glee found his heart.

He feigned intense shock, but the question was sincere. "What do you mean?"

"The army has taken the foundry for their own use." His friend looked over his shoulder, then back.

"Should we not alert the men in town and make ready to take back what should be yours?"

What should be mine.

At least someone understood that.

Philo filled his lungs. "When was this?"

"I do not know." Still panting, Maxim motioned over his shoulder. "But it can't have been long. Come. Let us—"

"No. Wait."

One hand on his friend, one in the air, Philo's mind followed the whisper that left crumbs for him to follow. Perhaps...

He caught Maxim's gaze. "Do nothing."

"What?"

"Do nothing."

Maxim jerked back. "You cannot be serious."

Philo dropped his hold and placed a hand on Maxim's back, careful not to have his friend see through his pretense.

"We must first be sure we know what we are up against." Remembering his mantle as a man of God, Philo reverted into the role he'd grown accustomed to, no matter how uncomfortable the cloth. "Providence does not work but with everlasting wisdom, does He not? Surely there will be good that comes of this. Prudence before haste. We must trust in His power to protect and provide."

"But does not God expect us to act?" Maxim's face curled with frustration. "You do not speak sense, Philo. Your daughter is—"

"She is fine." He put a hand over his heart. "I feel all will be well, Maxim. Aye, we shall proceed, but with caution. We cannot have any more of our men running to their deaths. Already there will be too many widows amongst us."

Only slightly subdued, Maxim nodded with a rough breath. "I suppose."

Striding forward, Philo knit his hands behind his back, pressing his lips together to hold back the smile that tickled his face. Such good fortune. Perhaps God was as displeased with Ensign as he. Feigning more fraught than he felt, Philo pursed his mouth and slowed his step, staring down at his feet.

"Let us return to Newcomb and see if we cannot somehow glean a bit more information from that Redcoat, hmm?"

Maxim's mouth bowed up, and he nodded with acceptance. "I can always be persuaded in that vein."

"Come. Let us see what we can learn."

Philo started again and glanced up to the clouds. Providence at work, surely. God was not well pleased with Ensign, that much was certain. Here was the chance Philo had been waiting for. The art of persuasion was delicate, but even soldiers were human, were they not? They had pride that needed stroking, egos that craved boosting.

Once they could be swayed to side with Philo, Ensign would have no choice but to give Eaton Hill to him after all.

Chapter Seven

A day had passed—one day and a full night—and they'd been on the road again since daybreak. The vast silence between them loomed like the snow, quiet and endless, surrounding and consuming. Hannah gripped the edge of the wagon seat beside Joseph, a giant flake plunking against her cheek. She brushed it away. The minutes passed more like hours. A bump in the road jostled her, and she gripped the seat harder to keep from bumping into his body, which rested not half an inch from hers. *Not much longer.* She shivered. Her cheeks and nose prickled, and her fingers ached with every movement. Having hardly recovered from the first journey when setting off on the return, she still had not fully shed the quivers of cold.

She flung a quick glance in Joseph's direction before focusing on the puffs of breath that left her mouth as she breathed. Not a word between them. For that she was both grateful, and not. Could they really make such a ploy believable if they could not at least be civil? Nathaniel and Captain Donaldson had made clear their mission, and she was both alive and sick with dread at the thought of not fulfilling what she'd vowed she would do at any cost.

A slice of bravery tempted her to look at Joseph again, and her heart skipped a pulse. Tricorne dusted with snow, blond queue resting between his broad shoulders, greatcoat barely able to contain the large muscles that filled it. He stared forward, the blink of his eyes against the falling snow the only indication he wasn't a mere statue as he held the reins.

He had insisted—nay, demanded he be the one to accompany her. Why? She didn't want to question, for her heart loved and loathed his presence far more than she would ever admit in words. She must tread with care. Their mission, short as it was, was long enough to demolish the fortress she'd erected, despite its thick towering walls.

"You wish to speak." His voice rumbled toward her, nearly startling her off the seat.

She straightened, gathering the composure his sudden words had scattered. "I am sorry to disappoint, but I do not."

He peered her way with the slightest move of his head. "You say I do not know you, Hannah, but I do. You wish to speak."

"I have nothing to say." She wriggled in her seat, her insides twisting.

He stared forward, offering an almost imperceptible shrug, waiting near a full minute before voicing his reply. "Very well."

The nerve of him. He did not know her. Well...not perfectly, anyway. She tapped her toes in her shoes. To keep the blood moving, aye, but also to ease the stifling anxiety. Fighting the urge to peek at him again, she stared off into the wood, the large flakes floating to the ground like goose down. Keeping the barricade of their broken past between them meant the raw, tender parts of her would not have to be touched, and such security allowed for rumination. This man had offered to be her companion. Nay, had insisted. The protectiveness and sincerity she'd seen in his eyes played wistful chords on the strings of her heart. But the ever-present dissonance overshadowed, as well it should.

This is no game, Hannah. And you are no fool.

"I suppose we could make the entire journey in silence." She breathed in, avoiding the battle of her own thoughts, which dizzied her. "But I hardly believe such would be good practice when we are supposed to make the British believe we are kin."

His jaw shifted, and he flung her a fleeting look before training his attention on the snow-covered road. "True."

After a beat of silence that testified indeed that one word was all he would say, she cleared her throat to speak, but no response readied itself. Nay, that was a lie. There were words that waited to be spoken. Oceans of them. *How have you been these past years?* Still, the deepest ones reached up from her heart to grip hard at her throat. *Why did you never return to me?* Even deeper still, *Did you not love me as I did you?*

Hannah released a shuddered breath, more audible than she'd hoped, and she could feel his sudden gaze upon her. The sensation pressed stronger, and she fought the urge to crane her neck toward him. If she turned now, he might note the pain—that chronic throbbing of the heart that sometimes burned behind her eyes.

"Are you well?"

She could only nod.

He tugged on the reins, pulling the horses to a stop.

"What is it?" Sure her emotions were buried once more, she looked to him. "Why have we stopped?"

His eyes trailed over her, and his brow twitched down. Reaching behind her into the wagon, he felt for something. "I fear you are becoming too cold. We've only ten more miles before we reach the inn." He retrieved a large blanket and handed it to her. "This should provide a measure of extra warmth."

She took the offering, careful not to meet his gaze or allow her fingers to brush against his. If only he weren't so kind. This venture was rife enough with conflicting emotions. She needn't the chafing cloth of his generosity to rub her raw. "Thank you."

Unfolding it, she carefully tucked the heavy covering around her knees and behind her back, watching the thick snowflakes land upon her lap, as if the large white flecks felt the need to blanket her as well.

When the wagon didn't immediately roll forward, she turned, and her gaze collided with his. She couldn't breathe, and yet her heart beat a frantic rhythm. All the strength she willed to pull her eyes away betrayed her, keeping her face toward him. Sweet heaven, but he was handsome. The years had not marred him but enhanced his rugged appeal, adding to the steep angle of his jaw and broadening the shape of his muscular frame. Not only was he pleasing to the eye. He was kind, strong, and as sincere as he had always been. She felt herself slipping, a gradual slide that would gain strength and pull her down a never-ending slope if she had not the strength to grip her nails into the mound and strain with her might against it.

A painful throbbing pushed tears through the crack in her heart. *What happened, Joseph?*

Putting a tight smile to her mouth, she tugged herself free from the power of his stare and faced forward, tucking her hands beneath the blanket. Shielding herself from his arrows of sincerity with a curt nod to the road, she questioned, "Why do you wait?"

Again, he didn't answer, his unyielding stare heating the side of her face. "Joseph, come now. This is foolishness." She flung another look, and his arsenal splintered to pieces the shield she'd so hastily constructed. His eyes, as endlessly blue as a summer sky, seemed to cup around her, holding her motionless as he studied her.

Determined to keep herself alert by the hurt that pricked, she huffed a light breath. What right had he to stare—to ignore the vast chasm that gaped open between them? "Why do you wait? We shall freeze here."

"Why have you not married?"

All the world stilled. Even the flakes drifted slower. He had not actually dared ask such a thing.

She blinked, her movements slow and words hushed by the disbelief that gripped her. "What did you say?"

He finally released her from his gripping stare and turned to the road with an irritated shift of his jaw. "Why have you not married? 'Tis a simple question."

Pins pricked her chest and the back of her eyes. "I need not answer that."

"I am in earnest, Hannah." He twisted toward her again. "We are to be cousins—not strangers. I would know this of you and more if I am to have a ready answer when asked why such a lovely woman has no family of her own."

Lovely woman.

Hannah lowered her gaze and turned away. What right had he to speak to her that way? To compliment her under the guise of only doing his duty for the cause they undertook instead of the honest truth of his curiosity?

Shame burned from the crown of her head down to her neck. She blamed him, but she was no innocent party. Deep down she'd wanted him to say everything that ripened on the air between them, for she hadn't the strength to reach for the low-hanging fruit of truth. Such a coward she was.

Sighing, she knotted her hands beneath the blanket, praying she could douse her sparking emotions with at least a cupful of truth. "My need to care for my family took my time and devotion." Which was true. Aunt Bea had always been of frail health, and after the heartbreak of losing the one thing that might have brought her and Joseph back together, Hannah had needed the distraction from her own woes by caring for the needs of another. The weight of memory pulled her vision to her lap. "And I suppose...I suppose I could not marry, since I did not love."

"You did not?"

The rich bass of his timbre lured her face to his and she stilled. *Not since you.* Numbed by all that was unspoken, the words streamed from her mouth.

"Did not you love? Why have you not married? I should know the same of you, should I not?"

His gaze trailed over her face, then drifted to the road. After a breath he straightened, reins in hand. "I never cared to marry."

With a flick of the reins, they jerked forward, Hannah's heart leaving a trail of crimson on the snow behind them. She clutched her knitted fingers so tight she feared her bones would snap. Neck cording, she made sure to breathe in long, steady strokes. All these years, she'd wished not to believe it. But so it was. Just as Father had said. *He is done with you, Hannah. He is not the marrying kind. You had best move on and forget him.*

Forget it, man. Leave it be.

Joseph ground his teeth. Such an easy thought for an impossible task.

Glancing to Hannah, he noted the pinch of her mouth, the rise of her chin. The woman had sat so rigid these days past he'd feared at every bump she'd fall from the bench.

Letting out a slow, quiet exhale, Joseph reined in the growl that nearly got away from him. *Why have you not married?* How could he ask such a thing? He hadn't intended to of course, but the question had whirled so harsh in his mind that his lips had begun speaking before he was able to stop them. Though as he considered it, his excuse was valid. They *did* need to have their histories straight, or their quest would be over before it began.

As he stared at the white road ahead of him, the flakes dotting the horses' backs as they walked, he submitted to the siren song of memory. Why she'd refused to see him after that night they'd become one burned like a winter bonfire, hot and high and fierce. Was it true what she said? That she'd never loved? He blinked, straining to focus on the snow that fell on the road, but his mind snatched him away to the night his heart had been taken. Nay, not taken. Given. Freely and with passion. Their vow to marry had not been taken lightly. Not by him. And he'd thought, not by her.

He breathed out and rolled his shoulders back. No use in trying to untie a knot that had been tangling itself for so long. He'd struggled for years to come to an understanding. He'd made no progress then, and he wouldn't now.

Ignoring all his former thoughts, he tried to communicate as if his insides weren't afire. "When we arrive, we must ever be cautious, ever alert. Do not allow yourself to be alone with them." He would focus on their mission. That and nothing else. Though no matter how he tried, his instinct to protect her surpassed everything. "Do you understand?"

She offered a cursory glance, then looked away and nodded.

"I cannot have you doing anything foolish, Hannah."

"Foolish?" She scowled. "You act as if I know nothing of what is ahead of us. I am not a young girl, Joseph."

"No, you are not." He stopped the horses again and turned to face her. "You are a beautiful woman.

You will attract the attention of every soldier—your *every* action will be watched. Closely."

Her mouth dropped open slightly, and she pulled back, as if the thought slapped her. "That is ridiculous. They shall be far more intent upon their own duties than upon me."

Leaning forward, he held her as motionless with his glare as he nearly did with his hands. His voice rumbled through his chest. "If you believe that, then you do not understand the ways of men."

She squirmed and averted her eyes. Good. Perhaps his need to frighten her was working. "Our utmost caution in all things is paramount. Especially your safety."

She straightened, her mouth a thin line. "We spoke of all of this before we left. Captain Donaldson and Nathaniel made everything clear, and I do take it seriously, no matter what you may think." She crossed her arms, the steely creases in her brow not as imposing as she might have thought. "I do not see why you should still be so concerned even after we've planned this so well. I begin to think you do not trust me."

"Trust has nothing to do with it." Small measured breaths ensured his volume wouldn't rise. "And what have we planned, exactly? Have we considered that you are known well enough for anyone in town to become suspicious should they see both of us at the foundry?"

"'Twill be over in two weeks, hardly time enough to raise suspicions." A dainty sigh left her mouth, and her chest dropped. "Visitors are rare, and all the workers have gone. Joseph, I cannot understand—"

"What of your father?"

The words made her freeze, the color in her cheeks slipping from red to pink. Another victory, though it pained him to halt her in such a way.

Her gaze fell, and her mouth twitched. "What of him?"

"When did you see him last?"

"I..." She brushed a snowflake from her cheek, glancing away. "When I refused to return to Sandwich with him six years ago, when I told him my home was with his brother, he vowed he would never see me again." Raising her eyes to him, she finished the thought, her tone a cold thread. "That vow he has not broken, though he never ceased his continual rain of hatred on Ensign. I doubt even the knowledge of his brother's death would entice him to mend anything between us." Flinging a look to him, a flash of pain darkened her eyes before courage turned them evergreen. "Joseph, I would not have accepted this had I any indication my father would make an appearance."

Joseph's muscles cramped as he wrestled the reality he knew and that she did not. Her gentle features strained as she stared at the wood at their feet. The vulnerability that lined her eyes and mouth tugged at him like a thickly twined rope. The battle against the desire to reach for her hand, to promise their safety and success, drained all the strength from his limbs.

Sighing, he turned forward, ready to flick the reins. Perhaps he should turn back. Perhaps he should force her to forfeit by revealing all that he knew. Aye, 'twas what he wished—for the safety of her life and the safety of his heart. But reason nudged his thoughts in line. "Keep in mind the mission and the danger. That is all I ask."

"I am committed in every way." She smiled, all ease and friendliness as if their very lives were not in the balance. "We shall not be discovered."

"You cannot be sure."

"I have never been more sure." She placed her hands in her lap. "If you are not, then I suggest before you retreat, depositing me back home, and I will do it all myself."

Blast it, woman! He bent forward, his nose almost touching hers. "It is my responsibility to keep you safe, and I will do that as best I can, but as I cannot chain you to my side, I must ask you to be wise."

The black centers of her eyes grew wide, and her brow plummeted. "You think I would not be?"

He dipped his chin, his voice low. "Nay...but I know your impetuous nature, your determined mind. And as you are under my care—"

"Under *your* care?" Cheeks scarlet, she faced him in full. "Must I remind you that we are merely reluctant partners in this venture, two people emboldened by a greater cause? So do not believe for a moment—"

"Hannah." His volume roared louder than he'd wished. "You cannot begin to think that—"

"I refuse to—"

A sound around the bend hushed them both, and they looked to the road, then to each other before assuming postures that told nothing of their argument.

Snatching the reins, he flicked them, rousing the horses to move. His instincts cocked like a ready pistol as he strained his hearing on the noise of the approaching riders. The drumming of hooves and mumble of several voices gave tell of at least three or four travelers, but it was the glint of red around the corner that made his blood chill far more than the temperature biting his flesh.

He glanced to Hannah, ready to shield her, ready to see a flash of fear in her eyes. But she only looked up at him briefly, her voice as smooth as glass. "We begin."

The riders came within view, five in total, coming at them in the center of the road.

"Halt!" The soldier in front raised his hand out toward them.

The knowledge that Joseph would from here forward be forced to do the will of the enemy seared his skin, but he obeyed, acting his part.

"Good day, sirs." He molded a small, polite smile on his lips.

The nearest soldier nodded and halted his mount beside Joseph. "What are you doing on this road?" He looked around the wood. "'Tis unpleasant weather to be traveling in indeed."

Joseph glanced to Hannah. Had she seen the soldier's eyes take her in in a single sweep? 'Twas just as he'd feared, and they'd not even reached the foundry. *Dear Lord, what have I done?* "My cousin and I are just returning home from Salem, sir."

The soldier's mount shuffled sideways, and he tugged on the reins. "Is that so?"

"Aye." He snarled the rest of it, not lowering his gaze from the men who now surrounded them. "The bloody Patriots ransacked my cousin's home because he refuses to join their cause. We went to help."

The same soldier nodded, flinging a glance to the man on the horse behind him. "You are loyal to the crown?"

"We are no friend to the Patriots." He nodded toward them, the next words burning a path through his throat. "God save the king."

A grin broadened the lines on the soldier's face. "God save the king." Sitting straighter, the man looked to Hannah, his gaze lingering overlong on her face. "I should hope you are near home. Your cousin looks chilled to the bone."

Joseph shook his head in reply, suddenly wishing perhaps they had posed as husband and wife. Then perchance the men would be less likely to pursue her. Then again, maybe not.

He flexed all his anxiety into his arms. "We are stopping at Greenborrow for the night, then on to Plymouth."

"Plymouth, eh? We have just come from there."

A nod was all he could offer. He glanced at Hannah, scanning her expression for any indication of recognition, but her painted geniality took center stage.

"Plymouth is our home." Her voice trilled like birdsong. "'Tis lovely there. I am surprised you would wish to leave it."

"I should have regretted to leave, indeed, if such loveliness as yours had been present." He tugged at the reins of his mount again. "But alas, the army does not have..." He stopped, his gaze suddenly gripping to her with a scrutiny that stabbed blades into Joseph's gut. "Forgive me. I do believe I feel as if we have met before. Have we not?"

Hannah's cheeks reddened, and she looked away. "Sir, you speak too freely."

His smile quirked at one end. "Deepest apologies, my lady." Again the man looked behind to the others with him, the bob of his eyebrows making Joseph's shoulders grow taut. "Greenborrow is still ten miles south, is it not?" He shook his head. "I should hate to see someone so lovely suffer in such weather as this."

Joseph shook his head, knowing full well what the man would say. "It will not be long—"

"As a point of fact..." The soldier looked back from where they'd ridden. "Though we have just come from there, I would be most happy to take you the rest of the way."

Had Joseph a ready pistol, he would have brandished it. "That will not be necessary."

"Nay, nay, I insist. 'Tis the least I can do for any colonist willing to stand up to the Patriots." The man's eyes narrowed in the corners, but his smile widened. He turned his attention to Hannah. "A ride on horseback would bring you to the warmth of the inn much quicker."

Never. Joseph all but leapt from his seat. "We thank you for the offer, but—"

"You will not let the lady answer for herself?" The words were barked before he grinned immediately after. "My lady, I would be honored if you would let me take you to the inn. Your cousin shall follow right behind. I do believe that warmth and a meal will do you good."

Hannah turned to him. "May I?"

The glance and accompanying smile she fed Joseph did strange things to his soul. He wanted to slay every other man who touched her and in the same second scold her reckless foolishness. Did she not know what horrors might await her if she trusted this stranger?

He swallowed and cant his head in the most *cousinly* way he could. "It isn't that much farther, and I promised Aunt Libby I would not let you out of my sight."

She slanted her chin with an equally slanted grin and reached out to touch his arm. "These are the king's men, cousin. They will treat me far better than the Patriots have, I am sure of that." That shallow dimple made a brief appearance before she lifted her face to the soldier. "I should be most pleased to accept your offer, sir. I thank you."

"My pleasure, of course."

She stood to climb down, but Joseph gripped her fingers, and she twisted to face him, fire pluming from the backs of her eyes, as he knew it did from his. But she would not be moved.

"Do not worry, cousin." Rising, she planted a chaste kiss on his cheek. "I shall see you before sunset."

The soldier dismounted and helped Hannah down from the wagon, his hands lingering at her waist far longer than they should. In truth, Joseph should not have let the man touch her at all. What was he thinking allowing her to go through with this? Yet how could he protest? She was not a woman to be contradicted no matter how he wished he could rope her to the seat beside him and never allow her to leave his side.

The soldier nodded to Joseph, an indication he intended to give every remaining attention to Hannah.

Nearing the horse, Hannah grinned. "To whom am I to offer my unending thanks?"

He bowed his head. "Lieutenant Matthew Greene, my lady. At your service."

She flicked a look to Joseph before the man aided her onto the saddle, her eyes wide and face as white as the snow on the trees.

Greene.

Joseph lurched but was held still, as if pulled back by an unseen hand. The man was astride and off with a nod before Joseph could put two thoughts together. Within moments, all of them were gone.

Every muscle, every vein and sinew strained until Joseph's entire body alternately ached and burned. He should never have let her go. What was she thinking to accept such an offer? What was *he* thinking?

'Twas that very man who had taken Ensign's life. *Dearest Lord, protect her.*

The fear in her face had all but cut through his chest.

He flicked the reins and kept the horses at as fast a pace as they could endure, but even then he would never match the speed the soldiers had taken. Accursed wagon. Accursed scheme!

If that man did anything to her—if she were not in a room, alone and content when Joseph returned, then Matthew Greene would not live to see another sunrise.

Chapter Eight

Joseph pounded on the rough wood planks of the door of the room he was informed Hannah occupied. Melted snow dripped from his shoulders and cocked hat. Why didn't she answer? He pounded again, then looked down the dimly lit hall. He didn't wish to disturb any others, but the longer he waited, the longer his nerves stretched to their thinnest.

He tried the handle. Locked. "Hannah, 'tis I. Let me in." He whispered against the wood, but still his tone sounded more frantic than he would have wished, but it couldn't be helped. The horrifying scenarios that had played in his mind since the moment she left his side refused to quiet their constant revolutions.

"Hannah, are you in there?" If she wasn't, if he didn't find her in the next second, he would—

The handle turned, and his heart leapt to his throat as the door opened. A weak smile on her face, Hannah motioned him to enter.

He rushed in, scanning the room to be sure she was alone before looking her over. "Are you all right? Why didn't you answer right away?"

"Forgive me. I was..." She closed the door, her expression lost and voice hollow. "I suppose I was so consumed by thought I didn't hear you."

Joseph stilled, claiming her eyes when he spoke again, this time clear and low. "Are you all right?"

Taking a deep breath, she nodded. "Aye."

He stepped closer, fighting the strange and sudden urge to touch her cheek, to study her face, to know if really all was as well as she claimed it to be, for that was the only way his reckless fears could finally be calmed.

A flash of her smile allowed him to inhale a bit deeper, but still he clenched his fists, arms rigid at his sides. "What happened on the ride?"

The indignant tip of her head he expected at such a demand never happened. She hugged her middle and went to the window, staring out at the huge flakes that floated aimlessly. "We spoke little. He asked our destination, and I answered him truthfully, saying we are returning to our uncle's foundry." She paused, her throat moving. "He acted as if nothing had happened there. As if he was not acquainted with that place at all. He said nothing of the British taking it. Nothing of Ensign's death." Her voice cracked, and a stray tear blinked from her red-rimmed eyes. "A death he is responsible for."

Dear Hannah.

The hungering need to hold her, to comfort away her grief, became too great to conquer, and he submitted. He neared from behind, ready to reach for her, but he stopped when, gratefully, she spoke again, saving him from a foolish act that could not have been unwritten.

"I told him we planned to leave again in the morning." She looked over her shoulder, the weariness in her eyes tensing his already stiff muscles. "And he plans to accompany us."

"What?" Joseph turned her at the elbow. "Tell me you are not serious."

She slowed her movements, staring somewhere past his shoulder. "I tried to dissuade him, but he was unmoved." After a shallow shake of the head, she brushed past him and moved to the other side of the room where a desk and chair rested. "I must write to Caroline and tell her not to call."

Joseph's stomach clenched. "Does she often?" A single unwanted visitor could destroy everything.

Offering a cursory glance, Hannah shook her head. "Rarely. But we cannot take the risk."

Foresighted. Joseph issued a slight, albeit needed inner reprimand. It seemed he gave her far less credit than she deserved.

Clutching the chair, she stopped, touching her forehead. When she didn't instantly look up again, Joseph advanced beyond the crouching enemy of risk and put a hand at her back. "I fear you are unwell."

"Only tired."

He moved her to face him, but she kept her hand upon her head, and 'twas then he noticed her red-cold fingers.

"You are still too cold."

Heedless of the danger, he took her hands, rubbing them between his own. 'Twas then the threatened enemy struck, as the feel of her skin against his ignited the sweet, torturing memories.

In a flood he could not contain, he tried to speak, to act, to move as if he were not nearly drowning. He continued to rub her icy hands between his. "I wish you would rest."

She stared up at him, eyes circled and full lips partly open. "I...I suppose I should."

He kept rubbing, hoping the action would erase not only the cold in her hands but the heat that suddenly burned a path up his chest.

"If you will promise to stay here, I shall go belowstairs and return with a meal."

Licking her lips, she nodded, her eyes speaking more than he wanted to believe. Did she feel it too? The tangible sparks between them? The sudden pink in her cheeks and quick rise and fall of her chest attested she did.

Slowly, he stilled his hands but could not find the strength to release his hold. Only a moment longer...

She peered up at him, her lips open as if she prepared to speak. Tugging her hands away, she grinned and moved her fingers to prove they had indeed warmed. The color in her face bloomed, matching the same tone of red that her fingers had been.

"Thank you." Her voice wavered, and she stepped back.

"I..." He cleared his throat, hoping to knock his tone back into place. "I shall return."

He hurried to the door, flaring his fingers to flick away the lingering allure of her touch. He gripped the cold metal handle and fled the perilous space.

Fool.

Closing the door, he descended the stairs, berating himself with every pulse of his far-too-heated blood. Why had he done it? He growled. He *knew* why but refused to acknowledge the answer that taunted him—laughing and pointing like a bullying schoolboy. But he stood his ground.

Never again.

Another touch, no matter how innocent or well meaning, would dispatch him to places he knew all too well. Places he would never go again.

Hannah's breathing refused to return to normal as she stared at the door Joseph had just closed. What had happened? She shuffled backward to the bed and sat, her pulse still forcing her lungs to pump as if she'd taken a long flight of stairs two by two. *Merciful heavens.*

She looked to the door again, shock infusing every weary nerve with shots of vibrant light. The tenderness in his eyes, the way he held her hands in his...and almost hadn't let go.

The rhythmic pulse of her heart drummed a warning cry in her ears. *No, Hannah. Do not do it.* She had taken this road before and knew its deadly path. 'Twas clear her heart would betray her no matter what she did to secure its loyalty. Groaning, Hannah covered her face. How weak she was. Could she not keep the past ever before her? If she blinked she might lose sight of what she'd already lost, and then the pain she'd suffered would be too much to bear. Having loved him once before, 'twould be all too easy to fall prey to him again.

Such reckless behavior should never be condoned. She must be strong, no matter what he did or did not do. The power to remain safe was hers alone. Like freshly scrolled words on a crisp parchment, Hannah hovered the memory over the flame of those pain-filled years. With a groan she collapsed back against the thin pillow and stared at the ceiling, unwilling just yet to touch that waiting flame to the precious moment. His eyes had turned such a deep blue as he'd looked at her, his strong hands giving their warmth. His breath was so soft. Did that mean he still cared for her? A man would not be so with a woman if he did not...would he?

She slapped her hands to her face. *Foolish woman! He cares for you as you care for him. Not at all.*

Hannah jerked upright, burning once and for all the memory of his touch upon her hand. Tomorrow would begin a new day, and tomorrow she would arm her heart with musket, sword, and dagger. For without defense, she would lose her whole soul to him as she had once before. And that she could never endure. Not a second time.

Chapter Nine

The next day was long and colder than the last had been. How that was possible, Hannah couldn't begin to fathom. Though the snow no longer fell as it had yesterday, the temperatures reached through to her bones. Thank the Lord the foundry was just around the bend. The trees were as familiar to her as if they were her very kin, welcoming her home. The five soldiers who went ahead of them were almost out of sight, certainly out of range of the sound of their voices.

She glanced to where Joseph sat beside her on the wagon, the protection she placed around her heart so far doing the job she'd intended. Neither had spoken of the touch, and neither even acted like the event had ever occurred. If she allowed it, she wasn't sure whether to be relieved or otherwise, so she settled on the former, promising herself he thought not of it, as she was working to do.

Clearing her throat, she stared forward. "We are nearly there."

"Aye." After a quick glance her direction, he stretched his shoulders back. "Be watchful. Be cautious. We know not what awaits us."

The reserved thunder in his whispered words made her pull her cloak tighter. She nodded. "I am ready."

"Our escort is not so innocent." He flung her a quick glance before studying the road.

She nodded. "There is something he does not tell."

A single brow slanted, as if he was surprised she had noticed it as well.

"We will gain our objective—we must." She inhaled a long, slow breath. "And I am not afraid, Joseph."

"I know you are not." Head twisting only slightly, his voice reached low to jostle her. "That is what worries me."

His words stung. How could her confidence bode ill? Yoking her shoulders between steadfastness and strength, Hannah pulled the weight of her conviction headlong into the future. *For you, dear Ensign. For the cause.*

"We're here." Joseph said the very words her heart whispered.

Chin raised, she rested her previous frustrations in the comfort of the view that consumed her as they rounded the remaining corner. *Eaton Hill.* At long last the house came into view—its shining windows and red door seeming to bid them welcome, while the foundry and small hill not far beyond sang a homecoming ovation.

There in the yard between the foundry and the house, the soldiers were dismounting and leading their mounts to the barn.

Play the part, Hannah. Live it. Breathe it.

"'Tis good to finally see home again." Hannah caught Greene's stare. "You are very kind to see us here. May I offer you something warm before you take your journey back?"

"Forgive me, my lady." Greene dismounted and nodded to another soldier to take his horse. "I may have neglected to inform you that your uncle's foundry has been commandeered." No more sweet civility in his words, but a strict man of business. "We quarter here now."

Hannah looked to Joseph, who spoke a hundred warnings in a single look. Her insides twisted like a sopping piece of wash, and she turned to Greene, who, from his firm features likely assumed she would protest his announcement. Pleasurably, she disappointed him. "You are? This is news indeed."

He pretended politeness, his eyes more squinting than smiling. "I shall inform the captain you have arrived." With a curt nod he made for the house.

Only once he was gone did Joseph finally speak. "Are you certain he does not recognize you?" He hurried around the wagon to help her down.

She swallowed, hoping he didn't hear the hesitation in her tone. "Aye. I am certain."

Jaw ticking, Joseph moved to the back of the wagon and pulled the first trunk forward, whispering so the piling snow could not stand witness. "Stay with me. If things take a dangerous turn I—"

"So you are the family Mr. Young spoke of."

Both Hannah and Joseph spun toward the voice.

The man stepped forward. Bold smile and stocky build, the older soldier stepped within only feet of them, his congenial nature so thick it reeked of fabrication. He prepared to speak again, when suddenly his gaze landed on her, and his stance eased, his eyes widening. "Major Ezra Stockton at your service, my lady."

Greene stepped forward. "Major Stockton, this is Miss Young and her cousin, Mr. Young." He looked to Hannah, then to the major once more. "Sir, these are the two I was telling you about."

Stockton grinned, a sickening kind of attraction flaring through his expression as he took her in from head to foot. "A pleasure to meet you indeed."

His voice unlocked the carefully guarded places she wished to keep hidden, snatching the phantoms by the throat and wielding them like the weapon they were. "Where is our uncle?"

Joseph's hand suddenly gripped around her waist. "You must forgive my cousin. The journey has been —"

"Not at all." Stockton put a hand to his chest and stepped back. "So many miles in so much cold. Nay, you both should come into the house immediately."

Stockton tipped his head toward Greene. "Have Private Peterson care for their horses and bring in the trunks." At this he turned back to Hannah, offering his elbow. She took it, and he started for the house. "I shall answer you, but first, I beg you to warm yourself by the fire."

Hannah's blood pounded in her ears. He spoke as if it were *his* home, *his* fire. She looked to Joseph, whose cautioning glance did little to buff away the scratching irritations she'd tried but failed to prepare for. God give her strength.

Stockton opened the door and motioned for her to enter, followed by Joseph before dripping his attentions on her once more. "You are surely chilled to the bone."

Once inside, Hannah took quick stock of the parlor. Just as she'd left it, but for two kitchen chairs that had been positioned near the fire in the front room alongside the others. Was all the same in the rooms abovestairs? Her pained curiosity begged her to look to the kitchen, to see the place Ensign had first fallen by the ball that hit him, but she schooled an even expression and took the first seat Stockton offered.

Standing like the officer he was, the major took his place in front of the fire, his back to the warmth, one hand grasping his coat, the other resting at his side.

He looked to Greene, who was already joining them inside. "Major Stockton, I have a matter that—"

"Yes, yes." Stockton's amiability waxed cold only in his eyes. "My lieutenant tells me there is something I must address ere we discuss anything else." Pausing, he allowed his stare to harden and linger. "He claims...he claims, Miss Young, that you were here several nights ago."

Dear Lord.

"Here?" Hannah flung a glance to Joseph, who stood behind where she sat as if ready to pull her to safety. All the blood in her limbs retreated to her heart. Releasing a sprite laugh, she looked to Greene, then back to Stockton. "Why, that is impossible, sir, as I have been traveling back from Salem."

Greene and Stockton shared a brief communication that only their eyes could detect before Stockton faced her. He inclined his head. "I have trusted Greene for some time now, and if he says you are familiar to him, I am tempted to take his word. You see, there was a young woman here when we first arrived, and we've been most concerned, since she seems to have run away."

Panic gripped her chest and refused to remove its claws. *Lord, I pray thee...* A brush of thought dislodged the stabbing, and she looked around before plaiting her face with sincere inquiry. "Do you mean Betsy?" The men glanced at each other, and she turned to Joseph. "Have you seen her?"

He shook his head, glancing around as if trying to distinguish any sign of this fabricated soul.

Stockton frowned politely, and she continued, praying the heaven-inspired idea would imprint upon their minds in place of everything else. "We hired a young woman to see to Uncle's needs while we were away. I would have expected to see her, just as I expected to see my uncle, and thus far neither have yet to make an appearance. Why in heavens name would she run?" Laughing, Hannah relaxed her hands in her lap. "I daresay the arrival of your distinguished men in arms may have frightened her away. Do you not think so, Major?" Tilting her head at a shy slant, she prayed the man would accept her teasing.

Greene's sharp stare cut from her to the major. "You hired a woman to care for your uncle while you were gone?"

"Aye." She didn't need to feign the sudden tightness in her voice. "He has just recently lost his wife, and we didn't wish him to be alone."

"I see." Stockton's face curled in a smile that would have seemed sincere had she not known the villainous truth that lingered behind the bars of his heart. He flung a glance to Greene that hurled so hard against him, he took a step back. "Forgive us. It seems this conflict with the Patriots makes us suspicious."

"I do understand. 'Tis no matter." She looked to Joseph. "'Twould seem it is difficult to acquire good help these days."

He shrugged a shoulder, his face a melding of emotions she hadn't time to decipher. Was he pleased? Dissatisfied with her explanation? He would surely tell her his feelings later, though she wasn't sure she wanted to hear them.

Sitting straight, Hannah poured calm over the ruts in her voice. "Now, please, sir, where is our uncle?"

She felt a hand on her shoulder and straightened, not needing to look to know that Joseph touched her. His large, strong hands were known to her through glove and coat. The touch infused her with a courage she hadn't known was missing.

Stockton looked to Greene, then tossed his gaze to Joseph before stilling it upon her. "It gives me no pleasure to inform you, Miss Young, that your uncle is dead."

The sudden swelling ache in her throat and burning in her eyes forced her to straighten. She swallowed and took in a deep breath before attempting to speak.

Blessedly, Joseph did before her. "When?"

"Four days past."

Stockton's expression drooped in degrees, and his tone mellowed to an even sincerity she almost believed.

"I can see it pains you. I am so sorry."

"How..." The question was so thick she could not speak. The sudden charade draped back, revealing only the raw emotions she had not the fortitude to hide.

Joseph's strengthening grip on her shoulder deepened as he finished what she could not. "How did he die?"

Stockton's mouth bowed down. "His heart failed him."

Large, heavy tears plunked from her eyes. The lie she had known was coming crashed against her with a force she miscalculated by harrowing degrees. She curled her toes in her shoes and gripped the soft cushioned seat to keep from fleeing. His heart had not failed him. He *gave* it. His life for hers.

"Was he given a proper burial?" The demand that carried in Joseph's voice startled.

Stockton nodded, his eyes trained with remaining distrust upon him. "He was. Upon the hill beside his wife. Captain Higley saw to his burial, and I can assure you, Higley would have treated him as his own."

A flick of rage sparked and popped like a dry log thrown onto a fire, and she clasped the major's stare. Ripened accusations stung her tongue. Instead, she swallowed the sharp words with a wince and focused her attention on her hands.

"The other question then begs an answer." Joseph's tone was humble yet commanding. "How does it happen that you should have stopped at our humble dwelling? I must only assume you are in need of something we can provide."

"You are right, Mr. Young." Tension rising around his eyes, Stockton paced toward the fire, hands clasped behind his back. "Fools that the rebels are, they have taken much of what belongs to the king, leaving our army with little to defend against their wily ways." His gaze went to Hannah. "So, my dear, we came to ask your uncle for the use of his foundry for the duration of the war, and he was most willing to oblige. But alas, he fell that night, and we were unable to revive him."

The lies continued to compound, their weight pressing ever harder on her back.

Thankfully, Greene filled the stifling silence. "We shall be here for some time, as the king will require our every effort."

"I may be able to be of some assistance." Smooth and rich, Joseph's timbre swelled through the parlor.

"How is that, Mr. Young?" Stockton eyed Greene before facing Joseph in full. "You would offer your services to the king?"

"I would."

The major cant his head. "Go on."

Joseph took another step forward, the imposing height and breadth of him demanding attention as much as his voice. "I am a blacksmith by trade, but I am well versed in the skill of foundry work. I could lead your men in the job. That is, if you have not already chosen a man for such an occupation."

Humming his reply, Stockton pivoted to Greene, whose expression remained ever unimpressed. Hannah peered at Joseph, moving her hands beneath her legs as she sat, both to warm them and hide the sudden shaking she couldn't ease.

"What do you say to that, Greene?" Stockton asked, as if he'd already made up his mind.

"I will accept your recommendation, sir."

Looking to Hannah, Joseph spoke again. "If you are willing to allow us to stay on here, my cousin could cook and wash for you while I assist in the production of goods. I do believe it would be worth your while."

As if enlivened by the thought, Stockton pulled his shoulders back. "That is a tantalizing suggestion indeed." He swung his gaze to Hannah. "And you would be willing to do such a thing? 'Twould be only myself—the main camp is stationed two miles from here, where the other men will be. Your work would be minimal."

She clung to the opportunity as one clung to the reins of a runaway horse—wanting to release the sobs of grief but needing the strength behind their sorrow. This was their chance. Had not God orchestrated it just for them? "I am grateful to serve the king in memory of my uncle."

"Excellent." Stockton's eyes seemed to take in far too much of her, and she shifted in the seat. "Most fortuitous indeed."

Tossing a look over her shoulder to Joseph, Hannah prepared to speak, but he did first. "You must understand that with my cousin the only woman in the house, there will be rules of propriety that must be respected."

"You needn't worry on that account, Mr. Young." Bowing slightly, he grinned. "In point of fact, there are things I would wish to speak to you about. Alone."

"I understand." Hannah stood, grateful for the forced solitude she hoped would quell pains that rained like a summer gale. "I should like to visit my uncle's grave."

"Indeed." Stockton bowed again, and she curtsied in response.

Joseph caught her arm as she passed, his hidden glare a warning only she could see. She grinned slightly and touched his hand with hers. "I shall return and prepare supper before long."

The grip he held her with through his eyes nearly tugged at her like a grasp upon her shoulders, but with a blink and a smile she pulled to freedom. Walking to the door, she opened and stepped into the white winter light, blinded by not only the glare itself but by the sudden veracities that fell around her like the very snow from the heavens. This was her chance, her way to not only keep her vow to her uncle but to overthrow the very men who destroyed the life she'd loved. The farther she walked, the more it seemed the fears sloughed away like sand to lapping water. Emboldened, she turned back toward the house, a bitter-cold breeze tickling the hairs around her ears as she smiled.

Let the game begin.

Chapter Ten

Joseph watched the doorknob latch into place after Hannah's exit. He should be with her. Confounded woman. Did she not realize there could be soldiers about? Chest swelling with a breath he hoped would ease the thump of his pulse, Joseph turned back to the loathed men in front of him.

Greene stared, mouth firm, eyes fixed. Clearly he didn't like them despite the act he performed yesterday, and he planned to make it known. "So you are familiar with blacksmithing?"

"Aye, sir." Joseph nodded, resting a hand on top of the chair beside him. "I've worked in that trade near fifteen years."

Stockton rolled his shoulders back and opened his stance. "You own a shop of your own?"

Shaking his head, Joseph recited the story he'd perfected. "I do traveling labor. Many shops need outside help for larger commissions, so I make my way around. I have a special skill set other smith owners will hire me to make use of."

A single brow rose on Stockton's face. "Such as?"

"Locks, gates, and the like."

Stockton shifted his feet and moved his eyes to Greene before fixing his gaze on Joseph. "Familiar with gun parts?"

A pointed question. Joseph was grateful he could answer in truth. "Aye."

Stockton looked to Greene once more, whose only movement was a slight shift of the jaw.

Facing the fire, Stockton rested his arm on the mantel. "I have an order for one hundred gun barrels." He pulled his bottom lip through his teeth, as if second-guessing his sudden and revealing statement.

Already the information flowed. "So many?"

"Aye. The more advantage we have over the enemy, the better."

Greene stepped forward. "Sir, is it wise to—" He snapped his mouth shut when Stockton hurled a glare at his face.

"Do you believe..." The major paused, staring down before gripping Joseph with a gaze he knew was intended to show the strength of his position. "Could you craft that many in a short amount of time?"

Joseph reserved the shock of such a question. "How short?"

"Six days."

Eyes fixed and mouth a firm line, Greene seemed ready to burst at the proposition that would shortly be extended. Why not make the devilish man a bit more uncomfortable?

Joseph tilted his head as his mouth pulled to a frown. "'Tis almost too short, but with help, I could manage."

"Indeed I am intrigued." Stockton's gaze flung to Greene, not as an invitation to speak his mind but to repress any impending contradictions. Slowly, he turned back to Joseph. "Sir, I find you and your kind cousin to be most genuine. And as we are to be staying here together for an unforeseeable future, and if you are truly amenable to offering your hand in the service of your king, then I should be interested in offering you the honor of filling this order and any others that may be called for."

"Major!" Greene stomped across the floor, his face twisted and red. "You cannot possibly trust—"

"Silence." Irritation ticked below Stockton's eye, and a menacing vibration settled off his shoulders as his voice rumbled from his chest. "You forget your place, Greene. Do not second-guess my judge of character." After a beat of suffocating silence, he spoke again. "I can tell Mr. Young and his cousin are sincere in their devotion to the crown, and if they wish to be of assistance, well...seems to me that Providence is at work."

Providence indeed. Joseph bowed in a reverent show of acknowledgment while the two men exchanged glares like enemies exchanging blows. How could this not be God's hand? Here he had just been offered such an opportunity—to learn the very needs and numbers of the British and to be so trusted by one in authority.

Stockton thrust his last stare and turned to Joseph. "What say you?"

Joseph's muscles tensed, and he willed his blood to travel with less force through his veins. Bowing his head again, he replied. "It would be an honor. But I do not wish to interfere if there is another man for whom—"

"Do not let Greene's irritation dissuade you." Stockton pushed away from the fire. "The remaining instructions are expected sometime this evening. I must visit camp to assess things there and will return sometime after dark." Striding to the door, he stopped and turned with his hand on the knob. "Greene, you will ride with me."

He offered a shallow nod. "Aye, sir."

Swinging the door wide, Stockton exited before speaking over his shoulder. "I will discover which men can assist you in your work, Mr. Young. Oh, and tell your cousin not to worry over supper. I shall see her in the morning."

The way his mouth quirked at the last few words made Joseph's stomach coil, but he smiled to cover the grimace that shot to his face. "That I will, sir." Joseph followed them out. "I should like to have a look at the foundry before dark so I may be sure I have the supplies needed to begin work in the morning."

"Aye, excellent." Stockton waited as Greene barked orders for one of the remaining men to bring his horse around.

Joseph stopped in the center of the yard between the house and the foundry, noting the few remaining Redcoats. They had better not be lingering for much longer. He coated his voice in indifference. "Will your men be going with you?"

"There is no need for them to stay here when camp is only two miles distant. They will work while I am here—arrive early, leave late." He frowned as his horse was led to him, as if he'd been waiting far too long. Mounting, he pulled the reins to the side. "Be sure you've checked well the supplies. If we need anything, we must hasten to acquire it, for we must begin immediately." Tapping hard at the animal's flanks, Stockton rode the way Joseph and Hannah had just come, with Greene and the remaining Redcoats following behind.

The biting cold nipped at Joseph's face as he turned toward the hill. There, Hannah knelt on the ground, her hand on the dark mound of soil, her head bowed. Did she weep? If she did, she was too far to be heard. His legs urged him forward, to be at her side and give her the comfort he'd yet been unable, nay, too cowardly to give. If he allowed himself too close...nay, he couldn't even if he wished to. She wouldn't want him near.

The urgency pooling in his muscles became too much, and he was forced to move to ease the tension. Her grief was deep, and if indeed she wept— He stopped as Hannah rose. Hugging her arms around her chest she stepped back before she began the short trek down the hill. Had she seen him?

Pressed on either side, Joseph couldn't move. The need to go to her, to be assured of her well-being, warred with the need to maintain a distance that would keep his heart from deeper wounds.

He stared as she neared, the cold air painting red circles on her cheekbones, a strand of gold hair trailing beside her ear as she walked. Were those tears? Blast it. He stepped forward, then halted when she stopped and looked up. Not three yards away, and still he could see the evidence of grief on her face. The urge to wipe the streaks from her skin made his fingers ache.

Opening his mouth, Joseph prepared to speak, but the crowd of thoughts jammed in his throat, and he was forced to close his teeth, offering only a weak smile.

In a hurried motion she dabbed at her eyes before glancing around the yard. "Have they gone?"

Her voice was fragile, as if the emotions she just bore still clung to her.

Joseph nodded, not allowing himself a step closer no matter how his body willed it. "They will return sometime after dark." He looked behind, then back to her. "They will not be here for supper, so you are relieved of duty for the evening it would seem."

A hint of a smile graced her mouth at one side, and he sighed out a smile of his own, grateful the bit of jest lifted a mite of her load.

He motioned to the side. "It seems God has looked down on us in mercy."

"Oh?" She crossed her arms and rubbed her hands up and down. "How is that?"

Joseph twisted to look behind, making sure they were truly alone before he bared the fortunate news. Even still, he lowered his tone. "Major Stockton has asked that I take charge of an order for the production of gun barrels for the king's army."

"What?" Hannah's large green eyes widened. "That is good fortune indeed."

"Aye." The spark of surprised joy in her countenance rained on him like tiny orange flares. "So it would seem our quest has the full blessing of heaven."

A sigh left her parted mouth, which bowed in a slight smile. "I can scarce believe it."

"I find myself hesitant, but we are in such a precarious spot, I can hardly decline. Though this is a boon, 'tis also more dangerous. For if we are ever suspected..."

Hannah's mouth shut, and that dimple appeared as she held her lips tight, but the expression vanished like her white breath on the air. "We will not be. We shall do the very thing Ensign would have wanted." She turned back to him. "We shall do what must be done."

"I'm so sorry, Hannah." Unbidden, the words he'd not had the chance to speak spilled from him. "Your uncle was a good man. I admired him very much. For his character as well as his work."

She offered a pained smile. "He shall be greatly missed." An untold number of emotions fought in her pained expression, and the driving need to pull her near and fit her head beneath his chin—to whisper all would be well and that he would keep her safe—surged blood to his unyielding limbs.

A quick shake of the head freed him from the suffocating captivity, and he took a step backward. "I shall be inside shortly."

"Of course." She began a slow walk to the house, her eyes still on him, before she hurried inside and closed the door behind her.

Alone in the yard, the silence of the winter air upbraided him as he stared at the path she'd taken. The portend of ill should either of them be discovered was almost too much to endure. He would forever upbraid himself for allowing her to come. There was no way of keeping her clear of the dangers that lurked within their very home.

A grunt lurched from him, and he bent inwardly to the truth that socked him square in the gut. 'Twas not the danger of his enemy he despised most, but that of a pair of green eyes that lured him like a rare and precious gem.

Closing his own, Joseph lowered his head and wiped a hand down his face. 'Twas only two weeks. Fourteen short days. Before he knew it, 'twould be over and he could once again put her out of his mind.

He growled. Out of his mind, perhaps. Out of his heart...

Joseph whirled and strode for the foundry, leaving the rest of his deriding thoughts to die in the frigid air, where they belonged.

Staring into the mirror atop her dressing table, Hannah sat, unmoving, as she had done since before the sun had begun to drain its light from the sky. A candle flickered in front of the mirror, lighting not only her small corner but also the thoughts that wavered before her.

The grave was as the major had promised. A proper sight, right beside Bea. Somehow she couldn't quite clasp to the truth that Ensign was in fact gone, despite the gruesome reality that still played in her mind. She'd seen it, witnessed the act with her very eyes, wept over his grave, and yet here in this house, with the scents of his favorite coffee and hard soaps still lingering in the air, 'twas impossible to believe he was gone.

Hannah ran her hand across the smooth wood of her dressing table. Simpleton. She dropped her hand into her lap. Aye, she'd wanted to make them suffer for what they'd done—to beat them at the very game they thought to win, but what did she know of such work? Gathering intelligence from the enemy? Dear Lord, why had she offered it? Moments ago at his grave she'd felt strong, confident. But now...

She blinked, tracing her reflection with her gaze. How old she looked. Only eight and twenty, yet... Leaning forward, she touched the shadowed places under her eyes, then sat back in her chair with a sigh. What had happened to her youth? Where had it gone? Did Joseph see her as she saw herself? An old maid—a woman with far too many years behind her to make her appealing to any man? An audible groan left her mouth, and she rested her elbow on the table and her face in her hand. She didn't care to appeal to anyone. Most certainly not to him.

Expelling an audible sigh, Hannah looked up as a sunrise of thought stretched its rays heavenward. And like the rising of the sun, the thought would not—*could* not be stopped—its ascent promising to bathe the earth in light no matter how much she longed for night. *He loved me once. Perhaps...*

A knock tapped on the door. "Hannah?"

She turned in her seat, her heart traitorously picking up its pace at the rich tones of Joseph's voice. She tried to keep her own even. "Come in."

The door opened, and he entered, leaving it ajar. "I thought you might be abed."

Hand on the back of the chair where she sat, she shrugged a single shoulder. "I will soon be."

He stepped nearer, narrowing the space between them when suddenly the air became so thin she could hardly take a breath. His gentle smile as he spoke did frightful things to her middle. "I shouldn't have offered your services in the way I did earlier. Forgive me."

"Services?" She prayed he couldn't see the wild thump of her pulse in her neck.

He continued forward, then stopped halfway, as if an unseen bar restrained him. "To Stockton. For his laundering and meals."

"I do not mind. And I believe..." She paused, calculating her response. "I believe 'tis a most fortuitous opportunity. As is yours."

A slight grin tempted one side of his mouth. "I thought so as well." He stared and shuffled a step forward, then halted. After a quick glance over his shoulder toward the door, he lowered his voice. "Hannah, I do not like the way Stockton looks at you."

The memory made a worming sensation start in her chest. "You warned me of such."

His jaw worked. "Do not allow yourself to be alone with him if it can be avoided. Your safety is paramount."

"Mine is not any more important than yours."

His chest rounded as he inhaled a long, deep breath. "Give me your word."

He stepped forward, and as the distance between them closed, the pace of her heart grew ever quicker. She flashed a brief, assuring smile to her face. "You have it."

Joseph took another step, when the sound of horses in the yard stopped him with a jerk. Vigilance chiseled into the slant of his jaw. "Keep your door latched."

"I will."

He took a step, and Hannah touched his arm. "Wait." She stood and went to the trunk at the end of her bed. Opening it, she retrieved a large quilt and offered it to him. "'Tis a cold night."

He turned, towering over her in silence. His gaze swept across her face before his velvety bass voice caressed her skin. "Thank you."

Taking the quilt from her hands, his fingers dusted over hers, and a spark bolted up her arm. Unable to move, Hannah raised her eyes to his and feared perhaps her knees would no longer sustain her. *Dearest heaven.* That deep, tender longing she'd seen in his eyes when their love had once flourished now swelled, and the armament she'd employed dropped to her feet, exposing her heart in full. His gaze flicked to her lips, making her neck and cheeks burn like a kitchen fire in summer. If he leaned any closer...

With a blink he stepped back, the longing look in his eyes replaced with mere civility, leaving Hannah suspended over a chasm, grasping for anything to keep her from falling into the gaping pit below.

Swallowing, he stepped toward the exit and looked back over his shoulder. He gripped the handle, motionless for a moment. "Hannah..." The tenderness in his voice reached across the space between them to cradle the very heart in her chest. "You are a brave woman."

With that, he left, securing the door quietly behind him, leaving Hannah alone to gasp through the confusion that beat against her like waves on the sea.

Hannah let her shoulders slump and her hands drop to her sides. Stunned to near numbness by such an honest admission, she breathed slowly, unable to move her eyes from the place where the floor met the wall. She shut her eyes, bemoaning the fate she faced. How could she abide him day after day? Especially when he was so kind. He had always been kind.

Shuffling back to her chair, she sat and faced the dressing table, pulling on the round handle until the contents of the drawer smiled up at her. There atop a folded neckerchief rested the white booties. Lifting them in her hands, Hannah marveled—as she did every time—how tiny they were, how delicate and soft. He must not ever know. Not that she wished to keep secrets, but...

Hannah lowered the booties to the table and stared into the drawer at what now stared back. The small iron nail Joseph had curled and made to fit perfectly around her finger seemed to cry out for her touch. How could she not? Picking up the cold, smooth metal, Hannah's familiar room melted away, and that night so many years ago lived and breathed around her like a visit to the past. The cool air of the barn, the quiet chirp of the crickets. The scent of earth and hay. The wild pulse of her heart and the knowledge that this night would change her from girl to woman.

A sound from belowstairs stirred her from the shadows and she gasped, the rising flood of memories having nearly filled her lungs. She dropped the ring back into place and covered it with the knitted treasure she could never bear to relinquish no matter how it pained, knowing that such a thing still lived in the quiet dark, day in and day out.

Was she brave? Nay. Desperate. Determined to find a way to keep living despite the wailings that still roared behind the thick walls of acceptance.

She must stay the course. There were far bigger matters now that required her strength and energy.

If her future was not to include that of husband and child, she must endeavor at least to secure it for Caroline and others like her. She must do it for Ensign—for the vow she made to him. This grand cause of freedom must be championed.

Glancing toward the ceiling, she imagined God peering down at her, and she smiled. She had sinned, aye. But the years she had spent begging His forgiveness had proved His love. She had what she deserved, what she wished.

Now all that remained was to go forward in it.

Chapter Eleven

Up and dressed before the rising of the sun, Joseph descended the stairs, the alluring aromas of bread and coffee tempting him to the kitchen. 'Twould seem he was not the only one already beginning the day.

Reprimanding the thought before it shaped in full, he stayed the course. Not allowing himself to linger on the tensions that grew ever stronger between him and Hannah must be his soul's purpose. However, his mind would not relent. The display of wishes and wants in Hannah's eyes last evening when he spoke with her in her room were too perplexing to ignore. Was it fear that made her breath hush and cheeks pink, or the forgotten longing of him?

A self-serving thought. She didn't feel for him at all. She believed he had abandoned her—used her and thrown her away. Dear Lord, why hadn't he the strength to tear open the roughly mended parts of him and bare all that wished to be spoken? A swelling pain billowed as it did every time he allowed the winds of thought to blow. 'Twas in the past, and there it should stay.

Belowstairs the parlor was empty, but the fire blazed. He moved to the kitchen and found Hannah crouched by the embers.

He paused. Had she not heard him enter? She poked at the fire with a tong, jostling coals around a pot. Hair neatly pinned behind her head, those few rebel strands floated free at her neck and around her ears. The dark morning still clung to the corners of the room, but the umber glow of the fire highlighted her frame, shadowing all the perfect curves of her body and face.

The temptation to linger and enjoy the sweet domestic view lured his clouded thoughts, but he cleared his throat. "Good morning."

"Oh!" Hannah flung her hand to her chest as a scarlet hue blew over her cheeks. "Joseph, I didn't hear you come in." Pushing against her knees, she rose and went to the table, giving him only a slight smile before darting her eyes away, focusing intently on moving a batch of biscuits to a waiting platter. "The others are already gone, I suppose. I haven't seen or heard them since yesterday."

"Hmm." Joseph glanced around for any sign they'd already been back and gone, but the dim light of the fire and two oil lamps did little to illuminate the space. If they were to be so elusive, perhaps their job of covert activities would be simpler than he thought.

He turned back to Hannah, her attention still intent upon the spread of bounty. Dishes of all kinds dotted the table. Cakes, bacon, bread, and eggs. How long had she been up?

Gnawing the inside of his cheek, he rebutted his instinct to tease her. The straightness of her shoulders and back preached of tension and angst. Better to not induce unneeded embarrassment if she weren't to catch his meaning. Then again...

She twisted her mouth in thought, and that dimple he loved seemed to wink at him, weakening the last bastion of his resistance.

Joseph rested his hands on the back of the kitchen chair, unable to keep the dry hint of humor from his tone. "Generous of you to go to so much work for me. I'm touched."

Her head popped up, and her ears reddened, almost begging him to continue.

A genuine half smile found freedom on his lips. "I'm famished to be sure, but I fear you may have overestimated my appetite."

Eyes never leaving his, the slight dip of Hannah's chin and twist of her mouth made the second half of his smile join the first. She bobbed a shoulder, then turned back to the skillet. "I didn't do it for you."

"Did you not?"

She looked up again, and a slight spark in her eye made his face rise in full before he immediately frowned. "But where are the turnovers? Surely you haven't forgotten my favorite breakfast? For shame."

Her skin flushed, and she batted a curl away from her ear in such a huff he couldn't tell if she was jostled by his comment or merely attempting to beat him at his own game.

"If you would like turnovers, you can make them yourself."

"Maybe I shall." Chuckling behind a closed smile, he snatched a cake from the table and went to the door where his greatcoat and hat waited on the hook.

He swooped the coat around his shoulders. "I shall get the forges going."

"But you haven't eaten." Her quiet voice chirped, pulling him back around. "You shall be hungry."

The gentle reprimand and the innocent roundness of her eyes stalled him, his arms sliding slowly through his sleeves.

She placed a hand on her hip. "And after all this trouble I went to make it for you..."

He froze, unsure whether to speak or leave or...speak. There had been a hint of jest in her tone, hadn't there?

Hannah spun and flung a look over her shoulder, a single raised eyebrow making his knees soften. She had teased him right back, and so artfully he'd hardly known it.

Somehow he couldn't feel his limbs, his heart pulsing so fast he could hear nothing but the thump of his own blood through his ears.

Studying the back of her shoulders, the slope of her waist, her dainty ankles at the hem of her skirt as she worked, a twist of longing pulled through Joseph's chest, the sudden need to linger growing as bright as the coral dawn that swept across the horizon.

All the protective caution that weighted him motionless scattered like dirt in a dry summer wind. Joseph left his spot by the door and neared her from behind, bending so close he could almost feel the curls around her ear tickling his chin.

Sure to keep his tone rich, and volume low, he moved his mouth beside her ear. "I shall be back."

Snatching a cake from in front of her, he whirled away, his body humming with masculine pride at the way she'd melted a little as she'd gasped a tiny breath.

Swinging open the door, the cold blasted against his face. The colder the better. For this rising heat would most likely burn him alive.

Hannah's ear still burned pleasurably where Joseph's breath had dusted her skin.

She peered at the cakes, which looked innocently away, as if they hadn't noticed the gooseflesh on her skin or the way her chest pumped. Hannah shook her head, but the action did nothing to dislodge the well-wedged emotions. And traitorously, her heart was glad of it. She huffed aloud and turned back to the fire, removing the pudding from its scalding bath. Joseph had always been prone to tease.

Bringing the pudding to the table, she carefully cut the string that held the cloth in place around the mass of cooked and mashed peas. She looked out the window and reprimanded herself for not having tread with caution. In truth, she ought not tread at all. That path was rife with briars that would only bring more wounds like the ones she already suffered and still, at times, bled from.

The parlor door opened, and she turned, her heart at her feet as Stockton's voice peeled through the room.

"Aw, Miss Young." He stepped into the house, motioning for two others to join him. The last soldier closed the door behind him.

"Good morning." Stockton caressed her with his eyes. "You are hard at work, I see. Forgive me for disturbing you."

"Not at all." She wiped her hands on her apron to scrape away the sensation of his gaze. Nodding her head, she curtsied. "Major Stockton."

He took a deep breath and stepped farther into the parlor. "I left early to settle a few matters at camp. But I must tell you, I was eager to return, not only for the scents of food that tempted me from miles away but to bask in the warmth of your smile."

Hannah sighed away the sudden nausea. "You are too kind."

Stockton came forward, one arm outstretched to her, while he motioned to his companions with the other. "Gentlemen, allow me to introduce Miss Young. Miss Young, Major Pitman and Captain James Higley."

Hannah's throat corded. Breathing in slow and deep, she nodded at the second major before pinning her eyes on Higley. He was the one who had buried Ensign, was he not?

His handsome features softened in a smile that somehow eased the taut muscles in her neck. Tall and near as broad shouldered as Joseph, his dark-auburn hair was tied behind his head but appeared to despise its captivity, from the way certain waves tugged away from his hairline. His mossy-green eyes studied her, as if he knew more of her than she knew of him.

She shifted under the strange sensation and looked back to Stockton. "May I offer you men some breakfast?"

Major Pitman bowed at the waist. "You are most generous, Miss Young, but I fear I must be going."

Nodding to his companions, the mysterious officer left without another word, closing the door behind him.

Stockton scowled at the door, as if his irritation at his peer's sudden departure could breach the barrier of the wood. A blink, and the look vanished. Lifting his face with a smile to Higley, he then turned to Hannah.

"I should be glad to partake. I am famished."

The stare he next shot to Higley had implied commands welded so thick even Hannah straightened.

Higley inclined his head, no pretended civility in his manner when he met his superior's gaze. "I shall see to my assignments in town, sir."

The kind stranger rested his gaze on her, and the need to cry out for him to stay bulged in her throat. She didn't know him, but the worthiness she sensed from his kind eyes made her wish beyond hope he wouldn't leave her with Stockton.

But he did. Another rise of his lips and he was gone, shutting the door quietly behind him.

Stockton neared, stalking more than walking toward her. He glanced past her shoulder toward the kitchen before once again clutching her with his eyes. "You will join me, I hope."

"Me?" The word squeaked from her throat. She pressed her hands to her stomach. "I fear I haven't any appetite." Nothing had ever been more true.

"Have you not?" Stockton strode to the kitchen and fingered a piece of bacon. "Higley will be here most days, as will Greene." He faced her. "If ever you need anything from them, do not hesitate to ask. They are under strict command to be accommodating to you."

"How generous indeed." She rounded the table to fuss with the pudding that waited like a patient child. Moving it aside, she motioned to a mostly cleared spot. "I fear our table is a mite small compared to what you are used to, but I think there is enough room for you to—"

"This is perfect, my dear. *You* are perfect."

A flare of attraction brightened the gray of his eyes, and a gag lurched at her throat.

She coughed to ease the discomfort. "Where is Greene this morning? Is he not with you?"

"He is on assignment, as is Higley." He rounded his chair but didn't sit. "A pleasant opportunity for you and me to become more agreeably acquainted."

All she could manage in response was a forced grin and tilt of her head. Anything else, and she might have lost what little she had in her stomach. Busying herself with preparing him a plate, she ventured an attempt at trivial conversation.

"Your men stay very busy."

"Aye." He smiled in gratitude as she rested the laden plate before him.

She turned to get him something to drink, hoping he would sit, but he did not. "Brave too. I have heard tell of the Patriots doing dreadful things."

"They are fools and will soon be made to suffer for their transgressions."

Her heart thrashed wildly behind her ribs as she rested the cup of milk beside the plate. What would he do if he knew why she was really here?

In a swift motion he took her hand in his. "I see you blush, my dear. Forgive me. I suppose I should refrain from mentioning such matters."

"No, indeed, sir." Careful not to reveal how his touch discomfited, she tugged her hand away. "I find such things most fascinating." She paused, her next words scrolling through her mind so bright she could not help but speak them. "In truth, I wish I could do more to help the king in this valiant effort. If only I could..."

Stockton tilted his head, his gravelly timbre deep. "You would do such a thing?"

"Aye." She fussed again with the pudding. "The longer this conflict continues, the more pain for all of us."

"You are a woman with wisdom beyond her years, Miss Young." Stockton stepped directly beside her. "An attractive quality."

The compliment stuck to her skin like a hungry leech, and she hadn't time to yank it free before he started again.

"There is something you *can* do, if you earnestly wish to be of service to your king."

She stilled, her stomach in her throat. What did he mean? Fear tugged at her lips, frantic to keep them closed, but curiosity opened them. "What is that?"

Stockton moved so near she could feel the warmth of his body behind hers. "I am in need of a scribe. Someone to help me pen messages to my fellow officers."

"A scribe?" She turned and ducked away, moving backward around the table. "I am honored sir, but would such a thing be most proper?"

He shook his head, following her. "'Tis common, and your acceptance would be of great help not only to myself but to the valiant efforts we strive to achieve."

Her insides squirmed. Valiant efforts to achieve what? The suppression of fellow British citizens? She exhaled away the smoke of anger that clogged her lungs. "I...I hardly know what to say."

"Miss Young..." He crept closer and stopped within inches of her, his voice growing rich, his words bold. "I have never met anyone so lovely, and I find I crave your company." He continued, his tone lightening, as if he feared alarming her. "That is, if you are willing to spend time with a lonely old soldier."

Now she truly feared she would be sick. She swallowed and dared to meet his hooded gaze. "Not lonely, surely."

"I am surrounded by soldiers, aye. But what companions are they?" He pinned her motionless. "I do not mean to make you uncomfortable, naturally. I simply wish for the help of one whose smile will ease the burdens of my station. You understand."

His last two words hit like the gouging stab of a bayonet. This was not for her to decline. She could see it in the fine lines around his eyes. Her answer must be yes. Both for his demand of it, but also... Her mind stilled and cleared, like a breeze that parted a cloudy sky. Aye. She must do it. Think of what she might learn from his very lips?

Thank you, Lord. This was His doing.

Molding a modest grin on her face, Hannah pretended reluctance. "'Twould be an honor, Major. But I must tell you..." A barrier should be in place, something that might hopefully keep the man at a distance. "In hopes that our relationship is quite understood, I must tell you that I am being courted."

Stockton's expression rounded, and his brow shot up before he relaxed his look with a sigh. "I cannot say I am surprised."

Hannah lowered her lashes in humble response. *Pray do not ask more.*

"You have dashed all my dreams, dear lady."

She looked up to find Stockton's smile heightened on one side. Was that teasing in his voice?

"Tell me, who is the fortunate gentleman who claims your affections?"

A few breaths, and the rest of the falsehood popped free. "He is at sea, sir. I expect him home next year."

Stockton tsked in disapproval. "So long? How can he bear to be away from you for any length of time?"

"We endure it as best we can." She sealed her lips to cover the fragile lie she'd just shaped before returning her attention to the various goods on the table.

"I do hope this will not keep you from assisting me. You must know how humbly I implore you."

Knife in hand, she hovered it over the waiting mass of pudding. "You are too kind, sir."

He took the place Joseph had occupied only minutes before. "Then you will accept."

A spark of rebellion ignited from the core of her soul, heating her entire frame. She could not resist. This man was as culpable as Greene in the death of her uncle. And now he offered her this chance, this *favor*? A grin rose to her mouth. Raising her chin, she spoke to the window. "Aye, sir. Most agreeably."

He straightened, voice subtly proud, as if he'd just won a battle. "I am most pleased. Most pleased indeed."

Chapter Twelve

"Who are you?"

Joseph stood in the open doorway of the foundry, fists rounded and ready. Two men, one at each forge, dropped their hands from their work with a quick nod.

The nearest man stepped forward, wiping his palms on his leather apron. Ruddy complexion and thinning hairline, the round man's face appeared much younger than the rest of him. "Private Sackett, sir." He nodded sideways with his head toward the other one. "That there's Private Deane."

They didn't appear threatening, but that meant little. "What are you doing here? Did Stockton send you?"

"He did, sir." Sackett reached out and offered his hand. Joseph took it, impressed with the firmness of his grip. "He said to have things ready so you could get started right away."

Impressive. It seemed Stockton took this work as seriously as Joseph did. He scanned the rest of the foundry to be sure there were no other Redcoats lurking in the shadows.

Closing the door behind him, Joseph locked in what meager warmth hovered in the giant room.

Taking another quick assessment, he removed his greatcoat and hat. A welcome sensation breezed through Joseph's frame as he glanced across the foundry. How right it felt to be surrounded by the blast of heat and scent of scalding metal. The itch to hold a hammer in his fingers and feel the bite of flying sparks on his skin warmed him despite the chill in the air. Wherever a bellows blew and iron glowed, there he belonged.

Both forges were at work, but with only three men the task would take longer than he supposed Stockton would like. "Anyone else coming?"

The short soldier at the second forge shook his head. "Just us. Sackett's got the order."

Sackett pulled a folded paper from his pocket. "'Tis straightforward."

Joseph unfolded the paper and schooled both his face and his breathing to show nothing, despite the scowl that tugged at his features and the excitement that tried to speed the pace of his lungs.

> *100 gun barrels to be made and delivered to Willis Plains in Duxbury by February 3.*

His mind charged at full speed, kicking up clods of questions as it raced. Why Duxbury? Would they ship them north? Were there other munitions they planned to get into British hands? Nathaniel and Henry would need this information immediately.

He refolded the paper and slid it into his breeches pocket. "Such a task will be difficult with only the three of us." He took Sackett's place by the forge and yanked on the chain, the bellows rushing the flames high and hot. "Who's Willis Plains?"

"Our gunsmith." In stride, Sackett poked at the coals. "Poses as a Patriot, but he's workin' for us. If those idiot rebels haven't figured that out by now..." A rough chuckle left him. "Eh, the job's not bad. We'll have to work morn' and night, but we can do it."

Joseph glanced to Deane, who was inspecting the growing glow at the end of his rod. "There's no one else in your camp who can help?" He turned back to Sackett, who still yanked on the chain. "We could work faster with more men."

"We're the only ones who know how this is to be done." Deane pumped the bellows. "Better this way instead of trying to teach someone who knows nothing at all."

"Perhaps." Joseph stopped to look behind at the water bucket. Ice covered the top, and he reached for the nearest hammer, breaking through the thick covering. The men would need this water to cool their iron. "You've made gun barrels before?"

Deane nodded. "So's Sackett. We both worked in smithies before recruitment."

Looking from one soldier to the other, Joseph measured their strength. Their intelligence was harder to analyze. "Best see what we can accomplish before noon."

"With focus and speed I believe 'tis quite attainable." Sackett pulled the swage block beside the anvil. "Deane, you need help with that?"

The man grumbled his reply. "I can't keep the flame up and poke the coals at the same time."

Sackett left his post and went to pull on the chain while Deane heated the iron.

Joseph grumbled. This wouldn't work. These two were obviously capable but lacked practice. They needed at least four men, or the work would take far too long. He glanced behind, the men mumbling between themselves. Perhaps that was a good thing. Delaying the shipment of gun barrels by the mere fact they could not be produced might be sabotage enough.

He shook his head. Nay. That could make Stockton suspicious. The man was no fool. What then? Craft all one hundred and deliver as planned, but with an attack at the ready? He bit his cheek. 'Twas too early for such plans. But what a sweet victory it would be to bring such an enemy to heel.

The next several hours passed with frustratingly little progress, the weight of the note in his pocket all but ripping a hole through the fabric of his breeches.

Glancing out the window, he attempted to assess the placement of the sun, but the thick white clouds shielded its location. It must be at least noon.

With a grunted sigh, he released the chain he'd been pulling. "I'm to the house."

The soldiers paused, sweat glistening their brows, questions in their eyes.

Joseph motioned to the pile of coal in the corner. "I miscalculated the needed supplies. I must go to town."

"Shall not I go?" Sackett stepped forward, obviously keen to be rid of the foundry for the time being. "Tell me what you need, and I shall—"

"Thank you, but I must do it."

Sackett tipped his head with an acquiescent frown and turned back to his work.

Hat and coat on, Joseph spoke before closing the door. "I shall be back soon."

Striding across the yard, Joseph made for the kitchen, leaving behind the mission he must now perform, to consider the woman who likely worked just beyond the door. Heaven help him. If Hannah were still there, he might not be able to resist another bit of banter. He growled inwardly. Foolhardy, that would be. Not even a simple interchange was safe. The slightest slope could give way to an avalanche that would cover him, forever sealing him in a mountain of emotions from which he would never have the strength to dig free.

He stood at the door, taking a long inhale of air he hoped would cool the rising temperature of his blood.

Two weeks. That was all. Nothing could happen in that time. He was safe. So why did he feel as if he had never been in more danger?

The clock in the parlor struck the nooning hour. Twelve chimes, each one louder than the last. From her place by the laundering she'd just begun, Hannah glanced through the kitchen window to the foundry. She cursed herself for the countless times she'd peered through the frosted panes, secretly pining for a view of him. Scrubbing the shirt harder in the basin, she wished she could as easily scour away the longing that held like an old stain.

Up to her elbows in hot water, Hannah rubbed the linen between her hands, the conversation of hours past still struggling to find a comfortable position in her mind. But it would not, she knew, until she told Joseph. A thrill beat through her. She now had a chance to move forward in their mission more quickly than she'd anticipated. 'Twas so simple, it seemed almost too good to be true.

All that remained was to tell Joseph and to pray he wouldn't be upset.

Hannah noted a fraying spot on the collar of one of his shirts and rubbed more carefully, making a mental reminder to mend it. She continued to wash the shirt more carefully, pondering how she would explain her opportunity to Joseph. Surely once she explained how innocuous it truly was, he would be understanding and allow it—how could he not? Removing the shirt and wringing the water free, she hung the damp fabric near the kitchen fire.

Just then the door flung open behind her, and she whirled. "Oh!" She pressed a wet hand to her chest. "Joseph, you startled me."

He shut the door, cutting off the blast of chilled air. His half smile did dangerously delightful things to her middle.

"Hard at work, I see."

Hannah reached for the nearest cloth to dry her hands and find occupation for her sudden nerves. "'Tis noon. You must be hungry." Of course he was. He'd hardly eaten anything. She should have thought to bring a basket out to the foundry. Ensign had always liked that. "Let me fix you a—"

"Perhaps later." His grin lingered a moment, fading only when his vision shifted to his musket over the mantel. "I'm off to town."

She stalled, hands still clutching the towel. "To town?"

Caution knit through his expression, mouth tight, brow creased. The silent message roared from his expression.

"Oh." She knew the parlor was empty but glanced there anyway. Stepping forward, she came to the edge of the table. "You've already a missive to send? Will they not find it strange to have you leave when the work has just begun?"

Joseph grunted his reply as he lifted his musket from the mantel and slipped the powder horn across his chest. "I've discovered I miscalculated a few supplies, so a trip to town is necessary. A fortunate happenstance."

He spun toward the door, but Hannah halted him with a touch on his sleeve. "Joseph, wait." She yanked her hand back. How could she touch him so carelessly? Her body tensed, and she curled her fingers. The complexities of their strained familiarity battled so hard she feared she might slip into those comfortable habits that seemed to return with frightening ease. "There's something I need to tell you."

The instant tenderness in the lines of his face, the way his thick muscles flexed under his greatcoat as he faced her, made pleasant tingles spray through her chest.

His voice was a deep, peaceful river. "Anything."

Anything?

At that single word, the kitchen faded. The warmth of the fire behind her, the scents of freshly laundered cloth, the snapping sound of the logs in the hearth softened as if the sun were setting, stealing with its waning light all she'd thought she would say, leaving behind only the things she longed to.

Lowering her gaze, she allowed her eyes to study the swirled etchings on the center platter of the table. If only—

"Hannah?"

All the blood had fled her limbs in an attempt to help her heart keep its sudden, wild pulse in check. She hadn't the strength to lift her head in response, hadn't the voice to answer. She closed her eyes, hoping she could rip her mind from the trance of him that her soul submitted to so willingly.

Rough fingers brushed against her elbow. "What is it?"

Her blood thundered in her ears. Why? Why was she so weak? How easy it would be to open her mouth and tell him all the truths that pined for revelation. *I waited for you for so many years, Joseph. I bore our son...*

"Hannah." Smooth and warm, the sound of her name was like a whispered prayer.

Eyes still closed against the sight of him, she drew a quiet breath. Cold knuckles brushed her cheek, and she pulled back, eyes flinging open and instantly colliding with his.

His hand hovered away from her cheek. He swallowed, slowly dropping his hand but not his gaze. A small apologetic smile flashed over his mouth before he stepped back. "What had you wanted to tell me?"

Hannah stared, blinking to try to snip away the strings of the tender, bewitching moment. A pleasurable burn singed her skin where his fingers had touched her. What *had* she planned to tell him?

After a quick inhale the last tie was cut, and she was able at last to form the words she'd forgotten, though her voice seemed as if she spoke from afar. "Stockton has asked me to be his—"

The front door burst wide, and they jumped. Hannah whirled to the door to see Stockton and another man stride in.

She looked back to Joseph. His face was drawn, his stance leaning toward her as if he were so full of anxiety he was ready to leap from his own skin.

She could read the question in his eyes. *Stockton asked you to be his what?*

"Good afternoon, Mr. Young, Miss Young."

Hannah nodded to Joseph with a promise in her grin that she would tell him later, then turned toward the parlor. Peering to the others from her position in the kitchen, she curtsied. "Good afternoon, gentlemen."

Bowing, Joseph responded in kind, his frustrations apparently restrained, however temporary. "Major."

Stockton gestured to the man with him. "This is my attendant, Private Reece. He'll be helping me and Greene occasionally."

"Good to meet you, Reece." Hannah nodded to the soldier, who looked more like a boy just fresh from home. "Your arrival is perfectly timed, Major." She stepped forward. "Do forgive my boldness, but

I've a basin of hot water and am in the middle of laundering. If you should have anything—"

"How thoughtful of you, Miss Young. I do indeed." All politeness left his tone when he turned to Reece and gestured to his quarters in the room behind him. "Retrieve my shirt and cloak from the end of the bed and bring them to Miss Young."

"Aye, sir."

The youth hurried to his task as Joseph stepped forward. "Sir, I too am glad you are here." He made his way to the parlor, gun in hand. "I am afraid I must go into town."

Stockton's dark brow jammed together. "For what purpose?"

"I fear I miscalculated a few of our supplies. I must purchase more coal and a few other items if we are to make real progress."

Stockton's small eyes narrowed, only shedding that sheen of disapproval when they flitted toward Hannah. "I suppose temporary suspensions are to be expected."

Joseph nodded. "A slight impediment is all. Once I have what I need, I shall return to work."

Stockton turned his back to the fire. "Of course."

Reece emerged, the articles bunched in his arms. He hurried to the kitchen, depositing the clothes on the table beside where Hannah stood.

"Very good of you, Reece."

His rosy cheeks lifted in response, as if such gratitude were rarely shown him, and his pale eyes brightened. "Aye, of course, miss."

"I shall be off then." From in front of the parlor door, Joseph's resounding voice echoed through the room.

He flung a look to Hannah that sailed across the small distance to coat her with a kind of reassurance, a kind of courage that seemed to all but lift her feet from the floor.

"I will return before supper."

With that, he was out the door and gone. Hannah tucked away the gift he'd secreted her in the clearness of his eyes and gathered the next items to be washed as both Stockton and Reece took their places in front of the parlor fire, discussing wagons, road conditions, and the petty arguments of soldiers that needed remedying. Nothing useful. Positions of regulars, plans of action, munition stores—those were the particulars she needed.

Hannah lifted the cloak and unfolded it, when a paper slipped from a hidden pocket on the inside of the garment. Slapping a hand to her thigh, she caught the paper before it landed to the ground. Pulse raging, she stood still, listening to the rush of blood in her ears and the undisturbed conversation behind her. Cautiously she craned her neck to glance back. The discussion continued undisturbed. Blessed heaven. Her heart thumped so hard behind her ribs she could feel its savage drumming through her stays. The paper singed her fingertips. She had only seconds...

She straightened and hung the cloak over her arm. Flipping the paper back to front, she looked for a seal. Nothing, not even the remnants of one.

Nerves charged like the sky before a storm, Hannah unfolded the paper close to her chest and read.

Four hundred troops arriving to Boston by week's end. Supplies on board. Forty cannon and two thousand rounds. Docking at Duxbury to get remaining munitions then marching north. Majors Pitman and Stockton will prepare for engagement—

"Miss Young?"

A hard grip of panic seized her throat as the sound of footfalls approached from behind. Clumsily refolding the note, Hannah whirled around and dropped it behind her. Smiling, she locked her knees to keep them from buckling. "Aye, sir?"

The rushing blood in her ears crashed loud and hard, like storming waves on the shore.

Stockton neared, that sticky sweetness in his face still present, still loathsome. "Do forgive me, but I've just remembered something." He gestured to his cloak, and she offered it to him.

She stepped back to allow him room, and he reached for the inner pocket. A scowl clawed his brow, and he spread the garment wide, flapping it twice.

"Is something..." High-pitched and tense, the voice coming from her throat sounded nothing like her own. She cleared her throat and tried again. "Is something wrong?"

He threw a pinched glance her way, then back to the cloak. "Nay. It seems...it seems I've misplaced something, is all."

"Oh, I see." She stepped back, turning casually, praying God would enhance her playacting to its fullest. "Dear me!" She bent and picked up the article, handing it to him innocently. "Is this it?"

A bright flash of relief lit his eyes before formality and business replaced it. "Thank you, Miss Young."

"How fortunate it fell to the ground and not into the water." The laugh she let out carried a heavy lilt of freed anxiety, but from the smile he offered, he heard naught of it.

"I shall find a way to repay you, Miss Young. You have saved me, I daresay."

"'Tis nothing, sir." No doubt her cheeks were red, for they burned, and not from shy embarrassment, as Stockton's satisfied smile professed.

Bowing, he took the paper and replaced the cloak beside the basin. "I shall leave you to your work." But before he left, he whispered, "We shall have a bit of time to ourselves before the day is over."

Hannah gripped the edge of the workspace where the basin rested, her fingernails biting into the wood. Smiling, she nodded, her mind scattering like a panicked crowd. She turned away and stared into the dark water. Pulling in long drinks of air, she waited for her pulse to calm and the blood once more to return to her numb limbs. But it did not.

The gravity of what she'd just learned weighed upon her so heavy her shoulders began a slow, pulsing ache. She had to get this message to Joseph—he had to deliver both his secret knowledge and hers.

Sighing, she spoke another silent prayer, invoking the powers of heaven to work on her behalf. She would have to leave in a matter of minutes if she were to catch Joseph in time. A quick glance to the parlor grounded her fledgling hope. The two sat in chairs, Stockton all but lounging while Reece sat with elbows on his knees.

Hannah closed her eyes, praying as she had not prayed before.

Chapter Thirteen

The hollow stump was a half mile out of town at the edge of the wood, Nathaniel had told him. *Leave your missive stuffed deep in the left corner. Another man will check it each day after sunset.*

Only partway through town, Joseph's legs itched to tap Anvil's flank and race to his destination, the message almost smoking from its hiding spot in his pocket. Keeping his spine relaxed and his smile easy took more strength than he'd thought. Would to God that Hannah would not have to harbor any such secrets. The thought of her enduring this harrowing anxiety made his stomach turn. Let him do the spying. And him alone.

He'd like to have this over and done, though checking on the availability of coal and supplies would be his first stop.

Anvil nickered, and Joseph patted his neck, nodding at a man who walked past. His fleeting inquisitive glance made Joseph sit taller and call himself the fool that he was. Traveling midday might be necessary, but it certainly was not prudent. Praise heaven there were only a few townspeople about, thanks in most part to the stinging cold, no doubt.

Joseph tugged Anvil to a stop and dismounted in front of the mercantile, securing his reins to the post. A chuckle bubbled through him at Anvil's wayward expression. "I know 'tis cold. I won't be long."

Ducking into the building, the pungent scents of mace and clove swirled in the air, tickling his nose. He closed the door behind him and dodged a row of baskets hanging from a rope that spanned the length of the room. Pausing, he grinned at the laden but organized shelves of wares. The aligned jars of soaps, polished crocks, and lines of thread and cloth pried open his heart, tucking in the open space a melancholy homesickness. His blacksmith shop had been just as tidy, just as strictly arranged. But he was never going back, though every hour that passed seemed to censure what once he called wisdom. Leo might have been qualified, but did he love the work as Joseph did? More, could Joseph endure Hannah's presence day after day when the war was over? He tossed the invading thought away and continued to peruse the empty shop, still void of its proprietor.

Joseph glanced to a row of children's toys and baubles, that unsettling melancholy pressing deeper. He stopped and fingered a cup and ball that resembled almost exactly the one he'd crafted for Jacob so many years ago. How did the boy fare? Had his smile begun to broaden under Kitty's care? He upbraided himself. Next time he came to town, he'd be sure to have a letter prepared.

"Welcome, sir. May I help you?"

Joseph spun on his heel, a ready smile on his lips. "Good day. I am looking for—"

"Forgive me—is that your horse?"

Following his gaze to the large window, Joseph's body clenched. A pair of Redcoats were stopped beside Anvil, untying his reins.

Bolting, Joseph burst through the door, careful not to allow his rage to hurl him unwittingly into prison, or worse.

"Gentlemen?" His neck corded as he strained to keep his voice even. "May I ask where you're taking my horse?"

The soldiers turned to him, mouths tight and eyes hard. The tallest spoke first, rampant disdain riding his words. "We've been instructed to check any and all mounts for hidden documents and missives."

"What?" His answer came out like a thrown fist.

Eyes thinning, the man spit his answer. "It seems there's an informant about."

Joseph's ears went hot. "You are looking in the wrong place, checking him." He nudged his chin toward Anvil. "Neither of us is culpable. I am working under the command of Major Stockton. You may ask him yourself."

Without a second look, the man began leading Anvil away as if Joseph had said nothing. Crimson clouded his vision. He grabbed the soldier by the arm. "Do not think of it."

Turning, the man's face cramped. "Let go."

Joseph shoved the soldier back, rage locking into his muscles' memory—how it felt to know that he was about to fight and that he would win. A bolt of strength shot down his back. He firmed his fists and widened his stance. "You will not take my horse without a fight."

Righting his posture, the soldier hunched, mouth sneering to one side. "You will regret this."

"Private Abrams!"

The two soldiers turned at the shout, but Joseph remained, fists ready, muscles taut, not willing to take his pointed vision off the enemy.

"Captain Higley, sir."

Higley?

At this, Joseph allowed a brief look, but his tension only increased, teetering on the edge of explosion. He'd fought three men many times before, but...Hannah's face flashed in his vision like a pleading apparition.

If he were taken, she would be alone.

Easing his curled fingers, Joseph brought himself to his full height, the incoming fire of demands and explanations seconds from impact.

"What's going on here?" Higley's impressive frame made the two privates look laughably small.

The tall one answered first. "I have just been assaulted by this man." His arm stretched out in full, long finger pointing.

Higley offered a cursory glance toward Joseph before marking the other two in his sights. "It appears to me you are taking a man's property."

"Property?" The second soldier finally spoke. "You know Major Pitman's orders."

Higley's expression was unchanged, but for his eyes that narrowed. "Nowhere is it stated we are to *take* anything." He threw a look to Joseph. "I can vouch for this man. He is working with us."

Again the spindly soldier stepped forward, his voice sounding more like a whining child. "You will let him get away with what he did—"

"On your way, Private Abrams. You too, Cotton." The gruff command made both men straighten. "I shall see you at camp."

Striking Joseph with a last hard look, the men huffed off, leaving Joseph and Higley alone.

Reaching for the dangling reins, Joseph nodded to Higley and tugged Anvil back to the post, grappling for a reason why the man would have come to his aid.

Once again tying Anvil secure, he spoke, blaming his frank remark on his spiked pulse. "An informant, hmm? Good luck catching him."

Whatever reaction Joseph expected, the slight chuckle and quick smile Higley offered wasn't it. "What are you doing in town? I thought you were to be at the foundry?"

His words were so genial and familiar, Joseph found himself strangely comfortable. He eased his stance. "I needed a few other supplies." He paused. Something about Higley's expression prodded him to expose the rest of his needs without a second thought. "Problem is, the work is difficult with only three men."

"You need another?"

Joseph gave a slight nod to the side. "With more we could work faster, but it seems there's only the three of us that know the workings of a forge. Making gun barrels is simple enough, but it takes a few men to—"

"Perhaps I could lend assistance."

"You?"

Higley turned his head aside and stroked Anvil's nose, and 'twas then Joseph noticed the scar that scooped deep across Higley's ear, the top part completely missing. A battle wound perhaps?

"I have only a little experience." Higley spoke again and looked up. "But perhaps enough to make your work less burdensome."

He would do that? "Could Stockton spare you?"

The angled muscle in Higley's jaw flexed back and forth before he answered. "He has Greene to help him. And Reece."

Such an offer. Joseph glanced to the shop behind him, mind reeling. Having an officer in the foundry every day, watching his every action, would make the work more onerous, not less.

Joseph rubbed his gloved knuckles against his jaw. 'Twas not his place to deny Higley, no matter how he wished to and no matter how innocuous the man appeared to be. "If you should like to, I cannot decline your offer."

Higley bobbed his head, lowering his hand from Anvil's nose. "I shall speak with Stockton."

A nod of thanks and Joseph prepared to turn, but Higley's voice rendered him motionless.

"And Mr. Wythe...they *are* looking for someone. I would be cautious, if I were you." He patted Anvil on the neck and moved back up the road.

Joseph froze, his heart igniting a cannonade of explosions with every pump. What had he called him?

That single word rammed into Joseph's mind, yet the blinding shock seemed to refuse it entrance until finally the truth crashed with harrowing force, exposing every tightly shielded secret.

He'd spoken Joseph's true name—as if he'd known it all along.

The cold was not thick. 'Twas thin. So transparent it passed through her like a spirit, freezing, it seemed, the very flow in her veins. Hannah walked faster, wringing her aching fingers, irritated that in her haste she'd neglected the thick scarf her neck and ears now cried for.

In the center of town, she stopped, scanning the road for any sign of Joseph or his giant black stallion. It had not been twenty minutes after her fervent pleading with Providence that grace smiled upon her, Stockton revealing he and Reece must go to camp until evening. God's goodness was so immediate, so loving that no matter how she worked to show Him her gratitude, yet she would be an unprofitable servant. But that would not stop her from trying.

The buzzing in her frozen toes pressed her to walk faster. If only she'd had a horse, she could make it to town swifter. But she feared saddling and preparing a mount would take more time than hurrying to town on foot. And if she were to meet Joseph on his return, they could easily ride back together to wherever it was he'd left the message. Nathaniel and Joseph had both insisted she not know the place where the messages were to be deposited, so if questioned, she could answer truthfully. At the time such judgment seemed wise, but now with her own message hurriedly penned and stuffed deep between her breasts, she wished she would have insisted. For if she did not meet up with him now, she could have delivered it herself.

Turning in a full circle, she frowned, reserving a none-too-ladylike huff. He was nowhere in sight. She'd missed him. Again wringing her fingers, she studied her former reasoning. Leaving it for another time would have been fine, would it not? Glancing back the way she'd come, she licked her lips. Then again, with Stockton at the house, Joseph couldn't leave every evening without raising suspicions. Nay. 'Twas good she'd made the attempt but folly she hadn't reached him in time. Now what was she to do?

"Miss Young?"

Hannah spun. "Captain Higley."

He neared, stopping a polite distance. Bowing, he smiled. "At your service." He straightened and glanced around, as if looking for someone. "What are you doing in town? Have you come alone?"

She swallowed, uncertain how to reply. "Uh...aye." The truth was rarely a poor choice, but she revealed only part of it, ignoring the first of his questions.

His lichen-colored eyes studied her before he too glanced around the mostly vacant street. "'Tis a cold day to be out."

"'Tis."

He continued his study of her, and her cold hands moistened. She opened her mouth to speak, but when nothing came out, she simply breathed a light sigh and smiled, castigating herself for her stayed tongue. Why could she not speak?

Thankfully, he did. "Miss Young, I should like at last to offer my sincerest apologies regarding the loss of your uncle."

Hannah stilled at the raw honesty of his words. "Thank you, Captain."

Gaze unwavering, his handsome face eased into a knowing kindness. "I know this must be of great distress to you, but I must ask you...I would *beg* you to not give up hope."

"Hope?"

His eyes flitted away for a moment, as if he searched after the words he wished to speak. Returning his humble strength to her gaze, he sighed briefly. "Hope gives wing to many a prayer, does it not? 'Tis the very basis for what we desire."

But desiring one who is dead to yet live was not something for which any could dare hope.

She met his kindness with her own, grateful that one who was supposed to be her enemy would show such humanity. "Your sincerity means a great deal, Captain."

The quick dip of his brow and bob of his chin said something she hadn't a chance to interpret before he spoke again. "On a separate subject, I should like to advise you, Miss Young, that if you must come to town, do not come alone."

She raised her eyebrows, the action not needing to be forced as she asked the necessary question. "Is there something amiss?"

"Nay, 'tis simply...I know not how to say this..." He craned his neck to look over his shoulder, revealing for the first time a ghastly missing section of his ear. Poor man. How had he come by such a wound? A battle injury perhaps? Thank the Lord 'twas only his ear that had been hurt.

Turning back, he took a single step forward. "There are too many soldiers about, Miss Young. They are quite suspicious. I should not like you to fall prey to any..."

He stopped, a tight smile on his lips. He knew he needn't say the rest.

Her heart slowed as her mind scrambled to measure the length of his meaning. Was she in danger?

"You are most thoughtful, Captain." Her voice was more pinched than she would have liked. "But I am sure I will—"

"I must insist. In fact..." He glanced around again, then held her with a stare that demanded he be trusted. And almost unwittingly, she did.

"Miss Young, if you would allow me, I should like to escort you home."

Her cheeks scalded. She knew he asked not for his own gratification, but still his generosity made her glance down, heavy with reticence. "That is very kind of you, Captain. I didn't see anyone on the road. And...and as my business here is...done...I will return immediately."

"I insist."

The charity in his unwavering stare seemed somehow to make her spirit incline to trust far deeper than she would have done on her own.

She lowered her lashes. "I will accept, gladly. Thank you."

"Higley."

A call from behind turned them both.

"What is it?" Higley didn't care to hide the irritation in his tone. "Abrams, I'm—"

"Major Pitman wishes to see you."

By the crouch of his brow and flex of his jaw, Hannah knew his thoughts as well as if he'd voiced them. He glanced to her, the heavy frustration replaced by strict kindness. "It seems I cannot accompany you as I'd wished. Walk swiftly. Do not stop. And do not come to town alone again, I pray you."

The concern in his expression made her stomach twitch. What did he know that she didn't?

"Of course."

She glanced to the road again, praying hope against hope that Joseph would ride into view. She slid a forced smile to Higley, who bowed and started down the road toward his companion.

Abrams spoke something to him as Hannah faced the way she'd come, battling the irksome knowledge she'd failed to accomplish the very thing she'd set out to do. She looked down at the muddy ice, her legs so weighted she could hardly get them to comply with her command to move.

Peering behind, she saw Higley speaking with two others, when another man came out of a large building, speaking as loud with his motions as he did with his mouth.

Kicking her legs into action, she hurried down the road, the missive at her chest chiding her like a scorned mother. She should have kept going—and perhaps would have if not for Higley. The moment she thought to question his admonition, his sincerity cut through, and she sighed a long, audible breath.

At least another half hour of walking, and for what purpose? And what was more, this extended solitude allowed her mind to toy with thoughts she would rather evade. But silence had its way of imposing on the soul the very thing one wished to avoid. Joseph's smile, his strength—both of body and heart—his sincerity and warm tenderness caressed her imagination.

He hadn't meant to touch her, surely. He was only acting in simple and natural affection as any person would do.

Affection.

Her mouth went dry at the thought. He didn't still care for her. Her feet slowed. But what if he did? Then she stopped completely. *Dear Lord, what if he did?*

A clomp of hooves against the ice-covered road made Hannah slow and move to the side of the road, sure Joseph would appear astride Anvil.

But he did not.

Two riders rounded the corner toward her, their scarlet coats blazoning their approach.

Her breathing stalled when the face of the first soldier met her eyes. Greene.

He stopped, the other beside him. His wiry smile curled up his face, not hiding his satisfaction at finding her alone. Resting his hands on his saddle, he glanced to his companion. "What have we here, Pryer?" He looked back to her and leaned forward. "Poor young miss. You must be chilled clear through."

Higley's concern of a quarter hour past blared like the warning call of a trumpet. She should never have gone out without Joseph.

"Should we not assist her, Captain?" The man called Pryer urged his mount a few steps closer. "It appears to me she is alone, and such a thing should not be. No, no." Sneering, he turned to Greene with a laugh.

Vile man. Shoving the block of fear from impeding her path, Hannah continued forward, chin raised, refusing with her silence to offer them the reaction they craved.

"Hold on now." Jumping down, Greene blocked her path, arms outstretched until she came to a complete stop.

Hannah struggled against a growl that churned in her chest and lunged to step around him, but he gripped her shoulder and spun her around. "This was the one I was telling you about, Pryer. Stockton's little pet."

The other soldier dismounted and came around the front of Greene's horse to where she stood. Tall and thick muscled, the man's face would have been handsome had not the gloss of lechery in his stare turned his visage to that of a gargoyle.

"She's a pretty one."

Eyes trailing her from head to foot, the downy hairs on Hannah's skin stood on end.

Grinning, he looked to Greene. "Now, what would you say she's doing out here unaccompanied?"

Hannah stepped back, throwing at them the rage that erupted and eclipsed the haze of fear. "I am returning home from town, and if you are at all a gentleman, you would let me pass..." Like a steady rope tied firm between anger and courage, her voice held firm. "Out of my way."

"What are you about, woman?" Greene's grip on her shoulder tightened, and he turned her to face him. "Don't think I will be taken in. Stockton is a fool, but not I. I know you were here before—there was no hired help."

A hotness crept up her neck, and she prayed to God he wouldn't see it. "I don't know what you mean. I've told you the truth."

His fingers dug deeper, and she yanked against his hold, but he wouldn't release.

"Let me go!"

"Major Pitman has discovered an informant." Greene looked to Pryer with a nod, and the man moved around to her back. "We are to question every person in town and on the road." His dark-brown eyes slipped to ebony. "How fortunate we have found you alone."

Panic's double-edged sword cut swift and deep. She tried to dart away, but the iron grip of both men held her firm, grinding their fingers into her arms.

Greene pulled her back, holding her just inches from his face. Looming like a black storm, he towered over her. "You are a fragile little glass box. We need only tap you before you break apart and spill your filthy secrets."

"I have no secrets!" With a hard pull she prepared to yank herself free, but Greene released at the same moment, and she flew backward against the ground, her head hitting the ice with a thud.

Tiny lights sparked her vision as a ruckus of laughter filled the quiet wood, making two voices sound like twenty. *Get up. You must get up.* Turning to her side she blinked harder and pushed to sitting. If only her head would stop spinning...

"Watch yourself there, little lady," Pryer chided, a satisfied stretch of grin over his face

Hannah scrambled to her feet but slipped in search of her footing, when a hard boot kicked her backside. She went sprawling with a yelp, the cold ice smacking her face with a stab of pain. A hot liquid drained down her lips.

Shaking, the reality hit as hard as the unforgiving ground. Slowly, she pushed up, drops of scarlet splattering the dirty snow beneath her nose. Fear's imposing shape shadowed her from behind as another spray of guffaws were thrown through the wood.

"Get up." Greene kicked her again.

And again her face smacked the ground.

"Get up and let us search you. I know you are not so innocent."

Dear Lord, help me!

Arms shaking, Hannah tried to right herself and to chase after the remnants of her courage that rolled away like a wheel down a hill. But she could do neither.

She pushed to her hands and looked at the soldiers who stared with faces devoid of all but hate. She spattered blood as she spoke, grimacing at the acrid taste. "I have nothing for you to find. And if you do this, you will live to regret it."

How she could say the words she didn't know. Perhaps fear provided more resistance than she realized. For the lie was thick, heavy. The rolled note she harbored would be found all too quickly, for surely that would be the first place they would check. *Foolish, foolish girl.*

Greene knelt beside her, the slap to her face quick and hard. Grasping her cheeks in his rough fingers, he forced her to look at him. "I will not be threatened. Especially not by a woman."

Launching to his feet he motioned to Pryer. "Hold her down." His voice scraped hard against her skin. "I'll find what I'm looking for. Then we will see who regrets what."

SO PURE A HEART

Chapter Fourteen

Joseph returned through town, feeling a bit like the powerful Atlas might have if he'd thrown the world from his back. His lungs could take in air, and it seemed even Anvil walked with a lighter step. Too bad this ritual would need to be repeated at least a few times more, perhaps every day until their two weeks were out, if the information continued to pour into his hands.

To the left of him, a handful of Redcoats argued at the corner of a two-story building. He strained his ears but could hear nothing of their conversation.

He continued on, not for the first time wondering how Hannah fared in the house alone with the men. There was naught he could do but pray and be at her side as much as possible. Anxiety pressed against his stomach like a pestle into a mortar. He should not have left her. Next time he would find reason for her to come along so his concerns wouldn't leave a hole in his middle.

"Joseph!"

Pulling Anvil to a stop, Joseph twisted on his saddle to see Higley hurrying toward him, his companions glowering from behind.

Higley's face was taut with creases across his brow. "Have you seen Miss Young?"

That anxiety ground harder. "Nay. Why? Was she here?"

Higley sprayed a curse. "I'd hoped somehow you'd met up with her." He pointed down the road Joseph was headed. "She left not twenty minutes past. I told her she should not travel alone. With the search on, I fear that if the men should find her..."

Anvil sidestepped, no doubt sensing Joseph's unrest. "She went this way?"

"Aye."

With a nod Joseph kicked Anvil to a run and raced down the road, his heart flooding his frame with heat.

Gripping the reins between ironlike fingers, he breathed hard. She would be fine of course. Naught could happen in so short a time. Yet the rise of panic hit like a hailstorm.

'Twas a handful of agonizing minutes before he rounded a bend. Two horses stood in the middle of the road as two men in red coats were—

The view struck him so hard he leapt from his mount before coming to a stop.

Hannah lay on the ground, one soldier standing behind, the other crouching in front of her, gripping her bleeding face with his hand.

Joseph yanked on Anvil's reins and launched from his saddle. Muscles flexed, anger ticking in his bones, he roared. Greene stood and turned in time for Joseph's fist to meet the soft middle of his belly, knocking him backward.

Vision sheathed in red, his urge to do more than simply fight raged through Joseph like a tethered beast. That was Hannah's blood on Greene's fingers. The knowledge clawed, and he grabbed the back of Greene's collar, again slamming his fist into his middle.

The other man charged at him, fists poised for impact. Joseph moved a step away from Greene, who held his hands between his legs and staggered back. Dodging the incoming blow, Joseph rammed his fist into the side of the man's face, a spray of blood leaving his mouth as he stumbled backward. A boot to the man's thigh and another elbow to Greene's face soothed only a thread of his anger as the men tried again to attack from the side. He dodged, knuckles meeting jaw, then ribs. They would get this and more for what they'd done.

Grunting, the unknown man stepped back, wielding a knife from his side. A grimace of pain twitched on his face. "Two against one."

Greene unsheathed his own dagger and lunged. Joseph whirled back but the cold blade sliced against his ribs. He growled and swung his arm around, locking his grip on Greene's wrist. With a rough twist and hard jerk, he forced Greene's fingers to open. Joseph kicked the blade across the road and lunged when the second man barreled forward. He plowed his shoulder into the man's chest and hurled him to the ground. Another hard hit to the man's face left him motionless and bleeding from his mouth.

"Joseph!"

Hannah's voice yanked Joseph around, and he stilled. Greene's pistol waited inches from his nose. Time slowed. Reaching up and around, Joseph grabbed Greene's arm and launched to his feet as he pulled the man down. With a grunt of anger, he jammed his bootheel into Greene's groin. Rolling in pain, the soldier grabbed between his legs and howled through clenched teeth.

Lungs heaving, Joseph stood over his spoils. "Stockton will hear of this."

"You think...he will believe you..." Knees up, hands between his legs, Greene struggled to speak. "You will hang for this."

Joseph spun to Hannah, his heart collapsing at the blood still dripping from her nose. Reaching her in a few long strides, he knelt beside her, examining her condition before quickly untying the cloth from around his neck. He held it to her nose. "Can you stand?"

"Aye."

Reaching around her waist, he helped her up and pressed her toward Anvil. "We must get back quickly."

Round, worried eyes clung to him. "What will they—" Her vision drifted down, and she stopped hard. "Joseph! You're bleeding."

The pain in his side had only now begun to wail, and even still it was more a faraway cry, for he could not think of himself before her.

"'Tis nothing." He lifted her on the horse and swung up behind her, holding her steady with an arm around her waist. "Yaw!"

Still on the ground beside his motionless friend, Greene spewed curses as they rode past. "Stockton will hear of this. He will hang you, Young!"

Joseph held tight to her as they rode. "Do you have wounds I cannot see?"

She shook her head quick and shallow. "Nay." She glanced behind, removing the cloth from her nose. "Joseph, I am worried about you. We must—"

"Worry not."

Her light hand smoothed over his arm that held her, and suddenly his lungs went weightless, almost floating behind his ribs. Did she know what her touch did to him?

Again she glanced behind. "I shall tend it the moment we return home."

He tried to protest, but she stopped him. "No argument."

Almost as if his body obeyed a command his mind hadn't authorized, he tugged her harder against him, speaking low in her ear. "We shall be home soon."

And they were, thank the Lord. Leaving Anvil in the yard, Joseph dismounted and helped Hannah down. She hurried to the door, swinging it open and racing to the kitchen. He entered after and shut the door behind him.

"Come in here." Her voice echoed toward him.

Obeying, he stepped into the kitchen, grinding his teeth against the pain that continued to crescendo.

She looked behind to see he'd joined her and motioned to the worktable against the wall. "Lean against here. I must have a look."

Hurriedly she helped him remove his coat and unbuttoned his leather waistcoat. Staring down at the top of her hair, feeling her touch against his clothes, the pain retreated to a low throb, his pulse thundering.

Jerking her fingers back, Hannah stilled, staring at the half-unbuttoned waistcoat. "Oh, I...I suppose I should let you...do the rest."

Turning, she busied herself with placing a pot of water over the fire and went to the cupboard for a sheet she tore into rags. Joseph finished with the remaining buttons and let only a slight grunt free as he removed his shirt. He twisted to peer at the still-streaming gash. Deep. He looked up just as Hannah turned his direction.

Her cheeks instantly pinked as her eyes trailed from his chest to his abdomen. Masculine pride swelled through him, and another measure of the dissonant throbbing eased to the back of his mind. Striding forward, Hannah directed her gaze at his wound, not allowing him another pleasant peek at the attraction he'd spied so clear in her rosy expression.

She stood only inches from him. "Raise your arm." Direct, calm, she plucked a bandage from the table and bent her head sideways, examining his wound from another angle. "I should not like to stitch it..." At that she looked up at him, solemn angst in the upward pinch of her brow. "I fear that shall pain you more."

He nodded. "Wrap it first."

She swallowed and folded a thick wad of dressing atop the draining gash. Another stab of pain jabbed, but the discomfort vanished as her dainty, cool fingers rested against his skin. Holding the dressing in place, she took another long strip and all but hugged him as she wrapped the long cloth around his torso. The neckcloth that covered her chest dusted just below his, and instantly the pain was gone and in

186

its place a full, consuming need. She pulled back, then hugged around him again, taking the bandage around a second time. His pulse tripled, carrying him like a fallen leaf on a warm autumn breeze—blissful and heedless of where it would take him.

After a third time, she paused and tied a careful knot just below the cut. "There. 'Tis fine for now, but I shall change it again when I've prepared the salve."

"Thank you."

Hands still hovering over his abdomen, she looked up, the striking green of her eyes deepening to a dark forest of longing.

The arm he'd raised for her to continue the wrapping, he lowered, circling it around her back to hold her against him. A thrill of pleasure sparked to life as her breath caught and her neck corded.

Gaze darting to his, Hannah's dainty hands splayed across the bandage over his abdomen, the cold tips of her fingers brushing his skin and setting fire to his chest.

His mind struggled to work, the pulse of his heart stealing all the function his body could muster. Swallowing, he leaned forward for a bandage, then turned to dip it in a nearby pitcher.

"Let me clean your face."

Hannah's throat bobbed, but she didn't protest—didn't speak, hardly even took a breath, for her chest was almost still.

Cupping her chin in one hand, he dotted gently beneath her nose and around her mouth. The flow had stopped, thank the Lord. When all the red had been dabbed away, he went to one last place above her lip, and the soft, warm breath of her nose tickled his fingers. Joseph froze, cloth hovering just above her mouth. Her eyes, vast fields of green, were round and laced with a desire his soul had yearned to feel from her for so long.

He lowered his hand and rested the cloth at his side. Unable to stop his gaze from dropping to her freshly cleaned and slightly parted lips, he felt his head drooping closer. Smoothing his hand from her chin and over her ear, he cupped the back of her head—wishing, wanting, hoping to be taken exactly where he knew he ought never to go.

Mercy.

Hannah stared up, Joseph's hooded eyes studying the shape of her mouth. They shouldn't be here like this. Any moment Stockton could enter, and if he saw them...

She tried to move, tried to find the strength to pull away, but her frame was intoxicated with the feel of him, utterly heedless of the tiny timorous warning that chimed somewhere in the back of her mind. Ten years she had thought of him, longed to tell him all she'd endured, prayed for the chance to see him again despite the endless preaching of such folly. Her father's words tried to save her. *He told me, Hannah. He's never loved you.*

A dozen times in the next fleeting seconds she reminded herself of what she knew. But what she knew of the past and what held her helpless in his arms collided, raining over her like tiny flecks of gold. From the way his firm chest pumped, the way his hooded eyes roamed her face and his fingers rubbed through her hair—it could not mean nothing.

His head inclined, slightly at first, his body moving closer to hers. Her lungs raced, trying to meet the matchless pace of her heart. She must move away. Yet she could not. Her body was not her own. 'Twas owned by something far more powerful. A small kiss would hurt naught. Perhaps it would prove away the girlish imaginings she'd unwisely harbored for so long. Hannah closed her eyes, willing the rest of her to move away from the edge of the black cavern, despite the promise that the bottom was near and soft.

Calloused but tender, a finger curled around her chin and nudged her face upward. Slowly she opened her eyes, and her gaze married with his, her heart leaping into the beautiful darkness. His hands at her cheeks, Joseph's nose dusted against hers, tempting her face to rise ever so slightly and bring her lips closer to his. She blinked her eyes shut, savoring the fresh scent and warm feel of his soft breath as his lips brushed over hers.

He whispered her name, and she raised a hand to his stubbled jaw, when the door burst open. She jumped back with a gasp and whirled toward the parlor.

"Miss Young? Are you here?"

Stockton.

Hannah's body went rigid. Had they been seen? Joseph's mouth was partway open, his eyes still upon her.

"Miss Young?"

Strong footsteps beat across the parlor floor and stopped hard when Stockton's frame shadowed the doorway of the kitchen.

In an instant Stockton's face flared the same shade of crimson as his coat. "Dear God, what's happened?" His gaze flew from her face to Joseph and the bandage around his waist. The last measure of ease fled his expression, and his shoulders went back. "Who has done this?"

Hannah's mouth was stuck open, no words forming.

Joseph answered, pulling his torn shirt back over his head. "She was attacked on the road."

Stockton's expression flashed white before an even deeper shade of red consumed his face. "Who?"

"Stockton!" Greene burst into the parlor, hobbling. "Arrest that man!"

The major pivoted, looking back and forth between the two men whose glares reached across the room, fighting already across the distance.

"I have a feeling I won't get an accurate report from you, Lieutenant." He turned to Hannah, strained eyes studying the wound on her face. "What happened, my dear?"

Her fingers quivered. Knitting them tight at her middle, she answered in truth. "I was on the road when..." Tempted to lower her gaze, she slayed the weakness, meeting her assailant's venomous gaze as she condemned him. "When I was assaulted by Lieutenant Greene and another solider."

"What?" Stockton spun, his coat flying on the air as he moved. "How dare you!"

Greene leaned against the frame of the open door. "We had to, sir. Major Pitman said to question all travelers, and when she resisted we—"

"You imbecile!" He marched across the floor, chest rounded. "How dare you lay a finger on that woman!"

The thunder of Stockton's words brought Greene to his full height, no longer leaning for support. "Pitman made it clear we are to find whoever it was that gave away the location of our latest provisions shipment, and I am not about to take such a command with anything but the utmost—"

"You are not in Major Pitman's company. You are in mine, and I did not issue any such demand."

"You should have!"

Stockton slowed, his voice frighteningly quiet. "What did you say?" Shock and rage twined over him until it seemed his very coat smoked from the fire of hate that turned his skin red.

Hannah glanced to Joseph, and his hard look told her to stay both motionless and silent.

Greene stepped forward, heedless of the danger that lurked in Stockton's narrowed gaze. "You should have, Major, but you are too blinded to see anything past that woman!"

"Speak of her again, and I will throw you out of this house."

"She was here that night. I know it." He neared, his volume full, neck veins bulging. "I saw her in the barn—I watched her ride away. Yet you will take her word over mine?"

An eerie calm settled over Stockton's tense shoulders. "You are relieved of your post, Lieutenant."

Greene balked. "You cannot—"

"Gather your belongings from camp and ready a mount. I am putting you on assignment in Sandwich."

"Major—"

"Enough!" His roared response shook the walls. Stockton stalked forward until Greene was forced to back his way to the door. "If I ever hear that you have come within even ten miles of this place, I will have you hanged." His gravelly voice grated the wood at Hannah's feet. "Get out."

Greene sneered, enmity pulling at his posture. "Major Pitman will hear you've become a slave to your mistress, and when he does—"

The kick to Greene's stomach was swift and hard. He stumbled backward through the door and out of Hannah's sight.

Stockton shot a rigid arm at Joseph. "Stay with her until I get back."

In a single giant step he was out of the parlor, slamming the door shut behind him.

Standing straight, Joseph's forearms rippled as his fists worked. "What *were* you doing on that road?"

The missive.

She stepped closer, speaking low and quick. "I made a copy of a message I saw hidden in Stockton's cloak and tried to find you so you could deposit the information with your own."

The muscles of his face tipped slightly, angling his features in rich concern. "What message?"

Thunderous yells volleyed back and forth outside as Stockton and Greene exchanged their hatred.

Hannah neared. "Four hundred troops are to arrive in Boston with supplies and cannon. But they plan to dock at Duxbury first to gather the munitions that you are helping to supply."

Joseph's scowl carved deep grooves between his eyes. "What else? Anything?"

Stockton's voice grew louder as he neared the parlor door. Hannah's pulse raged, and her whisper hovered over silent. "Stockton and Pitman are to prepare their men to engage, but I didn't see—"

Slamming the door open, Stockton barreled in. "The criminal!" Hurrying to the kitchen, he halted inches from Hannah, gaze trailing her face as if his look and gentle words alone could ease her suffering. "I take this upon myself." He threw a look to Joseph. "Major Pitman must come to trust you as I do." Pausing, he stepped back. "My dear, would you allow me to issue an invitation for Major Pitman and his wife to join us for dinner tomorrow evening? Higley will accompany me as well. But only if you are agreeable."

Panic swept through her like a broom over a dusty floor. Dinner for two officers. And a woman who no doubt had enjoyed a life of ease? To answer in the negative seized her throat, but such was not a request for what *could* be. Rather, a declaration of what *would* be.

"'Twould be an honor, Major. But..." She could feel her cheeks flushing with heat. "I am ashamed at the size of our kitchen. 'Tis unfit for such fine company."

"Not at all, Miss Young. Do not trouble yourself with such trivialities." He stepped backward, glancing between them. "I shall send word to the Pitmans immediately." Circling back to the parlor, he gestured to Joseph with a nod. "Come with me. I shall need a full report from you. I do not wish to cause your cousin any greater distress by having to relate again what she's suffered."

"Aye, sir."

Joseph bowed slightly and offered Hannah a concerned look before following Stockton out the house.

There, alone, surrounded only by the silent furnishings, Hannah's legs lost their strength. She reached for a chair and sank onto its safety, folding over the table, with her head on her arm. Of all the times she'd been foolish, of all the choices she'd made that were impetuous and gross, this defeated all those with fantastic idiocy.

Grief-induced action was one thing. Spying another. But agreeing to spend any time with Joseph was beyond her scope of understanding. Why had she done it? She pushed up, staring blankly at the center platter. Ensign did not die in vain, and 'twas she who must make it so. Elbows on the table, she groaned and put her face in her hands.

How was she to resist the pull of such a man? One for whom she'd loved and lost—one for whom her heart still reached? These two weeks would pass like a lifetime. Yet despite the risk, the longing that pressed upward beneath its shallow covering warned that it could not easily be contained. She knew, despite her efforts, despite the risk, their duty must be fulfilled, their work completed. There was no circumventing the days ahead. She had to go through them, and pray her heart was not in tatters at the end.

Tufts of dark smoke drifted lazily from the smithy's chimney, carving a thick path through the cloud-covered sky. Philo hurried across the street in front of a passing horse and wagon, preparing his most gracious smile. Clumps of dirty snow lined the road, and puddles of icy water dotted the pathway he tried to navigate. Slipping down the small alley beside the blacksmith shop, Philo rounded the corner to find the back door slightly ajar.

At the anvil, Leo pounded against a long strip, orange flecks jumping with every whack.

Unseen, Philo reexamined his practiced speech before entering. He rubbed one hand with the other. The soldier he and Maxim had tried to bait turned over nothing of value, but one fact remained. Joseph had given his shop at the same time Ensign had sold his, and the timing was too conspicuous to overlook. He prayed this fellow would divulge what information the other soldier had not.

Ease well in place, he strode in. "Leo. Good day to you."

Halting midstroke, Leo grinned slightly. Civil, but nothing more. "Reverend Young. What brings you here?"

"I understand congratulations are in order."

Leo's face went slack, and the brightness left his cheeks. "Aye?"

"This smithy is yours now, is it not?"

"Oh." The color returned in an instant, and he released a held breath.

Had he feared Philo might say something of Caroline?

"Aye, sir, 'tis true. I'm pleased indeed to have it."

Philo glanced around, sure to mold surprise and satisfaction in the corners of his mouth and eyes. "Quite a well-managed arrangement, I must say."

Leo went back to his pounding. "Joseph is a remarkable blacksmith. Meticulous to a fault and far more talented than I will ever be able to boast, though I shall try."

"You do him too great a credit." Why did everyone fawn over the man? He was no saint. A devil in sheep's clothing, more like.

Eyes darting him a sideways look, Leo brought the piece back to the forge and shoved it into the coals. "I give credit where it's due."

"Where is he then? I mean..." Philo pretended ignorance. "Why would he leave his shop? 'Tis clear he loves his work."

"He's off to lend his hand to Washington like so many others." He yanked on the bellows. "I should go myself, but Mother and the girls need care. Father says I cannot be spared." There was a thread of enmity in his voice. Was not the man old enough to make such decisions for himself?

Philo shrugged the thought down his back. "So Joseph will return after the war, is that it?"

Leo brought the radiating glow back to the anvil and once again began pounding. He remained silent as he hammered, then quickly bent the metal at a straight angle and dunked it into a trough of water, the metal hissing and steaming at its sudden bath.

"He's not coming back, 'cept to take Jacob to his new home."

The answer teetered just out of reach. He choked back the runaway thrill. "And where is that?"

Leo shrugged. "I know not. He wouldn't share it with me, and such a question wasn't mine to ask."

Wasn't it? Philo glanced around again, more to calm the restless anxiety than study the tool-lined wall.

"I venture it can't be far." Leo relieved the iron from the water and examined it. "He said he'll return on occasion to give me additional training if I should like, and I certainly shall, I can tell you that."

Genuine glee lifted the corners of Philo's mouth. *Is that so?* "Excellent, excellent." Philo backed his way to the door. "Well, I would not want to keep you from your work. I can see you are quite busy."

Leo halted. "That's all you came for?"

He chuckled. "Aye. Unless you should like to discuss my niece."

Leo's throat bobbed as the color drained from his face. His jaw worked, and he turned to a box of small tools. "Good day, Reverend."

Philo bowed slightly and touched his hat while amusement pulled a tight grin over his lips. "I hope to see you at Sunday services."

Only Leo's eyes lifted. "You know I attend with Reverend Charles."

"Of course." Philo shrugged. "But should you wish for additional enlightenment, you are always welcome." Turning, he marched out, leaving the musky warmth of the large space, eager to free his legs of the tension they'd borne since before he entered.

He stopped in the alley, staring at his shoes on the dirty snow. 'Twasn't much, but more than he'd had before. He looked up, scowling the information into place. Ensign must have sold the foundry to Joseph. The man had always had a weakness for Hannah, and should she have ever expressed any remaining inclination toward Joseph, Ensign might have lured him there for more reasons than simply business.

That discordant melody played its mournful tune, as it had from the time Hannah had left. Nay, since he'd forced her out. She had defamed him, she and that lecherous man. The whisper of Philo's conscience tried in vain to crack the pride that kept him standing. What he'd done, he'd done to protect her as well as himself. How could she have been so thoughtless to heap upon them such shame? He scratched the back of his head and started walking. He hadn't been wrong in his actions. He'd done the harder, more righteous thing. And after all this time, Ensign aimed to renew the pain and ruin that Hannah and Joseph's first tryst had caused them— had caused *him*.

In the street once again, he made his way to Newcomb. He craved not only supper but a warm seat while his brain simmered on the knowledge he'd been given—before he would make his way to Plymouth and unveil the secrets Ensign kept hidden.

'Twas time, at last, he paid a visit.

Chapter Fifteen

Hannah scrambled to place the last plate on the table and the last glass at its station before Stockton and the other guests arrived. The approaching evening swept a rich navy over the sky, a few sparkling stars already beginning their nightly watch. Peering out the window, her stomach coiled in knots. And not only for the visitors who were minutes away.

Ever since yesterday, ever since that bewitching featherlight kiss... Oh dear heaven. She was a fool.

Moving in front of the fire, Hannah placed a hand over her stays, securing every lingering sensation safely within their prison walls and tossing the key.

That moment was naught but a lapse, a fleeting of weakness. He had just rescued her from atrocity. Thus her actions were understandable, were they not?

Like a breath over steam, she sighed away the rest of her thoughts. She must think of *this* moment, this impending meal. Certainly that was enough for her palms to moisten over. Keeping her mind upon that would be no difficult task. She raised her chin, feeling more pacified already.

Hannah peered again out the window, then at the fried chicken at the center of the table, the meat pie, and bounteous dish of potatoes and carrots. The onion rings, succotash, and corn cakes infused the air with scents that made her mouth water, though she feared her appetite was less than minimal, her nerves having robbed any desire to eat.

Fingernail at her teeth, she studied the table. Had she forgotten anything? Stockton must be impressed. If not, his like for her might lessen, and if so, he might seal his lips to what knowledge she and Joseph worked so hard to attain. They must learn where the British planned to engage. And how. However much they nauseated her, his attentions might prove to be the nurturing ground for her and Joseph's secret works. She grimaced. At least, thank the Lord, she needn't till that ground for long.

Breathing deeply, she removed her apron and examined the azure floral design of her printed cotton dress for any impediment or smudge she might have overlooked. There was naught that she could notice, and she could only hope none lurked unseen. Though the gown was nearly six years old and more worn than she'd like to admit, 'twas passable, and wearing it made her feel less ordinary— younger, even.

Critiquing the spread one last time, she fiddled with a pin that tried to stray from her curled tresses.

"They have not yet arrived, hmm?" Of a sudden, Joseph's voice circled through the kitchen. "I should expect they will be here any moment."

Hannah raised her head, instantly wishing she still had something to grasp hold of. Wearing a pair of white breeches, white linen shirt, simple waistcoat, and tan jacket, his hair brushed and tied, Joseph looked more like a hero from a fairy tale than a man who had once called her "my darling."

Her heart sputtered, and she busied herself by fussing with the placement of the forks. "Such a fine jacket and breeches. Where did you come by them?"

Adjusting his neckcloth, his lips stretched to a smile that teased far more than he realized.

"If this were home, I would have donned something much finer. But as the army doesn't require more than passable attire, this was all I brought." His eyes softened as he trailed his gaze over her gown. "You look beautiful, Hannah."

Cheeks aflame, Hannah could only offer a swift meeting of eyes before she spun away for a serving spoon she'd neglected. Preparing something artful in reply, her voice failed her, and she could only eke out a small "Thank you."

"Such a meal. They shall be impressed, I am certain of that."

Had he known she was so nervous? She couldn't meet his stare, the sincerity in his face too dangerous to tempt further. "You are generous, I'm sure, but...I do hope you are right."

That pin began to push away again, and she shoved it in deep and firm, grateful for the innocuous distraction. "To own the truth, I'm...I'm nervous." Somehow the truth found freedom in her voice. A light laugh left her, followed by a mumbled grunt as she held the curl in place, preparing for another go at the disobedient pin.

"May I help?"

Joseph's head inclined toward her, his finger directed at her struggle.

No.

But her want slipped out, though in silence. She stalled and held out the pin, still unable to hold his gaze.

He neared, standing at her side where the errant pin refused its duty to her curl. He slanted his head to look at her. "I don't want to hurt you."

Her skin flushed with heat. "You cannot."

Straightening, he raised the pin. "Where do I put it?"

She tried to answer without the longing depth she knew would coat her words, but it did despite her efforts. "Right here."

Every nerve, every sense was afire. His scent of clean soap, freshly laundered clothes, and a spice she couldn't name lured her to breathe deeper. So she did. More to prove she would not be weakened by any such allure than to enjoy the memories that could be made. Yet somehow the ploy seemed only to make her wish they could stand there all evening, talking, laughing—healing.

"I shall have a go then." Gentle, slow, he smoothed his calloused finger over hers, holding the curl in place as he attempted to force the tiny traitor to submit.

His fingers at her hair, his breath on her ear made her body weightless.

All too soon, he stepped back, lowering his hands. "How does that feel?"

The question stalled her pulse. *Like a dream.*

A quick breath restored her reason. "I don't know how you managed it, but it feels very secure. Thank you."

"You're welcome." Stepping back, he spoke more with his gaze as his eyes flitted to her shoulders, up to her neck, and over her lips. With a shake of the head, he cleared his throat, only polite familiarity in his voice. "You look very lovely."

She studied his eyes, their almond shape, the rich blue of their color, the way they held her. Sighing her smile into place, she turned toward the window. *Lord, help me. I cannot give my heart to him a second time.*

Out the window, a carriage pulled up to the house, and she leaned closer to the glass to get a clearer look. "They are here."

She spun back, her heart dipping slightly that he was no longer looking at her but heading for the parlor to let them in. Hurrying to follow beside him, Hannah glanced up with a smile, and he returned one of his own, the kind that twined around her heart, securing it in warmth and strength.

Without waiting for a knock, he swung open the door, putting on an impressive display of hospitality—no false dignity, no force. Inwardly, Hannah grinned. Such a man he was.

"Welcome." He stood with arm outstretched to the parlor. "Do come in."

Hannah reached out as Stockton entered. "May I take your cloak?"

He grinned, more than simple gratitude in his expression. "I would not have you serve me, my dear." He almost winked, taking off his own cloak and hanging it on the hook by the door as the others entered. "Allow me to introduce Major Aldor Pitman and his wife, Mrs. Dottie Pitman."

Hanna curtsied deep. "We are honored to have you."

Major Pitman smiled as if he'd lost an inner battle against the expression, but his wife's eyes were genuine.

She neared, her smile lifting her full cheeks. "You are so lovely, my dear, as is your home."

Hannah took the woman's cloak and muff as her compliments continued.

"My goodness, what is that beguiling scent? Aldor, I do believe she has made your favorite. He could eat fried chicken for every meal and not ever tire of it—that is what I always say, isn't it, Aldor?"

He nodded absentmindedly at his wife, and she laughed at his indifference, taking Hannah by the arm and starting toward the kitchen as if she'd been there a dozen times before. "Do not mind him. He is notoriously peevish, but I do believe it is mostly for show. His heart is pure gold."

Hannah looked behind to see Joseph struggling to smother a grin, when she suddenly found it difficult not to fight her own. Quickly turning back to her companion, Hannah grasped for conversation. "Mrs. Pitman—"

"Oh my dear, you must call me Dottie." She strengthened her grip. "There are so few ladies in this town—delightful as it is—and I crave female companionship. Now that I know you are here, I daresay I shall be by to see you near every day."

Her heart pitched. *Every day?*

Squeezing Dottie's fingers in girlish friendship, Hannah pried away. "Dottie, you shall sit opposite your husband here and—"

"Forgive me for being late." The door opened behind them, and Higley entered, his red coat a perfect frame for his broad chest and shoulders. He closed it quickly and rested his cloak and hat by the rest. "I hope I have not missed the meal."

Stockton motioned to the table. "We're just being seated."

Higley hurried in, nodding his greetings to all before taking the seat Joseph directed him to.

Once all were seated—Dottie and Joseph sitting opposite Hannah and Pitman, Stockton and Higley at each end—grace was offered. With every plate filled, the conversation began, and it seemed, with Dottie at the helm, the evening's musings would not be dull.

"Mr. Young, you are quite a handsome fellow."

Hannah slid a glance his way, noting how Major Pitman shoved a large bite into his mouth.

Dottie continued. "I am surprised you haven't a wife. Are there not a crowd of woman pining for your hand?"

Joseph finished the food in his mouth. "Nay indeed, madam." He offered a charming slant of his mouth. "Though I may have one in mind."

The fork slipped from Hannah's fingers with a clang, and she snatched it back up, the tips of her ears burning.

"Is that so?" Dottie's pointed features creased with pleasure. "Well, whoever she is, I should say she is one fortunate woman."

Stockton cleared his throat, the personal nature of the conversation no doubt displeasing him. "Mr. Young is working in the foundry, smithing gun barrels for the army." He looked to Pitman, who was preparing another bite of chicken. "A very skilled blacksmith. We are fortunate to have such a man on the side of the king."

"I should say." Dottie reached for a drink, face toward Hannah. "And you, my dear, are you made to stay indoors all day, cooking and cleaning for these beasts? 'Tis a prison, I am sure."

"Nay." Hannah pressed her fork into a carrot. "I enjoy the work. Labor is good for the body and the mind, is it not?"

"Well, I cannot say anything to that one way or the other, but you make me almost want to try it." She laughed, sliding a potato to her fork. "But why are you not married, my dear? Someone as lovely as you, with such incredible talents as you clearly possess, I cannot fathom how you have not yet been snatched by some heartsick fellow."

"She is being courted," Stockton said between bites. "Or so she tells me."

Joseph's face shot toward Stockton, then Hannah, and her muscles went stiff.

Dottie's face took on a sly, piqued expression. "Do tell me. I live for such gossip."

"That you do." Major Pitman spoke his first words but promptly filled his mouth with another forkful.

His wife laughed, unaware of the slight he'd handed her. "Aldor, you know me so well."

Hot clear through, Hannah suddenly couldn't remember how to use her utensils. She offered what she hoped would be the sincerest of smiles and attempted to slide the conversation away from herself.

"Mrs. Pitman, how long are you to stay in town? Are you at the inn?"

It was a moment before she responded. As she finished her bite, an uncomfortable silence hovered between the candles on the table and swirled around

Hannah when Joseph's chest rounded as he inhaled a heavy breath. Was he curious? Upset? She kept the frustrated groan within by taking another bite of her own meat pie. She should have told him. Shame, embarrassment, self-inflicted discomfort all consorted in her belly, shredding to tatters what remained of her appetite.

"Aye, I am staying in town with Aldor." Dottie went on. "He craves my company. I knew I had to come see him when I hadn't heard from him in months—he was desperate without me. Weren't you, my dear?"

Pitman didn't look up. "I was doing just fine."

She frowned as if she hadn't heard him. "Poor man. But now I am here, and we all are having such a marvelous time despite the Patriots causing trouble." She grinned, glass in hand, and glanced down the table. "Captain Higley, you are most quiet."

Higley halted with a bite halfway to his mouth. "Madam?"

Her attention pinned to Hannah. "'Tis a shame you are being courted, my dear, because I must say, our Higley is quite a catch."

Higley chuckled politely, dotting a cloth to his mouth. He offered Hannah a comforting look before turning to the woman who seemed intent on knowing the details of everyone's romantic entanglements—in fact, creating some.

"You flatter me, Mrs. Pitman. I assure you, I am well pleased with my work in His Majesty's Army. I haven't time for female companionship at present."

"Nonsense. Every man has time for that." She turned again to Hannah. "If you were not already spoken for, I would insist that Higley accompany you to the ball we are having this Saturday."

Ball? She offered Dottie a slight smile and forced a bite into her mouth, despite the way her stomach churned. How had their conversation taken such a frightful turn?

The woman kept on. "Mrs. Bates has offered me her home for hosting, as I cannot be thought to host at the inn of all places—and I must say her home rivals any I have seen in the colonies. They've a ballroom near as large as the one at Blenheim."

Pitman eyed her suspiciously, and she scoffed. "Well, perhaps not *quite* that large, but wait until you see it." She looked again to Hannah, undeterred. "I must insist you come, my dear."

"Oh...well..." Hannah's chair became increasingly uncomfortable, and she squirmed, though from the reactions of her several companions, everyone seemed to be suffering the same malady—shifting in their seats, reaching for glasses, filling their mouths with food.

Dottie seemed the only one who could talk. "'Tis settled." Tilting her head forward, as if to be sure Higley would look at her, she grinned, showing all her teeth. "And I must insist that as Higley will be most available, you—"

"If she attends with anyone, she shall attend with me."

Stockton's full voice froze everyone at the table. Hannah's insides spun into a nauseous storm, stealing the last thread of comfort that clung on the cliff of her emotions. She turned to Joseph, who offered her a pointed sideways look.

Facing her, Stockton tossed her a smile with a kind of sickening rescue to it, as if she'd hoped he would speak out all along. "Miss Young, if you are inclined, I would be honored if you would accompany me as my guest." He darted a hard stare to Higley, who nodded submissively in response.

Hannah's palms moistened, and her neck and ears scalded as she struggled for an answer.

Dottie swallowed the rest of her drink, shaking her head, blessedly speaking before Hannah. "But she cannot accept, Ezra. Another man is courting—"

"He is at sea and not expected home for some time."

He paused, his eyes on her, but she could not look at him. Instead she rearranged the food on her plate as he continued.

"I would not expect him to believe Hannah would refrain from enjoying herself in his absence. What say you, Miss Young?"

A quick glance to Joseph assured Hannah of what she feared. Jaw set, mouth firm, she could see his masked glare, almost daring her to accept. He must know she hadn't any other choice.

"'Twould be an honor, sir." The weak thread that came out sounded nothing like her usual voice. She cleared her throat. "I shall look forward to it."

"Marvelous!" Dottie sat back and clasped her hands. "I can hardly wait. Have you a gown?"

This time, her voice wouldn't work at all. She could only nod, her voice no doubt mute from the secretive look Joseph hurled from across the table.

"I...uh..." Even another polite cough couldn't produce any response.

As if a blessing from Providence himself, Stockton took charge of the conversation.

He leaned back in his chair, his arm outstretched. "We are fortunate indeed, Aldor, to have both Mr. Young and his cousin here. As he is offering his efforts for the cause, so is Miss Young."

He looked to her, and suddenly the blood drained from her head.

"She has graciously consented to be my scribe."

The slow, downward tick of Joseph's brow, the nary imperceptible tightening of his lips clenched around her throat. Her shoulders went taut. *Blessed heaven.* How could she have forgotten to tell him that as well?

"Is that so?" 'Twas Mr. Pitman who now spoke, his timbre taut with suspicion. "Have you done such work before, Miss Young?"

"Uh, nay. I have not, sir."

His disinterested look morphed into strained attentiveness. "Are you sure that is the right course, Ezra? You hardly know the woman."

Stockton's cheekbones reddened, but his voice stayed smooth. "If there were anything to be questioned, I assure you I would have detected it." He toyed with the edge of the tablecloth, nodding his head toward Joseph. "That is the same for Mr. Young, as well."

Pitman glanced to Joseph, then Hannah. "You know our work is secretive. That you cannot share what you will learn."

"Aye, sir." Her heart crashed against her ribs.

His eyes thinned. "There has already been someone who has broken a trust, and though that person has not yet been discovered, they will be. And when they are, they will be hanged."

"Pitman." Stockton's polite reprimand stalled the major's words. "Is that really necessary?"

Dottie sat with face pinched, her hands in her lap. She gifted Hannah an understanding grin, but it did little to ease the vice of tension that squeezed the blood from her head.

"If anyone is to engage in the work of war, they should understand the risks and that they are not exempt."

Stockton released an uncomfortable chuckle. "I am sure Miss Young is fully aware—"

"Should we not speak more of the ball?" Higley's well-timed interruption seemed welcome by all but Pitman.

Stockton raised his almost empty glass. "Excellent suggestion."

Dottie began immediately a lengthy discussion of the plans and preparations that were already underway, but Hannah could hear nothing, could hardly see or taste or smell. She could feel only the heated skewer of Joseph's gaze that burned against her skin.

She couldn't imagine what scoldings awaited her. Seconds ago she was eager for the evening to end. Now, despite the discomfiting conversation, the long hours were welcome.

Joseph had much to say. And she knew the moment their guests took their leave, he would speak it all.

Chapter Sixteen

Joseph stood at the door, Hannah at his side, bidding farewell to their companions as Major Pitman and his wife ducked into the carriage. Stockton and Higley mounted their horses, touching their hats in final parting. The carriage door closed at last, the soldiers banking them on both sides as they rode away. Joseph allowed his chest to stretch as he filled his lungs with the cold air that spilled through the open doorway.

The hours-long visit had taken him to the very brink of distraction. So much had been revealed he could hardly get his mind to rest. It ran like Pheidippides of old, racing to the finish. Yet for Joseph there was no end—no place for his thoughts to find solace.

Hannah ducked away and headed to the kitchen, hoping, no doubt, to postpone the onslaught she must know was coming. Her stance told him she knew he would ask her everything once the door was shut. And he would. Man that he was, he wished to slam it closed and speak sense to her, make her see that accepting Stockton's offer for both the dance and the scribing was outright foolery. But wisdom prevailed, and he clicked the door quietly in place.

He followed her, patient. To pounce on her with his frustrations was not only unkind, 'twas perilous. He wished to gain back her trust, not rip it from its fragile roots.

She brought the soiled plates to the worktable near the basin of heated water. Joseph did the same, amused by the way she so artfully avoided his gaze.

"'Tis good Stockton has gone with them." She said the next almost to herself. "I can hardly breathe with him in the same room."

Then why spend so much time with him? Joseph tugged at the words, lest they escape.

"'Twas a delicious meal, Hannah." He caught her eye and held it, warmed by the way his compliment seemed to shimmer unwittingly in her expression. The following tease, he couldn't help. "Higley certainly enjoyed it. He couldn't seem to keep his eyes from you."

Joseph had spied the man gazing at her with more than simple friendship. And though he supposed he had nothing to fear from him, the truth remained. Higley knew Joseph's identity, and yet refused to confess it. Unknowns piled like dry tinder. A single spark could ignite them, turning everything they'd worked for into nothing but ash.

"Higley hardly noticed me, and good thing." Hands full, Hannah offered him a wry look before depositing the stack beside the basin. "My only hope is that this evening was successful for our cause." She scraped the plates clean, forcing the remnants into a bucket. "Pitman seemed no more moved than he was when he first arrived."

"If Stockton continues to trust us, I believe we are safe. Pitman is an obstacle, but not an impassable one." His next words were a gamble as he brought a handful of glasses to the basin. "However...he did not likely miss that your attentions were on me most of the evening."

A clank resounded as she almost dropped the plates in her hands and whirled around, her cheeks a charming shade of scarlet. Her hands flew to her hips. "I did my best not to look at you too often. I—" The moment the confession left her mouth, her eyes went wide and her face almost blotchy from embarrassment. Had she meant she wanted to look at him more than she did?

Smoothing her hands down her skirt, Hannah's voice was cracked and shallow. "I didn't mean...I mean..."

Joseph's insides swirled, and a shot of masculine satisfaction rose over him. The depth of color in her face, her hurried breath wasn't for naught—and it thrilled him.

Despite her obvious upset, he knew her well enough to know he could go further. "Do not blame yourself. I am a man of many charms, and if you didn't fall prey to them, I should be ashamed."

At this, that delightful display of color drained from her face, and she turned away.

Devil's spit. He *had* taken it too far. Idiot.

Removing the last of the dishes from the table, he stood by her, drying what she'd washed. Silence sat before them, bemused, he imagined, like a wily cherub waiting for either of them to talk. But they didn't. On and on they went, she scrubbing and he blotting away the rivulets of water on the freshly cleaned glass.

The longer they worked, the more ease replaced anxiety, until soon it almost seemed the rhythm they found felt familiar, practiced, right. Here, enjoying the peaceful mundane actions of family life, it seemed as if they had been married these ten years, not separated and hardly knowing if the other still thought of their past at all. Is this what their lives might have been like? A rip started deep and continued to tear even deeper. *If only...*

He braved a sideways look, instantly regretting the action. She was so close, her arm almost touching his as she rubbed and sloshed in the water, heedless of the drops that splashed on her sleeves. That curl at her ear...it needed tucking.

She offered another glass, and he took it, grateful he had a useful occupation for his hands.

He glanced at the clock through the parlor, squinting to make out the time. Stockton had been gone nearly three quarters of an hour already. If Joseph were to ask the questions he wanted to—nay, needed to—before Stockton returned, he had better act quickly.

Keeping as unaffected a tone as possible, he spoke the words he wished he needn't. "I didn't know you were being courted. Is he from Plymouth?"

Her motion stopped. Resting the plate in the water, she kept her hands at the edge of the basin. Head bowed, she sighed, then tilted her head to him. "No one is courting me, Joseph." She started up again, scrubbing the helpless plate more vigorously. "I said that in hopes of keeping Stockton at a more reasonable distance."

A cool breeze rushed through his muscles, and his shoulders eased. So she was not being courted? Such a thrill should not be entertained, but he allowed it to bask in the pleasant light of revelation a moment longer before moving to the waiting question in line. "Then why accept to be his scribe?" The next came too quickly and too curt. "Being that close to him, Hannah, I do not like it."

Her face shot toward him. "He is not a man to be denied, Joseph. Consider, if we are to gain what information we seek, how can I not do it? We must learn where they plan to engage, mustn't we?" She thrust him the plate. "I must do things I might otherwise prefer not. What does it say about the strength of my convictions if I am not willing to sacrifice for them? I believe in this cause, Joseph. I do it for Ensign, aye. But also, I do it for liberty."

Each of her words slashed through him, tiny blades of humility cutting him to his knees. How could he ever have felt anything but admiration? She had not been impetuous, rather wise, selfless. His heart swelled, and had he not a dripping plate in his hands, he might be helpless to pull her against him and twine his arms around her back, rest his cheek atop her hair.

"You will attend the ball with him then?"

A pained look tugged at the corners of her eyes and mouth. "How can I not?" Dunking the last plate in the basin, she shook her head slightly. "I will be grateful indeed when these two weeks are past."

His gut pinched. Would she be? He breathed away the discomfort. Of course she would, as he would as well. That was understood. He would join his friends and ready himself to face the greatest battle of his life.

Greatest battle? The irony almost made him laugh aloud. Nay. The greatest battle he fought was here, standing beside him in the kitchen. No weapon but the slant of her smile, no danger but that of her touch, no risk to his life—nay, but to his heart.

Hannah reached for the towel and dried her hands, wishing there were more items to clean. Standing beside Joseph, talking so easy, 'twas a sensation she'd not ever imagined she'd feel. A safeness, a serenity and rightness she'd known only in her dreams. The longing to look up and study his face ached through her neck and shoulders, but somehow she resisted. Did he feel it too? Or was she the only one who suffered this blissful malady?

Gathering her bravery, she walked to the parlor. His steady footfall followed, and the urge to slow and walk beside him, knit her fingers in his, became so strong she hurried her step lest she act out the fantasies her brain and heart seemed intent on savoring.

"I..." At the fireplace, she glanced down at her fingers, rubbing the chapped knuckle of her forefinger. "I hadn't the chance to thank you."

Hannah turned her back to the warmth of the fire. Joseph went to the lowboy, pouring himself a drink. Gifting her only a slight look over his shoulder, he questioned her with his eyes.

She shrugged and swallowed. "For...for helping me the other day."

He replaced the cask and came to stand beside her, facing the fire while she faced away. He held his glass as if the mulberry color of the wine fascinated him, though she knew his thoughts went far deeper.

Body still, 'twas only his face that turned to her. His eyes were rich, his voice tiptoeing across the inches between them to caress her heart. "I would do anything for you."

Dearest heaven.

Longing, the kind that only the fullest love begets, bloomed in his eyes. But with an exhale it vanished, and his attention was once again on his drink. He took a sip. "I fear if not for some unearthly intervention, I may have done more than just..." His jaw ticked. "In my estimation they got far less than they deserved. I cannot bear the knowledge that a man has done harm to any woman."

Any woman.

Hannah peered at the toes of her shoes that peeked from beneath her skirt, trying to calm the slight ache at such impersonal words. They should be welcome, for indeed the more intimacies of speech they shared 'twould only lure to light emotions she wished to keep well in the dark.

Yet it seemed her mouth refused to take any counsel, no matter how well advised. She began speaking, almost as if her mouth were a separate entity and she powerless to stop it. "You were always so strong, Joseph. No one could best you in a fight."

'Twas a few beats of silence before he answered. "I haven't swung my fist in years."

She was ready for the sideways glance he tossed to her, but not for its affect. Hannah's middle fluttered as his heady timbre curled around her.

"I would do it a thousand times over if I knew it would keep you from suffering."

The tenderness of his words touched her like his very fingers, brushing down Hannah's skin with a trail of heat. Again she pinned her attention to her shoes. She knew full well Joseph's sad boyhood. How his older brother Cyprian had baited him, teased him, and bullied to the point of savagery—forcing Joseph to fight boys bigger and older than he, simply for Cyprian's pleasure. It had forced Joseph to grow stronger, wiser, and quicker. The constant subjection to violence molded his body and muscles more than even his brother had anticipated. Finally, Joseph was not only larger in stature but larger in spirit and character, Cyprian shrinking in the shadow of the one he'd tried so hard to demean.

Unbidden, the sudden question popped free. "How is your brother?"

Joseph's thick chest rounded as he drew in and let out a long, slow breath. "He is dead."

"Oh, good heavens." How had she not known? "Joseph, I'm...I'm so sorry. I didn't—"

"He and his wife died on the same day, leaving Jacob alone."

Hannah's mind scrambled backward, trampling through the lanky silhouettes of memory. It took no longer than a second to recall the round-faced boy, his bright eyes and happy laugh. She'd met him once. The very night before they had...

A door slammed against the striding thought, and she hurried to continue where they were.

She peered at him. "What is he to do?"

Again, Joseph stared at the liquid in his glass before circling around to place his back to the fire. "He is in my care now." At that he offered her a fleeting glance. "I shall do everything in my power to give him the life he deserves. Which is why I now do what I do." He held her gaze. "'Twould seem we both have a motive behind what we risk. Both honorable, both mournful if we should fail."

Hannah straightened, figuring the sums in her mind. Her heart hitched, her knees suddenly weak. The boy would now be only slightly older than theirs if he had lived... She gasped for breath and stepped to the nearest chair, resting her hands at the back for balance, should her legs give way. What would Joseph say if he knew?

To rescue herself from the sudden fall, she clutched to the chair. "Have you left him in Sandwich then? Who shall care for him while you are away?"

Joseph adjusted his stance, his voice taking on a sorrowful quality that forced her eyes to his. "Nathaniel Smith's wife is caring for him. He...he lost a leg, from the knee down. Mrs. Smith is skilled with medicine, should he need particular care until I return." His tone went wistful. "I have promised to take him fishing upon my return from war. He loves the pond."

Time slowed. Everything around her blurred until she could see only him. What man was this? The strong, generous one she'd known, aye. But he was more than that now. He had grown, changed somehow. She had changed as well. Did he see that she was more perceptive, more cautious? More real. Or did he only see how her griefs had aged her—no longer the youthful beauty of eighteen but a woman familiar with the heavy cares of the world?

"He was apprenticing under me."

Joseph's voice brought her surroundings back in full. "He would make a fine blacksmith. An excellent trade for one with such an impediment."

Joseph chuckled, his eyes sparkling in the light of the fire. "Aye, had not Nathaniel's heroics after his accident made the study of medicine more appealing."

"Is that so?" His levity made her laugh lightly as well. "Well, I suppose I can understand that. But do you have another apprentice in mind? I assume you still have your shop?"

The moment the words slipped past her tongue, she rued the taste of them. Familiarity was dangerous. How was she to know he still had a shop? So many years had passed, and after what he'd just revealed, 'twas clear there was much they didn't know of each other.

"I, uh...have someone working the shop now, aye. But no apprentice."

Her insides went hard as the need to know more—the need to know everything—surged upward, frothing and rolling like an unstoppable sea. How had he fared these years past? Had he stayed only in Sandwich? Was he happy? Did he ever think of her? Did he remember the time she'd left turnovers at his window or that note atop his anvil? Did he recall, as she did, the time he'd first held her hand as they'd walked home from Nathaniel's that hot summer eve? Or the time by the pond he'd stolen that kiss...

Saved by the chime of the clock, Hannah nearly chirped in relief. "Good heavens, 'tis getting late. I should retire." She started for the stairs. "Tomorrow I begin my work with Stockton. There is much to learn, and I fear I must have rest if I am to keep my wits at their sharpest."

"Hannah."

Roped by his velvety sound, she halted but dared not turn back, replying only with her silence.

"Are you sure you wish to do this?"

Craning her neck, she glanced behind. "I am." A sideways smile warmed her face. "We must discover where they plan to engage. And who better to know than an innocent Tory?"

Before his answering gaze could immobilize her escape, she turned and started up the stairway.

"Good night, Hannah."

She stopped, aching to say everything that pressed like a boot against her heart. Blessedly, only two small words formed. "Good night."

The truth she'd spoken in the kitchen rang stronger with every rise and fall of the sun. She would be grateful when these two weeks were out—when their mission was done. And yet...

Hannah hurried up the final steps to her room, shutting the door against the thoughts that trailed her. She rested her back against the wood and stared at the darkened ceiling. What pained her more? This time with him now, or knowing she would once again be forced to find a way to live her life without him?

Chapter Seventeen

The next morning dawned like an exuberant suitor—cheerful and full of promises. At her usual perch, Hannah pulled a dish of perfectly golden turnovers from the fire and set them on the table, unable to suppress the smile on her lips. Joseph was already in the foundry, hard at work. If he didn't return soon for breakfast, she would bring him and the others a basketful. She couldn't help but anticipate the smile such a surprise would produce.

The door opened, and Hannah's heart leapt, pulling her from her position at the table to the doorway of the kitchen. She brushed her hands over her skirt and pinched her cheeks, only to have her rising hopes punched down like a fist in dough.

"Aw, Miss Young. Good morning." Stockton entered, his cheeks flush from cold, eyes too bright the moment they found her. "Smells marvelous."

Hannah bundled all the pleasure her voice could convey and shoved it into her words. "Good day, Major. May I get you some refreshment? Have you had breakfast?"

He shut the door behind him. "I have—thank you, my dear. But I should like some coffee." Swinging off his hat and cloak, he went to the fire, rubbing his hands over the flame. "Chilly day. The mercury shows five degrees."

"That is cold indeed." Hannah took her time preparing the pot and entered the parlor only after she'd allowed herself a peek through the kitchen window, but there was no sign of Joseph.

She handed Stockton a full cup. "You must warm yourself, sir. Let me add a log to the fire."

"Nay." He batted her away playfully. "I shall do it." Cup in one hand, he gripped a log with the other and threw it on the already billowing flames.

She looked to the door, her lip between her teeth as her mind worried over the thoughts she'd considered last evening. Thoughts she hadn't been willing to tell Joseph, for she knew his answer. He wouldn't approve, but she felt she must. How else could she most easily get the information they needed?

"I..." She ducked her head away, studying her fingers. "I do hope last evening was satisfactory for you, sir."

"Satisfactory?" The sincerity in his voice made her almost believe the ploy she was about to undertake was not so dangerous. "'Twas heavenly, Miss Young. A success by every measure of the word."

"But you do think, I mean to say, is Major Pitman still unsure of—"

"Aldor Pitman may be a man of few manners, but he is no fool."

Hannah stalled, unsure of his meaning. "Sir?"

"He was quite smitten, I daresay. With his wife enamored by you, I can safely believe you and your cousin are free to aid the king with no more suspicions leveled at your back."

Her tight stays eased around her chest. Inwardly, a cheer broke loose, but all she released was a smile. "I am very pleased."

Gaze never leaving her, he took a sip of his drink. "I've quite a few messages to send. If you are willing, is now a good time to begin?"

"Oh, of course." Moving to the desk in the corner, Hannah sat, retrieving the quill from the inkwell. Her fingers began to quiver, but a slow inhale helped ease the spike of anxiety. "I am ready to begin."

"How eager you are." He came forward until he stood directly behind her chair, the warmth of his body radiating far too near.

She peeked behind, swallowing away the disgust at the interest she was forced to feign. "Eager indeed to be of help to one so generous."

"Generous?" The compliment straightened his shoulders.

"Aye, sir. You have been more than generous with me and with Joseph, and 'tis the least I can do."

Almost lecherous, his eyes coursed over her. "Is that your only motivation?"

Unsure of his full meaning, Hannah decided on a half smile and turned away. "That and working forward in the cause of unity for England."

"Of course." Was that disappointment in his voice, or did she imagine it? "Are you ready?"

"Aye." She dipped the quill in the iron-gall ink.

"If I speak too quickly, you need only tell me."

"I will, sir."

Stockton took a long sip of his drink before resting the cup on the table. "General Howe." Stockton strode around the room as if the tiny room were a grand hall. "Our men are to remain stationed here to keep watch over the Patriot activity in the small towns skirting the coast. I have just had word that more troops are expected to arrive by week's end. I can only hope that is true." He stopped and once more came behind her.

Hannah frantically finished writing the last. "Is that—oh!" She turned and jumped at his nearness, laughing away her surprise before motioning to what she'd written. "Forgive me, Major. Is that all right?"

"Perfect," he answered, his eyes on her, not the paper.

Her cheeks were no doubt a shade of scarlet dark enough to rival his coat. She turned back toward the paper. "Do you wish me to do anything different, sir?"

"I wish you not to change anything at all."

Her stomach churned, and her palms began to sweat. "Shall we continue?"

He spun away, taking the stale scent of tobacco with him. "Pitman informs me that the troops in Boston are in dire need, with only five thousand fit for duty. It is my recommendation that we quit the city and make for New York. But if you insist we move ahead with our previous designs, I need only your word to do so."

What designs? Where will your men engage? A billowing quiet careened against her back, and she gripped the quill so hard she feared it would snap. Hannah finished scrawling the last words, hanging on, praying he would speak the very words she needed. But he did not.

"Miss Young."

Forcing her back straight, she pivoted in her chair. "Aye?"

Hands behind his back, Stockton peered at her from his place beside Ensign's favorite chair. He lowered his chin, as if gathering his thoughts. When he looked up, 'twas no more the face of a man but more of a youth, whose wide eyes and expression was bathed in unabashed infatuation. "Forgive me. I should not like to seem overly bold, nor cause you any discomfort."

"Nay, of course not." A cliff above a rocky sea would have been more welcome than enduring whatever he was about to say. But she must invite it. She inclined her head with a shy grin at her mouth. "I should like to hear what you have to say."

Her reply must have surprised him, for the softness in his features grew ever more wanting. "You...are you sincere in your wish to attend the ball? I had feared lest our guest forced the idea upon you."

Dottie had indeed done exactly that, but there had been no way to decline. Hannah squirmed behind a calm exterior. This was not how this interlude must go. Lord in heaven, how could she once again bring the conversation around? Only a few more words and she would have what information they needed.

Acting the demure woman, Hannah knitted her hands in her lap and tossed him a half smile. "You are most gracious, Major. I hardly know what to say?"

"Say you will come with me." He inched nearer. "I would be the happiest of men to have a woman of such beauty at my side."

The way he seemed to peer into places he shouldn't made her squirm.

"You are most kind, Major. I am humbled that a man of your station would take interest in me. The only impediment is that I fear I haven't anything fine enough to wear to such an occasion."

"Nonsense, my dear." Closing the remaining distance between them, he loomed over her chair. "I am sure you have something suitable. It need not be *so* fine. For truly, you have a way of making anything appear—"

"I shall see what I have." She cut off his words before their sickening nature made her physically ill. Tossing a last look, she turned back to the paper. "I am almost so overcome I don't know what to say."

He shuffled back a step. "Your humility is one of your brightest qualities."

She couldn't bring herself to do anything but stare at the paper as his voice continued to scroll on behind her. "We shall ride to Duxbury at four o'clock and I daresay return just before the sun rises."

"Oh my." Hannah's hands began to sweat again, as they always did when she was faced with a detestable situation. She pressed them on her skirt. "Well, I have no doubt 'twill be a...a remarkable evening."

"You do not feel you are being unfaithful to your seaman?"

Hannah stared at her hands atop her knees. *This could be a way out.* Then again, if she were to refuse, she might lose the opportunity to gain the additional intelligence that would aid the cause. Gripping to the standard of courage, she lifted it high.

"Not at all, sir. In truth, I believe he would want me to go, to enjoy myself in his absence."

"As well you should."

Hand extended, mouth open to speak more, Stockton jolted as the door burst open.

A soldier burst in, his face flush with embarrassment. "Excuse me, sir."

"What is it, Private Sackett?" The kindness in his voice vanished.

The soldier entered, closing the door behind him. "Major Pitman, sir."

"Major Pitman?" The honest surprise in his voice was both inquisitive and concerned.

"Aye, he is here." The soldier nodded. "He asked me to come fetch you, sir."

Stockton's arms hung at his sides, fingers of one hand tapping his leg. "Very well." He pivoted back to Hannah, posture formal but gaze at ease. "We shall finish the remaining part of the letter when I return."

"Of course, sir." She grinned, unsure whether to be relieved or anxious.

The tight smile on his mouth said far more of his frustration than the clip of his words. "I shan't be long." Nodding, he exited, shutting the door quietly behind him.

Fingers blackened, arms burning with the pleasant strain of labor, Joseph pounded his hammer against the glowing iron. The incessant clangs were a welcome tune compared to the odious silence Major Pitman flung through the room.

Arms crossed over his chest, the man looked as if he could heat an iron rod with his eyes only. Last evening he'd seemed at least civil. Now he appeared ready to explode from a mere spark, and there were plenty of those to be had in this room of fire and heat.

Joseph shifted the iron against the anvil and began striking again, this time harder. Pitman had arrived only moments ago, saying only that he'd come to inspect the work, but nothing more. 'Twas the benign admission that niggled, and the fact Higley had yet to make an appearance in the foundry, though he'd mentioned his interest to help several days past. Perhaps he could not be spared. The thought eased over Joseph, and he pounded one last blow to the glowing barrel before digging it back into the fire. Not having the man around was a blessing he could only hope would continue until he could at last return to the troops. The memory of Higley's parting words still throbbed down his spine.

How had he known him?

Sackett rushed back in, Stockton at his heels. The soldier hurried back to his place beside the forge, where Deane prepared another rod, while Stockton moved beside his brother at arms.

He bowed slightly, brows fixed. "Good day, Major Pitman. You've come to see our progress?"

"Aye." Pitman scratched beneath his jaw with his knuckles, his gaze shifting to Joseph. "You gave me such a pleasant description of your work that I wanted to come see it myself."

Expression light, Stockton's mouth bowed down in a pleased, contemplative frown. He marched to the far wall, where the finished barrels were stacked. "Much has been accomplished, as you see."

Pitman made his way to the small grouping of prepared barrels, inspecting the lot as if he were the general and they his troops. "You shall have to work faster."

Joseph stopped the bellows and brought the iron back to the anvil, noting the tick beginning beneath Stockton's eye. He no doubt disliked being spoken to thus by a man supposed to be his equal. Joseph began pounding, keeping one ear intent upon the conversation.

Stockton neared his companion, heavy brows folded, jaw firm. "I have only three men to do the work."

"I find that impossible to believe. With all the men at your disposal—"

"'Tis not a simple thing to teach a man this work, and only these two in my regiment were familiar with the trade. If you'd like to spare some of your own..."

Pitman's grunt could be overhead above the clanging. "What about Greene?"

Stockton leaned back against the table, expression taut. "I have sent him to Sandwich. He attacked Miss Young in town, excusing his behavior on the fact you are searching for an informant."

"Attacked?" Pitman's shock raised his brow before it lowered again. "When was this?"

"Two days past."

Pitman's typically stoic demeanor cracked. "And you didn't tell me?"

Stockton pushed away and held his arms at his sides. "I didn't feel it was any of your concern. He is in *my* regiment."

This conversation was growing dangerous, like two rivals circling each other for a fight. Stockton defensive against Pitman, the dominant force.

They could not long go like this, or it might be revealed who it was that injured the other soldier, and such a thing could not come to light. Stockton knew, but Pitman did not, and Joseph wished to keep it that way. There had to be another way to bring their escalating conversation back to the barrels.

As Joseph lifted up on the iron and pounded the end against the anvil, a thought sparked as hot as the very orange bits that sprayed in front of him. He halted, sure such a thing was folly. Driven by his hunger, no doubt. He'd come out to work before allowing himself any food, and the lack affected his thinking.

The men continued to speak, but of what he couldn't say. Again the thought came, and this time with so much strength, his hammer could not have struck with such force.

Almost as if an otherworldly power possessed him, he stilled and cleared his throat. "What about Captain Higley, sir?"

Both men craned their necks to him, as if somehow simultaneously surprised and satisfied with the sudden interruption.

A single brow on Pitman's thin, weathered face lifted. He tilted his head. "How know you he is familiar with smithing?"

"He told me, sir."

"Told you?" Body and face unmoving, he looked to Stockton, who raised a single shoulder.

Resting his hammer aside, Joseph hurried the still-hot piece to Sackett, who nodded and began finishing the work. "When I was in town not two days past." He wiped his hands on his apron. "Captain Higley informed me he would speak to you of this...perhaps he decided against it."

Stockton spoke almost on top of his words. "I couldn't spare him. He's only just been made captain, and to lose him to this work..."

His answer struck Joseph, and it strained his forehead not to furrow. Why would he not wish Higley—

Hannah.

Then he too had noticed the man's attentions. Joseph's insides knotted. Stockton was becoming far too familiar, too possessive. The sooner this charade was ended, the better. The farther Hannah was from this place...

"Perhaps you could have a word with him, sir." The words were out before Joseph could weigh their prudence.

Pitman turned, his head cocked at the unsolicited suggestion. "You are in that great of need?"

"Aye." He motioned to Sackett and Deane, still faithful in their duties but surely no less interested in the conversation. "We work hard, but we can only work so fast. If we had another able man, it would make the work—"

"Nay, Major, nay. Our lack is not so dire." That tick beneath Stockton's eye tapped harder, and Joseph's muscles thickened. There was an unmasked threat in his stare. Did Hannah have any knowledge of how dangerous this man truly was? All his pretended politeness was like an undetectable poison.

While again the men sparred with their words, Joseph's mind caught him in a vortex. He must get her away. He must try and dissuade her from going with Stockton to the ball—she could pretend herself ill if need be. The more Joseph knew of the dangers that surrounded them, the stronger the need became to keep her as far from them as possible.

As if an answer to an unspoken prayer, an idea, much like the first, lit his mind, and he spoke before he even had a chance to make out the full shape of it. "Sirs, if you are not opposed, I should like to travel to Duxbury."

Stockton's disapproval was instant. "Whatever for?"

"Forgive me, Major." He cleared his throat, praying Providence would soften his enemy's heart. "I've made these barrels, but I wish for them to be inspected before the rest are completed. If somehow they are not true, 'tis easier to make alterations now."

Pitman glanced back to the stack, his mind clearly working as he studied them in silence. Stockton shifted his stance, crossed his arms, then uncrossed them. 'Twas difficult to find fault with such an argument, though clearly the man sought frantically for one.

"He's made a clear point, Ezra." Pitman spoke in a tone more personal than he had even with his wife.

Shaking his head, the tick at Stockton's eye refused to abate. "I have orders to complete these, and our timing is—"

"You must let him go," Pitman interrupted. "'Twill take only a day. If you let him leave now, he will return before sunset."

Like ice being slowly chipped at, Stockton's features shifted to varying forms of frustration. Finally, after a long breath that could have been heard all the way to the house, he dropped his arms at his sides and turned to the door. "I shall want a full report upon your return."

"One more thing," Joseph called, his insistence as wise as throwing rocks at a bear.

Stockton's abrupt halt at the door made dirt spray around his boots.

"I shall take my cousin with me."

Stockton's sudden scowl was intended, no doubt, as a visual punch in the gut, but Joseph continued. "She will want to see if any gown or fabric can be had in preparation for the ball."

Frustration eased from Stockton's shoulders at the logical nature of such a request, and after a nod to both Joseph and Pitman, Stockton strode out.

Pitman looked after him for a breath before facing Joseph, that familiar lack of expression in his thin face. "I shall send a courier ahead and tell our man to await you."

"Aye, sir."

"I do believe I shall have a word with Captain Higley...then see if I cannot get Major Stockton to acquiesce."

A slight lift of his mouth almost had the appearance of a smile as he too left the foundry.

Joseph filled his lungs as one filled a powder horn, careful and full, praying that God would grant the future to not carry more dangers than it already did.

Chapter Eighteen

Ten miles of pitted road might seem a burden on any other day, but not today. Hannah glanced down at her gloved hands, mentally flicking away the budding melancholy that their little journey was nearly half over. The ride to Duxbury had gone far too quickly, their conversation so easy and familiar Hannah ashamedly wished it could have gone on for ten more bumpy miles.

Joseph pulled the horses to a halt in front of a shop, and she glanced to him. He'd not specified to her why he'd brought her along, and though she figured he must have a purpose, she nurtured a hope that perhaps he had simply wished to be with her.

Silent, Hannah prepared to step from the wagon, but Joseph hopped down and hurried around, helping her to the ground. His large hands spanned nearly her entire waist, and foolishly, she wished them to linger, if only a second more.

His grin did funny things to her middle. He motioned to the horses. "Stay here a moment while I inquire as to where this Willis Plains fellow lives."

"They didn't tell you?"

He shook his head as he secured the horses. "Nay. Admittedly, I wanted to leave quickly. With so much road to cover, and so little time..." He shrugged away the rest and motioned to her with a single finger. "I'll not be long."

Sighing, she turned away, though feminine curiosity wished to keep her vision on him—to linger over the way his strong arms swung as he walked, his long stride powerful and determined.

This town was not unlike the others she knew—both Sandwich and Plymouth were sea towns such as this—small but fair enough to claim the necessities of life. The scent of salt sat so heavy in the misty air, it seemed you could almost taste it.

Across the street was the mantua-maker, several gowns displayed in the large window. She turned at the waist to glance behind, but Joseph was not to be seen, so she darted across the road after a carriage passed and stood at the window, admiring the subtle beauty of the foremost gown. The elegant polonaise, with its simple lines and soft colors—cream with pink and green embroidered flowers at the edges—was perfectly tucked in back to reveal the pink silk petticoat beneath.

Never had she seen such a lovely gown. Not that extravagant gowns were much to her liking. She preferred simple beauty—like the azure floral she'd donned the night before. But this...this was a gown she could feel a woman in. Simplicity. Sophistication. Elegance. She might feel young again in such a gown. Not eight and twenty, far past her years of youth and beauty. Perhaps if she wore such a thing, Joseph would—

"If ever a gown were made for you, that one was."

Joseph's voice tapped her mind clear, and she turned as he stepped up beside her, his attention on the window display.

"Lovely."

She grinned full without and within, following his lead and staring at the heavenly piece. "Aye. 'Tis..." Hannah shrugged, struggling to find the proper description. "'Tis perfection."

Preparing to step away, 'twas Joseph's words that stopped her. "If I hadn't brought you here to dissuade you from going to the ball, I might have purchased this for you."

A furrow folded over Hannah's brow, and she was unsure whether to praise or protest. There it was. The reason for his bringing her along. The thought that he would be so concerned over her to insist she not attend tickled her insides in delightful ways, despite the questions that budded to life.

"I thought we already concluded my attendance was unquestionable."

Joseph nodded to a passing stranger on the road before answering. "Your attendance would be helpful, but 'tis not imperative."

He cocked his arm, and she took it, allowing a parting look at the beautiful creation before they crossed the street to the wagon.

"Stockton is becoming too possessive of you, and such a danger I cannot allow."

Pulling her bottom lip through her teeth, Hannah watched her shoes take turns peeking from her petticoat as she walked. Perhaps her pretended coyness was too convincing, even if she did so only to gain more trust, in hope of Stockton spilling his secrets.

Joseph helped her back onto the wagon, then stood there, looking up at her with such yearning in his eyes she could do nothing but fall helplessly into their blue depths.

"Do not go with him." It seemed almost pleading, the way he spoke. "For your safety, I must beg it of you."

She would have answered him anything. But somehow, in that moment as he gazed up at her, another vision slid between them.

Ensign.

Mouth open, ready to answer his request, she clamped her mouth closed and dropped her gaze.

"Hannah..."

She swallowed, trying to free herself from the image that waved unfalteringly before her.

He rested his hand atop hers. "You do not have to risk your life simply because he gave his."

She raised her now-burning eyes to his, embarrassed at how suddenly the memory had accosted her. "If I do not, how are we to remain in Stockton's trust? How are we to get what knowledge we—"

The grip to her fingers stilled her voice, while his took its place. "We shall find a way. Perhaps here and now, we shall know in what way our army may proceed, and you can at last find safety away from the foundry."

He slipped his hand from hers and rounded the wagon, at her side again in only a handful of seconds. Gently flicking the reins, he glanced to her. "I've a mind not to take you back."

"What?" The cold mist tickled the hairs around her ear, and she held firm to the cloak tied at her neck. "What do you mean? Are you in earnest?"

Joseph directed the horses left. "If we continue in this much longer, I fear Stockton will not let you go."

"Not let me go?"

His jaw worked, his next confession slicing her clear through.

"I plan to arrange for someone to take you back to camp."

"What?" The horses' ears swiveled back as her voice echoed through the trees. She turned in her seat and reined in her volume, shock riding her words. "Joseph, you cannot do that."

He shook his head. "I should not have allowed this in the first place, and after today—Hannah, that man is dangerous. I won't have you scribing for him, and I certainly won't have you attending a ball with him."

"He believes I am spoken for. I doubt that—"

"You think that will dissuade him from increasing his attentions to you?"

Shameful heat pricked her ears, and she moved her gaze away as he continued.

"'Tis too familiar, Hannah. If you continue to accept such offers, he shall begin to think you favor him, and what then?"

Hannah stared at her knees, studying the homespun fabric of her petticoat. The creak of the wagon, the muffled clomp of the horses' hooves on the road seemed to tap the sliver of truth ever deeper into her flesh. Joseph was right, of course. She'd known Stockton's attentions were gaining intensity, but she was ignorant of the severity. Was she not supposed to be a Tory? Was she not supposed to pretend all politeness and respect for the army so she could pry from them their best-held secrets?

Another thought shoved her so hard she gripped the edge of the seat. Perhaps Joseph simply wished to be rid of her? Like a radiating summer heat, the memory of their almost kiss warmed through her. He didn't seem to dislike her presence, but then again she didn't *really* know him, did she? It had been ten years since they'd last loved, and to think she could still read the quirk of his mouth or the slope of his posture was ridiculous.

Then, as if her voice was not her own, the truth jumped from her lips like an innocent from prison. "I don't want to leave."

He peered at her, the movement of his head and eyes toward her, though slight, carried a weight far deeper than his expression could contain. Deep and soft, his gaze washed over her like a calming pool. As if he knew her meaning even when she herself fully did not, he quirked his head to the side, his smile at that slant that made her stomach weightless.

"But you must."

"Why?" She swerved against the seat, her knees touching his legs. "Joseph, Eaton Hill is my home. I refuse to allow those barbarians to destroy it."

"I would never allow that. Just as I will not allow you to be placed in any more danger."

His firm sincerity stilled her forthcoming reply for only a moment. "But you shall not be there forever, and what am I to do when..." That future she'd been unable to see, unable or unwilling, crashed like a blow to the chest. What *would* she do? Once Joseph was back with the troops, when the soldiers raped the foundry for all it had, was she to stay there alone? The new owner of Eaton Hill would not return until after the war, and there was no telling how long this conflict with England would last.

She blinked, failing to clear her thoughts as she faced frontward. So many feelings crowded up to her mouth 'twas all she could do not to spill them out all over the quiet. The strongest of all pressed hard against her teeth. *I don't want to be without you.*

"I will make sure you are not alone, Hannah."

Joseph's calming timbre brushed against her skin like the delightful touch of his fingers. His hand covered hers, and she looked up, captured by the rawness in his ever-blue eyes. "I will be sure you are safe."

Like a flood, the worries she'd tried to hold back breached their barrier, spilling over into the dry places she wished to keep safe. "Joseph, Ensign sold Eaton Hill."

Only his eyes narrowed, and he moved his hand away, questioning her with his silence.

She went on, freeing herself from the weight of the harbored angst. "But he refused to tell me to whom he sold it, and now that Ensign is gone, how am I to know who this person is and if they will honor their agreement?"

Joseph looked forward, then at his hands, moving his thumb back and forth against the smooth leather. His mouth a firm line, he breathed hard through his nose. "Hannah, there's something I—" He halted and tugged the horses right, whatever he'd prepared to speak shoved aside as a small house peeked at them through the trees. "We're here."

The small cabin, so quaint with its smoking chimney and candled windows, was minuscule compared to the large barn behind it.

Hannah gazed at Joseph. Expression stern, his eyes were fixed, as if his mind was already struggling in battles that were yet to be fought.

"Stay with me." Voice taut, he swung her a fierce look. "Should anything happen—"

"Welcome! I've been expecting you."

Both Hannah and Joseph jerked at the sudden bellowed pronouncement. From around the cabin, a tall fellow, slight of frame and balding, waved them forward and around to the barn.

"Aye, aye, this way. You may leave your wagon right there, excellent."

Joseph shot Hannah another fleeting look that warned her to stay cautious despite the man's surprising hospitality before he leapt down and met the man in front of the horses. "Willis Plains?"

"At your service." The man extended his hand.

Joseph gripped it and grinned. "You received word of our coming then?"

"Indeed." Willis nodded and continued as Joseph helped Hannah from the wagon. "Your foresight is wise. I'm pleased you wished to make such a journey." He leaned forward and winked as he led them toward the house. "Though I suspect Stockton wasn't too pleased to have to say farewell to either of you for even a few hours."

He chuckled to himself as he opened the door and ushered them in.

One hand at her back, Joseph let Hannah enter before him.

Instantly the homey scent of the fireplace and hot coffee somewhere in a pot made the strange surroundings seem welcome, warming. She stepped farther in as Joseph closed the door, and Willis hurried forward, gesturing to a seat nearest the fire.

Small but powerful, the fire's heat reached out to her as if it knew somehow she craved its companionship. Joseph took the seat beside her, his long legs and large frame dwarfing the compliant seat he'd been offered. He tossed Hannah a look, more amused than solemn.

Willis peered out the window beside the door, then shoved the lock in place.

Spinning on his heel, the man marched the few steps toward them, sliding the last chair opposite Joseph. The bright merriment eased to pensive sincerity, that aimless tone to his voice replaced with a depth that rivaled even Joseph's.

Hand on his knee, Willis leaned forward, his gaze clutching Joseph. "I am very glad you have come, *brother.*"

Chapter Nineteen

Joseph sat up as Willis's admission drew his spine straight. *Could he be...*

He glanced to Hannah, whose knitted fingers and rigid posture told him she too was at a loss of what to say.

Unable to respond, Joseph slanted his head, studying the enigmatic figure before him. If indeed this man was a Patriot, their work against the enemy could be combined, but if he was not...

As if Joseph had spoken the questions aloud, Willis sat back, an understanding slide to his lips. "I do not blame you for questioning." He nodded, answering the words Joseph didn't voice. "I too am a spy and am under the command of Washington."

"Washington?"

"Aye." Willis pointed to the kettle over the fire, his eyebrows raised.

Joseph shook his head.

The man continued. "I was offered this post not long after Bunker Hill. My family are all Tories, and 'twas assumed I was one as well. The cover was perfect."

One word made Joseph's back prick. "Was?"

"It seems there is an informant about." Willis's expression dulled, but his tone sharpened. "Lieutenant Greene was here a few days past, prying where he ought not. Do you know him?"

Joseph needn't look to Hannah to know that she stiffened. "We do."

"You don't care for him either, I take it." He huffed, shaking his head. "I feared I might have been discovered, but thus far it seems I am not suspected, thank the Lord."

Joseph ventured further. "How do you know of our mission? We have told no one."

Standing, Willis went to the mantel and shimmied out a stone from the side. Retrieving a letter from the cavity, he unfolded the paper and looked it over. "I received word from Captain Donaldson about your arrival at the foundry and your mission." He handed the letter to Joseph. "I knew 'twas only a matter of time before you came."

Joseph read the message in pleasant shock before handing the note back to Willis. "It seems you know more of this than I."

"I am plagued with needing to know everything that happens." He replaced the letter behind the stone. "'Tis a burden, though I am pleased to bear it for what good will come...what good I *hope* will come of our efforts."

Joseph spied Hannah, whose tight features showed her surprise and continuing suspicion. She was right to worry, as they knew nothing of the man, but there was something about him that seemed far too sincere to be questioned.

When Willis was seated, Joseph moved forward with the mission at hand. "I've brought the barrels."

"Excellent. Get up a moment. There's something I would show you." Willis motioned for them to stand before he pulled away his and Joseph's chairs and removed the crude rug. Stooping, he raised a hidden door in the planked wood. Deep, and filled halfway with muskets, lead, barrels of powder and cannonball, the hidden cellar was cavernous. Joseph's mouth would have hinged open if he hadn't intentionally held it shut.

Hannah's eyes were wide and her lips tight, as if she too was attempting not to gasp in surprise.

Willis straightened like a proud bird showing his nest. "Two hundred and fifty muskets, two thousand rounds, and three hundred cannonball. Along with the gun barrels you are to deliver, I'd say that's a fair prize for the waiting men in Roxbury and Cambridge."

"Good heavens."

Hannah's half-breathed exclamation echoed Joseph's very thoughts.

"Incredible." She raised her head and caught Joseph with her awe-filled expression.

He answered with a raise of the brow and disbelieving smile. He'd never have imagined it either.

Willis motioned for Joseph to help him lower the floor's hatch. With rug and chairs back in place, they took their seats, as if they hadn't just witnessed a storehouse of the army's lifeblood.

"There is a raid planned for the early morning of Sunday, February fourth." Willis leaned forward, elbows on his knees. His timbre had gone from serious to lethal. "We have planned it to the minute. Several hours after your delivery here, the Patriots will make their supposed attack. I shall be abed, pretending to be shocked and horrified at their arrival yet completely helpless to stop them."

"But there are other soldiers about." Joseph sat back in the small chair, his leg muscles ticking with the rise of tension. "How can you be sure they will not get word of this?"

"There is always concern, which is why secrecy is critical." Willis glanced to Hannah then back to Joseph. "But we have cause for hope. We have organized it thus because that is the night of—"

"The night of the ball."

Both men turned to Hannah. Chin raised, resolve and determination radiated in her rich, green eyes. "All the officers will be frolicking at the ball several miles from here while the Patriots make off with their stores."

Approval and undeniable respect lit Willis's face as he nodded at Hannah's statement. "Aye. You are a wise woman. Wise and devilishly brave." He shifted his eyes to Joseph. "If you can obtain an invitation—"

"I have one," Hannah answered.

Joseph's stomach curled into stone.

"You do?" Willis pulled his shoulders back. "In truth?"

She nodded, expression earnest yet calm. "Stockton has invited me to attend with him."

A light breath left Willis's parted mouth. "This is surely a blessing from heaven. With you there to keep Stockton and the others blissfully entertained, we may with more security do what must be done." He reached out and took one of Hannah's hands in both of his. "Your offering will not be forgotten."

Dear Lord, no. No. Joseph's muscles were hot and pulsing with dissent. He could not allow it. How could he submit to her acting in such a perilous capacity?

Hannah exhaled a petite breath when Willis released his hold. "I am most pleased to be of service to a cause so vital."

Willis's smile didn't leave her. "And you will surely be protected, my dear. For God cannot but shelter one with so pure a heart."

She bowed her head, cheeks pink. Tipping her face toward Joseph, the look she handed him slashed his heart as the courage he'd seen on her face in the tent that first time showered over her once again. She knew it, as well as he. She must go to the ball—her work now more vital than it ever was before.

Devil's spit. How was he to endure the knowledge she would be there with that beast? Nay. 'Twas too dangerous. He would not allow it. But the objection he tossed to her from his expression was hurled away by the subtle drop of her chin.

Joseph's core tightened, and he looked down, studying the frayed edge of the rug beneath them. He would speak of this with her on the ride back. After a heavy breath that did nothing to relieve his angst, he raised his head. "Has anyone else seen what is below our feet?"

Willis shook his head. "I've several muskets hidden in hollow hay bales in the barn that I use to prove my work to the British. The Patriots know of this, but the Redcoats do not—and I pray to keep it that way." He rose and motioned to the door. "You should not stay overlong, lest prying eyes become suspicious."

Joseph followed Willis's lead and moved to the exit, Hannah behind. He shook the man's hand. "We thank you, sir."

"And I you." The lines around his eyes deepened as a smile lifted across his worn face. "I have never seen a more aptly paired team. Husband and wife in the secret service of Washington? Excellent indeed."

Husband and wife? Though he knew he should rectify the blunder instantly, the misunderstanding nurtured a long-forgotten yearning, and Joseph was reluctant to correct him. He could feel the heat rising in Hannah's cheeks though he didn't look her way, and he cleared his throat.

"Mr. Plains, we are not related—though we do pose as cousins."

"Aw, I see. Donaldson didn't say anything about that, so I assumed..." He raised his head and lowered it, as if amused, and cleared his throat. "Forgive me."

He bowed to Hannah, and she inclined toward him, a half smile revealing her endearing dimple. Joseph offered his hand to their new friend. "I look forward to our next meeting."

Willis's hearty grip infused a sort of brotherly kindness in Joseph that warmed through his spirit.

"Be safe. Be cautious." Willis released his hold and looked to Hannah. "And you, dear lady. God be with you."

That dimple sank deeper into her cheek as she smiled her good-bye before starting for the wagon. Joseph followed, already teetering on a precarious ledge. He helped Hannah into the wagon, touching her as minimally as possible, and climbed up himself, but his mind was elsewhere.

A strange brew of frustration and imprisonment bubbled, and he coughed to release the discomfort, but it refused to abate. Not two hours ago he'd decided on finding her a way to safety. Now, instead of Hannah being farther from danger, she was as close as she would ever be.

"It seems you cannot be rid of me so easily."

Immediately scowling, he turned his head to face her. "Rid of you?"

She looked up to him, then back to the road. "Until the raid is over at least."

"What do you mean?"

One of her shoulder's bobbed up and down. "Oh, 'tis nothing."

'Twas something and he knew it. Whether he would attempt to have her expose what she wished to hide was another matter.

He pressed a heavy sigh from his nose. "I don't like it."

"I know." Keeping her gaze forward, she nodded and continued after a beat of silence. "But I feel I shall be safe. I shall be at the ball at least two miles from the raid, and though Stockton's attentions are unwelcome, I do not believe he would wish me harm."

However he hated to concede, Hannah was right. The major's affections for her were not fabricated, and though Joseph pined to be the one at her side, Stockton would no doubt be sure she was safe. That was, unless he learned who and what she really was.

Unsure how to arrange his feelings about the developments, Joseph ruminated over the looming future as they rode back through town. The ball. The raid. Both necessary evils they could not circumvent.

Allowing himself a sideways glance, he noted Hannah's gaze was fixed across the road and followed it to the gown in the window.

He swung his eyes back to her, and she looked away innocently, as if she'd not just been gazing with girlish longing.

The irritations that had piled began to slough away. He couldn't control everything, even if he wished to—even if his intentions were sincere. He had to trust that God would indeed protect her, as Willis had said.

Shifting in his seat, he tested the waters of playfulness that would hopefully be the balm for his ire. "Since you will attend the ball despite my protestations, I suppose I must insist that you wear sackcloth. For anything else would bring you far too much attention."

"Is that so?" Her mouth held hard against a smile that seemed difficult to suppress, her eyes sparkling with unreserved delight. "I fear sackcloth would bring more attention than less."

A rich satisfaction warmed his limbs. He chuckled, easiness massaging away a mite of the former tensions.

On through town they went, the silence equal parts tension and comfort—part of him wishing they would speak, the other relishing the peaceful quiet between them. The kind of comfortable reticence that existed between two people so content in each other's presence no words needed to be spoken at all.

Without warning his stomach grumbled, and he tossed her a strained glance, to which she smirked.

He chuckled. "I suppose my lack of breakfast is making itself known."

Hannah reached down, pulling a basket from beneath her seat. "Then 'tis a good thing I brought you something."

How had he missed she'd brought a basket? She eyed him hopefully, and he teased her with a suspicious frown before tipping sideways to inspect what awaited him. She slipped back the cloth and bit her lip, as if awaiting his expression of approval.

Sitting straight, he kept a sideways glance on her, an almost girlish expression on her womanly face. She wanted to please him. The thought did terribly wonderful things to his stomach, and not from the thought of food. "You made turnovers."

Satisfaction, sweet and humble, dusted over her cheeks. "They *are* your favorite." She added the next quieter, "I hadn't forgotten."

God give him strength. All amusement, all hunger fled in the face of wanting. He stared overlong, fearing he would lose the battle that raged and pull over the wagon, at last to hold her to him and kiss her as he'd dreamed of doing for so long.

Wisdom intervened, and Joseph reached for a cold but perfectly browned morsel and filled his mouth, if not fully his hunger. That might not ever be satiated.

He finished the rest in silence, when he pulled on the reins and scowled. Something wasn't right. Joseph pitched sideways and tugged the horses to a stop.

Hannah turned her head. "What's happened?"

He hopped down. "A harness has come loose."

The next moment he heard her footsteps on the snow. "May I help you?" There was something untapped in her words, but what it could be, he'd dared not hope.

She stayed on the other side of the second horse, peeking around its neck and shoulders. Was that yearning in her bright eyes? Or did she simply want to be near him?

Joseph cleared his throat to dispel the mystifying imaginings. "You may pet his nose if you like. I don't know this horse as well as I know Anvil, but he's patient. A touch from a pretty woman wouldn't hurt in keeping him happy while I work."

Her cheeks bloomed to the loveliest shade of pink, and she nodded, ducking away before he could linger over that perfect dimple any longer.

He bent to discover exactly what had come loose, and within moments had righted the buckle, pulling it tight. Straightening, he stepped back, brushing his hands. "On we go."

Circling back to his seat, he was struck directly between the shoulders...by a snowball. Slowly he turned, spying Hannah's impish expression as she hid most of herself behind the safety of the horse's huge frame.

He stayed motionless, trying to decipher the strange form of such a moment. A laugh built up, exuberant and bright. This was the Hannah he remembered. Her beauty was one thing. Her strength of will another. But 'twas the playfulness and humor he found breathlessly irresistible—and something he'd seen little of since their lives had been thrown back together.

With the slightest tip of one eyebrow and cant of her head, she dared him to hit her back.

Bending, he scraped together a large ball of snow. If she wished to play, he was all too willing to oblige.

Dear heaven, what had she been thinking?

Joseph's frame disappeared as he ducked for snow, and she hurried for shelter behind the horse. She could hardly see over the top of the animal's back, and there Joseph would have the advantage. He could find her out more easily than she could him.

Bursting with a joy she hadn't felt in years, Hannah looked over the horse's back one last time, and not seeing Joseph, darted to the other side of the wagon. What had possessed her to do such a thing? Smiling, she nearly laughed aloud. He'd looked so surprised, but she couldn't seem to help it—the action almost springing from her without her knowing. Things were becoming easier between them...more as it had been.

This was how she'd wanted things. Easy, natural. *Husband and wife.*

Her neck and ears burned at the memory of Mr. Plains's mention of them as such. Oh, why did her heart have to cling to such a thing?

A cold lump smacked her in the shoulder from behind, spraying bits of icy wetness onto her neck and ears. She squealed, laughing. Joseph lunged from his place behind the back of the wagon, four more crude balls in his large hands. His face beamed with that perfect white smile that made her knees turn to pudding. Crouching, she grasped for more snow, when another ball hit her on the knee.

She hurled a hurried handful from her position at the ground, but it missed him, and he strode toward her with long, determined strides.

Hannah jumped to her feet and raced to the trees, her limbs weak from laughter. She reached the edge of the wood where the snow was untouched, when an ironlike arm grabbed around her middle.

Joseph's rumbling chuckle vibrated against her ear as he held her firm. "You wanted a fight, hmm?"

"You were so serious." She spoke between spurts of sprite laughter.

"*I* was serious?" His grip loosened slightly, and she took the chance, wringing free from his arm, but he caught her back again.

Struggling against his solid frame, Hannah lost her balance and tumbled into the snow with a yelp, he following after.

Cold snow on her face, she rolled to her back, blissful laughs bouncing through her. He moved his body from hers, though his arm was still beside her right shoulder, his face directly above hers.

Slowly, their laughter dispelled, his nearness consuming every nerve already alive with the joy of him. *Dear Lord, how am I to endure this?* The lines around his eyes softened, their rich blue deepening to match the color of his navy-blue coat.

His gaze brushed over her lips, and her mouth parched. Would he?

With a grunt he moved back and pushed to his haunches, snapping like a dry reed the moment she'd used to lean her hopes against.

"Come." Offering his hand, he helped her to her feet and brushed a bit of snow from her shoulder.

"We best be back before Stockton begins to wear a path in front of the fire."

She nodded but couldn't help the slant of her head or the words that matched. "Is that all? Or are you simply afraid I shall overtake you?"

"Overtake me?" With a half smile, he stepped back. "I believe, dear Hannah, you have done that already."

Chapter Twenty

The yard was empty when Philo rode in, weary and chilled from the twenty-mile ride. He slid from his mount and swept his gaze over the land that should be, nay, *would* be his. Eaton Hill hadn't changed, as somehow he'd expected, knowing the British had taken it. 'Twas as wild and lovely as it had always been. The land still vast and blanketed with trees, the view still...mournful. From where he'd stopped in the middle of the yard, he could easily detect the new mound on the hill. He squinted. Or was it two? Raw, like a grave freshly dug, a pit began in his stomach. He shook his head. Nay. It couldn't be. His vision played tricks upon him, surely.

He secured his horse near the front door, when the clanging from inside the foundry across the yard met his ears. Must be Ensign at work. Or the British, but likely they'd commandeered him for their purposes.

A smile tickled his cheek. Ironic that Ensign was for the Patriots and yet would be made to work for the enemy. Had he sold to Philo as he should have, perhaps Providence would have looked more kindly upon him.

Philo strode to the door, tugging at his jacket before he knocked, struggling to ignore the swirling in his chest. Any moment Hannah would open the door. He hadn't seen her in years. Would she look even more like her mother? The thought made his throat tighten. What would he say? What would *she* say?

He prepared to knock again, when the door immediately opened. His heart lifted and sank in the same moment when his daughter did not greet him.

"May I help you, sir?"

The ruddy cheeks of the soldier who looked not much older than nineteen were lifted in a smile that seemed far too friendly for one in the service of the king.

"I uh..." He hadn't expected this? And why not? Imbecile. "I am here to see my brother, Ensign Young."

A truth, aye. But his mission was twofold, and if his plot were to be completed, he must find the man in charge. Certainly that was no longer Ensign.

The soldier nodded. "I see." His mouth twisted in thought as he leaned back toward the parlor, then turned again to Philo. "One moment, sir—what is your name?"

"I am Reverend Philo Young, sir."

The soldier nodded quickly before closing the door all but an inch. After a few voices jumped back and forth, the soldier returned, swinging the door wide. "Major Stockton will see you."

Major Stockton, hmm? Philo tucked the name away and entered, taking stock of the house in a single glance before his attention was stolen by the imposing man in front of the fire. His commanding stance was enough to herald his status even if his decorated scarlet coat did not.

The young soldier motioned to Philo, then the officer. "Reverend Young, Major Stockton."

"Thank you, Private Reece." The major dipped only his head in greeting. "Reverend."

Bowing deeply at the waist, Philo encased himself in all the charm and ease of one who spent a lifetime learning how to gain a man's trust. "At your service."

Stoic, the man only nodded. "You are here to see your brother, I understand?"

"Aye, sir." Philo straightened, easing the muscles in his shoulders and neck to give the impression he hadn't a thread of tension, though the longer he stood in the same room with this stranger, the thicker it became. "It has been some time since I have paid a call. What is family if not to love and care for one another, hmm?"

The man's eyes flicked up and gazed over Philo's shoulder to the young soldier behind him. It seemed there was a message in his look, for the soldier who'd seen him in excused himself, leaving Stockton and Philo alone.

"Reverend." Stockton pivoted slightly, resting his hand on the mantel. "I fear I've some sorrowful news to report...had we known of any family, we might have sent word—"

"Nothing's happened to Hannah." Panic's pointed fingers clutched his throat. Did that account for the second grave on the hill? Though he'd not seen her in years, though he hated her for what she'd done, it didn't change that she was his child and her death would be a blow he couldn't bear.

"Miss Young is well, sir." Eyebrows knit tight, Stockton kept his expression hard. "'Tis your brother."

"Oh?"

Lowering his hand from the mantel, the man straightened with a look that gripped Philo around the shoulders. "He is dead."

Dear God.

Philo's gaze lowered by degrees as the gravity of such a revelation forced his eyes to the ground. He spoke, his stare at the place where the wall met the floor. "When?"

"Some days ago." Strangely sincere, the man motioned in the direction of the hill. "His body rests beside his wife. I assure you he received a proper burial."

Still as a windless summer day, Philo allowed the words to first cling and then drag against him, waiting for the grief to strangle. It did, aye, but not as much as he'd expected. In truth, the future gleamed like a light in a firmament of pitch. Through loss would come joy then, it would seem.

He swallowed, aligning carefully what he would say next before he spoke. "Eaton Hill is a family estate." Lowering his head, he directed a heavy dose of sorrow through his words. "I wonder what shall become of it now he is gone?"

When Stockton didn't immediately speak, Philo seized the quiet. "I am pleased you have made use of it. I do fear my brother may not have been friendly toward the king, but I for one would see those rebels hanged for their treason."

Only the man's eyebrows lifted, as if he knew such a response was expected, but his trust was still in the balance. "You are kin of Miss Young then, I take it, as you asked after her?"

"Hannah? Aye, she is..." Of a sudden he was pained with a distant longing. "She is my daughter."

"She said nothing of a father." Suspicion creased his forehead.

"We are estranged."

The rising skepticism that settled ever deeper in the soldier's weathered face would not serve Philo well. He needed the man at his side, not apart from it.

Philo at last removed his hat and moved politely to a chair, praying the unsolicited act would be taken as a statement of his grief and not his pride. "When her mother died, I feared caring for a daughter myself, so I...I gave her into the care of my brother and his wife, who had no children of their own. I fear she believes I abandoned her. A father can only do his best."

Something of the partial truth he'd shared must have struck a chord. Stockton's hard features softened at the edges, and he looked over to the window. "Your daughter is a good woman. A brave one."

There was more than simple kindness in his words—there was a familiarity that wormed against Philo's skin, but he ignored it, bringing the conversation around again to him—to Eaton Hill.

"Well, sir, I will have you know that I would like to do what I can in your efforts. If you are in need of anyone to oversee the property—"

"You are generous indeed, sir, but I do believe Mr. Young has everything well in order."

"Mr. Young, did you say?"

"Aye, your nephew of course. Quite a talented blacksmith, I must say. He's generously offered to look after the work in the foundry while..."

Stockton continued speaking, but Philo heard none of it, while his mind chased and bound what he'd not dared even to consider. Joseph? Here with Hannah and posing as a relative?

Rage, disbelief, and confusion suffocated him, filling his lungs with their vile stench enough to force him to cough it free. It had to be Joseph. Who else could it be? Had they been together all this time? Had Ensign known of their continued love affair and sold to him for that purpose? Were they even married, or living in sin?

"Reverend, are you well?"

Philo coughed again, waving his hand in the air. "Aye, forgive me."

He wouldn't reveal her now. He couldn't. If he wished Eaton Hill for himself, his hand must be played with ever more caution than before. He must find a commonality with this man, something to break the tension and form that bond that was the basis of trust. Only then would he be able to carve the needed path that would make Eaton Hill his own. With the war upon them, what of deeds and bonds? This man alone had the power, and Philo must harness it.

"If I may be so bold, Reverend..."

Philo peered up at Stockton's sudden change of subject. "Aye, sir."

"How old is your daughter?"

"She is eight and twenty and so much like her mother." Though he hadn't seen her in far too long, he knew such a statement to be more than true.

Stockton gazed to the window, a dreaminess in his soldierly expression. "I find it strange she has not married."

Realization dawned, the spikes of light rising into the black corners of his remaining questions. He might have known Hannah would be the very thing that would unlatch the shackles and send Philo's chains into a blissful free fall.

Philo stood, emboldened by this newfound knowledge. "I suppose...I suppose she never found a man to her liking."

"Hmm." Gaze unwavering from the window, Stockton nodded in thought. "I wonder what she shall do when the conflict is finished." He looked to Philo with a minuscule slant of the head.

A more perfect interlude could not have been crafted. "There will need to be someone to care for the property—and for Hannah—for I doubt my nephew will stay on much longer." *For I shall throw him out.*

Stockton's quick shake of his head noted his agreement. "His trade takes him far and wide, I understand."

Trade? What lies had the man told? "I worry over it, and my daughter."

Striding to the lowboy in the corner, Stockton poured two drinks. "She seems an intelligent, capable woman. Not to mention her angelic beauty." He handed Philo an amber-filled glass, secrets in his genial grin. "I daresay I must keep her from my soldiers, or she's like to be stolen away by one or more of them."

Bringing the cup to his mouth, Philo chuckled in politeness. However, the statement settled with little amusement. He took a sip of the tepid liquid. "I almost wonder—forgive me for speaking so openly—but I do almost wonder if my brother's passing was not meant to be. I have long wished to mend what I have lost with my daughter, and it seems now is the chance. But..."

He paused, staring into the glass, hoping the man would bite at his dangling bait.

"You worry she will not trust you?"

Philo strode to the window. "I must have more time with her." He turned back around, sighing in perfect choreography to his words. "But how to ease it upon her. I have made so many mistakes..."

Stockton's jaw ticked, and he remained quiet before he leaned his head back and drained the rest of his drink. A flash of some unspoken grief flared, then died in his eyes. "I believe every parent feels the depth of their inadequacies." Again he was silent, pensive. "I cannot speak for her of course, but...if you feel it needful, and as she allows, I will permit you to visit the property."

"You are most generous, Major." Wings of elation took flight, driving straight to the heavens, but he kept it hidden behind the slightest of smiles. "I should like to do my best to begin to mend my wrongs."

Chin down, Stockton stared into his empty glass. "There is a ball this Saturday eve."

"A ball?"

"'Tis for officers and other such of the king's men, but Miss Young will be there as my guest. The presence of a Reverend would be prudent, would it not?" Stockton made a quick gesture before bringing the cup back to his lips. "You are welcome to attend if you like."

Philo struggled against the urge to smile as wide as the cold winter sky. "I would like that very much. Very much indeed."

As they approached the yard after their journey to Duxbury, Hannah felt lighter and more joy filled than she had since her youth. She glanced up to heaven, pouring out her unspoken prayers to the One who knew her better than she knew herself. He'd known she needed that levity, that laughter and freedom from woe, however short it might be. She might not have been able to bear the return if she hadn't. All because of God—and Joseph.

She glanced up at him, the grin on her lips stretching over her face and deep through her heart. Looking down again at her hands as Joseph directed the horses and wagon to the barn at the side of the foundry, she flicked away the prick of disappointment, as one might a crawling pest in summer. Here they must shed what familiarity they'd enjoyed on the brief ride. They must don again the heavy cloak of secrecy. They were cousins. Nothing more. 'Twas the way she wanted it, of course. With a swallow and a cough, she labored to ingest that belief, but the jagged edges of truth scraped on their way down.

Once stopped, she secured that ponderous cloak around her shoulders with strings of reality. She was here for the cause, for Ensign—as was Joseph. He had made his choice ten years ago, and if she thought their nearness would change that—that a mere playful fight in the snow would unravel the mass of tangled emotions, she was as daft as she'd been before.

Joseph hopped down and came around to assist her.

Hands at her waist, hers at his shoulders, he lowered her to the ground, his grip and gaze lingering. The small, unopened grin that warmed his face mirrored hers, no longer as light or as wide as it had been, yet just as real. And the depth of it held her like an embrace.

For a moment they stayed motionless, neither of them speaking, fearing, it seemed, that words might dim the brightness of what they'd shared and snip away what had been mended.

Slowly his hands fell away, and she wrapped her arms around her waist, reluctant to let the warmth of his touch fade. Glancing to the house, she focused her eyes on the unfamiliar horse that waited out front.

Another soldier perhaps?

Sighing, she started for the yard, when a firm grip on her arm stopped her.

"Hannah."

Her whispered name, deep and filled with an emotion she couldn't name, tugged at her heart as real as his hand at her elbow.

Like a stern mother, she scolded the sudden yearning and hid it behind a questioning look. "Aye?"

"Would you..." He swallowed and licked his lips, looking briefly away.

In that moment she saw the same nervous expression in his eyes—that same tentative want she'd seen the first night he'd asked to see her home. Dear heaven. If he were to ask her anything, she would be powerless to resist.

Releasing a quick breath, he tried again. "Would you sit with me by the fire this evening?"

Keeping her tone void of the exuberance that whirled within her took painful effort. "Of course."

She hesitated just long enough to note the easing around his eyes and the drop of his chest, as if he'd been holding a heavy breath. With a nod she turned back to the house, letting out at last the smile that burst from her spirit. Even her steps were quicker, lighter, forgetting the admonition of minutes earlier.

Attempting to restrain the childish thrill was folly, but she tried nonetheless. He simply asked to spend time at the fire. They had done that before. 'Twas nothing remarkable. So why did her heart labor under the hope that it was something more?

Having crossed the yard, she glanced at the waiting horse before gripping and turning the cold handle of the door. Pushing it wide, she took a step in, and the two men standing at the fire twisted her direction.

Lord in heaven, give me strength.

Unable to move, she stared at the one man who stared back, her emotions fleeing every direction, leaving only fear in her center. Fear and its shadow, suspicion.

Philo's smile was hesitant, his voice equally so. "Hannah, my dear."

Her tongue welded to the roof of her mouth. Still within the doorframe, the cold nipped up Hannah's skirt, but she welcomed the sensation, preferring it to the type of cold that waited within.

Stockton smiled, that familiar protectiveness deepening the lines around his eyes. Cup in hand, he left his spot beside the fire, placing the unfinished drink on the table between the chairs as he came toward her.

"If you'll excuse me, Miss Young, I should like to speak with your cousin about your visit to Duxbury." He stopped beside her, reaching out as if he would touch her arm. His throat worked, and his eyes darted to Philo before returning to her. "If you should need anything..."

With a dip of his chin, he left. She wanted to call out, beg him to come back. Even his presence would be more welcome than solitude with this man.

"Come in, my child." Philo motioned to the fire, his actions hesitant and strained as his eyes trailed her. He shook his head, looking as if he might speak something genuine, intimate, before he coughed it away. "You must warm yourself. You look chilled."

So much of her was weak, childish. For now, in his presence, the young Hannah emerged—the Hannah that was, and always would be, a daughter peeking from around that looming pillar of fear, always hopeful, always wishing. But a blink was all it took to right her mind and her heart. She closed the door, once again feeling the woman she was, and all the heartache she'd endured that made her so.

"What are you doing here?"

He set down his drink next to Stockton's and took a step forward, then stopped. His gaze rained over her like a summer downpour, covering every inch. "You've not changed."

"I have. If you knew me at all, you would see it."

The light breath he pressed from his mouth, the drop of his eyes, said her words hit their mark. He spoke of things physical, she of things much deeper.

Lifting his chin, and again his gaze, he tried once more. "'Tis good to see you."

Hurt, with its thousand weeping cuts, throbbed hard in her chest. "You have heard the news of Uncle then?" What else would make him come these twenty miles? Certainly not her presence. But how would he have learned of it?

"Aye." Philo's throat bobbed. "I am grieved at the loss."

Hannah shook her head, a bitter breath escaping her nose at the lack of sincerity in his profession. She was no fool. "You wish Eaton Hill for yourself. *That* is why you are here. Do not let pretense paint over reality."

Finally, the man she knew emerged. That hard look found its place over his expression, and the girl within her shrunk further away as he spoke.

"Then let me be plain. Eaton Hill should always have been mine, but my brother had an idea that perhaps he could take the future into his hands."

If not for lack of strength, and the fact her shoes seemed fastened to the floor, she would have fled, his bitter presence bleeding a raw ache through her muscles.

She gripped hard to her unraveling rope of strength. "He wanted only what is best for the foundry—for all of it."

"Ha!" Philo's head bent back as the laugh shot to the beams above. "So he would sell to your lover then, hmm?"

Hannah blinked, unsure she had heard him. "I have no love—"

"Joseph!" Philo took a giant step, his arm outstretched as he pointed to the door. "Joseph is here, Hannah. Don't think I don't know it."

Knees quivering, her mind flailed about for something to grasp hold of. Her body went numb, and her tongue thick. She didn't know how to act, what to say—should she try to deny it or simply stand against his accusation as if it were nothing but a simple spring breeze?

She ground her tone into submission. "I'm sure I don't know what you mean."

He lowered his arm and his voice. "I am no idiot, Hannah. Ensign sold the foundry to Wythe, allowing that hateful man one last blow to my life. It is too much to be borne."

She could hardly formulate a response before he started again. "How long have you been with him, hmm?" Mouth tight, nostrils flared, his voice rumbled across the floor. "Are you even married? Or have you long since disposed of that formality?"

Hannah's mind struggled, stumbling and gasping as it raced uphill over the jagged rocks. Joseph had bought the foundry? Why hadn't he told her? She nearly protested the accusation, but halted. If she denied the claim, he would want to know why Joseph was here—and that she could not say. Then again, he hadn't seen Joseph, so how could he know for certain? Perhaps this was a ruse to get her to come away with him? Perhaps he lied—made up such a thing to get her to speak, to spill all she held close so Stockton could know her secrets.

"I owe you no explanation." She shook her head, flinging aside the grip of weakness. "You cannot know he is here. You have not seen him."

"One does not need to see to know."

A quick glance to the window eased some hidden fear that perhaps Joseph would return to the house. The yard was vacant. "And if he is, what of it?"

"I would know if my daughter lives in sin." 'Twas more an accusation than a question.

"You are not my reverend, and I am your daughter in little else than blood."

He stormed forward, skin scarlet. "What would people say of you if they knew? Have you no thought of my reputation? I hoped after your first ignominious transgression you would have—"

"I do not care what others think. I never have." Her chin quivered. "'Twas you who despised the ruin of flapping tongues—tongues that bespeak only shadowed, partial truths."

Philo's high cheekbones glistened with rage. "Eaton Hill will be mine, Hannah, no matter what you may say."

"I have never had a say in any of it, nor do I wish to." She stepped forward, feeling the spirit of Ensign beside her. "Before he died, I gave my word to my uncle that I would care for this land, and I intend to do so, and not even you will I allow to stand in my way."

Unmoving, Philo's stare darkened in the center, his stance strangely relaxed. "Your tenacity does you credit. But your ignorance does not."

She stood firm against the verbal blow.

"That man is, and always will be, unworthy of you. I tried to warn you, to save you years ago, but still you have a weakness for him. For all I know, 'twas you who put my brother up to this. Do you not remember how he left you? He wasn't the marrying kind then, and he won't be now. That sort of person thinks only of himself and none other."

Hannah stepped aside as a signal for him to leave, but she was not quick enough to escape the fiery path of his words. They hit and burned deep through her skin to scar her tender spirit.

She motioned to the door, her throat so bulged with emotion she hadn't the capacity to speak.

With a nod, he started for the exit, slowing as he passed her, such a tangle of emotions in his eyes she couldn't begin to unravel them. Disdain? Anger? Sorrow, perhaps? Regret? Nay, the last was a figment of her hurting soul.

He placed his hat on his head and peered back over his shoulder as he opened the door. "You are not to be rid of me so easily." Said with jest more than anything else, he nodded and stepped out. "Goodbye, Hannah."

The door closed, cutting off the last of her strength. She reached for the chair at her side, her lungs heaving for the air she'd denied them. Awash with questions, her mind hung heavy like a sopping garment. Had Joseph really bought Eaton Hill? Why had he not told her? Hannah quickly replayed Ensign's promise that he'd sold to an honorable, just man who would care for the land and foundry as he had. In truth, she knew few others who fit the description as well as Joseph. And yet...

Her father's words drilled through her ears like a burrowing insect. *Do you not remember how he left you? That sort of person thinks only of himself...*

273

The words circled her heart like wolves around their prey. Hurrying to the stairs, she pulled her skirts to her ankles and raced for the safety of her room, slamming the door behind her.

She stared at the dressing table at the opposite side of the room. It seemed to beckon her, oblivious to the turmoil that writhed within. The treasures it harbored whispered her near, but she would not allow herself to bring to life the pains that now clawed at her.

Joseph had left her. That truth would never fade. He had not known of the child she bore or the pain she'd suffered. Would knowing of their son have even changed his mind?

Tears burned hard at the back of her eyes, spilling over her cheeks and down her neck. She breathed through clenched teeth. Perhaps her father was right. Perhaps she hadn't changed at all. Perhaps she was still as blind and foolish as she had ever been.

Chapter Twenty-One

Joseph finished the last barrel, dunking the molded iron into the water, its hissing and wheezing a melody to his ears. Sackett and Deane were beginning to slow, their day nearly as long as his.

"Enough for today." He put back his iron and tipped his head to the door. "Get back and rest. Tomorrow shall be equally demanding."

A pair of sighs heaved through the room as the men placed their tools on the bench. Sackett nodded, smiling. Deane did the same, both of them talking between themselves, mounting their horses and hurrying to the food and warmth that awaited two miles away.

Joseph glanced through the partially open door to the light in the kitchen window, the pleasant sensations in his chest stealing the concentration he needed to tidy shop and prepare for the night. He'd not felt this way since...since her.

After arranging the tools the others had laid haphazardly on the table, he left, securing the latch on the door. His legs wished to race him across the yard, but he resisted. Peering quickly through the window, he noted the lack of Stockton, Higley, or Reece. Or Hannah. She must be upstairs.

He entered through the back, grateful the house was empty. He needed a wash, and desperately. Hurrying up to his room, he pulled his soiled shirt over his head and poured a generous amount of water into the porcelain basin on the table and scrubbed, the scent of the fresh soap a pleasant change to the smoke and grime he'd been covered with throughout the day. No woman wanted to converse with a man that smelled of soot and sweat. Almost deciding against it, he hurriedly washed his hair, content now that he was presentable. He dried thoroughly and snatched a clean shirt from the drawer but halted before pulling it on. A line of fine new stitches graced the edge of the collar. He'd seen the fraying but hadn't known what to do.

Like the delightful touch of new petals in spring, somewhere deep within him, a sweet softness began, spraying tickles over his skin. She had done this for him. Glancing across his shoulder, Joseph peered to the door. Was he even worthy of her? What made him think she would ignore the mountainous past that rose between them? He was willing to scale any height for another chance. And if *she* was willing, he could hold her hand—carry her if she needed—every step of the way, for surely the view from the top was far more beautiful than they could ever imagine.

A slow breath lulled him back to his task, and he slipped the soft linen over his head and snatched his fresh breeches and stockings, tucking and buttoning everything in place. Feeling even more stirred, he thought of the evening to come. She'd not denied his request to sit with him by the fire. 'Twas a step forward, was it not?

Brushing and securing his hair behind his head, he peered into the mirror one last time, then hurried into the hall, surprised that Hannah's door was still closed. Perhaps she'd already gone down.

"Joseph?"

'Twas Stockton's voice. He had taken to calling Joseph by his first name, and Joseph could only hope he didn't take such liberties with Hannah.

"Aye, sir?"

He went downstairs and entered the parlor just as Stockton exited his room, his scarlet jacket shed.

"Ready for supper?" Glancing to the kitchen, Stockton's face puckered. "Is your cousin not joining us?"

Joseph spun around to inspect what befuddled him. The table was set, the food in the center, but Hannah was still not at her regular perch beside the fire.

"I cannot say, sir. I haven't seen her since we returned." He glanced up the stairs, the beginnings of a worry in his stomach. "Perhaps I should see after her. Be sure she is all right."

"Aye." Stockton's attention was up the stairs before his eyes shifted to Joseph. "I worried perhaps this would happen. She seemed none too pleased to see her father."

Struck by the revelation like a club to the skull, Joseph shook his head and all but stuttered his reply. "Her father? He was here?"

"He was." Sighing, Stockton scratched his thumbnail beside his eyes. "I left them alone to talk, but I fear perhaps I should not have."

Nay, he should not have. He should not have even let the man on the land. If Joseph had known...

His pulse raged. How many hours ago was this? He whirled to the clock on the mantel. Four hours perhaps, maybe more? That small worry steadily deepened to a cavernous pit. She hadn't seen her father in years. If only Joseph had been with her. If only she had come to him, told him of her encounter, he might have been able to help her, ease what pains she suffered.

Bounding up the stairs, he knocked gently, though the energy in his muscles wished to break down the door to ease in an instant the writhing concern. "Hannah?"

Silence replied.

"Hannah, are you..." Heaven help him, he didn't know what to say. He glanced down the stairs to Stockton, who looked up, eyebrows cinched.

Putting his forehead nearly against the wood, he spoke quiet, gentle. "I haven't seen you since we came home. I simply want to be assured you are well."

Still nothing. He tried the latch, and it gave. Pushing it open, he hurried in, and his stomach rolled to his feet. She was not there. The bed was tidy, not a sign she'd even been there, but certainly she had.

He hurried out and halted at Stockton's hard stare.

"Where could she be?"

If only he knew. He descended two by two as Stockton rushed into his room for his coat.

"No, Stockton, wait."

The man did an about-face, his expression taut. "I must go look with you."

"No, sir, I beg you. She will not have gone far, and if she is truly so upset, she might wish her distress to stay only within the family." Waiting as if on eggshells, Joseph prayed the man would submit.

Shoulders dropping, Stockton pointed. "If you do not find her within the hour, I will come. Family distress be hanged."

After a swift nod, Joseph yanked on his coat, scarf, and hat.

Hurrying out the door and into the yard, he stopped, not allowing his eyes time to adjust to the pale light of the moon before he circled, scanning every which way for any indication of where she might have gone.

He gazed to the hill, and his heart hovered between beats. There she was. Lord be praised. Racing up the hill toward the graves, he called to her. "Hannah."

She didn't turn, didn't even acknowledge him until he stopped directly at her side. A cursory glance and forced smile shadowed her face.

"Hannah...are you—"

"I am fine." The hollow words were a lie. She couldn't honestly believe he would accept such an answer.

"'Tis cold. Will you not come back inside?"

She peered down at something in her hand, then quickly tucked it out of sight. "Forgive me. I hadn't meant to worry you. I needed only a moment of solitude."

Her attention went again to the snow-covered graves. So enclosed in sorrow, it seemed she hardly knew he was there. *Dear Hannah.* If there were some way to ease what ailed her. She wished for Ensign, for his wisdom and embrace. Could not Joseph impart that now?

The winter stabbed at his ears, as surely it did hers. He wasn't about to allow her to stay in the darkness alone and in such temperatures.

Hadn't she a scarf? He uncurled the one from his neck and placed it around hers. "I shall stay with you. It grows dark and is unsafe for you to venture out alone when soldiers abound."

Offering him another look that hovered slightly above civil, she thanked him with a stiff smile, quickly turning away. But not before he noted the glisten of her cheek. She cried?

She dabbed quickly at her face, and his suspicions were confirmed. *Dear Lord, what should I do?*

Before even a clear answer came, he spoke. "Hannah, I am so sorry. I only just learned your father was here. Had I known I would have—"

"Nothing to be sorry over." She raised her chin, her tone brittle. "I should have supposed he would come when he learned of Ensign's passing. Only I cannot figure how he might have heard of it. We have told no one."

Joseph's heart ached upward to his shoulders, cramping his already tight muscles. The need to hold her was too great. He reached out for her, but she swiveled away, as if she knew he would touch her.

He swallowed, sorting through a stack of responses before deciding on one be hoped would suffice. "Do not concern yourself. We can speak of it later." He stepped backward to the house, knowing full well he would never let her out of his sight until she once again returned safely indoors. "I shall give you the solitude you seek."

He turned but stopped when a fragile thread reached out to him. "Joseph?"

"Aye?"

The silvery moonlight reflected in her tear-moistened eyes, and it took every measure of strength, down to his very bones, not to reach forward and brush his fingers against her skin, to vow he would do all he could to ease every pain she suffered.

She licked her lips and darted her eyes away, as if she wanted to be sure they were alone before pinning them on him. "I...I have decided to leave Eaton Hill. After the ball."

Struck in the gut, he tried to be pleased at the news, but instead his insides roiled. Wasn't that what he'd wanted—her to be away from Stockton? The truth exploded through him with each thump of his pulse. Nay. He wanted her here. With him.

"Where will you go?"

Studying her fingers a moment, she nudged her chin forward. "I shall go to Caroline's."

He nodded, working his jaw back and forth as he gnawed on the emotions he resented. 'Twas right for her to go. Had he not stated such this morning? After a breath that brushed away the fog, he spoke. "'Tis wise to stay away until the conflict is over."

Hannah tucked that stray hair around her ear and looked back to the graves. "I...I shall not be coming back."

"Not coming back?" That familiar pang, one he remembered all too well, one he loathed and resented, breathed back to life in his chest after so many years of being secreted underground. "Why not?"

She shrugged a single shoulder. "I have nothing for me here. I see that now. And as the new owner will want to run the foundry and care for the land as he wishes—and with Ensign gone, I see no reason to return." Lifting her pained eyes to his, her soul all but reached for him through her darkened gaze. "Do you?"

Aye, so many. A hundred answers flocked to his tongue, ready to fly across the vastness between them, at last to give life to the very thing he couldn't say. Everything slipped to the background while his mind chased after the answer he knew he would never catch. Should he tell her? At last bare the burden he'd carried across his shoulders since the moment he and Ensign had spoken? But if he did, would she despise him even more—think him selfish for purchasing something she loved so well? Perhaps she would believe he did it only to get close to her, to force himself back into her life?

He cleared his throat, answering how he should, not how he wished to. "You must do what you think best."

The delicate sinews in her neck jostled, and it seemed another rise of emotions consumed her, for she nodded too quickly and turned away.

Not since that day Philo revealed Hannah's anger had he felt this depth of pain, this raw, biting agony that ripped him clear through.

He started for the house, mindless of the cold, looking over his shoulder one last time. Opening his heart was one thing. Offering it, another. And it seemed God was trying to spare him from more grief, for surely that was all that awaited him. And he'd had enough of that to last a lifetime.

Chapter Twenty-Two

The sun was reluctant to rise, as sleepy, it seemed, as she was awake. A few stars still sparkled around the edges of the perse horizon, where the pale light had yet to reach. Hannah tiptoed belowstairs, her thick wool stockings itching her legs as she hurried into the kitchen. She must leave before the men were up. Bending, she scratched the loathsome necessity. Irritating as they were, the stockings she'd knit last winter would keep her legs from numbing on the ride.

Snatching the basket of day-old cakes, she covered them with a cloth and rested her swiftly penned note beside it. So consumed she'd been since her father's abrupt arrival and Joseph's tenderness last eve at the graves, sleep refused to beguile her. And though she knew she could not yet leave for good, she must do this. Now.

A sound creaked from above, and she froze. Joseph was the last person she wished to see. Though somehow, he was the only person her mind seemed able to fix upon. She swallowed and looked upstairs, one part of her wishing for him to enter the kitchen and plead with her not to go, the other wanting never to see him again.

Sure at last that no one descended to meet her, she slipped out the door and dashed across the yard. Twenty miles on horseback—alone—was nothing when the company of Caroline was the only remedy for what ailed her.

When the horse was saddled, she mounted and exited through the back of the barn, lest Joseph had awoken and come down to the kitchen in the few minutes since her leaving. If he saw her, he would no doubt attempt to stop her, perhaps might even follow once her note was discovered. He would be livid. But that was an inevitability she was willing to endure for a few moments with her cousin.

Winter's grip tightened around her, as did the reality of her impetuous act. Joseph would be right to be upset when he learned of where she'd gone. Traveling to Sandwich was foolhardy. But was not all of it? Spying, scribing...allowing her spirit to once more fit itself alongside the man she was supposed to have long since forgotten?

With a quiet "yaw" and firm kick, Hannah raced along the snow-covered road, part of her alive in a way it had not been in so very long. But more alive from the solitude, than from *him*, she promised herself. Caroline would help her see more clearly. 'Twas a feminine perspective she needed—a listening ear and understanding heart. The ride would take only a few hours, less if the roads were more favorably conditioned. After revealing her sheltered aches, the secrets even her own heart seemed unsure of, she would begin the journey home and return before supper.

The brisk air, the crystal sky, and the sudden freedom pressed her onward. She leaned forward with the rhythmic up and down of her mount's strong neck, torn at the thought of leaving Eaton Hill for good. How could she do it? 'Twas her home. Yet how could she endure the presence of Joseph day after day, knowing he hadn't wanted her before—and still did not—when her traitorous heart wanted him more with every passing moment?

She welcomed the biting breeze on her cheeks. Nay, she did right. Caroline would help her see sense, clear her head and heart of him.

At least, the *hope* of him.

Joseph hadn't slept. Only tossed and turned atop his feather tick, but naught more. That blissful ignorance a restful night afforded was not to be had. Not when Hannah's sudden change and mournful confession kept his eyes wide and back stiff.

He left his room to find her door closed, as it had been last night. His chest tightened. Not wanting to actually believe this morning was a repeat of before, he went first to the kitchen, where his concern was not eased but incited. On the table sat a cloth-draped basket of yesterday's cakes with a note beside it.

Flinging a look over his shoulder, he peered at Stockton's room. The man was likely still abed. Or had he already risen and seen this note himself? Hastily unfolding the paper, Joseph read Hannah's feminine writing.

Please forgive my sudden absence. I have gone to visit my cousin and shall be back before supper.

Miss Young

Sandwich? Was she mad? Refolding the note with a gruff breath, he shoved it into his pocket, his mind grinding over what he must do. He had to go after her, no question. Yanking his coat and hat from their position beside the door, he marched out. Such strange behavior, and so abrupt. She was not the kind of person to do this sort of thing. Last night and today? Something was amiss.

Flinging wide the door, he jolted at the sight of Higley's arm in the air, ready to knock.

"Higley?"

The man lowered his hand. "I've come to fetch you." Foreboding bled through his tone. "Your presence in town has been requested by Major Pitman."

"My presence?" This day had a hatred for him, it would seem.

Turning back to his waiting horse, Higley indicated for Joseph to head to the barn. "Ready your mount. We must hurry."

Something in the way Higley held his posture made Joseph's stomach turn. "Where are we going?"

Higley's jaw was set, his eyes hard, and he replied with nothing but silence.

Joseph had not seen the man so riled. "I'll not be a moment."

Racing to the barn, he readied Anvil in a handful of minutes, his spirit spiked with a nervous edge. Never far from Joseph's mind was the throbbing sliver of truth, as real as if it were imbedded beneath his nail. Higley knew his identity and could use it against him. Was he now taking him away? Had

Higley forced Hannah somewhere against her will? Nay. Joseph mounted, no more than a slight tap needed to get Anvil on the move. Higley seemed too kind beneath his red coat for Joseph to believe him capable of anything nefarious.

Higley's dappled mare sidestepped as Joseph neared. "Last night Willis Plains was taken on suspicion of working for the enemy."

"What?" Joseph tried to keep the color in his face from fading. "What happened?"

"You were the last to see him before he was arrested." Higley's next words were hoarse and low. "If you will witness of your encounter with him yesterday and that indeed he is loyal to the king, perhaps he can be saved. If not, Major Pitman is prepared to have him hanged."

Hanged. "I will do whatever I can."

Higley tapped his heels against his horse and raced to the road. Joseph set Anvil to match his speed.

The cold breeze sighed past his ears as he rode, but he couldn't feel it. His concern was twenty miles behind him in Sandwich. Perhaps 'twas better that Hannah had gone—if she in fact was there. If he too were to be discovered, at least she could not be taken, and perhaps he could vouch for her enough to have it believed she was not involved in any of what they undertook. Thus the blame would be his alone.

The cadenced beat of horses' hooves against the hard ground drummed into Joseph's very bones. Praying, he gripped the reins harder, pleading with God to pour His spirit through him. Willis must be saved, their mission kept secret and the raid accomplished. More was at stake than merely their lives. In greater peril was their future.

Chapter Twenty-Three

"Oh, Hannah, my heart breaks for you."

On the edge of her cousin's feather bed, Hannah rested her hands in her lap, Caroline directly beside her. Hannah had laid out everything—Ensign, the spying, Stockton, Greene...and Joseph. Every sorrow, every pain now free to roam the air between them, her heart not quite as heavy as it had been.

Caroline took Hannah's hand in hers. "I had received your letter, but...'twas so secretive, I dared not reply."

"You were right not to." Eyes dry of tears, Hannah breathed out a bitter laugh. "I am a fool. 'Tis my fault alone that I am in this position. I should not have insisted upon returning." The last came out as a reprimand that she'd intended to keep silent. "I should not have allowed myself to look twice at him."

Caroline seemed to cradle the tender confession, examining it in her quiet before her eyes slanted to Hannah, her question reverent. "Do you still love him?"

Love.

Those four letters curled through the air and into her chest, circling her heart until the truth she'd never revealed began to flow like water from a tipped pitcher. "In truth...I never stopped." She looked up, claiming her cousin's kind gaze and finding the strength to release the rest of her harbored pains. "I know I told you before—how my father said Joseph came to the house the morning after he'd discovered our sin, saying Joseph wanted to see me, but I'd gone out. My father told me Joseph had wanted to reveal to me by his own mouth that he was sorry for what happened, but that he'd come to realize married life was not his wish, that he didn't want to be tied to only one woman. And though he cared for me, he didn't care enough to make good on his promise to marry me. He wished me well but didn't want to hurt me further by seeing me again. With that, he left and never came back."

Saying it aloud made the past seem almost unreal, as if she told someone else's story and not her own. 'Twas easy to relate it to Caroline. One who knew most of what had happened, she being a friend to both her and Joseph during those years.

Hannah looked to her confidant, the next words heavy, dragging like an anchor against the bottom of her heart. "I never told him about the child."

Caroline's light-blue eyes rounded gradually, as if her mind was slow to understand what Hannah had spoken. "You never told him?"

"How could I?" She spoke quickly, to relieve herself of the residing guilt as well as to remind herself why she'd done it. "If he truly didn't care to marry and wished to move on, how could I tell him of our child, and what difference would it have made? 'Twould have only hurt me further, and that I could not have borne."

Grip tightening in tenderness, Caroline's gaze drifted down, her dainty eyebrows folding in the middle. "I knew something was amiss. Hannah, I didn't believe it then, and I still do not." At that, her gaze rose again. "He loved you more than I have ever seen any man love. The only way for you to be certain of his feelings—to be certain of what happened—is to ask him."

"I cannot do that."

"You would live with this burden?"

She shot back with more force than she wished. "Have I a choice?"

"Have you a heart that aches? Have you a mind that will not rest?" Caroline shifted sideways, her strong hands holding hard. "It might pain you to your very bones, but you cannot let the rest of this go unspoken. Not when he clearly still cares for you."

Another breathy laugh popped from her chest. "He sees me as someone who he must care for during our mission—and I will concede that he..." Her words began to slow, but she pressed them through. "He is as kind and generous as he ever was, but I fear now that 'twas not for me he insisted on coming, but for Eaton Hill." She leaned her head back with a hard sigh. "What a fool I was. I saw one path, and I took it. Joseph was right. I didn't think it through, and now I am suffering for it."

Caroline straightened, her features rising in polite contradiction. "You acted bravely and in the right. Do not belittle yourself so." With a quick squeeze to Hannah's hand, she stood to face her, as if to impede any additional streams of self-deprecation. "Though I understand you are upset over the spying, I still do not believe what you say of Joseph caring only for

Eaton Hill. He cares for you Hannah. I do not doubt it."

"Caroline, please—"

"I have never doubted that." She spun away, her skirt whirling behind her as she circled in full. "Why must you keep so much inside, Hannah? Tell him!"

"I cannot!" Hannah stood, lowering her voice for fear the others belowstairs would hear her. "I have risked too much of my heart to once again lay it out to be trampled on."

Caroline gripped Hannah at the shoulders, the soft angles of her face hardening with sincerity. "You may not have seen him for these many years, but I have. And never has he looked at another woman—"

"You can't know that—"

"When he lost you, he lost the light in his eyes, the truth in his smile." Caroline's gentle fingers brushed down Hannah's arms, and she took her hands. "Part of him died when he lost you."

Hannah twisted away, a vain attempt to allow the words to bypass her, but they enclosed around her like a hopeful embrace as Caroline continued. "We do not know why he bought Eaton Hill or why he kept the truth from you, but one thing is certain, and that alone you must place your trust in. He has done nothing but protect you. Does he not deserve your understanding?"

"Understanding?" For a moment she neglected her volume. "What if I tell him I had a child? I never thought to see him again—I was almost certain he had forgotten about me, that he indeed wished to have other women, as my father claimed, since he never even attempted to write to me..." Her throat began a slow-burning ache. "If I allow myself to believe him good, if I even let my heart so much as peer past the wall I have built, that would be enough for me to unravel all the mending I have tried to do."

"But you must give him a chance."

"I told him I was leaving, and he did nothing to stop me."

"Of course he did not."

Caroline's almost frustrated tone brought Hannah's head around.

"Do you think he would force you to do something you wished not to do?"

"Well...I suppose—"

"From what you say, it seems all he has done is bend to your will. You would go back to Eaton Hill, so he let you. You would scribe for Stockton, and he let you. You say you wish to come here after the ball—and he supports your choice. If you show no interest in him, he will not force himself upon you, Hannah. He never has."

Caroline's words chafed, leaving a sore spot upon her conscience. 'Twas true. He had never forced her. She knew this as well as she knew everything else. Almost everything.

She looked to the door, her spirit willing, but her mouth almost too weak. "I do not know if I have the strength to do it."

In a swift movement, Caroline tugged her cousin into the kind of embrace she hadn't felt since the night Ensign passed. Pulling away, Caroline tilted her head, as she always did when she prepared to speak something wise. "You must sacrifice your fears, Hannah. You can only know the true freedom you seek when you are willing to give up what imprisons you."

Her voice wobbled. "But my prison is safe." So much revealed in so few words, her own mind at last understanding her silence.

Caroline cupped Hannah's face. "I know. But once you do this you will no longer wonder. You will *know*. And no matter what happens in consequence, you will not ever wonder 'what if.'" Her smile tipped slightly, and her voice softened. "Do you not think that God has given you this chance? That perhaps He has prepared more happiness in your future than you can ever imagine? Why not try it and see?"

Like a breeze gently ushering away the shadows of high summer clouds, Hannah's spirit stilled as the thought brightened through her. Had God arranged this? Tears pricked at the backs of her eyes. Perhaps Caroline was right. God knew her better than she knew herself, did He not? Deep within her, this had been the wish of her heart—to see Joseph again. To have another chance.

Lifting her eyes to Caroline's, she blinked back the tears, her tone weak, testing the taste of the words before allowing them full voice. "Do you really think I should?"

Confident, sure, Caroline's pretty face bloomed like a summer blossom. "I know you should." She grinned and took Hannah at the elbow, head inclined. "The shops are just opening. Why don't we enjoy a bit of dallying before you return? You must be in need of some soaps and a ribbon for your hair."

Lip between her teeth, Hannah ruminated. "I should go back. 'Tis a wonder Joseph hasn't come after me, and if I am out any longer..."

"Nonsense." Caroline put a finger to her mouth. "If we escape out the back door, my family will be none the wiser."

The way her cousin's eyebrows pinched upward in the center, her lips splayed out in a silent plea, made a reluctant giggle bounce its way up Hannah's throat. "Very well." She whispered the last. "But I must leave no later than two in the afternoon. I wrote them I would be home before supper."

"Not to worry." Caroline gave Hannah's arm a squeeze, then reached for the door, her voice merry as birdsong. "You shall leave long before then."

The short ride into town was made shorter still by the thrashing anxiety in Joseph's limbs. Higley had said naught, his angular jaw firm as an iron bar.

Higley slowed and angled his horse toward a two-story house at the edge of town and dismounted just as Joseph rode up alongside. Once on the ground, Anvil securely tied, Joseph stepped beside the man whose taciturn and evasive communications made the hairs on Joseph's neck stand rigid.

Voice taut, Higley leaned slightly toward him as he neared the door. "Speak not unless you are spoken to."

Joseph nodded, praying they wouldn't speak to him at all—and that God would hedge up the way of their enemies, allowing him and poor Willis a chance to go free.

Higley entered first, striding in with bold steps. Joseph matched the man's confidence, though his legs battled between strength and weakness. This could be a trap.

The conversation was fully underway. Pitman's slender face was scarlet as his coat. Stockton stood in the far right corner, arms crossed and eyes digging bayonets into Willis's chest. Bound and bruised, Willis sat motionless in a chair in the center of the room. Reece stood at attention in the opposite corner, and several other soldiers dotted the small room, but 'twas more intimate and informal an affair than Joseph had expected. Most likely they wished to keep this from gaining public knowledge.

The two majors looked up as they entered, expressions sharp as a blade's edge.

Pitman motioned with only the movement of his eyes for Higley to take Joseph to the back corner of the room. Higley strode to the rear, and Joseph followed, heightening all his senses. If he were to be attacked, apprehended, there would be no way to fight his way free.

"I am slow to believe a common colonial in place of one of my men." Pitman growled, indignation rumbling through the room. "Such a claim is not to be taken lightly, Plains."

Willis swallowed, his voice raspy, a sign he had likely been held at the throat, or worse, when captured. "I did not exchange letters with anyone, sir."

"You would like me to believe that Private Graves would fabricate such a story?"

"No, sir. But if you would let me explain—"

He coughed and swallowed again, the grimace on his face making Joseph's anger boil. They'd beaten him, 'twas more obvious all the time. Joseph knew that type of pain, and it burned him to the center to think these men had done it to such a man.

"You know we have been searching for an informant." Pitman didn't move, but his voice loomed through the room like a lion ready to pounce. "And now, I believe we may have found him."

Willis shook his head. "'Tis not I, sir. I give you my word. I was only—"

"Ha!" Stockton strode forward, his face scrunched with hatred. "What man goes about after dark for a secretive rendezvous with another man?" He placed his hand on the back of Willis's chair. "You haven't any wife. Perhaps...perhaps you are *that* kind of man."

Willis jutted his chin. "I *had* a wife. You know that!"

"Your word means nothing now, Plains." Stockton released his hold but still strangled the man with his eyes. "Everything you have said, everything you have done, is a lie. You are a Patriot and a spy." He turned to Pitman, voice cutting through the walls. "He deserves the noose, and now!"

Pitman's jaw moved back and forth, his own gaze unwavering from the man in front of him as he spoke to Joseph. "Mr. Young, come forward."

Joseph flung a quick glance to Higley, sure at any moment he would reveal his true name. Yet there seemed to be confidence in the man's eyes, almost encouragement. Hurling aside the rest of his blithering fears, Joseph stepped past the soldier in front of him and stood beside Willis.

Arms firm at his sides, he stood tall, gaze direct but humble, waiting to be spoken to before he opened his mouth. *Lord, fill my mind with what thou would have me say.*

Pitman sighed and stepped back, allowing Stockton to take his place in the forefront.

Boots clomping against the wood floor, Stockton took his place in front of Joseph, his sour breath searing past Joseph's nose. "Tell me again about your encounter yesterday with Mr. Plains."

"My cousin and I arrived just before noon." He met Stockton's pointed look with one of his own before glancing past Stockton's shoulder to Pitman. "He greeted us warmly and invited us in."

He stopped, the still, piercing voice of Providence trickling through his mind. The thought was quick and clear, and Joseph didn't allow himself even a second to question it before he gave it voice. "We spoke only of the work, and he showed us the stash of weapons and lead beneath the floorboards of his parlor. He said my barrels were satisfactory, and we went on our way."

Stockton's brow folded as he turned to question the soldier nearest the door. "Was there such a secretive stash when you searched the place?"

The man shook his head. "No, sir. We saw nothing."

Whirling back around, Stockton hurled a bone-crushing look to Willis, then Joseph. "Explain."

Joseph's heart crashed again and again into his ribs, though he restrained his voice, maintaining its calm. "Did your man pull back the rug? A hatch is underneath the rug in the center of the room, in front of the fireplace." He paused, examining Stockton's facial response before he continued. "Willis claimed the Patriots often suspect him, and he feared the stash being taken. Thus, he built a cellar for this purpose."

Stockton tossed a questioning look to the soldier behind Joseph. "Well? You said you checked the entire house. I assume you found such a stash."

The man cleared his throat. "Uh...we did not look there, sir."

"You did not?" Pretended kindness infused Stockton's sound, heavy mockery in his understanding expression. "Well, 'tis difficult, I suppose, for one so daft to neglect such simple orders." In a breath the act was gone and madness gripped his voice and stance. "Get out, Private Graves. I will deal with you later."

The soldier turned and stepped out the door. Stockton neared Joseph, his face only inches away. "Why would a man hide guns in his floor if not to evade our notice? Is he really so afraid of a few farmers? I don't believe it."

Muscles solid, Joseph eased his fingers that wished to curl, his volume that wished to rise. "If I may speak freely, sir."

With a hard, hot breath, Stockton circled round, responding in favor with the quick raising and lowering of his hand.

"As I stated, and is true, Plains is often questioned by those in town." The answer came to him one word at a time, and whether it be true or fabricated, he didn't know and could not care, only that it would be believed. "Storing such munitions in plain sight would be foolhardy and would invite far too many questions. You've asked him to store for you—what else is he to do? If the Patriots knew of the cache, they of course would seize it. If your soldiers knew of it, is it not likely they would reveal what they know in town where some active Patriot might overhear them?" Joseph's chest pumped, his breath heavy and quick. "You have taken him in wrongfully."

Stockton flicked his head around, brow so hard he could have cracked the wall behind him. "You would speak to me in such a way?"

Alive with rage, Joseph's boldness swerved past the fear that should have been his safety. "I am interested in baring the truth, not in how you might interpret it."

Pivoting back to Pitman, Stockton kept his arms crossed. "What say you?"

Expressionless as always, Pitman didn't move. His eyes alone were blinking, his mind clearly sifting through the information, studying it over and under, backward and front.

"Will you show us this stash?" Pitman's sudden question was directed to Joseph.

He nodded, stomach making rotations, turning slowly into solid stone. "Aye, sir." He could only pray to heaven that the guns were still there and had not somehow been moved without his knowledge. "I am ready anytime."

"Good." Pitman flicked a wrist to the soldier beside the door, then to the other in front of Higley. "You two, ready our mounts."

They nodded and strode out, leaving only the five of them in the too-warm room.

Stockton neared Joseph, resting a hand on his shoulder, his conversation friendly and familiar, a dark contrast to his declaration. "If we find you have lied to us..." He patted Joseph on the shoulder with a smile. "I fear I shall have some terrible news to relate to your cousin come sundown."

Mouth stretched in a most unsettling smile, Stockton started for the door.

Pitman motioned to Higley, who came to take charge of Willis. Standing, the man limped past, and Joseph stilled, clutched by his powerful stare. In the dark centers of Willis's eyes, past the bruises and the sheen of the unknown, was courage—an unearthly fearlessness that flashed and exploded, hitting Joseph square in the chest, and his muscles seized.

No matter what happened, their fight was not over. Nay, 'twas only just beginning.

Chapter Twenty-Four

Arm in arm, Hannah tugged Caroline out of the warm lavender-scented shop, spirit bright, shoulders stripped of the burdens that weighted her, at least for the moment.

"I must be on my way." She spoke the words but didn't feel them.

"Are you sure you cannot stay a half hour longer?" Caroline's pleadings had taken Hannah's short stay far beyond her allotted time.

She glanced at the sky and squinted. Indeed it must be nearing supper. Good heavens. She should go before darkness sifted its gray over the road. Caroline pleaded with wide eyes as Hannah attempted to navigate the turmoil that raged like a foaming sea. She didn't want to go back, and yet she did. There her heart nested, and not only because 'twas Eaton Hill.

Hannah groaned aloud, the weight of her quandary halting her feet. "Oh, Caroline, I must go. I have stayed too long already."

Her cousin swirled to face her, holding Hannah at the elbows. "Did you not say you were to attend a ball? Have you what you shall wear? You cannot go in just any gown—"

Hannah shook her head, a wry grin tugging at her lips. She sidestepped her cousin, pulling her to follow. "Even if I wished a new gown, I haven't coin enough to purchase one or time enough to make one." A feathery memory of the gown she'd seen in Duxbury tickled her mind, but with a shake of her head, it blew away. "Nay, I am content with this bit of ribbon for my hair—your graciousness in purchasing it for me shall not be forgotten."

Caroline tried to protest, but Hannah spoke over her playful pleadings with a light chuckle. "In truth, I must be on my way."

Lips scrunched and twisted, Caroline's pert expression made a smile form on Hannah's face.

Sighing, Caroline shrugged and continued walking in the direction they'd been heading. "This way is home then, so we shall continue—but do not look ill upon me if I cannot resist pulling you aside for another glance in the shoemaker's shop. I hear they've a lovely new pair of red shoes. Have you not always wanted a red pair?"

Grinning, Hannah hugged her cousin closer, wishing with all her soul she would not have to say farewell to such a friend.

They reached the corner where the shoemaker's shingle reached out, iced in place by winter's bony fingers. They hurried across the street, and Hannah gasped at the figure walking opposite them on the other side of the road.

Caroline followed her vision and sighed, her shoulders visibly drooping as much as Hannah's. "That man looks so much like your father."

Hannah swallowed and kept on, stopping in front of the window. "I fear seeing him again. Though I know I will..." She allowed both her words and thoughts to fall away.

Taking her hand, Caroline offered comfort in the softening of her eyes. "I know you wish things to be mended."

Would they ever? "I must place my heart only upon things I can control, I suppose. And leave the rest to Providence."

"You *can* control what you wear to the ball."

The sudden change of subject made Hannah smile once more. "You are more eager for that night than I am."

"I cannot understand why." Caroline's eyes went wide and playful. "You will look so utterly breathtaking—you shall steal every attention in the room." She looked forward, chin slanting up. "As I cannot go myself, I shall require you to inform me of every detail to exactness."

Hannah laughed through closed lips, forcing her reluctant feet to begin walking again. "That I will be most happy to relate, though I doubt I shall steal every attention in the room. I am hardly beautiful, and certainly not as young as I used to be."

With a gasp, Caroline stopped midstep. "If you believe that, you are hysterically mistaken." She must have sensed the demand in Hannah's stare not to argue the point any longer, so she continued walking again, not speaking until a mother and child darted into the cooper shop beside them. "It matters not what you think, for I know it to be true, and without question Joseph will think you the loveliest woman in the world. This I *know*."

Swept away by the thought, Hannah allowed her girlish imagination to tug her to the future. Would he think her lovely? Would he stare overlong and offer that bewitching half smile she loved so well?

"Caroline, there you are!" A woman approached them in the street, her arms laden with a full basket of fabric. "I have been in search of you."

Chirping with delight, Caroline turned toward the voice. "Anna, how good to see you."

The two shared a quick embrace before Caroline swung aside. "Anna, allow me to introduce to you my dear cousin Hannah Young. Hannah, this is Mrs. Anna Donaldson."

Donaldson? She couldn't be the wife of the man she'd met in camp, could she? Captain Donaldson's wife?

Hannah grinned, struck by the woman's unbound beauty. "'Tis a pleasure to meet you, Mrs. Donaldson."

"Such a beautiful name you have. And please, you must call me Anna." The lovely woman lowered her chin, her striking pale eyes beaming with warmth belying their color. She shifted the basket and rested a hand on the slight swell of her belly. "How good it is to meet you. Are you visiting? I have not seen you in town before."

"I am just leaving, in fact. I must return to Plymouth before dark."

"My goodness, you did not travel alone, I trust?"

The polite question niggled against her already sore conscience. "'Tis not so very far."

"Well, I hope you will travel safely. And do come back. I should be glad to get to know you better."

Such sincerity from a stranger? Light beamed from the inside out. "I should like that very much indeed."

Perhaps leaving Eaton Hill would not be so terrible. Her father might be here, but with such good friends to be had? She might find the distraction was just what she needed.

Anna moved her attention to Caroline, voice slightly more somber. "I must speak with you. Do you have a moment? I shan't keep you long."

Caroline glanced to Hannah, and she immediately insisted. "Oh, please. Take what time you need."

Turning around to allow the women privacy in what they spoke, Hannah focused on the street and shops behind her. Sandwich had changed little in the ten years she'd been gone. The print shop was new, but the rest seemed almost as she'd left it.

Absentmindedly, she strode a few paces away, looking into the window of the shoemaker's at that lovely red pair of shoes Caroline went on about. A movement inside caught her attention, and she glanced up, her spine instantly rigid.

Lungs refusing to take air, Hannah's fears careened down the slope of her already banked emotions. She would know that profile anywhere, with or without the red coat.

Greene.

Had he seen her? *Lord, no.* He seemed so interested in the conversation with another soldier and the shop owner, perhaps he hadn't.

Her pulse raged, and she took a step back when he turned and stopped, just as abrupt as she had, his glare crashing through the glass.

Racing away from the door, she grabbed Caroline at the arm. "I need to go."

Both women must have seen the way her blood drained from her head, the dizziness almost stealing her balance.

Caroline stilled, voice thin. "Of course." She nodded to her friend in parting and grabbed Hannah by the arm, racing around the first corner, stealing home the back way through the wood.

Not stopping for breath, they reached Caroline's house in a handful of minutes.

Gasping, Caroline spoke before Hannah did. "What happened?"

Hannah pressed a hand to her chest, unable to speak until she'd gained more of her breath. "I think I was seen."

"By whom?"

Dear God, what had she done? She froze, unable to answer. The foolishness of her actions bit her skin like the end of a snapped whip. If she were caught, Joseph might be discovered as well...

"Hannah." Caroline shook her at the shoulders, her attentive, wise eyes pouring strength into Hannah's empty vessel. "Are you sure? Perhaps 'twas just a trick of the glass. I heard no footsteps behind us."

That meant little. The man was wily, tenacious. Murderous.

Her mind refused to calm. "I don't know. It seemed as if he looked directly at me."

"I pray he did not." Again, Caroline tried to persuade her. "Should you not stay here? At least until tomorrow. Perhaps—"

"Nay." Hannah glanced around, her foolishness in staying overlong berating what bliss she'd enjoyed. "I must get back as soon as possible. If I do not, I fear

Joseph will come searching for me." Her mind shook, winds of fear and foolishness stripping bare her former strength. "I..." Shaking her head, she hurried to the barn for her horse. "I must go."

Caroline followed after her. "Hannah, please. 'Tis unwise to—"

"All I have done these past days is unwise." The bitter truth assailed her as she secured her saddle and mounted. "Pray for me."

Her cousin's solemn expression voiced so much in a single look. Worry, hope, love. She reached for Hannah's hand and squeezed, her throat bobbing, as if she restrained the emotions that etched her face, before pulling back and smacking the horse on the rump with a loud "yaw."

Hannah gripped the reins, darting down the back road toward home, praying as she had never prayed before.

Chapter Twenty-Five

Joseph rocked back and forth with Anvil's leisurely pace, straining not to reveal how the plague of anxiety stung him. He wanted to race home, find if Hannah had yet returned or was still in Sandwich. But his companion seemed none too concerned about their lack of speed.

Glancing to Higley, who rode beside him, Joseph pondered the man who'd been his companion since before the sun had fully risen. Joseph released a heavy breath. It seemed more like ten days than ten hours since they'd left Eaton Hill. Since then they'd been to Plymouth and Duxbury, at last to return when the sun was bidding a reluctant farewell, the pale sky deepening to a striking indigo.

Weary to the bone, he shifted in his saddle, the creak of the leather the only sound other than the soft clip-clop of the horses' hooves on the frozen ground. Thank the Lord they were now only a few miles from home.

"'Tis good Major Stockton chose to stay behind, clean up the rest of the mess." Higley's tone was easy, relaxed. "To own the truth, I can scarce believe the outcome."

Joseph turned his head toward Higley. The sudden and surprising confession from one so silent begged for more. "Aye?"

Higley's shoulder's dropped, and he sighed, rubbing the scar on his ear as if it still pained him. "I was certain we would witness a hanging."

"As was I." He spied the man, allowing his deeper thoughts to feel the air. "Major Pitman showed more leniency than I might have imagined."

"Aye. He's desperate to find the informant, but I have a feeling the man will never be found."

"So this man is...sharing information with the Patriots?"

Head bowed, Higley looked at the reins in his hand, then back up. "We know little. Except that certain of our information has in fact ended up in the hands of Washington. Exactly what or how much is unclear, but they know our movements." He looked to Joseph. "'Tis owed to you that Willis is still alive. Spying is not taken lightly."

Joseph's chest went tight. "If the guns had not been there, I am sure both Willis and I would have felt the bitter end of a rope."

The look Higley threw was sharp as steel. "If the guns had not been there, nor your story so convincing, I fear you would have suffered more than a sudden drop."

Scowling at the thought, Joseph stared forward to the vacant road, trying to lure his worries away from the one person they seemed ever eager to encompass. He wondered, not for the first time, what would have happened to Hannah if indeed he'd been taken...tortured...killed. Would they have done the same to her as well?

Higley rested both hands on the front of his saddle, his expression and statement comfortable. "You are brave to do what you do."

Did he really mean what Joseph thought he did? He couldn't. But Higley's words were so pointed it seemed there was something hidden behind their casual sound. Joseph's muscles turned rocklike, his jaw locking. Giving Higley no more than a cursory glance, Joseph kept his torso forward, his voice mute. Surely he didn't.

Higley went on as if Joseph had invited more conversation instead of trying to silence it. "I admire you—and your cousin. There is much to be feared, but that seems to not deter either of you."

Pressing on the stirrups, Joseph moved backward on his seat, pretending composure despite his piling suspicions. "Should not a man—or woman—do their duty despite the risks? Taking on such work is what Hannah and I wanted. The king must be defended, and I can only say I am glad we are believed. For as Willis knows too well, there is much of lies about, much of secrecy."

Higley pulled his lip between his teeth, his horse tugging at the reins, as if she wished to move faster. "I do hope you will be careful. Both of you."

Joseph shrugged the comment away. "We shall do our best, but there is little to fear from one's friends."

"Stockton is not your friend." Higley's voice became sharp as an icy barb. "You know not with whom you trifle."

He pulled his horse to a stop, and Joseph did the same, his skin bepricked with retained panic. His voice refused to work, his glare speaking loud enough to scrape the bark from the trees. "I'm sure I don't know what you mean."

"Nay, you do not." Higley answered in the kind of whisper that could crack iron. "He was prepared to have a woman hanged not five months ago. If not for Donaldson and Smith's intervention, he would have taken her life without a thought."

The blood drained from Joseph's head. Why had Nathaniel not said something of this? Why had not Donaldson? Confusion and fear plaited down his back.

Higley went on. "Do not suppose that his attraction to Hannah will make him any less likely to hang her should she be discovered."

Joseph swallowed, attempting to lubricate his suddenly hoarse voice. "Discovered? What are you speaking of?"

Anvil could sense the rising tension. He sidestepped, shaking his head and grunting, but Joseph could do naught to calm him, for his own anxieties were cinching around his throat.

The next Higley spoke seemed unreal, as if said from afar. "I know what you do and who you are— both of you. But how I know, I cannot reveal." Higley brought his mount as near to Anvil as he could. "If you do not use everything within your power to remain covert, you will be discovered and you will be killed."

Body numb, Joseph stared, struggling to read the man's hard expression. "You cannot be serious."

Higley's expression clutched Joseph at the chest like a vice.

"If you truly love her, you will get her as far from here as possible, as soon as you can."

A wintery breeze iced through him. There were too many revelations in Higley's words to settle on one. They flew around him like snowflakes on a circling wind. Who was this man, and how in heaven's name did he know so much?

More, how did he know Joseph loved Hannah when he wasn't prepared to admit such a thing himself?

Joseph sidestepped the swirling questions to face the one most glaring, no longer attempting to ignore the obvious. "What of Stockton? Will not he go after her—us—once we have fled?"

"If you leave now, you may have a chance." Higley looked up the road, then back the way they'd come and kicked his horse to move again.

Joseph followed.

"Once they discover your involvement, his shame will be revealed to all—that he trusted the enemy with secrets he should not have. He will not rest until you are found."

"You speak of the enemy, but do so as if I am not one."

Higley's jaw ticked. "What you are to *them* is what should most concern you."

Still, the man would be so secretive? So much information offered, but so little declared.

Joseph gnawed the inside of his lip, heart racing at a speed he hadn't known, filling his muscles with blood and resolve. "We shall make the decision we believe best." If Higley would be cryptic, so would Joseph. "I thank you for your warning. It is duly noted."

Nodding, Higley glanced away, visibly displeased with the reply. He motioned to the split in the road. "This is where I leave you."

Joseph tipped his hat, allowing them to part before he stalled, calling after Higley, freeing the question that burned a path through his chest. "Captain. How know you I love her?"

"It lives in your eyes." Higley inclined his head, a smile ever so slight. "Take care. I doubt you will be able to conceal it much longer."

With that, Higley pulled his horse around and charged into the darkened road, leaving Joseph's shredded disguise to fall to pieces around him.

Dear Lord. He was surely not that transparent, was he?

Anvil grunted and nudged his head toward home. Joseph tapped him to a run. He had much to tell, much also to conceal. Hannah should not learn of Higley's knowledge of them. 'Twould cause too much alarm, and she dealt enough with burgeoning anxieties.

His pulse charged. Hannah had best be home. If she was not...he would make sure she never left the house without him again.

Despite the biting cold and the way her breath froze on the air with every exhale, Hannah's body pumped with heat. She rode into the yard, slowing her mount to a trot, startled at the darkness of the house. No lamps or candles flickered in the windows. Though the sky had yet to wrap fully in black, she knew naught could be seen in the house without the aid of a flame. Was no one home?

Limbs buzzing, unease afresh in her veins, she pulled to a halt and slid to the ground. Racing to the door, she flung it open, shoving aside the childish fear that some unseen ill awaited her in the shadows.

"Joseph?" Her voice echoed through the vacant room.

Blackness spilled through the parlor like ink across a table, pooling in the corners. She fumbled to light the candle at the table beside the door, only fully breathing when its yellow glow offered a pale flickering through the room.

"Joseph?" She closed and latched the door, unable to smooth away the ripples in her voice. "Joseph, are you here?"

Hannah darted through the parlor to the kitchen, and alarm raised the tiny hairs at her neck. The entire house appeared untouched. Even the biscuits she'd placed in the basket that morning were as she'd left them. But the note was missing.

She spun back around, looking toward Stockton's room and called for him, but again silence mocked her. Panic increased the pace of her lungs. No one was here. She peered through the window toward the foundry, which looked equally abandoned. Her hands began to slick with sweat on the swooped handle of the candlestick.

The stale scent of the neglected fire brought to mind a hundred frightful scenarios. She grabbed her petticoat and raced up the stairs to check the rooms and nearly choked with despair as another, more frightening thought cut her at the knees. Perhaps

Joseph had been discovered? Perhaps even now he was—

The sound of an approaching horse snapped her thought in two, destroying her composure. *Greene.*

Within seconds the handle of the door jostled, light at first, then after a pause, violently, followed by a hard pounding. She held her breath, a stream of prayers rising to the heavens as she stared at the door. There was no place to run, no place to find safety.

The pounding persisted. "Hannah? Hannah, are you there? Let me in."

"Joseph?" Fragile and fractured, the voice that left her barely reached beyond the first step.

She flew down the stairs and placed the candle on the table. Unlatching the door, she hurled it open and gasped as relief stole her strength at the sight of his tall silhouetted frame.

Pressing a hand to her chest, she stepped back to allow him in, trying to rein in her runaway pulse. "I'd feared you'd been taken." The confession blurted from her mouth, sounding far more self-serving than she'd wished.

"You feared *I'd* been taken?" He entered, stare trained upon her, boots stomping against the floor. His height seemed even taller as he stopped inside. Candlelight shadowed the angles of his jaw, the downward arch of his nose.

Little compassion laced his words. Instead, his own relief was speckled with frustration. "What in God's name were you thinking?" He entered the rest of the way and closed the door with a gruff motion. Leaving one hand upon the wood, he pointed with the other in the direction of Sandwich. "Traveling such a distance? Have you gone mad?"

Pride all but shattered, her attempt at valiance in the face of her failing was futile. She stepped into the parlor, unable to answer, her frame trembling more as the walls of her carefully constructed calm began to crumble in large chunks. What had she been thinking? She couldn't speak it aloud. Would he believe her even if she did?

The flameless hearth cried mournfully for heat, and she went to oblige—more to ease her own need for occupation than anything else. She couldn't long stand motionless, or she might give in to the need to spin back and put her arms around him, tell him all she'd rehearsed those twenty miles home—how she'd wished things would have been different, how she had never stopped thinking of him. Tell him of their child.

"Hannah." Joseph's firm timbre stopped her midstep.

She needn't turn to know his face was etched with questions, lined with the same vexation that knit his voice.

"Why would you do that? Why would you leave? You cannot be so ignorant of the danger. 'Twas foolish."

Gripping her from behind, his tone knocked free the last stone of her hiding place, leaving exposed every piece of her.

"Did you not remember what happened with Greene?"

She grappled for strength. "I needed to speak with Caroline."

"About what? What was so urgent that could not wait?" His boots stomped behind her. "Heavens, woman, our people are at war. You and I are working toward something far greater than ourselves. We cannot—"

"I went to talk about you!" Chin quivering, she circled back, a flood of long-concealed hurts consuming her as they unwillingly spilled from her heart to her lips. "For years I have endured this pressing on my heart, and with you now here to make my pains even greater, I was desperate."

His head jerked back, as if her words had struck him. "Your pains?" His throat bobbed, but he didn't speak. His jaw ticked, but he didn't move. The blueness of his eyes faded in the wan light of the solitary candle. "Tell me how I have grieved you, so I may find a remedy."

Spurred by his humble petition, Hannah trembled all the more, the rest of her splintered soul willing her at last to pull free the shards of hurt and reveal what she'd harbored so many years. But she could not, the familiar agony of her prison more inviting than the unknown.

She moved to the fire, but his voice reached out to grab her as real as a grip on her arm.

"If you wish to leave Eaton Hill...I will not stop you. In truth, you must leave as quickly as you can." He stepped forward and tugged her to face him, his expression tender, pleading. "I have learned more of Stockton's nature, and I will not have you here a day longer."

Unsettled by how the closeness of him weakened her knees when it should rally her hurts to anger, Hannah swallowed to moisten her parched throat and covered the past she'd been so near to revealing. "I cannot leave. Not yet. You say you do not wish Stockton near me, but if I do not attend the ball, I fear his suspicions will be even greater. I owe Ensign this."

"Stockton planned to have a woman hanged, and I refuse to submit you to this any longer." He paused, his chest rising. "Higley petitioned me to take you away."

"Take me away? Does he think Stockton will do me harm? I do not believe it."

His gaze roamed her face, his fingers light at her sleeve. "Once it is discovered we have betrayed him, he will stop at nothing until we are killed." His dark brow dipped. "I could not live with myself if anything were to happen to you."

Joseph's rich voice and the tenderness in his firm touch began to undo her. She moved her arm free from his grasp but hadn't the strength to do the same with her gaze. "What of Eaton Hill? What is to become of it?"

He paused, the question reaching his eyes before it reached his mouth. "You said you would not return."

Hannah looked away. Aye. A vow spoken in a moment of feminine hurt. But did she feel the same now? Of a sudden, the question blurted raw and ugly from her lips. "Why did you not tell me you bought Eaton Hill?"

Joseph's expression went flat. "Hannah, I—"

"Why would you purchase this very land if you didn't want me to know it?"

"I didn't want you to think I'd done it only to be close to you—"

"You don't want to be close to me."

He raised his hand, irritation crouching his posture. "I didn't say that."

"You wanted to make us think you were fine with us staying when you were simply waiting for the right time to let us go?"

He stormed forward, inches from her. "I made a decision for my future, and you happened to once again be a part of it."

"Once again?" Bitterness chirped free. "I was never part of your future."

Towering above her, his timbre throbbed with aching. "You were *everything* to me."

Grabbing for her waist, he pulled her against him and covered her mouth with his. The room dispelled, his hot mouth and strong hands consuming every sensation. She should push him away, not give in to this longing, but she was helpless as the years of wishing and wanting commanded more than she could resist. His lips toyed with hers, begging them open, and she complied, wrapping her arms around his back. Moaning, he knit his fingers through her hair, cupping and angling her face to more fully expose her mouth. She succumbed, rising on her toes to press even closer, her own hands kneading the firm muscles of his back. Never could she have imagined such a moment, though she'd dreamed of it endless times. Never until now did she truly know how desperately she wished to be his wife, as she always had.

Almost as if she had whispered the wish against his lips, he trailed kisses to her ear, his warm breath tingling across her skin. "Marry me."

Light of breath, knees weak, she rested her forehead against his, willing him to speak the words over and over, that their mellifluous sound would drown away the discordant voice of the past. *He isn't the marrying kind.*

Hands still in his hair, bodies still close, she whispered back. "Why?"

His tender words dusted her skin like a soft touch. "My heart has never stopped aching for you." His lips brushed atop hers again, soft and hungry. "Whatever has happened between us, whatever has kept us apart, matters little when our hearts still beat as one."

Hannah stilled, the gross sorrow of her secret looming like a dark spirit. "Joseph..."

Hands gently cupping her head, he brushed his thumb against her cheek. "Say yes."

She closed her eyes, praying God would give her strength it seemed her body hadn't of its own. "There's something I—"

The sound of an approaching rider tapped lightly against the door, and she pushed free from his arms. The same panic rimmed his gaze. Her hair was mussed, her lips red. If Stockton saw them...

Not waiting another moment, she raced up the stairs and into her room, closing the door only seconds before Stockton burst into the room.

Back against the door, Hannah pressed a hand to her constricting chest, listening to the muted voices of the men volley quietly back and forth belowstairs. Two steps forward and she collapsed on the bed, the humming of her soul still heating her body.

Joseph's words curled before her like gold-dusted lettering. *Whatever has kept us apart matters little when our hearts still beat as one.*

Lies did not burn as hot as the truth. And here, in this moment, her heart was afire. She loved him more than she ever had. Mayhap, after all this time, at last she could have the life with him she'd always wanted. He cared for her—she knew it. But then...mayhap he would leave her again?

Yet, somehow the thought didn't curb her longing. Nay. In truth, she would prefer a life of pain in want of him rather than ignore the pleading of her heart. Perhaps 'twas time to trust again.

Chapter Twenty-Six

Sleep did not always beget peace, though Philo wished it. He stared at the blackness of the ceiling, willing his eyes to close and the hours to drown away the vision of Hannah's pain-filled expression, the sorrow in her voice. But the memory howled, long and lonesome. He sat up, the milky moonlight draping across his quilt. Rubbing his head, he picked apart all the reasons he'd acted toward her the way he had. Each action right, each choice just. So why did his conscience plague him like a possessed body, railing over and over that somehow he'd done wrong?

Grumbling, he threw off the quilt and tucked his feet into his slippers before pulling his banyan from the chair beside the bed and shrugging it on. Candle lit, he went belowstairs. Not to answer a hunger or ease a thirst as he might have done on nights before, but he must try something for his unsettled state, and tea might prove a remedy.

In the chilled kitchen he reached for a mug, unable to escape the memory of her words. *I am your daughter in little else than blood.* 'Twas true, but how could he have changed it? She had made her decision—she had gone against God and chosen Joseph and her need of the flesh over all else. Such was not to be borne from the daughter of a reverend.

He grabbed for a pitcher of water and prepared a stash of tea leaves. Even now she betrayed him, living with the very man who had taken from him all that should be his. The unease of his stomach began to abate even without the tea. Nay, he'd been right to speak to her thus, and she had been in the wrong. She had always been wrong.

The dim glimmer of the candle gifted only a slight halo, but somehow it seemed a light glowed in the parlor, illuminating the small wooden box atop the mantel. He knew what lay entombed inside, though it had been years since he had read it. Perhaps if he did now, 'twould ease his disquiet all the more.

He finished his descent to the darkened parlor and rested his companion of light on the space beside the box he loathed to touch, but must. The box was lighter than he'd remembered when he lifted it from its home. Top pulled free, he raised the letter from its coffin and returned the box to the mantel.

Candlelight gleaming over him, he swallowed and unfolded the paper that crackled and snapped with pleasure at being released from its prison. This one thing he had kept, and rightly so, never letting Hannah know of its existence. If any other of Joseph's letters had been secreted to her, he knew not, but Ensign's compunction for dishonesty made Philo believe his brother would have told him.

Almost as if the letters waved with pleasure at being read, Philo allowed his eyes to roam over the flowing script.

July 27, 1765

Dearest Hannah,

You must think me the vilest of men, as well you should. I cannot begin to wish for your forgiveness, though I would seek it endlessly. You are right to despise me, and if you truly desire never to see me again, I shall with full respect honor your wishes. However, I must in deep humility beg one last request from the depth of my heart that still bleeds from the loss of you. Do not doubt, my darling, how sincerely and most painfully I have loved you and how I will continue in such sweet agony until the day my spirit leaves this earth. Never shall I forget you, and never shall I forgive myself for the selfish and foolish actions of a lovesick boy. For if I had acted a man, I should have tread with tenderness, not lust. If I could take back that night, I would, only to offer you my love when we are first made one in the Lord.

If you can find the grace in your heart to forgive me ~ as I have petitioned Providence in His mercy to do ~ and to consent to be my wife, a thing which I have longed for since the day I first beheld your heavenly face, I would be your most humble servant the rest of my days and live every moment to bring a

smile to your heart, a heart that I know
and love even more than my own.
My darling, I shall always be yours.

Forever,
Joseph

Philo lowered his hand, staring off into the coal-black shadows of the parlor's sleeping corner. A strange disquiet rustled in his chest, but he slammed the emotion deep into the cellar of his heart. Nay, those were not the words of a man of repentance, no matter how sincere they seemed. Joseph had only written these flowery petitions in an attempt to soften Hannah's heart toward him. He wished again to take advantage of her and further soil her body and her name. A snarl ticked upward. And it seemed Joseph had done just that, despite Philo's efforts.

Snatching the candle, he lowered the corner of the letter into the flame and watched the hungry ribbons char the memory he should never have retained.

As he watched the paper curl and blacken, a light knock tapped at the door. Startled, he threw the piece inside the fireplace and looked up. He raised the candle to the clock on the mantel and squinted. 'Twas nearly two in the morning. Who called upon a preacher at such an ungodly hour?

The knock came again, and he neared his face to the door. "Who is it?"

"Reverend Young, 'tis I, Mrs. Smith. I've come for you urgently."

Mrs. Smith? The doctor's wife?

He yanked opened the door and took in her weary eyes, the bulge around her belly. Was she ill? "Dear woman, what brings you to call in the middle of the night?"

The grief in her face made him almost reach out to steady her as she clutched the shawl around her shoulders. "I have been sent to fetch you. You must come straight away."

She begged so emphatically he nearly raced out the door in his nightclothes. Stranded between thoughts, he gestured for her to enter. "Wait while I dress."

"No, sir. I must go." She stepped away. "Come to my home at the back. I shall let you in."

He nodded, and she hurried up the dark street. Worry snaked about his heels and up through his limbs. Philo raced to his room and dressed, snatching his Bible before he left, his stomach aching at the thought of who it was that she called him for.

Ready with coat, hat, and scarf, he left the house with lantern in hand, his legs aching to run but his bones too weary to comply.

Arriving only a few moments later, he knocked on the back door as instructed, his nerves a jumble. Though he didn't care for Joseph or his young ward, 'twas terrible to see a youngster go before his time. For surely who else would he be called to administer to?

The woman answered instantly, ushering him in. Candle in hand, she motioned to the stairs. "Follow me." She started, then stopped and turned, pinning him where he waited. "You are a man of God."

"Aye." He didn't know how to answer, for it seemed more an affirming statement than a question.

Licking her lips as if to allow her mind time to finish her thought, she breathed out slow but hard. "You must not speak of this to anyone. For his safety, as well as your own."

Dear God, did this woman hide a fugitive? She seemed ready to see him back out if he would not agree, so he obliged her with a curt nod. "I give you my word."

An abrupt about-face and she was at the stairs, taking them quickly for one so great with child. He stayed behind her, fear at the unknown weighing his steps.

The room was large, fully furnished but dark. The fire in the hearth at the far wall spewed an umber glow that failed to reach but half the room. Mrs. Smith turned at the head of the bed, voice pleading as much as her eyes as she handed him the candle.

"I will leave you now."

He followed her with his gaze as she descended just as quickly as she'd come up. Shaking his head, he turned back around to face the one who'd summoned him.

The sight impaled like a harpoon. *It couldn't be.*

His breathing went shallow. "Brother."

Upon the bed, Ensign looked already passed, his face ashen, eyes sunk away. If not for the wheezing of his breath, Philo would not have believed he lived.

Ensign rolled his head against the pillow, his raspy sound unearthly. "I am glad you have come."

"You are alive."

There was a deathly pause as he swallowed. "Disappointed?" A weak smile tugged at one side of his mouth. Even at death's door, his humor had not altogether been snuffed out.

Yet Philo didn't find the laughter in it. "The British told me you died."

He gave a weak cough. "They would have liked that." Finally raising his gaze to Philo's, Ensign's voice gained strength.

"What happened? Who brought you here?"

Pain scrolled across Ensign's face as his mouth contorted. "They were after Hannah." Groaning, he sighed through his words. "Where is she? Is she safe?"

Remnants of Philo's anger, his grief and shame flared to life, turning to ash any worry or lingering fear. "She is living with the man to whom you sold the foundry. If that is what you deem safe, than you and I have different understandings of the word."

Pressing out another weak breath, Ensign allowed his head to lie flat on the pillow, as if he could now die in peace. "Praise God. She lives."

"Why didn't you tell me?" Philo bypassed his brother's response. "Why did you sell to him?"

Blinking, Ensign tried to speak, but his voice became ever more hoarse. "'Tis God's doing more than mine. She loves Joseph, Philo. God will mend what has been broken."

So his brother would play both matchmaker and guardian, hmm? "I refuse it. I have always refused it, and you have always defied me, despite the fact that *I* am her father."

Ensign coughed again, this time violent, but the fit quickly calmed. Now when he spoke, he could hardly be heard. "Read me God's word before I pass."

"You will not die, Ensign." Philo spoke the words the dying wished to hear, though he didn't feel them.

More, because he wished not to open the book in his hand.

Philo rubbed his head, scrunching his eyes against the vision before him. How could this have happened? Ensign's death had meant his vindication. But this blinding discovery made all that impeded him crash upon his future yet again.

"Who brought you here?" The holes widened, clamoring to be filled. "There is much I must know."

"What does it matter if I am to die?"

"I would know the full depth of the dangers my child is amongst."

The sigh Ensign released was not simply a breath. 'Twas patience and reticence. More, 'twas the signal that his brother would speak nothing of what Philo wished him to say.

"Read to me, brother." The words hardly passed Ensign's lips, his eyes fully closed. "I must hear something of comfort before I go."

Comfort? What comfort was there to give? Between them both in the years since Hannah's betrayal, there had only been heartache and strain. Yet...beside all of that, Ensign still had called for him, still asked *him* to read from God's holy book. He, the woebegone preacher who shunned his own child for a life of loneliness and misery. Despite it all, Ensign would still make such an entreaty?

The thought, as if coughed free from his mind, allowed for a moment, a brighter, clearer vision—an illumination of something never before shaped in his mind. Had he been wrong and Ensign right? Could it be that all this time...with a blink he closed that light into the dark where it belonged. Nay. Ensign always wished to prove his worthiness above Philo's, even here. Even at his death. The benevolent elder brother taking pity on the younger in his last moments.

"Please." Ensign's pitiful sound lifted Philo's head. "Anything, please...I go quickly."

So benevolent to the last.

Philo took the chair Mrs. Smith had no doubt occupied in dutiful watch and put the candle on the table. He sat with a hard breath and opened the book. Brushing his finger down the page, he read the first passage he came to. "Hear me when I call, O God of my righteousness: thou hast enlarged me when I was in distress; have mercy upon me, and hear my prayer."

Psalms. Philo held his tongue between his teeth to keep from balking aloud. Of course God would have him open to such a verse. Where was God's love for *him*, hmm? Hadn't he suffered as well? He deserved a child who honored him, a brother who respected him—a God that would deliver him and grant him what he was owed.

Again he rubbed his head, wishing for the sleep that was forever out of reach. Wiping his hand down his face, Philo looked again to the book, another verse striking him as he read in silence. *Offer the sacrifices of righteousness, and put your trust in the Lord.* The truth beat his chest like a club. Hardly a verse could match his brother better.

Philo glanced up, looking at Ensign—what remained of him—when another verse brushed over him, coating his entire frame with its piercing whisper. *Greater love hath no man, than a man lay down his life for his friends.*

Such a fine prick, but it went deep, striking like a needle of ice to the very center of his heart. He stared forward, looking but not seeing when again that thought filled his soul. Could it be? Had he been thus blinded? But as it struck, the sensation melted, the heat of the past dissolving it to steam. Ensign was not so saintly.

Again he looked to the Bible, the last verse a hard slap to his pride. He read the words aloud as if God were forcing the sound from his throat. "I will both lay me down in peace and sleep: for thou, Lord, only makest me dwell in safety."

After a beat of silence, Ensign wheezed. "Thank you." He moved his hand across the bed. "You must tell Hannah I loved her, that I hope she will soon have the joy she seeks."

Philo's chest clenched. Such pretty words from a dying man. The sentiments sat uncomfortable in his belly, but he couldn't locate the source.

He shook his head. There were greater needs to focus upon, and he took the chance. Perhaps his brother would, in his last moments, in his weakness, give him what he desired if perhaps he showed even a shadow of penitence.

"Leave Eaton Hill to me, brother." He scooted closer to the bed. "I give you my word that I will work to mend what has been broken with Hannah. I shall try to be a better father. Let me, I beg of you, have care of the land, the foundry. She and I can care for it together."

Ensign swallowed, grimacing in pain. "She yearns for your love. But...there is much you do not know of her."

Patience, man. Philo took a breath to ease the rising tension with a painful humility. "True. It has been many years but—"

"She has lost a great deal."

Philo nodded, while inwardly he huffed. Lost? Her fine reputation, aye. Any favorable future she might have had, aye. But what else?

"Patience and love, Philo. Those virtues are the healers." Ensign's mouth hardly moved now. "You deserve peace as well, and I believe you may at last regain all that you have lost."

Pins dotted over Philo's skin. Where those words an indication that perhaps...he would finally say it? Would Ensign bequeath Eaton Hill to him after all this time? 'Twas so close Philo could feel it.

"Hannah needs you." Ensign wheezed. "We loved her as our own, Philo. 'Tis your turn now, to love her as well."

How dare he.

Philo shot to his feet, the rage he'd almost shunned in place of penitence securing his loathing. "You think yourself so far above me because she loves you in a way she doesn't love me."

Ensign coughed, grimacing in pain. "Your prison is a wretched one. Such pride and anger..."

Philo lifted the Bible in his hands. "He who casts the first stone, brother." He stepped back, rage fuming through his sleep-weary frame. "You must know, whether you live or die, my errand will not change. I will fight until my last breath for what should be mine."

Spinning on his heel, he turned to the door but stopped when Ensign's waning voice stalled him like threads of iron.

"Then pray I live. For if I die, I will be sure to haunt you."

Philo glanced over his shoulder, unsure whether to be amused. His brother's humor again? He hoped. Not that he believed in such things, but the mention of it made his skin writhe. He rubbed his head. Tomorrow eve was the ball, and that would make two nights without sleep. Though 'twas worth it. For the more he could be with Stockton, the more he could convince the man of his worthiness and that Eaton Hill must be his. He peered at his brother one last time.

If Ensign did die, and if he did choose to haunt him, at least he would haunt in a place worthy of it. Ensign would witness him living in happiness with the daughter who was truly his own. A thing the dead could never boast.

At that he grinned, welcoming the ball. It seemed, of a sudden, it couldn't come soon enough.

Chapter Twenty-Seven

Morning had come far too soon. Hannah pinned her hair back, shunning her obligatory cap. She leaned toward the mirror and smiled. Was it her imagination, or did her skin look brighter, younger? A trick of the sunrise, most like.

She glanced out the window at the blush of morning, the shimmer of the sun promising to crest the horizon in minutes. Smiling, Hannah placed the last pin in her hair. She should have been down long before now. But sleep had lulled her so temptingly, and her dreams had been so real she'd been loathe to open her eyes.

A noise from downstairs flicked her pulse.

Joseph.

Her chest fluttered as she rehearsed the beautiful words over again, pulling them as close as he had held her when they'd kissed. *Marry me.*

Hope was not a fragile candle's flame, easily snuffed out with the smallest breath. It burned sometimes forever. Mayhap this time she had little to worry over. He appeared so sincere, as if he truly wished it. Then again, he had before...

Hair in place, she slid open the drawer and brushed her fingers over the booties, but they cried for cradling, so she picked them up, stroking the soft yarn. And suddenly that hope dimmed as the memories fleshed to life. Though she would never repeat her actions, never again be with him till they married—*if* they married—that wouldn't stop her spirit from dying should Joseph repeat what he'd done before.

Whatever has kept us apart matters little when our hearts still beat as one.

She must hold on to his words—to his sincerity that she knew could not be feigned—despite the way the past hurts threatened to strangle. The booties grew heavy with their accompanying memories, and she replaced them, but not before the ring next called out to her like the bells of a chapel. When had she last slipped it on her finger? Years, at least. She glanced to the window, the light growing. The men must eat, and she must prepare the vittles. Morning would not wait for her daydreams to find a happy end.

But she could not resist. Gripping the primitive trinket between her finger and thumb, she slipped it on, wondering if Joseph even remembered making it for her. What would he think if he knew she still had it?

Another sound clanked from below, and she hurriedly removed the ring and rested it beside the booties. Pressing the drawer closed, she did the same with her eyes, praying God would grant her strength to move forward with her future. Strength to endure whatever He would give her.

A third time a sound echoed through the floorboards. Oh dear...perhaps 'twas not Joseph. Had

Stockton refused to wait for her and cooked his own food? He hadn't done that before.

Rushing downstairs to the kitchen, Hannah's skirts swished around her as she stopped hard in the doorway. The grin she felt over her face spread like sunshine. "Are you making turnovers?"

Joseph twisted toward her from his crouched position by the fire, the half smile on his face leaping to her across the room. "You are always cooking for others. I thought I should return the favor."

Hannah bit her lip at the endearing sight, reining back the need that made her want to rush forward and hug him from behind, kiss his cheek and ear. But that would have to wait until they were...

She started forward, leaving the thought behind, focusing instead on what sizzled over the fire. "Not turnovers, but eggs, I see."

He moved the pan to the cool stone and pushed up, brushing his hands against his thighs. "The chickens were good enough to lay a few. Surprising, but perhaps 'tis a good omen."

"Perhaps."

When he was slow to act at all familiar, her stomach churned. *'Tis your fault.* She'd set herself up for disappointment. Did she expect he would grab her and kiss her again? Stupid, childish wish. Of course he would not. Stockton was about and could enter any moment.

"Is Stockton here?"

Joseph glanced behind through the kitchen window. "He's in the foundry speaking to the men. 'Twould seem he and Higley have some business to discuss."

In a flash he spun around and grabbed her at the waist, tugging her firm against him, pressing his mouth brusque and then tender against hers.

Delight sprayed over her, and she returned his hunger before dread forced her to push away.

"Joseph, we cannot. We shall be seen." She tried to wriggle free, but his stone-hard muscles held her close.

Dusting light, warm kisses over her jaw, he nudged his nose into the curls at her ear, his voice a deep, tempting pool. "You never answered me."

"Answered you?"

He rested his forehead against hers and brushed his knuckles over her cheek. "Be my wife, that I may be your husband."

Hannah closed her eyes, savoring the moment, attaching to it all the little things—the scent of the breakfast he'd cooked, the quiet sound of his breath. The way the pink sunrise filtered through the window, the crack of the morning fire.

"Say it," he spoke, his lips above hers.

She whispered in kind. "I will."

He moved back, disbelief painting his face. His masculine smile burst wide, and he picked her up until her feet were fully off the ground. Suddenly, he stilled. "Why not today?" He set her down, solemn earnestness in the lines around his mouth. "Why must we wait? We've time."

"Today?" His eagerness nourished her own, but one of them must use sense. She placed a hand to his chest and pushed him away, failing to keep a grin from her mouth or her voice. "We haven't time. Tomorrow is soon enough, and even then we will not have waited for banns to be read."

Determined, hungry, playful, he kept his eyes on her. "There is plenty of time."

"Nay, there is not."

He reached for her. "There *is*."

She backed away, hand outstretched as she laughed. "Nay." Joseph lunged for her, and she batted his hand away. "Joseph!"

"Miss Young?"

All the air evaporated, and she whirled at the sound of her name to see Stockton standing inside the parlor. His set jaw and hard eyes made her stomach turn. How much had he seen?

She could feel the blood retreating from her head. Her hands went clammy, and she wiped them against her skirt. "Aye, sir?"

His expression morphed to a scowl as only his eyes went past her to Joseph, who stood behind. "Is everything all right?"

Clearing her throat, she moved toward Stockton, hoping he would take her approach as a boon to his ego. "I am glad to see you, sir. May I get you some breakfast?"

Stare unmoving like an aimed weapon, he answered her. "Nay, I thank you." Finally his eyes went to her. "But I'm in need of your help. I've a letter to dictate."

"Of course." Not looking back, she went straight to the desk, her side vision taking in the lancing glare that Stockton threw to Joseph.

Joseph spoke from the kitchen. "I shall see to the work in the foundry."

Silent, Stockton didn't move until Joseph exited and the kitchen door closed. "Miss Young, you look flushed. Are you sure you are well?"

She placed a hand at her cheek. Aye, she was flushed. More from panic than from anything else, though perhaps she could use this to her advantage. "Oh..." Sighing with a quick look over her shoulder, she shrugged. "I'm only overtired, I suppose."

The writing desk beckoned her to take refuge at its station, and she obliged, sitting quickly.

"The ball is this evening." Stockton stood directly behind her. "I should hate for you to be unable to attend."

There was too much truth in his words. Hannah twisted in her seat, feigning weariness. "My faculties will rally, I am sure."

He shook his head. "After this, I insist upon you resting."

"But, sir, the day has only just begun—"

"No arguments." His words edged with demand, his eyes with dominance. Had she missed that before? Nay, 'twas now only more clear because of what Joseph had told her last eve. Her spine cinched when he commanded the rest. "You will retire to your room the remainder of the day." He tried to ease the rising tension with a light sigh. "Besides, I know women take their toilette for fancy affairs as quite a ritual. I would not wish you to think I expect my clothes laundered on such a day."

She looked away, pulling a slip of paper from the drawer. "You are generous, Major."

"I am selfish." He chuckled to make light of words that she knew to be true. "I wish the woman on my arm to be at her best, for I daresay there shall be none in the room to match you."

Selfish indeed.

Leaping over the comment with naught but a civil glance across her shoulder, she dipped her quill in the inkwell. "Shall we begin?"

"Aye." He turned his back to her, his typical haughty stance pulling him rigid, his arms behind his back. "General Howe, I have received your report and concur with your assessment of the men, but must advise against your suggested advance on Dorchester Heights. Unless it can be done swiftly and before Washington is able to secure it, I believe such would likely be an inevitable and futile repeat of the disaster at Bunker Hill."

He stopped there, and she knew he peered at her from the way his shoes shifted over the floor. She scrambled to finish the rest, her heart thrashing behind her ribs. *Dorchester Heights?*

"Have you got it?"

She quickly scrolled the rest and dipped her quill again with a nod. "Aye, sir."

"Excellent." He shifted again and began to stroll around the room. "As requested, I will speak of this with Pitman and the others tonight, gain their approval, and prepare for engagement as soon as you require it, unless you find my recommendation agreeable and wish for us to further discuss such an action. Signed, etcetera."

Hannah's fingers trembled so much she could hardly finish the last without the quill quivering against the paper. At long last. This was the information they had been waiting for.

She dropped the quill in the well and lifted the paper, blowing the ink dry before handing it to him, praying he wouldn't notice the shaking of her hand.

In silence, he turned, his stare looking far too deep as it brushed down her frame. He took the paper from her hand. "Now, upstairs with you."

She swallowed, pretending to be humbled by his generosity instead of sickened by it. "You are most gracious. But I must plead to be allowed to finish my duties in the kitchen before I comply. I shall not be long." Injecting the sweetest sound to her voice and slanting her head just so, Hannah did her best to portray the feminine sweetness she believed he would be unable to decline.

As suspected, he could not. He grinned, admiration deepening the lines at his eyes. "Do what is required, but only that. We must be prepared to leave at four this afternoon. Mrs. Pitman should wish to see you from the start, I've no doubt." Her stomach sickened when that carnal look returned. "Until tonight."

Hannah nodded with a smile of her own. "Until tonight."

So much in so few words.

He hadn't any idea what tonight would bring. What tonight meant for the Patriots. What it meant for her. For Joseph. For their future.

In the foundry, the hammer seemed lighter in Joseph's hand as he pounded on the freshly heated iron. The memory of their kiss, of Hannah's smile as she accepted his proposal, of her fingers twined with his, imbibed him with strength.

"We are only five from our goal." He spoke to Sackett, who yanked on the bellows at the forge behind him. "I imagine we will be done before the ball. Will you be attending?"

'Twas Deane who laughed in response. "We don't go to such gatherings. We're as good as dross to them." He began banging his hammer, sparks flying. "You? I hear Miss Young is attending with Major Stockton."

"She is." A fact he still could not accept, but must. He lifted the glowing barrel and pounded its end on the anvil. "I've not been invited."

"Perhaps you will be."

Joseph looked up at the sound of Higley's voice as he entered. Nodding in greeting to the others, Higley stopped in front of Joseph, a paper in his outstretched hand. "This just came for you."

Clearly already read, Joseph took the note and brushed away the forming scowl with an inhale. Did this man really not harbor ill intentions? 'Twas too dangerous to suppose otherwise. Why else would Higley have read a missive meant for him? The only ones who knew he was even here were his friends in camp at Roxbury.

He moved to place the note in his pocket to read another time, but Higley stopped him. "Read it now. Perhaps 'tis urgent."

Fighting a questioning scowl, Joseph flipped it open and scanned the note penned in the familiar hand of Nathaniel.

> *Good day, old friend.*
> *I pray this note finds you blessed and*
> *well.*
> *I am writing to inform you that the*
> *wedding will go as planned, thanks to*

*your abundant generosity. We know you
will not be in attendance, but I could not
move forward without telling you that
your goodwill will not go unnoticed or
unappreciated.*

   *We shall think of you, as you surely
will think of us.*

   *Come again when you can. Salem is
solemn without you.*

Joseph folded the paper, smiling his thanks to Higley. Would to God the man hadn't deciphered the hidden message as easily as he had. The raid was on, as planned, and his friends were part of it. This was as much a note to relieve him and Hannah of their post as anything. After tonight they could leave without any lingering guilt that in fact the army might still need them, and it had taken far less than the two weeks allotted them. But he would not "come again." He had Hannah to care for. And Jacob. Though he wished to join his friends at arms, he must take them away and only return when the war was over—if it ended at all. He would never risk their lives knowing Stockton was anywhere near Eaton Hill.

Where would he take them? West? Virginia perhaps? Another thought gripped him at the heels. Hannah knew of Jacob. She must understand 'twould not be only the two of them. 'Twas such a natural inference, perhaps she would not...nay, she was the most loving woman he'd known. Surely she would welcome the thought of caring for the boy.

"All is well, I trust?" Higley's sudden question snapped Joseph back to the present.

"Uh...aye." He slipped the note into his pocket, then reached for the long barrel that needed another good heating. Shoving it into the coals, he reached for the bellows. "Family wedding. Seems I shall miss it."

"It seems you shall." Higley's jaw ticked, and his tone went dark. "Have you seen Lieutenant Greene?"

Joseph straightened. "Nay. Not since Stockton banished him to Sandwich. Why?"

Neck muscles tight, Higley swung a glance to the others before continuing. "One of my men tells me they saw him in town today."

"Today?"

"Aye, and I have a feeling he is wishing to prove himself, much like Stockton's son did. He doesn't like to be told he is wrong."

"Wrong about Hannah, you mean."

Higley nodded.

Joseph wiped a hand over his face and looked behind him to be sure the others were well occupied and hadn't stilled to listen in. Thankfully, they talked between themselves. Joseph turned back to Higley. Did Greene still think he could sway Stockton?

"You think he will try to come back?"

Higley threw a quick glance to the soldiers as Joseph had done and stepped closer, nearly whispering. "I suspect he will be about. Be careful."

He spoke of tonight—the drop he must make to Willis. Joseph only dipped his chin in acknowledgment. Why did this man seem so intent upon helping him? Was he not the enemy?

After a sigh, Higley began again, speaking of something different yet equally pressing. "She will need you there tonight."

The pronouncement made Joseph yank the bellows harder, the flames in the forge roaring. "If you think I will let her go alone, then you don't know me at all." He didn't speak again until Sackett spoke to Deane over the clanking of his hammer. "I shall follow and watch from outside. If I could attend, I would, but 'tis a private gathering. I've not had an invitation."

"But of course you have." Higley smacked him on the back, speaking so low the fire would be hard pressed to eavesdrop. "If anyone asks, I delivered an invitation to you in person." He looked behind, then continued. "Make the expected delivery and arrive after dinner. Your name will be on the list, and I daresay Stockton will be pleased to hear your report."

Could this man do that? "Who *are* you?" Joseph regretted the question as soon as it left him, but the curiosity was too much to retain.

There was a pause before his reply. "Just a soldier." Higley touched the end of his hat and signaled his departure to the others, his volume rising above the din. "Men."

They nodded in acknowledgment, more intent on their work than paying attention to anything else.

Joseph stared after Higley as he left, struggling to balance the questions atop the peaks of revelations that were glaringly few. Higley was a soldier, but not the kind Joseph knew. That kind would be more willing to aggrieve than assist. Where Higley...with all his secrets he was far too trustworthy to be seen as a mere Lobsterback.

Joseph breathed easier, hardly knowing he'd been so tense. God be praised for this cryptic stranger. Without him, he would have been forced to watch from afar, but now he could protect Hannah at her side.

He pulled hard on the bellows. Tonight it would be over. And tomorrow, they would at last, *at last*, be one.

Chapter Twenty-Eight

Pressing the needle up and down through the fabric was a pitiful occupation for one so rife with anxiety. Hannah glanced up, allowing an audible sigh to free some of her angst as she sat at the kitchen table. If Stockton returned to find her here instead of abed, she could plead his understanding that staying warm by the fire with easy occupation of her hands was rest enough. In truth, she had to find a way to keep her mind estranged from what ailed it.

The note she'd copied and folded sat like a brick in her pocket, so heavy she feared it would be seen bulging from the side of her skirt. The courier had taken the original hours ago, and she prayed once she gave this to Joseph and the Patriots received it, it would not be too late.

A knock on the front door spun her on her seat. Standing, she peered through the kitchen window to see who it was before she ventured to answer it.

'Twas Reece.

Hannah hurried to the door and opened it, balking in surprise at the large package in his hands. "Good afternoon, Reece. What brings you here?"

Those ruddy cheeks widened, and his eyes smiled. "You do, miss."

She laughed through her reply. "I?"

He extended the package to her with a polite bow. "A package for you. I was instructed to be sure it made it into your hands."

A package for her? Mouth open with happy surprise, Hannah took it. "Why, thank you."

Reece stepped back, his boyish expression genuine and innocent. "Of course, miss."

"Will you be attending the ball tonight?"

Grinning, he shook his head. "Nay, miss. 'Tis an affair for those higher in rank and status than I." Such a thing seemed not to dim his spirit. "Mrs. Pitman is known for throwing quite a party. I am sure you will have an enjoyable evening."

"I am sure I shall."

Too bad he would not attend. At least then perhaps Hannah might have someone with whom she would like to converse.

Hannah curtsied slightly, reaching for the door. "I thank you, Reece."

He touched the end of his hat. "Miss."

Turning, he started for the yard, and she closed the door.

A package. No one had ever given her anything like this before. Mouth twisting sideways, she pulled her lip between her teeth, examining the bundle in her hands. Of medium weight, the package was wrapped in simple brown paper, twine crisscrossing over the front and back. She lifted it up to see if a note was attached, but there was none she could detect. Suddenly realization poured like a crisp rain.

Caroline.

She must have sent a gown. Face blooming, Hannah released a joyous breath. Such a dear she was. Hannah couldn't curb her girlish enthusiasm and hurried abovestairs. Sitting on the bed, she untied the twine and unwrapped what she knew it must be. Folding the paper away like curtains to a spring garden, Hannah held her breath.

Oh dearest heaven.

A note rested atop the gift. A single small card bearing words she could hear as well as read. *For you, my darling.*

Hannah's breath stilled in awe. *My darling.* He hadn't called her that since...oh, how she'd missed the sound of the words.

Holding the cream gown up—the pink petticoat folded beneath and peeking hello—Hannah's eyes began to burn. When had he purchased it? Her throat ached. She didn't deserve him. How had she been so blessed to gain a second chance?

Like a cry from the past, the last untold secret wailed for revelation. She could hold it in no longer, and she put a hand to her head. *Lord, grant me the right moment to tell him, and swiftly. He must know before we speak vows.*

When surely the gift was intended to lift her spirits, it did the opposite. He gave her gifts and made her promises for the future, and she would give him the knowledge of something so mournful?

She laid the gown aside and went to the door, latching it shut before beginning to unfasten her bodice. Slipping it from her shoulders, she moved to the table and sat, staring blankly at her reflection in the mirror.

After tonight...if he would still have her, they would be one at last. Their lives joined as she had always wished.

After the ball. After the raid. After this final missive made it into the hands of the Patriots. Then they would be free. Where they would go, she knew and cared not, for *he* was her home.

She reached two fingers between her breasts and removed the message she'd copied.

Dorchester Heights.

Reading again the possible fate of her friends in Roxbury, Hannah shuddered. Washington must learn of this and take the hill as swiftly as he could. Another devastation like that at Bunker Hill would be unimaginable. But perhaps Washington had enough men—more than even Howe—and such an end could be averted.

Sighing out the storm, she replaced the note and reached for the pitcher, pouring the cool water into the basin atop her dressing table. The soaked cloth slicked over her skin as she began the process of cleaning, smoothing, brushing, curling. With help the task was difficult enough, but alone, 'twas nearly impossible.

The longer she toiled, the more her anxieties domed over her. What if the raid failed? What if *she* failed? She was supposed to keep Stockton well entertained, but could she? *Lord, be my guide, I pray thee.*

Dotting rosewater at her neck, she pinched her cheeks and pulled on her stockings, securing them with a ribbon above her knees. Hair artfully styled with two thick ringlets draping her neck, she pinned the ribbon Caroline had gifted her up and through the curls atop her head.

She reached for the gown, running her fingers over the small, delicate flowers embroidered at the edges. Exquisite. Almost too beautiful to wear. She grinned. Almost.

Once on, panniers perfectly placed and stomacher pinned, Hannah stared at herself in the mirror. How many years had it been since she had felt this beautiful? Her lips pulled upward, her smile unable to fully release the humble joy, the fullness of peace that stroked her from the inside. 'Twas not the gown that made her feel so. 'Twas love. The love of and for a man she'd longed for since her youth.

Lord, how do I repay thee for such happiness?

She sniffed away the brimming tears and opened her drawer, reaching in the back for the pearls Ensign had given her, when a knock tapped at the door.

"Hannah?"

Her pulse jumped at the sound of Joseph's voice, and she looked one last time in the mirror before going to the door.

She gripped the handle, holding her breath, aching as she tried not to show her longing—the need to see his eyes widen and lips stretch when he saw her. Twisting the handle, she pulled. The space between door and wall grew, their eyes meeting at the smallest opening. Her mouth went dry as his gaze combed over her. He put his hand on the door, pushing it open, slow and commanding.

His throat bobbed, and she could see his pulse throbbing in his neck. "You look beautiful." Voice soft, he stepped in, eyes all over her. "So beautiful, in fact, I do not wish you to go."

Heat crept over her cheeks and she ducked her head. "Joseph...I don't know how to thank you." She looked up. "'Tis such a grand gift, and I have nothing to—"

"You gave me your consent." He stepped closer. "That is all I have ever wanted." Reaching for her curls, his silken timbre caressed her skin. "A wedding dress. I am glad you approve."

"Approve?" She glanced down, the gown looking even more magnificent from that angle. "'Tis beautiful..." Her words trailed away as God's gentle nudging brought to mind the miracle she had cradled and buried. And how desperately she must reveal all to the man she loved.

The sound of the parlor door opening and closing made them both jerk.

"Miss Young?" Stockton carried too much eagerness in his rough voice.

Was it four already?

She swallowed, glancing to Joseph before speaking toward the open door. "I'll be right down."

Facing Joseph, she bemoaned the time that had slipped away. She'd wanted to tell him about their child before she'd left—unburden her spirit before the night's labors, in hopes her mind and body would have greater endurance for what awaited. But God knew when was best. She must trust in that.

Resting those thoughts aside, she held out the pearls, her hands trembling too much for her to tie the ribbon. "Would you?"

Joseph nodded, enclosing her hand in his as he took the necklace. His expression grew soft, and he smoothed his rough thumb against her skin, his voice a warm cloak around her worries. "You're trembling."

Hannah sighed and looked away, detesting the truth that shamed her. "I'm afraid."

"You needn't be." Gently, he tugged her body against his, nuzzling his nose beside her ear before whispering. "I shall be—"

"Miss Young? Are you ready?"

Suddenly her throat forgot its function. Swallowing, even speaking, was too difficult. Joseph's gaze gripped her, infusing courage through her as he'd done so many times before. She released a shuddered breath and closed her eyes. For Ensign. For the cause.

For our future.

She turned without allowing herself the chance to look back, for if she did, the fragile strength she carried might slip from her fingers and shatter at her feet. Snatching her crimson cloak and muff from her bed, she stepped down the stairs, anticipating the look Stockton would give her with as much glee as one might a fall in an icy pool.

Finally below, she offered him only a fleeting glance. 'Twas enough to have both her suspicion and sickness confirmed. Stockton's face went slack, and his eyes devoured her with ravenous hunger. Her skin crawled, and any appetite she might have had fled in the face of such revolting lechery.

He neared, reaching for her cloak. "Allow me."

In character as she was, she allowed him. Gloved hands reached from behind, placing the cloak around her shoulders and lingering there too long, draping slightly down her arms before he moved around to face her. "Miss Young, you are a vision."

"You are too kind, Major." She ducked away just as Joseph descended.

"The barrels are loaded, sir."

Stockton looked up and nodded. "Excellent. You deliver at seven."

"Aye, sir. All is in readiness."

Stockton's mouth bowed up in approval before he moved on. "We shall not be back until morning."

Joseph bowed in response, a soft grin masking any emotion he might have felt—all but polite understanding. "I do hope you enjoy yourselves."

"I assure you we shall." Stockton extended his elbow to Hannah, and she took it, grinning as she knew he wished her to, unable to bring herself to look at Joseph for fear her wanting of him would slip through her eyes.

At the door, she stopped when her empty hand reminded her of its lost companion. "Oh...I've forgotten my fan."

"What was that, my dear?" Stockton cocked his head sideways.

She twisted and motioned up the stairs. "Forgive me. I've forgotten my fan. I'll not be a mo—"

"Allow me." Joseph stepped backward. "Where shall I find it?"

Hannah's chest fluttered at the shielded love in his stare. "In the drawer of my dressing table."

With a nod he bound up the stairs and disappeared into the room.

She turned politely to Stockton. "Forgive me for the delay."

"'Tis nothing." His response was airy, as if he hadn't really heard her. And likely not, for the way his gaze still crawled up and down her frame.

Hannah glanced to the stairway, when panic drained all blood and feeling from her head and limbs. *No. Oh heavens, no.* What had she been thinking? If Joseph opened that drawer...

"Joseph!"

Gripping her petticoat, Hannah raced through the parlor and up the stairs, praying beyond hope he would see the fan and nothing else.

Halting with a jerk at the open doorway of her bedchamber, Hannah's lungs heaved with terror as fear tackled her forward. She gripped the door to keep from losing her strength. *No, no, no. Lord, no!*

Back to her, Joseph stood motionless in front of the dressing table. His broad shoulders were drooped, his head slightly bowed.

Hannah's hands went clammy, her breath shallow. "Joseph?"

He remained still, every passing second making her blood pound harder in her ears.

She tried again. "Joseph, I—"

"What is this?" He moved at the waist, peering to her over his shoulder, his voice deep and quiet.

Hannah swallowed, willing her strained voice to produce words, sound, anything. "I..." Her throat cut off her words. *Lord, help me.*

His face had lost a sheen of color, and his strong brow pinched low. Lifting the booties in his hand, he asked a second time, though now his tone was darker. "Hannah, what is this?"

She could neither think nor feel. The truth she longed to share was branded on the inside, and she yearned to show him her scars, yet somehow her lips had no strength to move.

His throat worked, and he looked down at his hand, finally turning the rest of him to face her. Gaze gripping like an iron vice, his voice cracked, and the muscles of his face flinched. "You had a child."

Eyes burning, Hannah held the doorframe harder, the apathetic wood giving no comfort to her failing strength when by grace alone, the answer slipped free. "Our son."

"Miss Young? Is everything all right?"

The clomp of Stockton's shoes echoed up the stairway, and she turned to the hall, the effort it took to move and speak without weeping as painful a thing as she'd ever known. She smiled down at Stockton, where he'd stopped halfway up the stairs. "It seems my fan cannot be found. I shall go without it."

He nodded, smiling. "Of course." Hand extended, he waited for her to come to him.

Though her eyes burned with an unquenchable fire of grief and regret, she blinked away the rising moisture. She wished nothing else but to throw her soul at Joseph's feet, reveal everything and beg him to forgive her. But with Stockton's unfaltering stare upon her, she could not show the emotion that threatened to slay her soul—could not peer even one last time at Joseph as he stood beside her dressing table, holding the treasure of their child in his strong hand.

Lord, give me strength.

Descending, she took Stockton's arm, and he led her down the remaining steps and out the door. She had to remind herself to breathe, but even forcing air in and out took strength she didn't possess. 'Twas a dream. Or so it seemed from the way the world moved in and out around her, the way the sounds of voices and shoes and doors seemed far away as

Stockton helped her into the carriage. All she could hear, see, feel, was Joseph. His hurt, and pain, and shock stabbed through her very bones.

The carriage moved, but she was too numb to feel it. Joseph had loved her that morning—did he still now? The memory of the lack of life in his eternal blue eyes drained more of her strength. He thought her selfish, cruel for keeping such a thing from him. And mayhap she was.

Hannah pressed a palm to her chest and closed her eyes when the paper between her breasts shifted, and she wrenched her spine straight. Her eyes sprung open. The note. A groan built in her throat, and she closed her eyes again to force it away. She had meant to give it to Joseph before they'd left. *Oh!* Hannah dropped her head in her hand. She'd failed. She was no spy. All the work they'd volunteered for would come to naught.

"Miss Young? Are you unwell?"

She looked up and gasped in surprise at Stockton's sudden question. A small laugh she hoped would ease the tension did nothing but stir it. "Aye, indeed. I was...I was just pondering over my fan. I can't think of where I might have left it."

Giving the laugh another hopeful try, she shrugged and circled her fingers deeper into her muff, falling instantly backward to the pit that gaped behind her.

Joseph. Joseph, I am so sorry.

Perhaps if he had come back as she'd hoped he would those many years ago...if her father hadn't shunned her and forced her from town...if she had told Joseph of their child.

Perhaps then all of this would have been nothing but a bitter dream and she would wake in the morning wrapped in the arms of the man she loved.

But 'twas not a dream.

And she could only hope the rest of what awaited her that eve would not crush what remained of her spirit. For the night had only just begun.

Joseph stared, his arms and legs heavy and numb. He tried to swallow, to dislodge the emotion that clogged his throat. But it wouldn't move.

Again he lifted the tiny, soft booties, shock so consuming him he could hardly form a single thought but the memory of Hannah's mouth forming the words he couldn't believe she spoke. *Our son.*

Why hadn't she told him?

He turned back to the dressing table and yanked open the drawer in full. There must be something else—a journal, a letter perhaps. Something to answer the questions that writhed through him. Privacy be hanged.

There, in the center of the drawer atop a folded cloth, sat something he hadn't seen since that night ten years ago—something, to own the truth, he hadn't even remembered. Though now that he looked at it, the memories crashed against him like a wave, dragging and pulling him under.

Joseph rested the booties on the table and took the ring in his fingers, the touch of the metal opening a sacred closet, one he'd locked but not forgotten. With this ring he'd asked for her hand. And she'd accepted.

He breathed out a soft breath, thick with hurt...and love. Not enough money to purchase a more fitting semblance of the marriage they wished for, he'd made it that morning. Rolling it between finger and thumb, a pain-filled grin pulled at one side of his face. How she'd smiled when she'd seen it, begging him to slip it on her finger. How she'd loved him then.

The stabbing he'd felt from the time Philo told of Hannah's hatred of him throbbed, the wound never having healed.

But she'd kept it. Why? It seemed foolish to keep such a trinket that would only remind her of what they had lost, if she truly hated him as much as Philo had claimed.

Lost.

Joseph groaned deep in his chest and shook his head. To bury a child all alone? How had she endured such grief? If he had known, nothing in heaven, earth, or hell would have kept him away. Didn't she know that of him? Was his unfailing devotion not so profoundly felt?

"Joseph?"

The deep voice from the parlor tapped at his shoulder, bringing him around and rousing his mind just enough to respond.

"Aye?" He paused to rest the ring and booties in the drawer and went to the top of the stairs. "Oh, Sackett." He descended almost too quickly, needing to move his body and force away the blinding confusion. "The barrels are finished?"

"I figure we will be done just in time to make the delivery."

"Excellent." Joseph slipped his arms into his greatcoat, enough anxiety in his limbs to give him the strength to run the ten miles to Duxbury. How would he ever endure the three-hour wait? "Stockton informed me I should make the drop alone, but you know that, of course?"

Sackett nodded, almost chuckling. "I've no trouble with that."

"Good." Flinging open the door, Joseph marched out with Sackett following, grateful for the weighty distraction. The delivery, the raid, and the evening's ball were enough to keep his mind and his body engaged without combustion. But only for tonight. For tomorrow would come. And with it the realization that more sorrows lay between him and the woman he loved than he had ever known.

Chapter Twenty-Nine

"Aw, we've finally arrived."

Hannah stirred at Stockton's announcement as the carriage slowed to a stop. She pressed out a weary breath. The lights from the torches lining the road slipped through the window of the carriage, but she couldn't bring herself to look. They might have arrived, but her soul was ten miles behind, crouched and crying.

"Are you all right, my dear?" Stockton cleared his throat. "Miss Young?"

At the sound of her name, Hannah raised her head, slapping her mind awake. "Oh, aye. Forgive me."

"If I may be so bold, you do not appear well." His expression took on a protective angle, and he reached out, resting his hand atop her muff. "I fear perhaps...I fear your cousin is making unwanted advances."

"What? Oh...no. Nothing like that." Was that what he'd thought? He'd seen them in the kitchen and no doubt noticed her lack of color since they left Eaton Hill. "Not to worry."

He inclined his head, unconvinced. "If he has done anything to—"

"Nay." Hannah tried a relaxed laugh that came out as a high-pitched squeak. "All is well. I...I have just been overtired, but today's rest did wonders."

Stockton's stare refused to leave her. "If you require anything of me, I should hope you would feel comfortable to speak to me of it, Hannah."

Her stomach rolled, and she forced a response to cover the gag that built in her throat. "Of course." She roused a smile with a slight nod, sucking in a deep breath that did nothing to calm her storming belly.

Blessedly, the footman opened the door, bringing the conversation to a quick end. Stockton exited first, offering his hand to Hannah. As she stepped from the carriage, she raised her eyes, and slowly, her mouth opened in awe. Dear heaven. Large as any estate she'd seen, the home was magnificent. Wood built and whitewashed, the wide walk of the three-story home was lined with large Greek-style carvings, and though snow blanketed most of the greenery, 'twas clear the gardening was meticulous.

The torches washed their orange light up the handful of brick stairs to the large doors that opened as if someone had seen them approaching.

A wigged man bowed and reached for her muff and cloak, looking to Stockton as he spoke. "You are most welcome, Major Stockton."

Stockton placed a possessive hand at Hannah's elbow. "This is Miss Hannah Young."

The stranger stepped aside, motioning to the ballroom. "Jones will announce you."

Another fellow walked before them, leading them down a vast hall. Candles lit the walk, portraits and busts seeming to nod with pride as Hannah passed.

To the left, the large doors were already open with two men standing at attention at either side. The guide stopped at the doorway, the soft yellow glow beaming from the chandeliers as his voice boomed through the room. "Major Ezra Stockton and his guest, Miss Hannah Young."

The man stepped aside to allow her and Stockton to enter, all eyes intent on them as they stepped in.

Stockton offered his elbow and leaned her direction, whispering, "Did I not say you would be the most lovely woman here?"

"You are too kind, Major." Sound drifted from her throat. Her lips moved, but 'twas mechanical, forced. All she could see were her failings. Scrambling to gather what strength she'd had earlier, Hannah gripped Stockton's arm, holding him for fear her legs would weaken. The wood floor seemed more like soft soil beneath her shoes, giving way with every step. *Lord, help Joseph forgive me.*

Stockton looked down, placing his other gloved hand atop hers, his unabashed stare drifting to her chest before lifting back to her eyes. "I do hope this evening will calm whatever ails your spirit, that we may at last become even more acquainted."

"Oh! There you are!" A mirthful chirp resounded from the right of the large room, the other guests already interested in the next announcement that blared from the entrance.

Dottie Pitman came bounding toward them, her ample bosom bouncing. "My dear, I have been awaiting your arrival with such anticipation."

Hannah curtsied. "'Tis an honor, Mrs. Pitman."

Plump and jolly, Dottie's cheeks widened as she smiled. "My dear, I know you feel you must be formal since we are amongst so many, but please, you must call me Dottie." She glanced up to Stockton. "I can see you will be reluctant to release your hold on this lovely woman, but Aldor is at the refreshment table and has something to speak with you about."

Dottie looked to Hannah, her eyes growing wide, as if she were confessing through her expression that she fabricated the statement simply to be rid of him.

Stockton bowed before stepping back. "I would be pleased if you would do me the honor of the first minuet, Miss Young."

Hannah looked to Dottie. 'Twas not his place to ask her, even though she'd come as his guest. As a woman of lower rank, she could not dance with those of a higher station, and she prayed from the depth of her that Dottie would hold to tradition.

But she did not.

Dottie frowned, happily tsking. "I see that worry, my dear, but you mustn't think of it. With that gown, and attending as Major Stockton's guest, no one will judge you."

Stare still intent upon her, Stockton didn't move until she faced him. "'Twould be an honor, Major."

"The honor is all mine." He stepped back, holding her with his stare before turning to locate the companion he'd been sent to find.

Dottie reached out, and Hannah took the woman's hand with both of hers, grateful to have someone else to cling to. "I am so pleased to be here." Hollow words, but ones that must be spoken.

"My dear, you are positively radiant." Dottie quieted, as if she wished to hide her voice from listening ears. "I am pleased you were willing to attend with the major, but I daresay there are a few others I wish to acquaint you with." She walked Hannah to the side of the dance floor where a row of seats lined the edge. "Higley is to arrive later, and he is simply—Oh! Mrs. Harper, there you are. You simply must meet my new friend Miss Young. Miss Young..."

'Twas easy to pretend she heard as the two women prattled on. Hannah need only nod and smile, curtsy and offer an occasional "hmm" or "aye" while her mind moaned over her heartache. Where was Joseph now? She looked to the clock in the far corner of the room. She'd been there only twenty minutes. Oh, how would she survive another ten hours?

"I'm most curious, Miss Young?"

Hannah shook her head, grasping wildly for the trail of unheard words her mind struggled to follow. She ducked her head apologetically. "Do forgive me. I...I didn't hear—"

"Oh, not to worry, dear." Dottie patted Hannah's arm. "Mrs. Harper wanted to know who made your lovely gown."

"Uh...'twas in town. Already made."

Another woman began to speak. Something about how she thought she'd seen it, when another rang in saying she was sure it was the prettiest thing she'd ever seen. Hannah's eyes began to burn, and she smiled over the pain, breathing long and slow.

Dinner could not come soon enough. Then she could busy her hands and keep her mouth full despite the fact her stomach rolled and was likely to reject anything she forced into it. But dinner was still another four hours away.

"Ladies and gentlemen, please take your places for the minuet."

Hannah whirled and jerked back to see Stockton already inches from her. She placed a hand at her chest. "Forgive me, Major. I didn't see you there."

He swept around, motioning to the floor, where couples were beginning to gather. "Shall we?"

Perhaps a dance or two would do her good. Not that she wished to be any closer to this man than she must, but the music and the motion might dull her anxieties.

She placed her hand on his and practiced a smile, praying he didn't detect the pretended sincerity. One minute, one hour at a time. That was the only way she would make it through the night.

The drive was awash with heavy shadows, the sliver of moon offering little light for Joseph's arrival at Willis's yard. He pulled the horse to a halt and jumped from the wagon, the hairs at his neck already on end. Higley's warning tapped endlessly through his memory, and he scanned the wood for any sign of movement. There was heat in the wintery air, as if unseen eyes burned through the blackness.

So far the yard appeared vacant, and God willing 'twould continue to be so. He patted the horse's neck, wishing not for the first time it had been Anvil with him and not the wagon horse. Rounding the front of the animal, Joseph glanced to the darkness of the surrounding wood. If Greene was hiding somewhere, he had better not be alone. If he were, Joseph would prove how dangerous attacking him would be.

At the door, he knocked twice, and it swung open.

Bathed in a soft light, Willis motioned Joseph in, that jolly exterior slightly dimmed from the recent beating, but still afresh. "Come in."

After Joseph entered, Willis shut the door, his tight expression speaking something different than his mouth. "You are ready?"

Joseph nodded, understanding the unspoken meaning. "I've the barrels in the back. Waiting to be put to good use." Should any listening ears be privy to what they spoke, their conversation would be taken as naught but their already proposed plans. "Shall I help you unload them?"

With his eyes alone, Willis looked to the window, then back to Joseph, his arms crossed and voice eerily low. "Were you followed?"

"Nay." Joseph mimicked Willis's volume. "I saw no one outside. Is the house being watched?"

Willis breathed in deep. "It was. But I haven't seen anyone since noon." At this he allowed his regular volume to resume, speaking in coded words. "I had hoped Pitman would keep a few soldiers stationed here as before. There are too many risks at having such a load in one place."

"Indeed." Joseph glanced to the floor, where beneath his feet rested the incredible stores, then to the wagon through the window. "We best hurry."

Willis uncrossed his arms and strode to the door. "I owe you my life." He swung it open, stopping long enough to hand Joseph a look that hailed of gratitude before he stepped outside. "If not for you..." He needn't speak the rest.

Joseph clapped him on the back, keeping every comment he might have spoken behind the barrier of his teeth. The stars might be listening.

They moved the barrels in only a quarter hour, securing the last remaining muskets below the floor without so much as a clink of iron.

Willis dropped the rug back into place and gripped Joseph with a stare that chipped a corner of his courage. "Be careful. I've had a foreboding...an ominous feeling that refuses to leave me."

"About tonight?"

Still they spoke carefully, saying so much more than their words. "I worry. They are everywhere."

Joseph neared, inclining his head as he placed a hand on Willis's shoulder. "Everything is planned to the moment. Worry not. You shall not be taken."

"'Tis not for myself I have concern."

The comment sat hard in Joseph's gut.

Willis went on, his voice stringing tight enough to snap. "If tonight goes awry...you must be ready. She will need you."

A chill dashed over Joseph's skin. He must get Hannah from here as soon as possible. Though she was two miles away at the house in town where the evening's gaieties were taking place, should the intended raid go bad, such a distance was still close enough to... A curse cut over his tongue. If only he could race there now and snatch her from that den of lions. But no matter how he wanted to, he couldn't arrive until after the dinner had ended. Higley had insisted Joseph's name would be on the list, but arriving then without an invitation would have him thrown out. Arriving during the dancing, when the wine was draining their sensibilities, would provide at least a measure of the cover he needed to take her to safety.

"I shall protect her—I promise you that." Joseph dipped his head and stopped at the door before exiting. "Thank you, Willis. You have been a good friend."

Willis didn't smile, hardly spoke for the undercurrent of caution that swept through his tone. "God be with you."

Quiet carried the words for a moment before Joseph could answer. "And you."

He stepped away and patted the horse before bounding up to the wagon seat, his earlier anxieties colliding with his newfound worries.

Joseph bent and readjusted the lantern at the side of the wagon when the horse's ears perked, a sure sign he heard someone—someone near.

"Who goes there?" Instantly straight, Joseph reached for the pistol inside his jacket, when a man stepped cautiously from the wood.

Joseph jumped from the wagon and rushed forward, his blood racing hard through his limbs.

The figure stopped at the edge of the trees, one hand raised, the other at his mouth.

The signal alone was enough to flick Joseph's memory to light. He took several more steps, glancing left and right before whispering. "Nathaniel?" Stopping beside his friend, he gripped the man's arm. "What in heaven's name are you doing here?"

Nathaniel's volume was nearly inaudible. "I thought I heard your voice." He motioned behind him with his head. "Donaldson and I came before the others. We want to be sure what we are up against before we descend on Willis. He is ready?"

"Aye." Joseph turned, looking to the home across the yard he'd just left. "I saw no one, though that means little. There is talk of one who might be preparing to do you ill. Where is Donaldson?"

"Around the other side." From the wan light of the wagon's lantern, Joseph could see Nathaniel's jaw tick. "We will return again in half an hour to—"

"Are you mad?" Ire twisted through Joseph's chest, and he pointed right. "You cannot come here again until you are in greater numbers. That barn is massive. There could have been a dozen soldiers in there, and you would have been walking into a trap—"

"Aye, but there aren't, and we are not." His silence scolded Joseph's reprimand. "We do what we must regardless of the risks."

"Do not balance your lives on such fragile luck."

Nathaniel's grin slid sideways, and he tapped Joseph on the shoulder. "There is no luck when God is at your side."

Joseph huffed and shook his head, the comment wriggling down his conscience. Without God they would surely lose at this devilish game. All those he cared about were suffering from it. If anything were to happen to these men...to him...what then? His stomach lurched. It was too much. *Dear Lord, help us all. I must get Hannah to safety.*

"Where is Hannah?"

Nathaniel's inquiry brought to life the chimera that ate Joseph from within. His mind was stolen away, and he stared toward the road. What was she doing? *How* was she doing? He thought of what he'd learned before she'd left. Her face had gone so white when she saw him...

"She is well?" Nathaniel neared, his brow plunging low. "Has anything happened?"

Joseph nearly laughed aloud, but he ground his teeth together. Had anything happened? Everything had. And nothing. His legs began to twitch. "We cannot stand here talking like mindless women."

A rustling in the snowy wood axed their words, and they whirled toward the sound.

"Nothing and no one to be seen." Donaldson appeared, his lungs heaving as if he'd been running. He nodded a quick greeting to Joseph before looking to Nathaniel. "Is all in readiness?"

"Aye," Nathaniel answered.

"I must go." Joseph lowered his chin and his volume. "And so must you. Your men will be awaiting your report, as Stockton will be awaiting mine."

"Donaldson, go ahead." Nathaniel's clipped words said something Joseph didn't care to hear. "I will be right behind you."

Joseph knew that pointed look. Nathaniel wanted more out of Joseph, but he would have to pry open his jaw to get it.

Donaldson turned without so much as a parting look, his experience no doubt making him tread with far more caution than Nathaniel seemed keen on using.

"What's happened?" Nathaniel neared. "I have known you long enough to hear the tension in words you haven't spoken."

Even in the blackness, Joseph's vision nearly went red. Did Nathaniel believe that here and now he would—

"Is she untrustworthy? Has she been fooled to work for the other side? Is she—"

"Hannah?" He couldn't be serious. "Nay. She is valiant as ever."

"What then?" Nathaniel insisted. "There are concerns you have not voiced, and I must know what—"

"She had a child." Joseph spoke through his teeth. He growled and turned away. "I just learned of it."

Nathaniel's question came slow and hesitant. "A child?"

Thinking of it was enough to drain the blood from Joseph's head. He couldn't reply. He needed to flee this moment and escape to the next occupation that would busy him.

Shaking his head, he found the strength to move his legs, and he hauled up to the wagon seat, then halted. Remaining motionless as the realities crawled over his back like demons, he let the sorrowful truths spill from his lips. "She never told me. I wonder if she ever would have if I hadn't found..." His voice stopped, his mind at the spot in front of the open drawer, the booties blinking up at him.

"Nathaniel?"

Donaldson's quiet call brought Nathaniel full around. He glanced to the wood, then to Joseph, sympathy in the drop of his expression. "We shall speak more of this later. Our work begins. God be with you, my friend."

He darted into the arms of the shadows, both his frame and his footfall being swallowed up in the blackness.

Joseph released a breath heavy with an imbalance of dread and relief. He flicked the reins, and the horse started, pulling Joseph into the vision of Hannah that wavered before him. He'd never seen her so pale. What would he say to her now? What would she say to him?

More, what other secrets did she carry in her heart, and how, if at all, could he tempt her to share them?

The pain he felt, though wrenching as any he'd known, 'twas nothing beside the knowledge that she had suffered such griefs alone. Above all, 'twas shame that beat him. He should never have accepted her father's word. He should have written more than once, should have waited below her window every day and night until she was certain of his devotion, no matter how her father threatened.

Fool. Utter, worthless fool.

God willing, she would tell him all. God willing, at long last, she would trust him.

Chapter Thirty

Standing beside the far window in the ballroom, Hannah put a hand to her stomach and closed her eyes. Blessed, blessed solitude. The conversation at dinner had been engaging enough that her lack of appetite had gone unnoticed. Stockton had been in rapt attention with the officer and lady at his side of the table, allowing her a full hour in which she'd not had to speak with him. A tender mercy.

She breathed in deep through her nose, the floral notes of perfumes and colognes beginning once again to dance through the air, as did the voices of the guests as they filled the room. Outside the window was freedom, and it taunted her. Hannah gazed through the glass, her thoughts refusing to leave the place they'd claimed so many hours ago. What dread her future held if even such a gathering could not distract her. When she returned, what would Joseph say? How could she face him?

"You are looking well this evening, Miss Young."

Hannah spun with a small gasp. "Captain Higley." Grinning, she tried to act at ease, though somehow she feared her charade was as clear as the wine-filled glass in his hand. "Forgive me. I didn't hear you...I didn't know—" She cleared her throat and tried again, grateful a more dignified sound emerged. "Were you at dinner? I didn't see you."

He shook his head. "I had business to attend to. I've only just arrived. And please, do call me James."

James. She'd forgotten 'twas his name. It fit him well. Yet she'd grown so fond of his surname she hadn't the heart to discontinue the use of it.

"Quite a gathering." He pivoted and gestured to the groups of threes and fours dotting the vast space.

His presence allowed her spiked nerves to dull their edges, and she breathed more freely. "Indeed."

Taking a sip, he offered a handsome sideways grin. "I have yet to see such an estate as this outside of Boston." His brow bent slightly, eyes keen, as if he were looking for someone before he turned back to her. "And in so small a town. Remarkable."

"I agree." Hannah's tension eased from her shoulders at the welcome conversation he offered.

Again he took a sip and glanced from one side of the room to the other, allowing Hannah a long look at the missing section of his ear. It seemed to fit him—rough and harsh as it was—proof of his fearless soldiering nature. His red coat was pristine, every polished buckle and clasp reflecting the bright glow of the candles that surrounded them. For someone so tall, and of such a rank, he carried an easiness about him. Yet there was a cloaked alertness that never rested. His eyes ever watching, his spine ever straight.

"Oh, there you are, my dear."

Dottie's arrival signaled the end of Hannah's blessed quiet.

Round and bouncing with exuberance, the woman seemed to gain in mirth as the evening wore on. "I was searching for you, and here you are."

Higley tossed Hannah a smile, a single eyebrow bobbing as he stepped aside for the woman to come between them.

Her vision was planted at Hannah's face. "You left dinner so early I was beginning to—Oh! Higley! My, my...how dashing you look. Doesn't he look dashing?" Eyes wide, she lowered her chin at Hannah, expecting an immediate answer in the affirmative.

Hannah licked her lips, allowing herself a moment to mold a proper response before opening her mouth. "Captain Higley is most kind. And most handsome."

The declaration she offered Higley was taken as she'd hoped—a friendly gesture and nothing more. He responded with a gentle grin before turning his attention fully on the woman who seemed intent upon matchmaking.

"Mrs. Pitman, what a hostess you are. I am sure I have never attended such a ball as this."

Clever. He turned the conversation to her.

"And you have ordered such magnificent refreshments. This wine is extraordinary."

"Oh."

Dottie's cheeks pinked, and she appeared more the smitten schoolgirl than a married woman as she giggled. Perhaps she had taken a bit too much of the wine already herself.

"Well, the music will begin soon, and I do think the two of you would make elegant dance partners."

Hannah grinned and glanced away. She would be pleased to have Higley take her hand, though she could hardly be the one to second the suggestion. The thought of Stockton once again standing opposite her made her belly want to cast up what few bites she'd taken. He'd looked at her with such intensity the first few dances she could almost feel the touch of his stare on her skin.

"What do you say, Miss Young?"

Higley's voice tempted her gaze back up, and for the first time that evening, she smiled with real meaning. There was knowing in his eyes, as if he had read the reluctance in her posture and wished to calm it. Relief massaged away the knots in her neck. What manner of man was he?

"Thank you, Higley. I would be—"

"Captain Higley, there you are."

Hannah's stomach rolled to her feet when Stockton strode through the crowd and joined them.

Higley bowed. "Good evening, sir."

"Ladies." Stockton grinned at them before aiming his glare at his captain. "Higley, there is someone I should like you to meet."

He stepped aside, and Philo took the empty space, grin wide and feigned as ever.

What was he doing here? Bile crept up Hannah's throat, and she grit her teeth, breathing carefully through her nose. *Dearest Lord, I cannot endure yet another tribulation.*

"This is Reverend Philo Young, Miss Young's father." Stockton turned to Dottie. "Do forgive me, Dottie. I took it upon myself to issue him an invitation, as I figured you would be—"

"Why of course! You know I do not take such things too seriously. The more there are, the more jolly a crowd." Amiable as always, the woman curtsied. "You are most welcome."

"'Tis an honor, Mrs. Pitman." Philo flowed with charm.

Hannah fought the urge to laugh openly at his charade and nearly choked when he pinned his eyes on her. "Hannah, how lovely you are. 'Tis a joy to see you, my dear."

Like a bird in a trap, there was nothing she could do but offer the kind of grace that was expected of a woman in such a place at such a time. "You are too kind." Surely he caught the hurt that flung out with her words.

Philo straightened and twisted toward the dance floor. "Stockton was good enough to invite me, and I must say I was eager to attend. I see my daughter but little these days, and I crave any chance to be with her."

Lies. Hannah shielded herself against their penetrating hurt, but the girlish yearning for fatherly love leapt out, as always. And as always, the barbs of truth cut. He didn't care for her, no matter how she craved it.

"Think nothing of it." Dottie moved forward, stopping just beside him. "I adore your daughter and see why you would wish to be near her. Now if you will excuse me, I should like to see about the musicians. They should have begun to play by now."

"I shall go with you." Hannah hurried forward, unwittingly brushing shoulders with her father as she passed him. Though she didn't look, she could feel his stare and wished she could shove it away with a glare of her own, but she resisted. Taking the woman's arm, Hannah exuded more geniality than she felt. "I should be most pleased if you would introduce me to the players."

The comment widened the woman's eyes, and she seemed almost exuberant at the simple request. "Certainly, my dear. You know, I first heard these musicians while I was..."

Dottie kept on, but Hannah's hearing faded to low throbbing sounds. The clomp of her shoes on the floor seemed almost louder than the din of voices clamoring through the room. Her father? Here?

It could not be borne.

Why had he come? Why had Stockton invited him? She thinned her lips to keep from scowling. There was more than simple fatherly sentiment that lurked in his self-serving will. This had to do with Eaton Hill, no doubt. And his hatred of Joseph. A revolt began in her belly, and she grit her teeth to keep the sensation at bay.

Dottie looked her way with peaked brows, obviously having asked a question Hannah hadn't heard. She nodded, hoping the response was requisite, and when it seemed so, she braved a glance behind her. The three men conversed, her father with his back to her.

If she could avoid him all evening, and by some divine intervention Stockton as well, she could perhaps endure the night and make it to the heartache that awaited her at Eaton Hill.

Philo watched her go, fleeing from him as if he were a leviathan and she an innocent seraph. Of course she would see him thus, and it stabbed in a way that a cold blade could not. Despite what she believed, the deepest yearning of his spirit was not so self-seeking. Not entirely.

Ever since seeing Hannah those few days past, a ticking had begun within him, the slightest shift he could feel but not distinguish. If only she knew how truly he cared. She had grown—changed so much. Though in other ways she'd not changed at all. Even ten years later she was still willing to succumb to a man such as Joseph Wythe.

Staring across the ballroom floor, the hatred he'd nurtured for the man who'd ruined his daughter, the devil who'd cheated her life away from her, loomed like a haunting apparition. Joseph and Ensign had prepared this scheme together for some time, that was clear. Hannah didn't know herself—she couldn't make decisions for her future. Joseph didn't deserve Eaton Hill, and he didn't deserve Hannah.

Philo alone must own the land that was meant for him from the beginning. Ensign's pretended benevolence be hanged.

"Reverend Young, allow me to offer my condolences."

Philo twisted back, questioning the tall soldier in front of him. "I'm sorry?"

"Forgive me. I am Captain Higley." He nodded forward. "I refer to your brother. I grieve for your loss."

Who was this man, and how did he know of Ensign's supposed death? As if a stranger would care. For all he knew this was the very man who'd tried to kill Ensign. Philo lifted his chin to tip away the sarcastic thread. "I thank you for your kindness. He shall be most sincerely missed."

Ensign had been so close to heaven's gate last evening. Was he already there? Perhaps he had been denied entrance for his treatment of Philo these past years. Such wouldn't surprise him.

Though the moment the thought found the center of his mind, a niggling discomfited his belly. If anyone was to get to heaven, 'twould be Ensign. Somehow he could hear his brother's voice behind him, reprimanding Philo's stiff-necked ways. He should tell Hannah that Ensign had been living...in fact, that he might in this moment still be breathing. Philo shook his head. Surely he wasn't. If he was, Philo's purpose would be thwarted, and he'd come too far to turn back now.

He glanced over his shoulder, spying Hannah as she kept her back to him, speaking with a gathering of musicians and several other women keen on garnering attention with their flapping fans.

If nothing else, this evening he would harness the future for himself and his daughter, as he should have done long ago. She would not be pleased with the outcome. But 'twas for the best. And that was all that mattered.

Chapter Thirty-One

Joseph tugged on his waistcoat and then his jacket and bound up the front steps, his nerves tumbling like a rowdy bunch of schoolboys. The agony in waiting until dinner had long past made him almost writhe, but he'd endured, and at last he could make his appearance.

The doors of the large house were fast, and he was about to knock, when they creaked opened.

A wigged man appeared from behind the door and gestured him in. "Good evening, sir. Your name?"

He cleared his throat. "Joseph Young."

"Aw, yes." The man shut the door. "I saw your name on the list." He started down the hall. "This way."

Joseph's limbs buzzed. So his name had been on there. He stretched and curled his fingers to ease the building tension. Would Hannah be pleased to see him? Upset? She would be surprised of course, as she didn't know Higley had told him to come. He prayed her reaction would be one of acceptance if not pleasure, but he doubted the latter. She'd looked near to tears when they'd parted.

He spied the immense portraits in the hall, the detailed rug at his feet, and situated his mind on the person who would surely detest his arrival. Stockton likely hoped to enjoy the evening with Hannah to himself. But that was about to change.

At the entrance of the ballroom, the man motioned for Joseph to enter. "You have arrived just in time. It appears the dancing will soon begin."

Joseph bowed and entered, grateful his arrival seemed to go unnoticed.

As if tugged by unseen hands, he turned and was struck motionless. In the far corner stood Hannah with Mrs. Pitman and several other women. The lot of them seemed nearly giddy with their lively conversation, while Hannah's posture and thin smile conveyed something else entirely. And he was to blame.

He hadn't intended to speak so tersely with her. 'Twas shock that had stripped him of his civility—his soul so violently shaken he could not then, and *still* could not, find the words to express how he felt and how desperately he wished to hold her. To tell her he held her no blame. To ask her in humility to tell him everything, so that in some way, if 'twas possible, he could try to make it right.

Scanning the room, his vision landed on Stockton and Higley, and he made straight for them, loathing how he must make this last report instead of take Hannah by the hand and lead her immediately away from this place. The heavy scents of wine and candle smoke stung his nose. There were many reasons he was not drawn to such gatherings, and the decadence was only one of them.

"What the devil are you doing here?"

Stockton's greeting, though churlish, was less hostile than Joseph had expected. A good omen perhaps?

Joseph inclined his head. "Good evening, Major. Captain Higley." He looked up and froze when the last man turned toward him.

Philo.

Devil's spit. What was *he* doing here?

Stockton shifted his weight over his feet. "I don't remember you receiving an invitation."

Joseph opened his mouth to respond, but Higley's answer cut off his own.

"'Twas my doing, sir." Higley rested a hand on Joseph's shoulder. "I must ask your pardon, but I had supposed you would wish a report after..." He looked to Philo, then stopped and swallowed. "After he finished his duties. So...I invited him to attend."

Stockton's glare reddened, that twitch under his eye starting up as it did when he was irked. "I'm surprised at you, Captain." He sighed with gruff resignation, then motioned to Philo. "Being that you two are family, I do not need to make introductions."

"Indeed." Joseph dipped his chin, his stare cutting through the stream of hate that poured from Philo's small eyes. He prayed the man would keep his mouth shut and not reveal the true nature of their strained past.

Why was he here? Sandwich was no small distance away... The thought smacked him across the head, and he set his jaw. Eaton Hill.

Philo's ever-abiding disgust stabbed, but Joseph parried with his own. If the man thought to better him, he would soon see his folly. Joseph's own brother had treated him thus for so many years. He was well acquainted with how to take command of one who attempted to control and demean.

"Well?"

Stockton's singular question stepped between the fight, and Joseph swallowed, battling the urge to see if Hannah peered his way. Did she know her father was here? Perhaps 'twas the very reason she chose to stand at the other side of the room.

Taking a full breath, Joseph rolled his shoulders back. "'Twas successful."

Stockton's eyes narrowed, then eased, as if he understood the reason for Joseph's laconic answer. In place of a response, Stockton offered only a brief grin before looking away.

Joseph followed the man's gaze to Hannah, and his muscles hardened. The musicians were beginning to take their places.

Bowing, he stepped away. "If you'll excuse me."

He would not allow Stockton near her again. From now on 'twas *he* who would be at her side. Tonight and forevermore.

"Merciful heavens!" The woman beside Hannah tugged at her arm. Though Hannah had known her all of three minutes, the woman acted as if they'd been friends since girlhood. "Who *is* that man?"

She pointed across the room, and Hannah's blood drained from her face. Knees suddenly more weak even than before, she gripped the woman's arm in return, staring.

Joseph.

When had he arrived? What was he doing here? Though she pleaded with herself to look away, it was impossible to turn her eyes from him as he stood with Higley and the others. His blond hair was fastidiously tied and contrasted perfectly with the dark-gray jacket that seemed to strain against the muscles beneath. Taller than all but Higley, he demanded attention simply from the way he held his broad shoulders and angled his head.

"Have you seen him before?" she asked again.

Hannah could not respond, but only watch him. By the goodness of God he hadn't looked her way. Or perhaps he had and she hadn't seen him.

The woman tried again, this time entreating the hostess. "Dottie, dear, who is that dashingly handsome fellow speaking with the major?"

"Oh!" Dottie stepped beside her, face aglow. "My goodness, this is a surprise." She faced the all-too-enchanted stranger at Hannah's side. "That is Miss Young's cousin."

The woman gasped and pressed a hand to her large bosom. "My dear, do tell me he isn't married."

"Virginia!" Dottie's voice sounded surprised, but her expression was gleeful.

Not at all shamed by her exclamation, Virginia waved her fan. "Is it so sinful for a single woman to be interested in a single man?"

Hannah's palms grew clammy. "He is..." Keeping a disinterested sound in her voice proved futile. "He is not married."

"Really!" Virginia leaned in and prodded further. "Spoken for? Courting? I pray not, for I must have my chance at him."

Hannah clung to the sudden and healthy stream of irritation that buoyed her draining strength. She breathed in deep for the first time all evening. "Nay, neither, but I do think he may have someone in mind." The last came out with more force than she'd intended.

The overly endowed woman reached for Joseph with her eyes. "Oh, Dottie, do you think you could bring him over here? I crave to know how he dances."

"Certainly, darling, but first—"

"Mrs. Pitman, are you ready?"

One of the musicians bent forward from his place on the stand, eyes keen and violin in hand.

"Oh, aye, aye." Dottie waved her hands. "You may begin with the cotillion, Billy."

He smiled, her flightiness likely known to all from the way he offered a polite and patient nod. "Of course, Mrs. Pitman."

Over their heads, the violins began singing, and Virginia gripped Hannah's arm, her pinched whisper spraying into Hannah's ear. "He comes! He comes!"

Hannah spun around, and her heart stopped.

From across the room, Joseph walked toward her, stride determined, eyes hungry but gentle. Her pulse went from stalled to charging. Virginia's fingers squeezed and then released as Joseph neared and stopped before them. Virginia curtsied low, but Hannah's knees wouldn't bend.

"Hannah." He bowed at the waist, his gaze holding her like a warm embrace.

Her throat ached. "Joseph."

Eyes still upon her, he extended his hand. "Will you do me the honor?"

Her mouth was dry, her mind vacant. She couldn't. Could she? She glanced to Dottie and Virginia, who gazed at Joseph with soft smiles and tilted heads.

Hannah blinked, her heart bound by so many sorrows she could hardly move her lips in response. Unbidden, she reached for him, and instantly his fingers folded over hers.

Guiding her to the floor, Joseph stood opposite her as the other dancers took their places beside them. She shouldn't do this. 'Twas dangerous to be so close to him, to engage thus when her longing for him was already on a cliff's edge, ready to fall backward at the slightest breeze. She braved a glance, and the look Joseph gifted her swung around her and pulled her fears to safety.

He did not hate her then? Where was the hurt she'd seen in his eyes, the shock and anger?

Lyrical and melodious, the music began, her body remembering the gentle movements as easily as she remembered the feel of Joseph's touch. Curtsying, she dipped down, then back up, her breath chasing wildly at the longing that glowed from him when he bowed, his stare never leaving her as they began to dance. Close together, away again. Fingers brushing, air curling around them as they circled one another. They danced as if they had never been apart. Again he drew near, his gentle touch on her hand as intimate as a kiss.

Her breath stalled, while her heart fluttered in beautiful rhythms. Whispering, her lips spoke what her mind had wished to refuse utterance. "Why are you here?"

At that moment, they parted and stood opposite as two others danced around them. She read his silent, mouthed response. *I came for you.*

'Twas their turn, and they moved together. Circling her, he whispered. "I cannot think of anything but what you told me."

Again they parted, moving around the others before standing in place once more. Regret pooled in his pained expression, the pleading so heavy she could feel it in his stare. Hannah's skin flushed. His were not the eyes of a man who hated.

Pivoting, four of them took hands in a line, lightly moving up and back, releasing and crossing paths to wait at the other side.

When she met Joseph again, he drew her with his yearning, his quiet beseeching almost more than she could bear.

Bodies nearly touching as they turned, he whispered, "If I had known..."

There was no accusation, but still she felt it. "How could I tell you, knowing you had changed your mind—the idea of marriage being so disdainful to you."

His frown was instant as he took her hands to turn her. "I wanted nothing else. But you hated me, and I would never force you to—"

"I never hated you."

The floor wobbled, and she hurried back to her place before the other couples began. Standing motionless, the truth she once believed fell in severed pieces at her feet. Hannah raised her eyes to where Philo stood, and her blood chilled. *Lord in heaven.*

The dance continued around her, but her mind was stolen. All this time she'd believed one thing when the truth had been buried alive in a deep and loathsome grave. How had she never seen it before? How could he have done it?

"Hannah?"

Joseph spoke her name, but she couldn't move. Her vision wavered, and her eyes burned, the stays around her chest growing ever tighter.

Losing balance, she put a hand to her chest and hurried from the ballroom, heedless of the chatter that whispered behind her. Let them think what they would, though they no doubt believed she fled to a fainting couch. And in truth she did, her lungs gasping for air as the cracks in her understanding flooded with cold realization.

"Hannah!"

She made it to the door, when strong hands held her shoulders, steadying her.

Joseph's tone was warm with concern. "Come. There is a couch just here."

He led her into the library and helped her to sit. Crouching in front of her, he kept one hand beside her, the other at her knee. "What can I get you? A drink, a cool cloth?"

She closed her eyes against the dizzying thoughts, but the darkness only filled them with life. Like a book of paintings, the past sorted through its ignoble portfolio, flashing visions of grief and unanswered questions, as if hoping this new revelation would at last provide the resolution it had long sought but never found.

Her breath came quick and shallow through her mouth. Somehow, her tight throat allowed a few words free. "He did it."

"Who, my darling?" Joseph leaned toward her. "What do you speak of?"

She raised her eyes to his, grasping at the strength that flung to her from his gaze. "My father."

In a swift motion Joseph rose and looked to the door, then sat beside her, taking her hands in his. "What did he do?"

The facts were nearly too painful to voice, their blades cutting up her throat as she spoke them. "I see now what I had not seen before." She spun her head toward the man she loved. "He made us each believe..." Nay, 'twas too harrowing to comprehend.

The breath she inhaled was shallow, choppy. "He told me you came to the house when I was out. He said you wished to bid me farewell, that you realized after our...our indiscretion that you didn't want to marry. That you wanted a life free of vows. That you never wished to see me again."

Joseph stood and spun to face her. "I came to tell you I was ready to marry you. That very day." Shock pulled his brow low and his posture straight. "I came to tell you I didn't care what your father or anyone might think—that I knew we had done wrong but I wished to make it right. I wished to be your husband as we planned. But he..." His face reddened and fists curl. "He told me you hated me. That you despised me and blamed me for what had happened. That you never wished to see me again."

"Nay!" The ugliness of such a lie jerked her from her seat. Her head shook, the disbelief consuming to such a degree 'twas as if her body attempted on its own to fling the bitter revelations from her mind. "I never hated you. Even after I lost our son..."

"You never hated me." Tender and draped in longing, Joseph's whispered statement cracked her fragile composure.

"I *wanted* you." Her chin quivered, and she pressed a hand over her mouth, the pains she harbored for so long finally bursting free, unwilling to stop their wild run to freedom. "I believed you would return to me." She moved her hand to her chest and met his gaze. "'Twas that belief that kept me living. I almost lost my life along with the child, but I saw you returning so many times, and such a dream, however vain, was what kept my soul from slipping away." Her voice wobbled. "For three years that hope lived within me. I could not believe you could have loved me so strong only to abandon what we had shared. But then...you never came."

Motionless, Joseph stood rigid, his arms at his sides, eyes red rimmed and jaw ticking madly. Rage prowled in the back center of his stare. "I am taking you away. Away from this place, away from him."

Pools of tears filled her eyes, then drained over her cheeks in hot streams. "You really loved me?"

In a single stride he was beside her, his arms encircling her as he held her firm against him. Lips and nose against her hair, he whispered through a voice fraught with love. "My darling, I have only ever loved you."

My darling.

Hannah closed her eyes, feeling the very fissures in her heart mend at his words. He had always loved her. He hadn't left her for lack of wanting—but for lack of knowing.

And 'twas all her father's doing.

A whimper of sorrow echoed through her throat, and she gripped him tighter, when suddenly he reached behind and unhooked her arms from his back. Her face scrunched, pleading that this gesture did not bode ill news. She could not bear it. But there was a promise tucked in his grin, and the sudden cramp in her brow eased when he spoke.

"Do you think we can begin again?"

She turned her head in question. "What do you mean?"

In a swift motion he curled a finger in his waistcoat pocket, an ache in his angled expression. Slowly, he raised his hand, revealing the ring he had made for her so long ago.

Her eyes burned, and she flung a hand to her mouth.

"Come away with me tonight." He moved closer, circling his other hand around her ear to cup her face. "We can at last be married and begin the life we wished for ourselves."

Hannah blinked the moisture away, straining to speak against the heated stone in her throat. She was consumed. So consumed with love, surely she could live forever on the life it gave. While deeper, a blackening sorrow brewed. How could Philo have done this? He might have despised their impetuous youth, their sin, but how could a man take it upon himself to destroy the lives of anyone, let alone his own child?

Joseph brushed her cheek with his thumb. "We are done now—no more spying. No more secrets. Our future awaits us." Gently, he took her hand and slid the warmed ring over her finger as if 'twas a reverent act. "Your father will never come between us again."

He swooped his head down and captured her mouth with his, and she responded, pressing against him, when the note in her stays burned her skin like a singe from heaven, and she pulled away.

"What is it?" Worry bit into his face. "You have not changed your mind?"

"Nay, I..." She turned from him to pull the paper free from her bosom, then whirled back. "I meant to give this message to you earlier, but I was so distraught, I..."

He took the missive and read it, the tick in his jaw indicating he understood the gravity of the intelligence even deeper than she. He refolded it. "The Patriots need this."

"I know. Forgive me." Had her mistake cost the lives of her friends? Or would God grant them another chance? "What can we do?"

Ducking his head, Joseph kissed her again, his mouth warm with vows of more yet to come. "This last missive we will take on our journey away. Then our lives will be our own. Come."

He stepped back and took her hand in his, when a voice outside the hall sent a shiver down Hannah's spine.

Nay. Their lives would never be their own.

Chapter Thirty-Two

"A fine evening for such an occasion."

Philo sipped the drink he'd acquired and attempted menial conversation while Stockton stared in bitter silence at the way Joseph and Hannah moved in effortless grace around the dance floor.

Stockton answered in a toneless hum before taking a drink. Jealousy was never difficult to detect, but this man's was blatant. Perfect for manipulation.

Shifting his feet, Philo took an even more casual stance and tossed the other officer a smile before speaking. "I must say I am quite surprised they are able to endure each other's company so well."

Stockton snapped at the bait. "How do you mean?"

Philo shrugged, encasing himself in the most fatherly tone he could. He tilted his head and shook it slightly, as if he regarded the past as only a minor impediment, not a sheer-sided precipice he must scale to attain his goal. "Youth, you know. Many years ago Joseph loved Hannah and tried to win her, but I helped her see the error of him as a choice." He slid a quick glance to Stockton, whose face was pinched with question, so he went on. "I do not like him at the property. I should feel more comfortable if

I were there in place of him. I could oversee anything as well as he, and then Hannah would not be at his mercy."

"I did not know this." Stockton's tone gained a level of piqued animation. "They said nothing of—"

"And of course I am sure Joseph prodded her not to mention it. No doubt he brought her to Eaton Hill with the intent of wooing her again." Diving ever deeper in the pool he filled, Philo sighed, eyebrows pinched up. "I have been considering it since you informed me of the situation, and I cannot say it sits well with me. As her father I cannot help but—"

Stockton cut the air with his hand, his stare gouging through the crowd.

God himself could not have organized a more flawless chronology. Escaping the dance floor was Hannah with Joseph at her heels. Philo's chest lifted and lowered with gaining bliss. Perfect.

Jutting his drink toward his officer, Stockton moved forward. "I should like to see what—"

"Sir."

Stockton whirled, his nostrils flared. "What, Higley?"

"Did Major Pitman tell you about Lieutenant Greene?"

His brow plunged. "Cannot this wait?"

The soldier shook his head apologetically. "I meant to tell you earlier, but—"

"Well?" Not even a shred of patience filtered Stockton's voice.

Philo looked to the door of the ballroom. Joseph and Hannah were gone, but to where was unknown.

Higley motioned sideways. "He was seen in town and is believed to be about some business—"

"What business? I told him to stay in Sandwich." Stockton growled and swore under his breath. "How long has Pitman known?" Again he swore and marched forward. "Never mind. I have more urgent —"

"He might be the informant."

This stalled him. Philo again glanced to the door, his muscles ticking. He'd nearly had him. Blast. If this man were not so intent on speaking...

Stockton turned to fully face the one who'd borne the news. "How do you know this? Has Pitman sent for his arrest?"

"It seems he fled."

"Fled? Impossible." Jaw working, he whirled, scanning the ballroom. "Where is Pitman?"

"I don't know, sir."

Without even a second glance, Stockton marched from the room, storming across Philo's carefully laid trail. He inhaled, neck cording. This was not meant to be. He was supposed to throw Joseph out, banish him from Eaton Hill—place *him* in charge.

Then like a glimmer of light in the center of his mind, a thought was born. Perhaps there was still a chance.

Stockton plowed through the doors, then to the right. Philo followed but went left down the long, wide hall.

From the nearest doorway, light spilled over the carpet. As he approached, the sound of voices rustled the air, and he hurried forward, then slowed when he was within inches of the opening.

Back pressed against the wall, he turned his head just so, and the two of them came into perfect view.

He dulled his hearing to all but their hushed words. That ignoble man would think to—

Philo's thoughts skidded to a jerking halt when Joseph pulled something from his pocket and spoke in such tender tones Philo could almost believe the man was sincere. If he didn't know the deeper depravities of Joseph's soul, he might have been convinced—certainly any woman would be.

"Come away with me tonight." Joseph neared her until their bodies nearly touched, one hand at her face. "We can at last be married and begin the life we wished for ourselves."

Liar!

Rage clawed through Philo's muscles, and were it not for his need to know more before he acted, he would have charged through the room and tackled the imbecile. Philo might not have been a perfect father, but hadn't he taught her enough to be wary of such men?

As Hannah gazed at Joseph, eyes shimmering and expression so full of longing, something faraway in Philo's mind stirred. A memory, so many years hidden, rustled beneath the dust and cobwebs of forced forgetfulness until his heart quivered. *Mariah.* That was how his wife had looked at *him* when they had first twined their hearts and their hands. That same longing and hope he'd buried with half his soul when he'd placed her in the ground.

He blinked to be sure he hadn't imagined the look on his daughter's face. Nay. She couldn't feel love. They were living in sin.

Joseph's voice grew quieter, and Philo had to strain to hear him.

"We are done now—no more spying. No more secrets. Our future awaits us."

Spying?

Philo glanced away, his pulse thundering. Could Joseph be the informant Stockton and the other soldier searched for?

All such thoughts fled when Joseph began again, and Philo flicked his vision toward them, his stomach at his feet.

"Your father will never come between us again."

Philo scoffed inwardly. He thought to take her away, hmm?

A scuffle at the front of the hall tugged at him, and he craned his head back. Several soldiers rushed in the front doors, their voices taut and animated. Stockton and Pitman appeared, each with rigid backs and wide feet. Something was wrong. Philo spun around to the two he spied as Hannah handed Joseph a note. Joseph's eyes narrowed, and his brow plunged low.

"The Patriots need this."

The voices at the other end of the hall increased, and three words met his ears. *Raid. Patriots. Spies.*

Stunned, Philo's mind lunged for the first thought and clung to it. He stepped away and pointed at the library, yelling. "Here! He's here! The spy you're looking for is here!"

Every man at the front of the hall spun toward him, and he ran two steps into the room. "You cannot escape now."

Hannah's face went white, hate spewing from her eyes before she turned to Joseph and pointed to the window. "Go!"

Joseph's face crunched. "I won't leave you."

She rushed to the window and grunted as she pulled the pane upward. At her side in seconds, Joseph shook his head. "I can't—"

"There!"

A brush of wind moved past Philo as the soldiers rushed in.

"Go!" Hannah's voice screeched through the room. Agony bled through Joseph's face. Ducking, he leapt from the window as the soldiers dashed across the room.

Shoulders straight, Hannah seemed heedless of the commotion, the yelling. Her stare gripped Philo at the throat, saying far more than her voice ever could.

Philo's limbs went weak. He had done right, hadn't he?

Stockton rushed forward, bumping Philo as he barreled into the room. "Where is he?"

Another soldier hurried to him, pointing to the window. "He escaped."

Stockton's voice boomed like cannon fire, his face as scarlet as his coat. "Go after him!"

The two others raced from the room, and Philo dared a question. "What's happened?"

"There's been a raid." Unmoving, Stockton stared at Hannah. "The Patriots somehow knew of the stores and would have taken them all had not one of my men followed a hunch and gone to check."

Hannah's throat moved, but her chin was raised in pretended surprise. "How would they have known?"

Stockton moved a single step forward. "I should like for you to tell me that, Miss Young."

Philo's stomach pinched. The man wouldn't do anything to her, would he? 'Twas Joseph he was supposed to suspect.

Dainty eyebrows pinched, she shook her head unconvincingly. "I don't know what you mean."

"Do you not?"

Stockton spun on his heel and went to the hall, his thundering voice flickering the candles. "Higley!"

In seconds the man was bounding toward them. "Aye, sir?"

"Stay here while I go see about this raid—and apprehending Joseph."

"Sir—"

The man's words were put short by Stockton's cutting motion. "Stay here and guard these two until I get back."

Stockton stormed down the hall, yelling commands as the soldiers rallied to attention.

Philo's pulse still raced, but it charged even quicker at Higley's sharp glare.

Higley pointed to the room. "In."

Was Philo's loyalty to be questioned now too?

Hurrying forward, Philo made it to the center of the room before the heat in Hannah's glare became so hot he could go no farther. Still beside the window, she stared at him, chest rising and falling, lips pinched white.

"What have you done?" The cry that left her splintered the air with a thousand pains.

What did she think? That he'd done it to spite her? A burning started in his core and moved outward. He braved a step forward. "I act when I deem it right, and what I saw was—"

"When *you* deem it right?" Her chin quivered. "All you have ever done is attempt to pull us apart."

"For your good."

"For *your* good, not mine."

Supported by his foundation of righteousness, Philo spit through his reply. "Since the beginning you have been too foolish to see past that man's wickedness. So much so you allowed yourself to be dragged through the muck along with him, and I refuse to have my daughter—"

"You tried to protect me, did you?" Her voice went eerily calm while her exterior quivered. "You thought that making either of us believe such falsehoods would in some way shield me from a life of grief?"

Aye. At last it seemed she understood. But the hate in her stare said otherwise.

Philo flung a glance to Higley, wishing the man would stand outside the hall while the two of them spoke, but from the strength of his stance, 'twas clear the man was going nowhere.

Shaking his head, Philo stepped forward. "You do not understand my struggle because you have not loved a child of your own."

Her face went slack.

There. He'd caught her. "If you had, you would know the weight of feeling you had done all you could and still failed."

Eyes instantly red, she reached for the chair beside her. Her quivering increased, and she licked her lips. "You did not do all you could. Had you done so, you would not have shunned me from town. You would not have hated me for my transgression so much that you refused to see me."

He hadn't hated her. Not in the way she thought. Philo's mind floundered against the rising tide. He hadn't meant to—

"I told you I was sorry." Volume rising, Hannah's voice wobbled as much as her chin. "I craved your love and forgiveness." She paused, tears streaming over her cheeks. "If you loved me as you claim, you would have been there for me as Ensign and Bea had been when I bore and buried Joseph's child!"

Impaled, Philo stared, blinking as the pain started in his gut and bled over the rest of him. She could not be in earnest. Dear God, it could not be so. "You never told me this."

Face crumpled, she turned her back to him. "I never wanted to."

Was it true? He flung a look to the soldier who stood with them, peering at Philo with the same disdain he felt from even the portrait over the fire.

Philo faced her, scrambling for a scrap of dignity in the rubble of his broken spirit. "Why didn't Joseph return for you then? If he was as good a man as you claim—"

"He would have if he had known." She whirled back around, her expression hard. "He was led to believe I hated him, and I was led to believe he wanted nothing more to do with me, so he learned of it only today, as you have." She paused, inhaling an unsteady breath that cracked Philo's bones. "I have had this pressing on my heart for so many years. I believed my life would be spent alone, until once again God brought into my life the only man I have ever loved, and once again you have stripped him from me!"

"Hannah...I am so sorry." Barren and lost, Philo shook his head, his mouth and mind dry as a desert plain. "Hannah, I...I hadn't meant to hurt you."

"But you had meant Eaton Hill for yourself." Tears easing, she dabbed at her cheeks with the back of her hand, anger lacing both ends of her words. "Do not think me ignorant of your central desire. Still, I had a part of me that craved your goodwill, that hoped perhaps you wished to be close to me, but you have slayed that now. I should learn never to dream of things that are impossible."

The blade of her confession stabbed through Philo's spirit, and it fell to the ground, knees bent and hunching while the rest of him stayed rigid. *This* was not what he had wanted. He had wanted Eaton Hill, aye, had wanted Joseph away, but he hadn't wanted to hurt the daughter he loved. Like a haunting remembrance, Ensign's words preached from the pulpit of his memory. *She yearns for your love. But...there is much you do not know of her. She has lost a great deal.*

Taking quick shallow breaths, Philo's sins berated him, beating away the hard covering of pride with every stroke until finally the humble center of him glowed through.

Ensign had been right. These many years when he'd thought himself so noble, 'twas he who had been dishonorable.

Dear God, what have I done?

Philo reached forward, too fearful of upsetting her further to take another step. "Hannah...Hannah, I..." He stopped. What could he say that she would believe? He prayed God would give him strength— that He would help turn her ear to him. "Forgive me, my child. I see now that I was wrong. Please, I wish to make it up to you."

Hannah's gaze raised to his as a slight breath left her mouth. "'Tis too late." Her eyes shifted to Higley before returning to Philo with the force of a winter gale. "You have taken from me the man that I love and sentenced him to death."

"No." A violent resistance overtook him. "No, he will—"

"If he is caught, he will be killed, and I would rather lose my own life alongside him than be doomed to live the remainder of my days without him!"

Wailing and gnashing, the demons of Philo's actions swirled around him. There must be a way to make this right. Joseph was strong, was he not? He could outrun his pursuers. But if not, and if the note were found, these men would do more than hang him...

Philo's body scalded with the need to act. Wounds began to open in his gut, as if somehow he were feeling for the first time what she had felt—the wounds *he* had inflicted upon her. He must atone. He must show her his devotion, his change. His love.

Another silent prayer slipped through the enclosing panic, and the reply was instant. *Thank you, Lord.* God might not be pleased with what he had done, but 'twas clear Providence would look after Hannah.

"I will make this right," he said, wishing his pledge were enough to dry the sorrows from her eyes.

In a quick about-face, Philo marched to the door, speaking as he went. "I'm going to the raid." He paused at the door and twisted to look at Higley. "I don't recommend you try and stop me."

"You are going where?" Hannah lunged.

But her father didn't stop, didn't turn to look when she cried after him—only ran.

She looked frantically to Higley, who stared through the open door where Philo had gone. He'd said he wished to make it right, and as much as she wanted to believe that were true, there was little that told her she could trust him.

Grabbing her skirts, she raced across the room and snatched Higley by the arm. "Will you just let him go?"

Higley's angled jaw ticked as if part of his mind were running after Philo's retreating form, the other part calculating. "I will let him go. But not alone."

Chapter Thirty-Three

Thighs burning from exertion, lungs afire, Joseph ran from the house. The frigid winter air did nothing to cool the anger that flamed him. *Philo.* The man had always found reason to hate Joseph for his love of Hannah, and now it seemed he would have his revenge.

At the first horse he came to, Joseph leapt onto the saddle and kicked the animal into a run as a clamor of commotion defamed the night's earlier calm. Pitman barked orders from the front step. Soldiers splashed through ice-covered puddles in the road. Joseph tugged his borrowed mount right, praying that amidst the fray, his path would be lost to his pursuers.

Once in the covering of the wood, he was forced to slow his pace, which only escalated his pulse. Time was fleeting, and its value inestimable. This note must make it to Washington.

Joseph growled and yanked the horse sideways only seconds before they barreled into a hidden tree stump. Grinding his teeth, he opened his heart toward heaven. Only Providence could help him now.

He stopped in the wood, glancing around at the eerie quiet that hovered in the midnight black. Where were the Patriots? Had they already fled? Who had the muskets?

Devil's spit. Where was Nathaniel?

Lungs heaving, muscles flexed and full of blood, Joseph dismounted. Spying through the wood, he squinted, cursing the lack of moon. He could make out nothing but shadowed forms in the yard in front of the barn. There were only a handful of remaining soldiers, it would seem. Though more were on their way, that was certain.

A shadowed figure rose ten yards to the left. From the lack of coat and crouched way he stood, 'twas clear the man was a Patriot, ready to dash for safety. Throwing a whisper as far as he could, Joseph called out to him. "Halt!"

But the man ran, and Joseph gave chase. He took his chance and spoke the code word Nathaniel had told him. "Fox!"

The man stopped hard, but his posture was ready to start again. Like a frightened animal, the Patriot's eyes were round, his breath loud and quick.

Joseph took him by the arm. "What's happened here?" The man didn't answer, so Joseph gripped harder. "Tell me, man. Where are the guns? Did the Patriots get them safely away?"

He shook his head. "Have you not seen?"

"Tell me!"

"We got them away." His body was trembling, and 'twas then Joseph noticed the slick of blood trickling down the side of his face. "But not before—"

"Where are Captain Donaldson and Dr. Smith?"

Joseph released his hold, and the man took a few steps backward, preparing once more to run. "They made it away, but not before four of us were shot. A few taken." He spun and gasped as if he'd heard something. "Get to safety while you can."

Turning, he dashed through the snow-crusted wood. Dear God. 'Twas worse than he'd thought. Four shot? How many taken?

Something firm and hard struck him in the back, and he stumbled forward.

"Here's another one, Lieutenant!"

Joseph circled back and cocked his arm for impact, but resisted by some unseen hand. The eyes of the young Redcoat in front of him appeared ready to bulge from his head.

"Mr. Young?"

Joseph lowered his arm. "Reece?"

The faint light reflected in the boy's questioning stare. "What...what are you—"

"What is it Reece?"

Joseph gripped the boy at the shoulders, impaling him with a dozen sharp petitions. His voice was a raspy whisper. "Let me go, Reece. I beg of you."

The call from the yard came again. "Reece? Who goes there?"

"Uh..." Reece shrank back, face pinched and voice wavering. "Uh...I've just..."

"Well...this is a pleasant surprise, Mr. Young."

Joseph's spine jerked straight at the familiar dark sound, and he dropped his hands from Reece.

Twisting back, it took Herculean strength not to plow his fists across the man's face. "Greene."

So Higley had been right.

Greene tilted sideways to look past Joseph, slapping Reece with a glare that would no doubt leave a mark. "When I ask you a question, I expect an immediate answer."

Reece bobbed his head and stepped out of Joseph's shadow. "Aye, sir."

"Make yourself useful to Pryer."

After a shallow bow, Reece finished the last ten feet through the wood, leaving Joseph to fight his need to destroy the enemy without the company of one whose obvious innocence might stay his hand.

But even without Reece, Joseph knew he couldn't retaliate. There were far too many others, and he'd be too quickly overtaken.

Failure was a bitter reward for all he and Hannah had done. Their work was discovered, their message thwarted, and now, without God's intervention, their very lives would be ended.

"I'm glad you've come." Greene yanked on his arm and led him toward the yard where Reece had gone. "I may have been banished, but it served my purposes well. I have never stopped trying to discover who it was that was feeding messages to the Patriots. Seeing your *cousin* in Sandwich with known rebels was enough to solidify my suspicions. I knew you two were never to be trusted."

Did he mean Caroline? Joseph's hands ached from clenching. Had Hannah known she'd been seen?

Once out of the trees, Greene shoved Joseph forward and pointed a rigid arm toward a soldier who stood in front of the barn across the yard. "You there!"

The soldier jogged forward. "Aye, sir?"

"Tie this man. Find a place for him inside while we wait for Stockton to arrive."

"Aye, sir." The man who grabbed Joseph's hands could not have been more than twenty. Tall and lanky, the soldier's cold fingers circled around Joseph's wrists and brought them around the back of him, tying the rough rope hard enough to slow the flow of blood.

Yanked at the elbow, Joseph stumbled toward the house. *Oh dear Lord, no.* Joseph had to hold his teeth together to keep his anger from thundering free. There, in the center of the yard, lined with three other bodies, was Willis, eyes open, a gaping hole in his chest.

Joseph flung his vision to the other bodies, praying he wouldn't find the faces of any others he knew, but the soldier shoved him into the house before he could place them. "Come on."

Too pleased with his occupation, the soldier pointed to the small chair Joseph had occupied when he and Hannah had first visited—when Willis had been vibrant and fearless.

"Stay there."

The soldier marched out the open door and began throwing questions to the others, but Joseph dulled his hearing. Willis. What had happened?

His legs began to numb as a horror consumed him. Once the note in his pocket was discovered, he and Hannah would be accused of treason.

He scrunched his eyes and growled. If only he could break these bands. The rage pulsing through him no doubt gave him enough strength, but what then? What would happen to Hannah if he were to flee? He could not leave her at the mercy of the enemy. *My darling, forgive me.*

They had been so close.

If only God would grant one last blessing—one last miracle. But the flame of Joseph's hope for such a thing was snuffed by this last drop of irony.

The one who had wished them apart so long ago, the one who they'd believed would never harm them again, had been the one to press his bootheel in their future. Philo had won.

"Where is he?" Stockton's unmistakable thundering shook the walls of the cabin seconds before he burst through the door. "Aw, Mr. Joseph Young."

Joseph steeled himself against the incoming attack, refusing to retreat inwardly or out. A cold thread knit through him, and he clung to it as Stockton loomed beside his chair.

Deny.

"It seems you have been caught." Stockton tsked and shook his head. "A shame. I rather liked you."

The rake of hate in Stockton's black stare cut a path up Joseph's chest. *God, spare Hannah. Do not let her suffer this man's vengeance.*

Wiggling his fingers to lure even a tiny stream of blood to his stinging fingers, Joseph locked his stare to Stockton's. "You must believe me. You have the wrong man."

"I should like to believe that." The muscles at Stockton's mouth curled. "But to think you would actually believe I would accept your word—the word of one who has lied to me from the beginning."

"Lied to you?"

"*You* are our informant. Greene has made that very clear to me now." He went to the rug and flicked it back with a single swipe. "I was a fool not to see it in the beginning." The next he added under his breath. "Such a fool." Bending, he swung open the door and snarled. His vision snapped up, stabbing Joseph in the neck. "Where have they gone?"

Deny.

The petition came again, and he leaned what remained of his future fully upon it. "Sir, I give you my word I had no knowledge of this—"

"Where have the Patriots gone? This cellar is empty, and I refuse to believe you had nothing to do with this!"

"I did not!" Speaking the lie twisted hard in his gut, but he prayed such a falsehood for a greater good would go unpunished. He must do it, if not for himself, for Hannah. "Philo spoke without knowing what he saw. He knows not what he has done—"

"Then why run?" Stockton leaned forward, breath sour, as he seethed inches from Joseph's face. "'Tis you who has done this, and 'tis you who will pay."

"I tell you I did not do it, sir." Hannah's face flashed before him, and his voice began speaking ere he had time to stop it. "Hannah would never allow me to do such a thing. She is too devoted to the king. And I...too in love to gainsay her."

Stilled at the unexpected statement, Stockton straightened, his facial muscles slacking. He blinked and looked to Greene, who had suddenly occupied the open doorway. "Keep watch. Should anyone else arrive, inform me immediately."

Greene nodded and turned, but Stockton halted him with a second command. "And tell all the other men to return to Major Pitman. I have the matter under control."

"Aye, sir." Stepping out, Greene shut the door behind him.

Stockton folded his arms and spoke again the second they were alone. "You have always had designs on her." His thick chest lifted and lowered as he filled his lungs with a deep sigh. "And once you saw her inclination to me, you were besieged with jealousy."

Joseph swallowed, his blood stilling. The way to save her opened up like a crack in the earth. If Stockton believed Hannah was available to him, perhaps her life could be spared. Joseph would willingly fall over any cavern and allow her to walk across him to safety. But what security would she have without Joseph there to protect her? Philo cared not for her, and Stockton would use her in ways he dared not consider.

Yet for her to lose her life...to be drawn and quartered? *Dearest Lord...*

Joseph shifted in the hard chair, molding determined truth across his face. "I have always loved her. I cannot deny that."

As if he were the father and Joseph the son, Stockton stared down at him. "But she cared not for you."

Again Joseph worked his wrists against the strangling rope, his mind doing the same with the words that bound him. He could not answer. Not until he'd had a moment to disassemble the welded parts of memory. *She cared not for you...* 'Twas that very belief he had endured for so many painful years. Until this very night he had thought she'd felt the obverse of love—that she had despised him and wished a life without him.

But now, knowing that she'd wanted him, knowing she'd given life to the fruit of their love and grieved over an unthinkable loss, made a hot swelling start in his throat.

The answer breathed free. "She did. Once."

"Once, hmm?" Stockton untethered his arms and shifted his feet. "So you'd believed that perhaps by forcing your closeness you could draw her heart back to you?"

Had Stockton no son to lecture to? Joseph would not speak of love with a man who clearly had romantic designs of his own. But if it would save her life...

Joseph swallowed. "I did."

"I knew something was wrong." Stockton circled around. "I knew—"

"Major!" The front door flung open, and Greene charged in. 'Tis Captain Higley, sir. And another man—"

"Joseph!" Philo burst past Greene, eyes red and chest heaving. "How dare you!"

Launching to his feet, Joseph tried to dodge the incoming attack, but Philo's rage made him quick. With a roar he tackled Joseph backward. Like a man possessed, Philo grabbed at his coat, scratching and snarling. Joseph kicked and rolled to get himself free, but 'twas Stockton who yanked Philo back.

"Stop!"

A trickle of salty blood streamed into Joseph's mouth. Pulse heaving, he looked across the room as Stockton pushed Philo back, and whatever horror he might have felt tripled when he saw whose frame filled the doorway.

Eyes circled in fear, face devoid of color, Hannah's gaze was on him as one in a dream, ever reaching out but ever moving away.

Why had she come? Did she not know the danger?

Stockton whirled and yelled at Higley, who came to stand beside her. "I told you to keep them at the house."

"She could not be stayed, and I—"

"Enough!" Veins bulging in his neck, Stockton pointed to Greene. "Search them."

"No!" Hannah stumbled forward with arms outstretched. "Please, Major, I beg of you."

Something that resembled compassion rippled through Stockton's eyes but died at the shore of his pride.

The look he threw Joseph kicked like a boot to the face. "Get up." Again he turned to Greene. "Search them all."

Chapter Thirty-Four

All strength fled, and Hannah's legs buckled.

"No!" Higley gripped her arms to hold her steady. "Major, please."

The note she'd handed Joseph would be found in his pocket, and then they would both hang. Their hopes for love and happiness destroyed by a man who should have loved and cherished. Instead, had forsaken.

Stockton flicked his head toward her. "We've no time to wait. Lieutenant, get it done."

"Aye, sir." He stepped toward her. "I always knew you were not one to trust. And here at last I have the chance to prove it."

"Stop!" Joseph's cry stalled Greene's steps and turned all heads to him.

But 'twas Joseph's eyes that were upon her, and the look in them chilled her blood. She shook her head, silently pleading for him not to do what she read in his face that he would. If he sacrificed himself, 'twould be grief that stole her life in place of a noose.

On his knees, Joseph leaned into his words, resolve casing his features. "She is innocent—if you will check anyone, check me."

The tiny muscles under Stockton's eye began their familiar tick. He swung his glance from Joseph to Hannah and back again. "I do believe you are right. 'Tis you who I must question first."

Lord, this cannot be! Her limbs nearly lost their ability to hold, and she gripped harder to Higley. Hot tears burned her eyes before searing down her cheeks.

Stockton flicked his wrist to Joseph, and Greene marched to him. Yanking Joseph to his feet, Greene's gruff hands reached quick and hard into every pocket.

Hannah raised her eyes to Philo, who stood motionless, arms heavy at his sides as he watched. Why? *Why?* A cry built within her, guttural and black. Why had he never forgiven? She had wished for nothing else, but he had not been willing to offer anything more than begrudging civility. Did his hate of her reach so deep that he would place her own life and the life of the man she loved in such peril? Did he not know they would be killed? Did he not care?

Clinging madly to her sensibilities, Hannah focused her vision on Joseph, who looked at her as now Stockton came to inspect, then quickly stepped back, his mouth a hard line.

He said nothing, gesturing for Greene to search Philo. Cold relief washed through her. From across the room, Joseph's eyes blinked, communicating the same bafflement she could hardly assemble into thought. Had the note dropped from his pocket? How could they not find it?

"Raise your arms, preacher. You're next." Greene shoved Philo's arm high and dove his hand into his pocket. Suddenly he stilled and looked up, gripping

Philo's absent expression with a victorious smile. "What have we here?"

Slowly, he raised the folded note and circled on his heel toward Stockton. "It seems we may both have been misled, Major."

Hannah's mouth hinged open as Philo turned his face toward her. Her thinking ceased, impeded by the shock that shot from the sea of her fears. There was something in her father's eyes...something she hadn't seen since she was a child. 'Twas beseeching and sorrowful, yet sweet and entreating. An unheard melody seemed to groan out of him, his spirit speaking with hers in mournful, euphonious strains, as if to say, *I love you.*

Greene stomped forward, shoving the paper at Stockton's chest before he looked to Hannah, snapping her bleeding heart away from a pain she could not understand. "This does not absolve you of involvement, Miss Young." His glare squeezed. "You shall get what's coming to you."

"They are innocent!" Philo reached out hard and fast. "I confess."

The young soldier twisted back, mouth firm. "You confess?"

"Aye." Philo swallowed before speaking the rest, praying Providence would fill his mind with anything that would convince the crimson-faced soldiers he spoke the truth. "'Twas all my doing."

"You?" Stockton stepped forward, arms rigid at his sides.

Eyes narrowing, he gouged Philo with a stare that made his stomach physically tighten.

"You told me you were friendly to the king. That you were pleased we used the foundry for these very purposes. And we find *this* in your pocket?"

Philo licked his lips and adjusted his weight over his feet. By God's help alone he'd been able to snatch the note from Joseph's pocket and secure it in his own without detection. And the ruse of anger had worked so well, it seemed to be believed by everyone. But there was more to feed them, and he feared perhaps they would not bite.

If only God would show mercy in this time of his humility. That He would show His hand and rescue Hannah from Philo's sins that had brought them all here.

"Well?" Stockton snarled.

Philo straightened. "I have been watching the house since your arrival and secretly intercepting all messages leaving the house."

"Impossible." An almost imperceptible slant tilted Stockton's head. "I have not seen you. Neither has anyone else." He swiveled his head to Hannah. "Was he making you give him my notes—"

"No!" Philo's panic clawed. His well-meant but senseless attempt at persuasion could have her taken as well. *Lord, help me.* "She knew nothing of this. I..." 'Twas clear the man was more confused than convinced, and Philo poured a heavier dose of truth atop the rest of his fabrication. "I wanted Joseph away from Hannah, and when I learned they were both at the house, I knew I needed to keep an eye on things—not only to relay messages to Washington but hopefully to keep them apart. And so, this evening when I saw them together, I knew..." Such falsehoods scraped bloody paths on their way to his lips. If only he would have a chance to tell Hannah how sorry he was. To dissect the real regrets from the lies he used to protect her. After a tight breath, he finished. "I knew that if I could make you believe that Joseph was the one with the missive, I might be able to escape...but, as you see, I have not had such a luxury."

The following silence and dissatisfied grins on the faces of the men he'd hoped to convert razed the remaining pillars of his confidence. He swung another look to Hannah, whose ashen expression squeezed every unspoken pain from his heart.

He'd not wished to hurt her yet again. Had he known...Philo slammed his eyes shut. Nay, if he had known, then his rage might have been even more ferocious. His only hope remained in this feeble effort to atone for all the grief she'd suffered at his hand.

But that effort seemed doomed to fail.

Unless...

"Let them go." His spirit breathed to life as the passion for his daughter's freedom consumed. "I am ready to tell you what I know and would gladly give my life for the cause—if only you will give me your word that Hannah and Joseph may go free."

"Father!" Hannah gripped the arm of the soldier at her side. She threw a weeping glance to Joseph, whose fallen expression was frozen with shock.

"You've been blatantly vocal in your ill favor and disdain for Joseph." Stockton crossed his arms. "I find it puzzling that you would not wish your daughter free of him."

Philo pitched his eyes toward Joseph. "I refuse to allow an innocent man to suffer despite my eternal dislike of him."

A hard, staccato laugh jumped from Stockton's throat as he looked to the other soldiers in the room. He moved back and faced Philo, eyes black. "You are willing to be treasonous yourself, wishing no harm to come to a man you claim is innocent, but whom you hate." Again he laughed. "You Patriots are dichotomous."

Philo's very limbs numbed as the pronouncement of their fates hung like a sword above their necks. Philo could only hope that his was the neck that would be stretched and not theirs. *Lord, please not theirs.*

"Lieutenant, take this man and oversee the construction of a gallows."

Greene nodded as Stockton continued his commands. "Captain Higley, I give you charge of these two until dawn, at which time Reverend Young will be hanged for treason."

"No!"

Hannah's cry split the air, and she sank to her knees, her sobbing spilling through the room. Higley crouched to help her up as Joseph launched forward, clearly aching to be at her side. Somehow 'twas only the two of them that Philo could think upon, not the quivering fear of a rope about his throat. Nay. 'Twas the hope of their freedom and future that filled his soul like a pool heaving beyond its bounds. They must have what he had denied them. At any cost.

Once Higley helped Hannah to her feet, Stockton shoved the note at Higley's chest, his voice clinging to calm. "Keep this as well." Stepping back, he rolled his shoulders straight.

The young Redcoat almost grinned. Philo's heart split open and cried out to heaven. *Lord, let my death be the end of their sorrows. Bless my sacrifice for their gain, Lord. I pray thee.*

Stockton flicked his wrist at Joseph, commanding in a single gesture that Joseph march toward the door.

Hannah shook her head violently, craning her neck to see past Higley as he ushered her outside. "Father! No, Father, please! You cannot die!"

Joseph stopped at the door, shoving Stockton with the hate in his eyes. "Untie me so I may assist her."

Wrath plumed from Stockton's flaming eyes, the fetor of confused animosity as strong as the man's breath. With a quiet grunt he reached to his side and unsheathed the dagger and, with a swift swipe, cut Joseph's wrists free.

Pivoting back, Joseph's expression was hard at the edges and addled in the center. His jaw worked for a moment before he turned and hurried out the door.

From his place by the doorway, Stockton rested all his fierce attention on Philo. "Someone must be made to show what will happen to those who go against the king. And you, Reverend, it seems will be the one to help me make such an exhibition."

There was no fear, as he'd thought perhaps there would be. In its place, peace nestled. The likes of which he hadn't relished in far too long.

With a nod, Philo answered. "So long as you give your word that my daughter and Joseph will be set free." He glanced to Hannah, whose cheeks were wet as she held a hand over her mouth.

Stockton's eyes narrowed, and his head cant to one side ever so slight. "I must be sure they have not themselves committed treason—"

"They have not—"

"I will do as I see fit!" He gestured for Philo to exit. "You will spend your last evening in the barn, where Lieutenant Greene will extract from you what information you have to share."

They would torture him then? Would that God might fill his head with something, anything that might persuade them he had knowledge to share and that they would find his fabrication plausible.

Philo started for the door, and Hannah reached for him, her face pleading. But Greene yanked him away and through the door, into the biting night. Greene continued to pull Philo across the yard, but he wrenched his neck around to peer at the child he loved—the child who called for him through her tears. Past the few soldiers that still shuffled around the yard, past the bodies that lay side by side on the cold ground, Philo opened his soul to God. *Oh Lord. Have mercy.* That would be him in a matter of hours. His mortal vestiture to at last become one with the earth.

Entering the dank barn, he was shoved against a bench seconds before the door was slammed and blackness consumed him. He knit his fingers and pressed his hands against his head, a surge of emotion writhing through him in gasping waves.

He fell to his knees and wept. The grief he had caused, the compassion he had withheld—the love he had not shared and should have, racked him with the pains of a soul already damned to hell. Gritting his teeth until his jaw threatened to crack, Philo strained to keep his wailing silent as tears spilled over his cheeks.

Lord, I thank thee for allowing me to offer myself in their place, that I may take upon myself the punishment. Forgive me, I pray thee. Forgive me. Grant my daughter freedom. Give her the life she deserves with the man she loves. And, Lord, grant me thy everlasting grace, that despite my transgressions I may be permitted to come into thy kingdom.

He inhaled a gasping breath and gripped his fingers into his hair.

In a few hours he would meet the very One he prayed to. Then he would know what God would decree for him, whether he was worthy of an eternity of rest and peace.

But even then, there was only one thing he truly wanted. A thing he feared he might not ever have but was more precious to him than salvation.

If Hannah could forgive him, 'twould be enough to give peace to his writhing spirit no matter where he spent eternity. And for that very need, he held his head in his hands and prayed as he had never done before.

Chapter Thirty-Five

Joseph gripped Hannah around the shoulders and helped her up the front steps of the home where the party went on in disinterested bliss. Her trembling frame unsettled what feeble inner strength Joseph had remaining. He still could not comprehend what had happened. How had Philo attained the note, and why would he—

"There you are. Oh my dear!" Dottie rushed from the house, arms extended. "Come. Come. I will take you inside and give you some tea by the fire."

Hannah's pained smile showed her thanks, but the red rimming her eyes lay bare the raw emotions that pierced her as real as a weapon in her flesh.

Joseph pressed a kiss to Hannah's head and nudged her face toward his. "Warm yourself. I shall not be long."

Her cold fingers gripped his, and her words cracked. "Why did he..." She shook her head, a tear falling.

He brushed it away, hoping she would finish the rest—unburden her heart of the questions she bore.

"What happened, Joseph? Why would he do it?"

Again, he dotted his lips against her hair. "I do not know, my darling."

He replayed the scene, and still he could not settle on anything that would calm his frenzied spirit. The woman whose father had hated them would now suffer a fate that should have been theirs. The questions hung from his shoulders, pressing against his back, and there was no amount of shrugging that would release their hold. Only answers. And he must have them. For Hannah, if not for himself. She could not endure a life with an unknown that harrowed such as this.

Joseph glanced to Dottie, whose pointed features were soft with concern. "Thank you for seeing to her. I shall not be long."

"Of course." She nodded, taking Joseph's place at Hannah's side and leading her into the house.

He didn't move as he watched them enter and close the giant door behind them. Shaking his head, Joseph exhaled a hard breath from his nose. If only there were a way to—

"You should not stay here long."

Joseph turned his head behind him at the sound of Higley's voice. "Nay." He knew that much but had yet the luxury of considering what he could do— where he could take her, where they would be safe. And should he bring Jacob as well? Or would that place the boy in greater danger should they be caught? *Lord, grant me thy wisdom, I pray thee.*

Stepping beside him, Higley looked at the door just as Joseph had done. "Stockton is not a man to easily forgive or forget." At that, he turned his solemn stare to Joseph. "Though he now has one whom he can unleash his rage upon, that does not mean you are free. You must take her where his reach will not find you."

Unbidden, his lips spoke the very thing his mind struggled to subdue. "I must speak with him."

"Who?"

"I cannot allow him to die when..." He looked to the house. His own need to know consumed, but 'twas Hannah's pains he must find a way to ease. "I must speak with him."

"You cannot." Higley's answer was firm but gentle. "You must focus upon getting to safety first, and then—"

"The woman I love is about to lose her father without any chance to say good-bye to him." Joseph gripped Higley's arm. "Help me find a way to speak with him. I only need a moment."

"Nay." Seething, Higley answered through his teeth. "If you are found there, you too might hang, and what then?"

"So you will not help me?" Confusion and frustration made their way to anger, and he released his hold with a push. "Then I shall go alone."

"Wait." Higley stopped him with a hand on his shoulder. "I shall get you into the barn, but not for long."

Tension quieting, Joseph studied the man beside him. "Why do you help us?" Once the cached questions began to spill from his lips, they would not be stayed. "Why be so intent upon helping us find refuge? Why is a man in the king's army so willing to help the enemy when you know well the consequences?"

Higley's jaw flexed, and he looked away, dropping his grip. With a breath he turned back, a slight grin at his mouth. "We best get going."

'Twas clear he would offer nothing more, and Joseph struggled to place the spilled questions back in the box that seemed too small to hold them.

Higley went to his mount and swung his leg up. "I can grant you five minutes."

Feeling began to return to Joseph's anxiety-numbed limbs, and he hurried to the horse beside Higley. "Let's ride."

'Twas four in the morning, the sky still as black and morose as it had been when he'd first arrived at Willis's yard an hour before. But activity buzzed as if the noon sun were in the sky. Having left their mounts some yards behind, Joseph followed Higley wide around the back of the home, where no soldiers patrolled, and up to the back door of the spacious barn.

Hand on Joseph's shoulder, Higley's usually stern expression hardened to a deep glower. "You must speak quickly." He looked over Joseph's shoulder as if he'd heard something. "I will do my best to keep the guards in front occupied, but should you hear anything, you must leave immediately."

He nodded. A handful of minutes was not much time...but 'twas ample when his barren understanding stretched like a never-ending wilderness.

"Here." Higley reached in his side pocket and produced a small book. "Stockton will not provide any traitor with the peace of a reverend's word before his execution. As he is one himself, he might not need this, but I have a feeling that your sharing God's word with him would be welcome."

Joseph took the Bible from Higley's grasp, his chest tight and heavy. "Will they draw and quarter him?"

With a sigh, Higley released his hold and straightened. "I've seen Stockton hang a good many, but never does he insist upon the rest. I feel he doesn't care for the mess of it."

The mess of it. A shiver chased down Joseph's spine. Thank the Lord for that. The knowledge eased some of the churnings in Joseph's gut, but 'twas little solitude when one's life would end in a matter of hours.

Higley raised a finger to his lips and opened the door, entering halfway and craning his neck from one side to the other to be sure no one waited within. He pulled back and nodded that 'twas safe to enter.

Hurrying through the door, Joseph was struck with the cold, stale scent of hay and dust in the room that welcomed as much as a slatted coffin. He stood motionless to allow his eyes to fix upon the minuscule stripes of light yellow that squeezed through the boards of the main door, behind which the soldiers built the gallows by light of torch and lantern.

At long last, his eyes adjusted. There, at the other side of the barn, Philo sat with his elbows on his knees and fingers knit in prayer. He didn't look up, though surely he must have heard Joseph enter.

"Philo?" Joseph whispered as he stepped quietly forward, lifting his own prayers heavenward that God would prepare Philo's heart. If the man suspected

Joseph were there for some ill design, they would both be forced to endure a more terrible end.

"Philo."

Finally he looked up, the beams of faint light gleaming in his eyes. He looked to the door beside him, then rose in silence and hurried to Joseph, arms sweeping wildly. Stopping only inches from Joseph, he placed a hand on Joseph's shoulder, the other pointing to the door Joseph had just entered.

"What are you doing here? Are you mad? You must leave now."

Firm but quiet, Philo's tone resembled nothing of the hard man Joseph had known.

"I came to speak with you—"

"Go back to my daughter. 'Tis not safe for you here."

Joseph held Philo by the arm and pulled him to the back of the barn, where their whispered communications would be even more shielded. Chest pumping, he opened his mouth and refused to close it until all he'd come to speak had been liberated.

"I will go back to Hannah, but not until I have the answers we seek." He released Philo's arm but continued to grasp the man with a stare that seemed to hold Philo motionless. "You knew I had the note. You had them pursue me, so why then come to my rescue? Why take the blame for something you didn't do or even know about when you clearly despise me and want me nowhere near your daughter?" He stopped just enough for breath. "Philo, I have long since begged your forgiveness, as has Hannah. We did not formulate some plan behind your back. Aye, I purchased the foundry, but I did it for my own benefit and for the advancement of my skills as a blacksmith, not to lure her back to me. As for the rest, it simply happened. And I know you disapprove, but I—"

"I do not disapprove."

The four words blew against Joseph and froze him as if he'd been gripped by an icy blast. The man could not be serious.

Rolling his shoulders back, Joseph's brow crimped down. "You have always hated me."

Philo's gaze drifted downward as a sigh heavy with regrets breathed free from his mouth. "I did." His stare swept up and circled Joseph in pleading. "But I was wrong."

Confusion settled like a heavy fog. This was not the man Joseph knew. "I don't understand."

Even in the dark Joseph could see grief creasing in the corners around Philo's eyes.

"I learned this night that all these years I had felt myself to be the one that was wronged...but I see now I was the one *doing* it." He stopped, his voice fragile. "My regrets are a prison from which I cannot escape."

Regrets? Hadn't Philo always made it clear he'd wished them apart? He'd not seen much of the man since that awful day ten years past, but the cut in his soul had throbbed even so. Philo's hurtful words never fully found refuge in forgetfulness. Joseph inhaled, but a deep breath could not blow away the clouds that grew ever more turbid.

Philo's bereaved tone groped in the space between them. "I blamed you for what happened— both of you—because I feared more what others would think, when I should have embraced you." His voice wavered. "All I can do now is beg your forgiveness and pray my daughter will as well, for I will never see her again in this life, and I have no one to blame but myself."

The more Philo spoke, the more Joseph's heart pulled apart at the seams, bulging with a dolor that even the deepest of hopes could not contain. The man was in earnest. "You say you have just come to see this now—how? How is it you make this change and choose in the final moments to take such a thing upon yourself? Philo, I do not understand. Hannah is beside herself with the pain of questions she has no answers to."

"I suppose..." Philo looked away, a quick breath huffing from his mouth. "I suppose I have felt the tickings of change within me but was too prideful to admit my wrongs." At that he looked to Joseph and rested a hand on his shoulder. "The pain I feel for having caused her too much sorrow destroys my soul. Now I can make it right."

"By standing in our place of judgment?" Joseph pointed a rigid arm toward the rising gallows outside the far doors, straining to keep his volume from reaching past Philo. "You will die, Philo."

"I know." The resolve in his tone was serene, strong. Peaceful. "I must do it. My daughter deserves to have the happiness I denied her. She deserves a family—with the man she loves." Philo looked away again, clearing his throat. "She told me of her child, your child." Again he paused and coughed, his voice a fragile thread. "I had not known any of this. All I could see was my own suffering, my own selfish desires. I...I wish there was a proper way for me to beg your forgiveness. I hope what I offer you now is enough to prove the depth of my contrition."

Joseph stilled, his entire frame numb as Philo's entreaty and offered love reached out to cup his sorrowed heart, mending it with not only words but with sincerity as real as the blood that flowed within his veins. His throat thickened with hot emotion. Hannah must hear this. She must feel this love, this unspeakable peace—she needed it more than he.

He swallowed and took Philo at the wrist. "You cannot die." Joseph turned back to the door, heart pulsing. There must be a way to save him. He turned back, staring at the man who by all accounts should despise him, but whose sincerity swelled so rich that Joseph believed he could bottle it and store it for times when he and Hannah wished to relive this memory.

Philo shook his head. "Do you expect if we attempted to escape now that we would not be caught?"

Gritting his teeth, Joseph refused just yet to relinquish the seedling thought, but Philo continued to cut it at the roots.

"If we fled, we would both be captured, both be killed, and what of Hannah then? The woman we both love would have no future at all." He took Joseph by the shoulders. "I have placed my sins upon the altar, Joseph. I have sacrificed my pride and anger, and I have never felt such supernal freedom. 'Tis a peace I should have allowed myself so long ago. But now, and after I am dead, I will continue in that peace—if God, in His mercy, will see me into His kingdom."

The voices out the door increased in volume, and both stiffened.

Philo pushed Joseph to the back door, speaking through closed teeth. "Go. You must leave now!"

"I will not leave before—"

"I shall get him right away, sir."

The soldier's voice outside the large barn doors was loud and strong. Panic-stricken, Philo shoved Joseph deeper in the shadows. "I will not have you taken." He took the Bible from Joseph's grasp and pressed it to Joseph's chest. "Tell Hannah I love her."

"Philo, please. There must be a way to—"

"Go to Ensign. I pray he lives."

Joseph almost stumbled backward. More answers, and yet at their side came more questions. "What do you mean he lives?"

"If he has not yet been called to heaven, you will find him at the home of Nathaniel Smith. I cannot watch your family grow in joy, but perhaps he can."

A rustling at the door made Joseph's breathing stop. "I would stay with you until the end."

"I refuse it." Loving anger made Philo's tone heavy. "Stay, and you risk destroying the very thing I wish to give you. You cannot be discovered."

Just then the back door opened and Higley rushed in and whispered through closed teeth. "Come now."

Philo reached out for Joseph's arm. "Tell her I love her. Tell her how sorry I am. Tell Ensign—"

The large doors opened, and Higley jumped back. Joseph pressed his shoulders against the wall, where the shadows were thickest.

"Where are you, prisoner?"

Philo turned. "I am here."

The soldier pushed the door fully open and stood motionless, the glow of the torches giving his frame a dark silhouette. "Ready to meet your maker?"

A hand gripped Joseph's arm, forcing him into the pitch of the shadows.

"I am." Philo stepped forward, not once glancing back. Though as he moved away, his shoulders and straight posture were like a petition, a secretive message that only Joseph could see. *Go*, it seemed to say. *I am not afraid.*

Holding tight to the hope that reached across the space, Joseph collected it in his heart and prayed God would grant him the strength to share that peace with the woman he loved. If only he could hurl out of the shadows and bring the man to safety.

But that was not to be. Philo's future was decided. And there was naught Joseph could do but pray.

The soldier stepped forward and yanked Philo by the arm. "Get a move on." With a crisp jerk, he shoved Philo out of the barn and into the yard where the gallows loomed, high and hateful. Torches flickered. A smattering of soldiers littered the otherwise empty space. Some with lanterns, others motionless, arms crossed.

"Major Stockton doesn't want to wait." Reaching for his arms, the soldier tugged Philo's hands behind his back and tied them into place just as Stockton exited the house.

Hat affixed, sword at his side, the man carried his shoulders high and chest out. "Is there anything you wish to confess? Any last words you want spoken before you can speak no more?"

Philo shook his head. Thanks to the mercy of the Almighty, he had said all he wished to. He now prayed God would carry Joseph to Hannah, that he would give her the message Philo had so wanted to give himself.

With a brusque exhale, Stockton turned and nodded to the man beside Philo. "Prepare him."

Pulling him forward, the soldier held him at the elbow, Philo's vision bound to the rope that in moments would unwittingly be the means of his escape from this mortal travail. It hung motionless, almost as if it drooped in sorrow for what it knew it must do.

Philo put his foot on the first step when a movement beyond the group caught his attention. Somewhere in his heart, a cry went out—a beseeching he hadn't wished to expose but that refused to be withheld. *A friend, Lord, I pray thee. In these last moments.*

He blinked away the hot threat of tears as the soldier led him to the platform, pushing him to stand upon the stool. As Philo stared forward, the rough rope circling his neck, his vision found him. There, far in the back, almost at the trees and illuminated by the faint light of the torch-lit yard, was Joseph atop his horse. He kept there, a clement witness to Philo that God had heard his prayer.

Across the yard, through the darkness, Philo poured his love through his gaze, not moving, not blinking. Though he could not discern Joseph's eyes, he imagined—hoped—he felt a strength whispering through the wood toward him. The rope tightened, and a quiver snaked down his back.

Closing his eyes, a tear wet his face.

Lord, forgive me. I have sinned against thee and against those I love. If only he had been granted a chance to read God's word before this moment.

Then like the breath of an angel, the passage he'd read only one night past rose through his soul.

Offer the sacrifices of righteousness, and put your trust in the Lord. The tears flowed, his neck cording as Stockton ordered his face covered with a sack. This must be, but how could he die with such regrets? Would Hannah forgive him? Would God?

All his senses faded as he narrowed his mind upon the only thing that would give him comfort. *My Lord, my God.* And 'twas there, as Stockton called for the stool to be kicked free, that God's warm voice opened the heavens.

My son, greater love hath no man than he lay down his life for his friends.

Chapter Thirty-Six

The moment the stool was yanked away, James could see Joseph's back stiffen.

He kept his volume around a fragile whisper. "You must go."

As if the quiet declaration pulled him by degrees, Joseph nodded and turned his head. "Thank you."

There were grief and gratitude in his expression too deep for anything else, though James could see more words in his eyes. If only he could have done more for this courageous pair. "Take Miss Young away immediately. Stop at Eaton Hill to change horses and head directly to Sandwich."

Joseph glanced right, then turned away again, the scene in the faraway yard likely too terrible for him to witness further. "I will." He gripped the reins and sat straighter, ready to ride the back way to the house where Miss Young waited. "We are indebted to you, Major."

"I shall hope to see—" A movement behind him made James's spine rigid. "Go!"

Without a second glance, Joseph kicked his horse and raced into the cover of morning's inky shadows.

James sat motionless, his mare nickering and sidestepping. She could feel his angst. Tapping his heels against Ginny's flank, he led her onto the road, trying to keep his mind from straying to the past, but it would not obey. He ground his teeth. If Joseph had been caught, he too would have been hanged, and the mere thought made James's muscles cramp. Joseph Wythe was brave to a fault. As was Miss Young. Pray to God they would remain unseen. They must make it to Sandwich. For the boy, aye. But also for—

"Delinquent in your post again?"

Fate would not allow him a moment's peace. James breathed out a smooth, quiet breath before answering the man who had been the thorn in his side from the day they'd met. "You should be happy, Lieutenant Greene. Your informant has been found. And killed."

Also atop his mount, Greene reined in his horse beside James's, looking toward the small crowd of soldiers who worked busily in the yard to disassemble the hastily made gallows. "So it would seem. Though I am not convinced."

No wonder this man and Stockton's son had been such keen companions. They were so much alike. "You believe an innocent man has been killed, is that it?"

"Nay, he was guilty of working for the enemy, that much is clear, but I do not believe the informant Major Pitman is searching for was that man."

James caged his disgust behind his ribs with a long inhale. "What now then? Will you continue your search? I understood Major Stockton had banished you to Sandwich."

"Oh, he had." The laugh Greene let out was harsh and low. He trained his eyes on James as if the directive he prepared to issue would cut him from head to foot. "But I have just returned from issuing a report of this evenings events to Major Pitman and it seems he is so impressed with my efforts, that he has requested that I be transferred to his regiment so that I might be put solely in charge of discovering this elusive traitor." The triumphant grin curled up his face. "I shall soon have full authorization to use any and all tactics to sniff out the one who will feel the tight end of a rope."

So much pride. But pride's companion was often cowardice. "I heard tell you were the informant."

Greene's expression coiled. "By whom?"

James eased his posture. "By several."

"'Tis a lie."

Shrugging, James tilted his head in the direction of the gallows. "None of this business with the Youngs happened until you made your appearance at the foundry."

"I was the one who found out Willis this very evening! Do not tell me—"

"I am telling you nothing except I wonder if Major Pitman has requested your transfer because he trusts you or because he believes you culpable." He paused, watching Greene's expression evolve from indignant to hateful. "Keeping you closer to him, he can watch you with greater scrutiny."

Greene's jaw shifted back and forth as he chewed on the tack James had tossed him. "I will find this informant, and when I do, I will discover who it was that first slandered my name and I will be sure they regret it."

That worn-out threat Greene was so quick to throw at the first rustle in the grass made James almost chuckle. "Good luck then." He almost added a sarcastic remark to crown his enjoyment but swallowed it back before it could feel the morning's biting air.

With a glare that Greene no doubt wished would stab, he clicked his tongue and finished his advance to the yard.

James stared, grinding his teeth as he calculated the work he must now do. Pitman was no fool. So why wish a man like Greene to oversee such an operation? In truth, instead of murmur over such a development, James should give thanks for it. The man was as dense as a dung pile. If he didn't know who the informant was by now, he never would.

He'd been meticulous, careful, even cautious to an extreme. But if he didn't begin to take even more care, James's work for the Patriots would be discovered, and that was something he could never risk.

A grunt from Ginny lurched James's thoughts into place, and he tugged her the opposite direction. The note in his coat pocket clawed for freedom. And he knew just the place to leave it.

In the barn of Eaton Hill, Hannah secured the last bag of goods to the side of Anvil's saddle. The frigid midnight air pinched under her skirts. How grateful she was that they'd stopped, if only for a moment, for without her wool stockings, journeying so far in such cold would have been crippling.

Joseph strode through the open barn doors, urgency in his step. He rounded Anvil and stuffed the remaining knapsack with what he'd gathered from the kitchen. "We must hurry."

Hannah looked to the darkened house across the yard. "I am ready."

"Anvil is swift." Joseph's lips pulled tight in a sorrowful grin. "We shall not be overtaken."

"Joseph...I know we haven't time to speak..." The pale light from the fragment of moon illuminated the plume of her breath. "There is so much I don't understand. I..."

A heavy breath left him, as if he'd already read the hidden missive in her expression "I know."

She closed the space between them and rested her head against his chest. "What of the note? Will the soldiers be safe? 'Tis all my fault—"

"'Tis not your fault." His warm embrace enclosed her. "Do not blame yourself." He rested his cheek against her hair, hands stroking her back. "God will see to that."

Closing her eyes, Hannah tipped her heart toward heaven, praying that Providence would protect the valiant men-at-arms. With that stone of worry now free, the larger rock of her sorrows toppled upon her. "I didn't get to say good-bye." Her chest seized, and she choked on the heated lump in her throat. "I didn't get to tell him I loved him. Despite everything, I truly did."

"My darling..."

Joseph's rich tone shoved aside the boulder that threatened to crush her.

"I spoke with him."

"You did?" She pulled away and looked up. "When? Tell me."

"I shall—I give you my word. All you need know now is how desperately he loved you." Joseph's gloved finger brushed against her cheek. "He wanted you and me to be happy."

Closing her eyes, she leaned her forehead against his chest, refusing to give way to the sobs that pressed on her spirit. So why had he done it? After all the years of hate—how had he come to such a change? And to have accepted such an end?

"There is much more to tell, but it shall have to wait." Joseph kissed the top of her head. "Though I will tell you this."

He pressed her away, the love in his face enough to carry her beyond the travails that impeded them. "What is it?"

Joseph lowered his chin. "Jacob shall need a mother."

Jacob. Like a spark to a paper box, the thought was small in its dawning but in seconds burned bright. "Of course he will. I shall do whatever I can—"

"And Ensign...he will need you as well."

Hannah frowned. "What do you mean?" She had misheard him, surely.

Joseph smoothed his hands down her arms. "He is alive."

"Alive?" Her once cold limbs jolted with heat. "How can that be?"

"I know little more than you." Something drew his attention to the house, and he gripped her elbow, leading her closer beside Anvil. "Your father said he spoke with Ensign two nights past at Nathaniel Smith's home and that he still lived, though Philo seemed to believe Ensign's condition was grave."

Oh dear Lord. If her uncle was still alive... "We must go to him."

"Straight away." Expression rich with longing, he held her at the waist. In a swift motion he pressed a quick kiss to her mouth, the promise of passion in the tender touch of his lips. "Sandwich awaits."

Stepping around Anvil, Joseph went to check the saddle one last time. Hannah reached up and prepared to mount but halted when a chill rushed over her skin. A voice...

Chest tight, Hannah spun around, her heart racing. But she could see no one and blinked away her foolish imagining. Her mind played tricks, surely. Yet something kept her looking. 'Twas so real. It was as if her heart had heard something more than her ears.

Perhaps...she shook her head. She was merely tired.

Preparing to turn round, she heard it again and halted. This time the soft, sweet sound was so familiar, so rife with heavenly strains it reached deep through her soul.

I love you, my child.

Hannah's breath caught, and she pressed a hand to her chest. *Father.* 'Twas almost as if she could see him smiling at her as he had when she was a child, that familiar warmth and joy in his face. He had given his all, and though he was gone, yet would he live.

A hot tear streamed over her cheek, and she whispered into the night. "And I shall always love you, Father."

Epilogue

Six months later...

The scent of sun-heated grasses and flowering brush made the air as delicious to her nose as the sound of birdsong was to her ears.

From her spot on the blanket some steps from the pond, Hannah leaned on her arm, gazing dreamily at where Joseph stood at the edge of the water, Jacob beside him with fishing pole in hand.

"I can hardly believe six months have passed." She turned to Ensign, who sat beside her, legs cocked up, arms around his knees. "Can you?"

"I cannot." He smiled as he answered. "Life is but a breath, and then we are gone." He looked at her, wisdom circling his vibrant eyes. "I am so pleased we have at last returned to Eaton Hill. More pleased than I can say."

Such simple words for a meaning much deeper. "'Tis a blessing Joseph is more needed at the foundry than on the battlefront." She gazed down at a small black beetle that seemed to find her petticoat a pleasant place to rest. Picking it up, she rested the happy thing in the grass. "I am not sure I could have borne the grief of his leaving...and the fear of him not returning."

A hand grazed her wrist, and she looked up, Ensign's grin warming her more than the summer sun on her back.

"God has given you a gift, my dear."

He had given her many gifts indeed. A memory tickled her heart, and she gazed back at the grass. Hadn't Caroline said that very thing—that perhaps God had more happiness planned for her future than she could ever have imagined? How right she had been.

She raised her eyes again to Joseph. He bent beside Jacob, smiled, and said something as he straightened and pointed into the pond, raising his arms with a triumphant laugh that filled her soul. 'Twas then he looked to her, his white smile beaming. Tapping Jacob on the shoulder, he nudged the boy to look at her, and his bright expression shouted with myriad pleasures as he waved.

Sitting up, Hannah waved in return as a heated lump formed in her throat. They were a family. At long last. It seemed only yesterday they were riding through the winter night to safety. But 'twas only two months after their arrival in Virginia they were told that the British had left Boston for New York and that Joseph had been requested to return to Eaton Hill and produce goods for Washington's men. The Patriots needed much in the way of munitions, and Joseph was eager and willing to supply.

Hannah watched as the two of them chuckled and pulled at the fishing pole as something in the pond fought back with intrepid effort. It filled her soul to see Joseph so happy. He loved the boy as his own, just as she did. A flutter began in her chest, and she bit back a smile. And soon more joy would greet them...

"What are you smiling about so secretly?" Ensign ducked his head, a single eyebrow slanting up.

Hannah giggled, the news nearly bursting from her lips, but she held it back. Joseph must be the first to hear. "Oh...I am simply...simply happy." She leaned toward him and rested her head on his shoulder. "I owe Mrs. Smith so much for caring for you. And how desperately I wish I could thank whoever it was that saved you. God will surely bless such a person."

"I pray for him morning and night." His gaze drifted away, the past luring him backward. "I remember so little...I felt sure I would not make it through that night."

Hannah quirked her head to look at him. "You still do not remember anything of that night?"

Brow cinching, Ensign gazed forward. "I have been pondering it at great depth, but I can only recall a few vague details." Pausing, he sighed. "I remember being carried by someone very large, very strong. His ear was deformed or scarred, it seemed to me." At that he looked to her. "But it was so dark, and I was in such agony of pain I feel my memory cannot be trusted."

Illuminating her mind like a candle in a hall, a light settled on a vision she'd forgotten, and a chill rushed up her spine.

She turned to Ensign. "Is that all you remember? Is there anything else?"

An incredulous smile tipped his lips, and he scratched the back of his neck. "It seems unreal, I know. But...I remember his red coat." At that, he turned to her. "Hannah, I believe...I believe I was saved by a soldier."

Dear Lord! Higley had been Ensign's rescuer. A cooling breeze dusted against her skin, and it seemed her spirit stepped away from her, falling into the clarifying clouds of memory.

Captain Higley saw to his burial, and I can assure you, Higley would have treated him as his own.

Hannah's breath began to chase.

Miss Young, I should like to at last offer my sincerest apologies regarding your uncle. I know this must be of great distress to you, but I beg you to not give up hope.

Dearest Higley. She flung her gaze to Joseph. All that he had done for them, and they the supposed enemy...

Bless him, Lord.

"You think me mad." Ensign gave an apologetic chuckle. "'Twas they who intended my death, so why should one risk to save me?"

"I do not think you are mad." She rested her hand on his arm. "Though one wished you dead, that does not mean they all did."

"Look!"

The mirthful call of Jacob's voice brought her head around, and she smiled as he hobbled forward, crutch in one hand, a fish in the other.

"See what I have caught?"

"My goodness." Hannah hurried to her feet to clutch the boy in an embrace. Grinning wide, she rested her hands on his shoulders. "The second one this week. You have a talent, Jacob, I do believe."

Joseph stopped beside her, circling his arm around her waist. "Have you ever beheld a catch of this size? And to own the truth, I did not but help him pull it in."

"I am truly impressed." She tousled Jacob's hair. "Why don't you place it in the basket and tell Uncle Ensign the details of your conquest while I speak with Joseph for a moment."

Jacob nodded, grinning almost as wide as the fish was long. He stepped closer to the blanket, and Ensign rose, helping the boy onto the ground.

With the fish in place and the two once more seated, Hannah hooked her arm around Joseph's and tilted her face to him. "Walk with me."

A playful smile quirked over his lips. "Gladly."

The hot August air cooled in the shadows beside the water. Hannah led him into the grove and craned her neck to be sure Jacob and Ensign were out of sight.

"Joseph, I—"

His kiss cut off her words. Passionate but tender, his lips covered hers, and she answered his want with her own. Smoothing her hands up his firm chest, she skimmed her fingers over his smooth jaw and lifted on her toes, pressing harder against him before she pulled away, her news too eager to be revealed.

She laughed spritely. "Can you not wait until we return home?"

He shook his head, eyes hooded. "I cannot."

He descended again, and she stopped him with a coy look and a finger to his lips before painting the worried look over her expression as she'd practiced. "There is something I must tell you."

The slight backward jerk of his head and pinch in his brow spoke before his voice did. "Something is wrong."

"I..." She dropped her hands and tilted her head, hoping to lure him further. "I haven't mentioned this for fear of worrying you, but I have been feeling quite peaked of late."

Joseph's features slackened, and his eyes trailed her face, as if searching for signs of her ailment. "What do you mean? You are ill?"

Such an effort it took not to smile. Hannah cleared her throat and looked down for fear her joy would spill over her face and he would discern her secret before she was ready. She studied her fingers. "I haven't been able to eat as well as before and—"

"I had noticed."

She couldn't help but look up. "You had?"

He nodded, concern darkening his eyes. "Aye, but I thought perhaps 'twas—" He stopped himself and shook his head. "We must call for a doctor right away."

That smile inched upward, and she tried fruitlessly to stop its growth. Marrying her gaze with his, she allowed it to bloom in full. "I do not think we need one just yet."

"Of course we do. I won't let you..." His words stilled, and his eyes rounded, while his mouth hung open. He stuttered. "You are...do you mean you are..."

"Aye." Her heart nearly burst from happiness. "You are to be a father. Again."

His breath went airy. "You are in earnest?"

She laughed merrily through her smile. "I am."

"I...I can scarce believe it. A child." Joseph's throat bobbed, and his eyes misted as they drifted to her belly. Stepping forward, he closed the few inches between them and enclosed her in an embrace that filled every tiny crevice in her soul. His velvety tone was fissured with joy. "I am so happy, my darling."

Hannah gripped his strong back, savoring the ethereal beauty of a moment she'd thought would never come. As she gazed out over the shimmering water, birds trilling, insects humming, her eyes brimmed with emotion. "I am not sure how to carry so much joy."

"All this we owe to our Father in heaven and to your father." Joseph stroked her back and rested his chin on her hair. "I cannot bear to think of what our lives might have been without his sacrifice."

Hannah could only whisper her reply, her throat so thick with sorrow and gratitude. "I think of it every day."

"As do I." He made little circles on her arm with his thumb. "I pray I may live worthy of it. And now, knowing we shall have a child…"

"God has given us so much." Pulling away, she took his hand in hers. "I am so pleased that at last our past sorrows are no more."

"'Tis our past that brought us to where we are—our griefs and our joys." He tugged her back into his arms and rested his cheek against her hair. "We cannot know what awaits us, but I promise you this. Whatever comes, we need not fear, for we shall face it together, my darling. Hand in hand. Forever."

Bless you for reading Joseph and Hannah's story. Your willingness to turn the pages means more to me than I can ever express.

I loved bringing these characters to life and including those vibrant, gripping historical details that are too beautiful to neglect.

Book five, *So Bright a Hope*, will feature James Higley and Caroline Whitney. And I must say, I can hardly wait to share their romance with you.

If you would like to contact me, you can visit my website, www.amberlynnperry.com or visit me on Facebook—Amber Lynn Perry, Author. I would love to hear from you!

For liberty,
Amber

66073156R00272

Made in the USA
Lexington, KY
02 August 2017